THE WELL OF MANY WORLDS

THE WELL OF
MANY WORLDS

LUKE METCALF

First published in 2018 by Rebel Youth Productions

ISBN 978-1-912892-11-2

Also available as an ebook
ISBN 978-1-912892-12-9

Typeset by Jill Sawyer Phypers
Cover design by Richard Augustus
Printed and bound by CreateSpace

To my parents

Preface

Never had Emily imagined that her death would come like this. Not that she had given the subject much thought. But nothing that had happened in her life previously could have prepared her for the events of the last two weeks.

He tore off his mask, revealing the crazed obsession that burned in his eyes. He advanced upon her and gave her an almost friendly smile and a wink.

Emily felt a terrible sadness that she would never be able to avenge the murder of her father. She then thought of her love. Had he been destroyed? Her fear vanished and was replaced with a feeling of overwhelming gratitude for having been able to find something so transcendental. She was unconditionally and inescapably in love with him and it was the most thrilling experience of her life. The thought filled her with courage.

Emily raised her chin and stared into the demon's eyes defiantly, daring him to kill her.

One

"So, you have no idea who would have wanted your father dead?"

Under the harsh fluorescent lights of the police station, Emily Bliss struggled in vain to control the tears. Her eyes were already red and puffy from hours of crying.

Detective Scannel leaned back and sighed, the wooden chair creaking under his weight. His face was meaty, and the corners of his eyelids sagged with exhaustion after a career filled with sleepless nights.

"What about the people who broke into his store?" Emily asked.

"We're following that up. But do you have any reason to suppose there is a connection between the break-in and your father's murder?"

Emily shrugged and the tears welled up again. Whenever she had thought about her childhood in the past it had always appeared as one long, beautiful summer's day. Now she felt that golden world drifting further and further away, replaced by images of horror and uncertainty.

"Had your father been acting strangely in any way? Had he said anything to you that seemed unusual?" The detective rocked himself back and forth in the flimsy chair. It was getting late and it looked as though he just wanted to get home. Emily shifted uncomfortably in her seat, remembering the last conversation she had had with her father that morning.

She had been sitting on the sofa in the tiny living room of his cramped one-bedroom apartment, worrying about him as usual. He was in his bedroom on the phone, having a heated argument with a customer, but she couldn't make out any of the conversation clearly as the bedroom door was shut. She lay there, channel surfing while finishing her bowl of cereal.

"So what was that all about?" Emily asked as her father finally emerged from the bedroom.

"Hmm? What?"

"On the telephone just now."

"Oh that." He gave a dismissive wave of his hand. "Just some new customers. They want me to track down some piece they're looking for but they're unbelievably rude and pushy. I really don't want to do business with people like that but they keep harassing me." He frowned and stared pensively at the ground for a moment. "Listen." He tapped her knee. "I put a box in the back of your mother's garage last night so if you stumble across it you'll know I put it there and to just leave it there."

"What is it?"

"It's uh… It's your eighteenth birthday present. It's in a big package, all wrapped up in brown paper, buried under all that crap stored in the back of the garage."

"Why did you put it in the garage?"

"It'll be safer there. I don't have any room here, and don't tell your mother this, but the store was broken into a couple of nights ago."

"What? You were robbed?"

"Yes, but don't make a big deal out of it. I don't want to upset your mother. She has a lot on her plate right now." He lit up his phone screen and began checking email messages as if wanting to end the conversation.

"But, Dad… who do you think did it?"

"I have no idea. Probably just some kids."

"Why would kids want to rob an antique store?"

"Yeah, it's odd, I don't know." He shook his head. "I don't know who it was. Anyways, just promise me that you'll keep it safe, until your birthday. And don't open it. And do not tell your mother about it. Promise?"

"Okay, I promise," said Emily, standing up and hugging him.

"Well, you should get going now," her father said. "Time for school. Oh, I almost forgot – I won't be able to see you next weekend."

"Why?" She felt the familiar sense of hurt surging up inside her. "You're not going to come for my birthday?"

"I'm sorry."

"Why do I even ask? You canceled on me the last three weekends in a row and now my eighteenth birthday? You know what would make things easier? Maybe just don't waste my time making plans with me in the first place."

"I'm sorry, I've been very busy."

"Well," she snapped, pulling on her coat, "let me clear some space in your schedule. Don't bother about the weekend after that either. I've got other things to do." She threw her backpack over her shoulder and headed for the door.

"I'm sorry, Emily, but I have a lot of research to do, and there are important things…"

Before he could finish his sentence she had walked out of the apartment.

"Yeah, and I'm obviously not one of them," she muttered.

"Emily, wait," she heard him say as she shut the door behind her. If her father wasn't interested in being an active part of her life anymore, then she couldn't force him, but knowing that didn't make the disappointment any less painful. Reaching the street, she threw open the door of her car.

"Emily!" her father called to her from the balcony. She didn't look up at him as she got into her seat, started up the engine with an angry roar and drove off down the street, ignoring the spikes of guilt urging her to go back and hug him again.

"And you have no idea who this person, this 'new customer' was who your dad was arguing with?" asked Detective Scannel, twirling a pen around his fingers as though it were a cheerleader's baton.

"No," said Emily. "Can't you trace the numbers on his phone?"

"We're looking into that, but so far it hasn't led us anywhere."

"Do you think he was the one who robbed him?" She wondered if she should mention the mysterious birthday present waiting for her in the garage but decided against it. It was the last thing her father would ever give her, too personal to just hand over to the police as evidence. She wanted to open it and see for herself what it was before she told anyone else of its existence.

"Don't know." The detective handed her a photo of a man she had never seen before. He was Caucasian and looked to be in his thirties with wild eyes, like a rabid animal. He had thick dark hair, square, prominent features and a solid jaw line. His face was terribly scarred, and he was missing most of his right ear.

"Ever seen this man?"

"No."

He set the photo up against his water bottle, so she could continue to examine it. "He was spotted in the area of your father's store around the time of the break-in. His name is Cady Sunner. He's a go-between and a mercenary, works for some organized crime bosses."

"You mean mafia?" Emily asked. "In Portland?"

"Drug smuggling is expanding to the smaller ports up and down the east coast. Fewer police," he explained.

"Oh."

"Yeah, Asian triads, the Russian mob, bikers… we've got it all now," he sighed.

Emily shook her head. "I've never seen him. You think he robbed my father's store?"

"We don't know. Whoever did it ransacked the place but the only things missing were his books."

"What books?"

"The records of all his sales and purchases."

Emily stared hard at the photo, trying to imagine why anyone would want her father's sales records.

"He only kept hard copies of his records as far as you know, correct?"

"Yeah, my father wasn't big on computers."

Detective Scannel took back the photo and placed it in a manila folder, clipping it to the top edge before taking out another. "How about this man?" he asked.

Emily took the photo and looked at it. It was a picture of an Asian man who she guessed was in his late fifties. He had high cheekbones and a mustache. He was dressed in some kind of military uniform.

"No, never seen him." She shook her head and handed him back the picture. "Who is he?"

"He goes by the name Commander Claw. We don't know much about him, other than that he is affiliated with the Asian triads and we believe that Cady Sunner is working for him. We'll do everything we can to figure out who broke into the store and who killed your father, Emily, I promise. One last thing…" Detective Scannel glanced about, clearing his throat. He looked uneasy. He handed her a piece of paper and pointed to some words written in blue ink. "Do these words mean anything to you?"

The words read: THE BLOOD OF THE WORLD IS THE BLOOD OF THE GOD.

Emily recoiled, as if bitten by a snake. "No. What does that even mean?"

"Are you sure you've never seen them?"

"Yeah, I'm sure. Why?"

He cleared his throat again and looked at her as if gauging how much he wanted her to know. "Because," he said eventually, putting the paper down on his desk, "these words were written on the wall of your father's apartment. They were written in his blood."

Emily went straight to her garage when she got home from the police station, lost in thought. Her birthday, Halloween, her favorite day of the year, was just over a week away and her father wouldn't be at that or any other birthday of hers ever again. She found the package containing her present at the back of the garage under a heap of junk, including a dust-covered plastic turtle pool. It was quite a large box, wrapped in brown paper.

"Okay, Dad," she whispered to herself, "I've found it." She felt a knot of excitement tightening in her stomach as she pushed aside the bicycle and toys piled on top of it. Is this what those men were looking for? she wondered. Is this the reason my father is dead?

She tore the paper from one end of the box, cutting through the packing tape with her house key. Taking a deep breath, she lifted the flaps of the box and peered inside at her birthday present.

From the brass plaque on the side, she could see that it was a desk from a ship. It was crafted out of walnut with a leather top and drawers down one side. It looked as if it had recently been refurbished, and whoever had done it had done a fairly decent job. Judging from the untouched base it had previously been in very rough shape. The small brass plaque on the side read *Pinalute*.

Emily frowned. Why would her father give her a desk? Why would he consider it something she might like? Was it really her birthday present or was he just saying that? And if this was the item the robbers were looking for, why would they or anyone else, be interested in it? It couldn't be that valuable. It was kind of junky, to be honest. Then again, maybe it was owned by someone famous or was used in some important historical moment and was worth a ton of money.

She opened the drawers, but they were empty. The top flipped up to reveal a small storage area, but all that was in there was a piece of paper, a record of purchase. Emily remembered that the thieves had stolen his record books. I guess the thieves don't know for sure if he had this desk if they couldn't find the purchase record, she thought. If that's even what they were looking for. As she picked up the piece of paper she noticed some words roughly carved into the wood of the storage area underneath that said "VADAS ASGER" in capital letters. The word "demons" was carved below it. It looked as though dried blood had sunk into the carved letters.

She shivered as she stared at it. She turned over the piece of paper and noticed that her father had also written "VADAS ASGER?" on the reverse. Emily put it back in the desk and resealed the packaging as best she could, hiding it under the junk where she had found it. Her mother never cleaned the garage so she knew it wouldn't be found. Going upstairs to her bedroom she opened her computer and looked up *Pinalute*. Apparently, it was the name of a merchant vessel in use over two hundred years before. There was no mention of anything particularly special about it. She then typed in the words "Vadas Asger". Nothing came up.

Emily clapped shut her laptop, dropped her head into her folded arms, and breathed quietly. She wondered why her father had been so insistent that she not tell her mother about the present. After a moment she got undressed, brushed her teeth, crawled into bed, fell asleep and plunged into a vivid dream.

She found herself lying in a large four-poster bed in a castle bedroom redolent of ancient times, the polished oak of the furniture gleaming in the candlelight. She was wearing a white nightgown and a beautiful pearl necklace with a ruby and diamond pendant around her throat. Her face was wet and her eyes swollen from crying. Above her stood a young man more handsome than any she had ever seen before. He looked to be about her age, perhaps a year older. He stood over six feet, was lean and powerfully built with pale skin and unnaturally bright emerald eyes. He already displayed more than a hint of the maturity of the man he was becoming. Because he was shirtless she could see his extraordinarily athletic physique and broad shoulders. He was chiseled like a sculpture, taut and hard.

She opened her mouth, tasting the tears on her lips, and drew in a long breath. Thick, messy, golden-bronze hair framed the young man's face. Her heart pounded. His intelligent eyes glittered as they stared at her. His eyes were mesmerizing. Desire exploded deep inside her. At the same time she could see a carnal hunger smoldering in his stare that sent a thrill of danger through her whole body. She was vaguely aware that her skin was prickling wet with sweat. Emily opened her mouth to speak but no words came out. Her throat felt tight beneath his powerful gaze. Lightning flashed outside and thunder cracked and rolled across the sky. A window blew open, knocking over a vase of flowers, which shattered across the floor like a gunshot.

She was unable to move or speak as he stepped closer, his eyes changing; now blazing with an inhuman, crimson glow that filled her with terror. His skin became even paler, as though he were a corpse, a delicate blue spider's web of veins spreading through it.

Emily screamed as the dream switched and she found herself falling and falling from a great height. The ground rushed toward her, she was going to die… then… nothing. She was lost in an endless darkness, staring about her into a limitless void.

From the darkness a shape began to form and even before she could see it clearly she knew it was a demon. It was humanoid, but horribly deformed. Its red lizard skin was on fire, hunks of flesh bubbling and peeling off. Its yellowish-green eyes blazed and it had horns and teeth that were rotted and crooked as old tombstones. The demon lunged toward her.

Two

The young man from Emily's dream strolled along an avenue of trees in the early evening, heading toward the Palace of Versailles. The tension in the air was tangible, a slowly building storm.

He ran a strong hand through his golden-bronze hair as he stared up at the palace in all its splendor, its Baroque extravagance perfectly merging with the French classical style. A constant stream of carriages came and went from the courtyard at the front. The young man was dressed as a nobleman, radiating an aura of strength and confidence. He appeared both wealthy and powerful. His fashionable clothes were tailored from the finest materials to fit him perfectly. He wore thick gold rings with finely cut gemstones on each hand and a long sword hung at his side. As he drew close to the walls he stayed in the shadows and then, silent as a ghost, he ducked into a grove of trees. Unseen by the guards stationed on every corner, he made his way round to the south side of the palace.

Glancing about to make sure no one had seen him, he climbed straight up the wall with cat-like agility, carefully opened a window and slipped inside.

Pausing on a high windowsill he looked down over an expansive storage room at a group of four men and three women who were all dressed spectacularly for a masquerade ball. They all had the same pale skin and bright eyes as him, and held their masks in their hands as they stared up at a structure that was about fourteen feet high and covered by a large sheet.

One of them, a man who looked to be in his late twenties, stepped forward with a flourish and spoke in French. "Ladies and gentlemen," he said, "I give you Madame Guillotine!"

He ripped off the sheet to reveal the machine beneath. A tailor's mannequin had been positioned with its head on the block, ready to be sliced off.

"The perfect killing machine," he continued. "We are going to make hundreds of them, which will mean we will be able to take off tens of thousands of heads in the coming months!"

He pulled a lever and the blade plummeted down with a fearful, metallic, rushing sound, taking the head clean off the shoulders of the mannequin, dropping it neatly into the waiting basket. The others gasped in awe and then clapped with an excited delight.

"It will be a glorious blood sacrifice for Mezzor," the young man declaimed. "The blood of the world is the blood of the God! We will turn it on any who oppose us. Finances are all in place. Robespierre is ready. The hour is nigh. We will make terror the order of the day!"

A beautiful woman in her early twenties stepped forward. "How amusing," she said, reaching out to touch the guillotine, "that the aristocrats commissioned its creation with no idea that it will be used on their own necks."

Everyone laughed and chatted as they exited the room in search of the party.

With the same cat-like agility, the young man jumped down from his perch, landing silently. Pulling a gold Venetian mask from his pocket he covered his face as he followed the others through the door.

Ahead of him in the magnificent corridor, the walls adorned with mighty paintings and sculptures on pedestals, the group had also donned their masks and were entering a huge, ornate ballroom filled with crowds of laughing, drinking, gossiping guests. The young man followed them in.

Marie Antoinette's grand masquerade balls were legendary displays of decadence. The costumes and jewels on display were amongst the most glamorous in history. The young man stared about for a moment at his surroundings, enjoying the music. Performers and acrobats in outlandish costumes were everywhere, dancing and juggling amongst the noisy revelers. Aristocrats on the balconies above threw confetti down upon the hundreds of people swirling around on the polished floor below. Dozens of immense chandeliers hung above their heads, their crystals sparkling from the flickering flames of thousands of candles. The intruder headed toward the young woman he had heard talking in the storage room as she stood talking to two other extravagantly attired ladies.

She noticed him approaching. "What do we have here ladies?" she said, hiding her smile behind her fan as she sized the young man up. "Gorgeous!" The two other ladies turned to follow her gaze and smirked their approval.

"*Bonsoir, Mesdames,*" he said, sweeping them a gallant bow.

"*Bonsoir, Monsieur,*" they replied as they curtseyed.

"You are English," said the woman from the storeroom. "I am Comtesse LeDuijou."

"*Enchanté,*" he bowed again. "I am Mitchell Keats."

"This is Madame Marie Blanche," said the Comtesse. The second lady nodded at him.

"And this is Madame Angelique DeBrey." The third lady curtseyed again.

"I am afraid that I have arrived late and missed the unveiling of the wonderful Madame Guillotine," said Mitchell.

Marie and Angelique shot the Comtesse puzzled looks. Behind her mask the Comtesse gave a small frown of displeasure before regaining her composure and addressing the two women in French. "Ladies, if you will excuse us for a moment."

The two women nodded their understanding and left Mitchell with the Comtesse, giggling conspiratorially as they went.

The orchestra struck up a waltz.

"Comtesse," said Mitchell, offering her his hand. "Would you do me the honor?"

She took his hand and they moved gracefully together to the music.

"I should give you a good thrashing for your stupidity," the Comtesse growled as they whirled around the gleaming floor. "But since you are positively the most gorgeous thing I have ever seen and you dance so beautifully I shall be merciful. When did Baelaar turn you? Or was it one of the weaker ones? Foolish man. Did he not tell you to keep your mouth shut about our doings in front of mortals?"

"My apologies, Madame. Baelaar created me but he was in a rush. I was simply given orders to come to the palace and seek you out for instructions regarding the guillotine."

"Hmmm. Well," she said, looking him up and down from arm's length. "Baelaar certainly made a good choice. I am going to demand that he give you to me."

"Give… me to you?"

"What on Earth is the matter? Do my looks not please you?"

"The Comtesse looks most lovely this evening."

"Oh, you wicked dog." She gave a light, silvery laugh. "You may call me Celeste."

She raised an eyebrow and stared at him for a moment. "Come with me," she said, taking his hand and walking toward the doors of the ballroom, nodding to two of the men who had been in the storage room with her as she went.

Mitchell followed her out of the ballroom, down the hallway, through another set of doors and into the most beautiful gardens the world had ever seen. They covered two thousand acres, most of which were landscaped in the French classic style. There were perfectly manicured lawns, groves of orange, lemon, oleander, palm and pomegranate trees, spectacular flower gardens and dozens of beautiful fountains and statues. There were two hundred thousand trees, over two hundred thousand flowers, fifty fountains and six hundred and twenty water jets to delight the guests who wandered through them. As they strolled along the avenues of trees in the low light of evening, Mitchell breathed in the flower-scented air.

"You have a very important decision to make," the Comtesse told him.

"And what might that be?"

"You become my personal servant and pet forever, or be destroyed."

Mitchell was aware that the four men from the storage room had followed them outside. He turned to glance at them. When he turned back the Comtesse was holding a sword.

"In the ballroom you tried to read my mind," she said, "but you made a mistake. You thought I was much younger and weaker than you and that I would not notice. You were wrong. The fact that I cannot read your mind means that you are at least the same age as I am. You are not one of the Priests of Mezzor. Are you are a member of the Niveus Gladius?" He stayed silent. "No, I do not believe you are. Who are you? And what information were you seeking in trying to read my thoughts?"

He heard the sounds of the other vampires unsheathing their swords as they circled around him.

"I will never be your servant – that you can be certain of."

She laughed and looked him up and down. "No one refuses me. No one has ever refused me. I do not tolerate disobedience. Not for one second."

"That sounds like a personal problem."

"You will live to serve me!" she snarled.

Mitchell gave her a cocky, mocking smirk. "I would agree with you, but then we would both be wrong."

"How dare you!" she shouted and stamped her foot, eyes blazing. "Destroy him!"

As Mitchell drew his sword the other five vampires attacked. Mitchell fought with amazing focus, speed and precision. He was a master swordsman and within a few seconds he had slashed open the chest of one of the vampires and had thrust his sword through the thigh of another, but even he was not fast enough to battle all five at once. The sound of clashing swords and groans of pain brought guards running from every direction. Spotting an aristocrat on horseback, apparently dressed for the ball, who had stopped to watch the fight, Mitchell leaped through the air, kicking the man out of his saddle, taking his place as he landed on the ground, lying on his back, winded and gasping for air. Gripping the reins, Mitchell spurred the horse at full speed toward the palace since either vampires or palace guards now blocked all escape routes.

A couple of the palace guards shot their muskets at him and he heard the balls of lead whizzing past his ears as he galloped through a set of double doors into the Hall of Battles. Partygoers screamed and scattered as he clattered on down the hall past paintings of legendary battles. His horse halted and reared as a vampire appeared in front of him, slashing at him with his sword. Bringing his own sword down in a wide arc Mitchell sliced the vampire's arm open, sending him snarling and stumbling backward. Mitchell spurred the horse on through more rooms and out into the Royal courtyard.

He swung the horse's snorting head left; galloped to the end of the Marbre courtyard and through another set of double doors, back into the palace. Charging through more revelers in the Hall of Mirrors he saw three vampires running toward him. With one mighty kick he sent the horse crashing through an enormous window, out into the gardens. As he passed under a tree he grabbed a branch, allowing the horse to continue on its way without him. Mitchell clambered up quickly into the higher branches and waited.

A few moments later three vampires ran past in pursuit of the horse. Once they had disappeared into the darkness Mitchell dropped out of the tree and ran like a shadow back toward the palace. Again he scaled a wall and slipped in through a window, finding himself in the Mars Room, beneath the ceiling painting by Claude Audran of the god Mars on his chariot being pulled by wolves. He took two steps into the room and froze. A young man was lying on the floor, moaning. It looked as though he had been knifed. His clothes were soaked in blood, his body wracked by spasms. With each seizure, his back arched and contorted so far it looked as if his bones would snap. Mitchell stood watching as the man's body finally went limp, apparently drained of strength.

He knelt over him. The man opened his eyes, looked up and smiled, his white fangs gleaming in the lamplight. He was handsome, a strapping lad in his early twenties with thick, shoulder-length blond hair and sea-gray eyes. Mitchell noticed puncture marks in his neck. They were healing and closing with unnatural speed.

"Who did this to you?" he asked.

"Is this a new world?" the man whispered, slowly sitting up and staring at his surroundings in awe. He sounded American.

"Yes, in a way."

The man rose to his feet, casually flipping his hair back as his strength returned. "Good. I was tiring of the old one." He laughed. "My name is Sylvain DeLune." He held out his hand.

"Mitchell Keats. Pleased to meet you."

They shook hands and Mitchell couldn't help but smile at the man's studied air of casual arrogance.

"Well, Sylvain, do you understand what has happened to you?" Mitchell asked.

"Not in the least."

"I will explain to you the basic elements of your new nature. But first, what can you tell me about the man who did this to you? Tell me every detail of what occurred. Start from the beginning."

"I was at the tavern…"

While Sylvain was speaking, Mitchell read his mind. He saw him in a tavern, sitting at a table with an unkempt man who looked to be in his late thirties. His nose was red and bulbous, his hair greasy and ragged, the features of his grubby face sagged in worry. Two men entered the tavern. Both of them moved with strength and authority like prowling leopards. One was wearing a long black cloak made of the sort of fine threads favored by noblemen, and riding boots carved from the softest black leather, his face was obscured by a Venetian mask in the form of a demonic-looking goat. The other was dressed in fine riding boots, long coat and high hat and wore a mask in the design of a ravening wolf. He carried a half-full bottle of absinthe. The two men sat down at the table.

"It has come to my attention, Henri, that you are a doubter," said the man in the goat mask to Sylvain's companion, speaking English. He spoke slowly with a deep voice and enunciated every word.

"My name is Alain," said Sylvain's companion, frowning.

"You see, Henri," continued the man in the goat mask as he took a vial of yellowish liquid out of his cloak and placed it on the table, "there is something that you must be made to understand. Faith is what makes the man. A man of little faith… is a little man."

As Sylvain and Alain exchanged glances the man in the goat mask snatched three empty glasses from the next table and poured the contents of the vial into them. There was enough for about an ounce of liquid in each. He pushed one of the glasses toward Alain.

"Who are you?" asked Sylvain reaching for the hilt of his sword.

The man slowly removed his mask. He was handsome, in his late twenties. He wore his hair slicked back and it was brownish red. Sylvain realized it was the color of dried blood and a chill ran down his spine. The man's skin was pale as milk and there were dark circles under his black and hypnotic eyes. The moment Sylvain looked directly into them he found that his gaze was trapped.

"I am darkness visible."

The other man took off his mask. He looked to be in his late thirties and had a large nose and high forehead and curly brown hair that fell to his shoulders. He took a swig from his bottle of absinthe.

"You are quite the lady-killer," continued the first man, addressing Sylvain. "Do you think he is as much a lady-killer as you?" He nudged his companion with his elbow. "Perhaps you should slay that wench." He gestured to a waitress with his chin as she walked by. Sylvain sank backward in his chair now released from the hypnotic gaze. He felt shaken and confused.

"Bah!" snorted the other man. "I can do better than that," he said, also in English. "Like Cupid I aim for the heart. But unlike Cupid I am not blind. I aim only for the heart of a peach, a sweet heart, not the heart of some sour artichoke, for that would choke my art." He laughed and took another drink.

"But I would wager that you would happily choke a tart," said the first man.

"Haha! Indeed!"

"Cheers," commanded the first man, holding up his glass as he stared into Alain's eyes. Alain and the two men clinked their glasses and drank.

"Woo that has a bite!" shouted the second man drunkenly as he slammed his empty glass down upon the table.

"Delicious!" said the first man, sticking his pinky finger out pretentiously.

As soon as the liquid was down his throat Alain began choking and sputtering. His face turned beet red as he clutched and clawed at his chest and then collapsed on the ground.

"What have you done? What have you given him?" demanded Sylvain as two waitresses rushed over to help Alain who was now foaming at the mouth and convulsing on the floor.

"I collect the venom of the deadliest snakes in the world," said the first man as he placed his empty glass upon the table. "A truly refreshing beverage. This is Squire Griffith" – he gestured to his companion with his chin – "and my name is Baelaar. And you will be coming with us."

The two men stood up, grabbed Sylvain, each taking an arm, and dragged him toward the door of the tavern. As they passed a table of drunken revelers Baelaar reached into his cloak with his free hand, pulled out a live snake and casually tossed it at them. Shrieks erupted from the table as the three men exited the tavern. Once outside they released Sylvain.

"Good sirs," said Sylvain slowly backing away, "I... I am an upstanding citizen. I am not interested in becoming involved in anything..."

"An upstanding citizen?" guffawed Squire Griffith. "You'll be a horizontal citizen if you don't do as you're told." He roared with drunken laughter at his own joke and jabbed Baelaar in the ribs with his elbow. "Did you hear that? Horizontal citizen."

"Shut up," snapped Baelaar before he turned his attention back to Sylvain. "I only wish to hire you to drive my carriage since my manservant has disappeared and my friend here is far too drunk."

"Sir!" bellowed Squire Griffith. "I protest. I am only just getting started."

Mitchell saw in Sylvain's memories that he had driven them to the palace in an elegant ebony carriage. Upon arrival Squire Griffith had disappeared into the ballroom and Baelaar had taken Sylvain by the arm, leading the young man into the Mars Room. Once out of sight of all prying eyes he had turned Sylvain to face him, placing a firm hand on each of his shoulders and staring deep into his eyes. As he held Sylvain with an iron grip Baelaar drew him close, holding his gaze until the moment he lowered his face onto Sylvain's neck, sinking his fangs deep into the young man's veins, slaking his own thirst and then feeding him some of his own blood from a gash he cut in his wrist with a dagger, transforming Sylvain into a vampire.

Once the deed was done Baelaar released the boy from his grip, allowing him to crumple to the floor, where Mitchell had found him.

"This is the greatest night of your life," said Baelaar, looking into Sylvain's eyes as he stared up at him, drained of blood and helpless. Sylvain again noticed that Baelaar always enunciated every word and often paused to stare into his eyes. "I am going to answer all of the most profound questions of humanity for you. I am going to reveal the true human condition to your inquisitive mind. 'Who am I? What is the origin of the universe? What does it all mean? What happens after death?' Tonight you will have the answers to all of these questions."

Baelaar cleared his throat and struck a scholarly pose. "Earth, the planet itself, is a demon, a vampire god named Mezzor, it means 'the Reaper.' It creates all life – humans, plants, animals, insects, everything – in order to gain awareness through their life experiences. Then, when they die and return to the earth, Mezzor feeds upon their awareness, the sum of their life experiences." Baelaar paced back and forth as he pontificated. "We are Mezzor's high priests – demigods, if you will, as we are the only immortals. We are his chosen servants. It is our sacred duty to make regular blood sacrifices." Baelaar knelt down and stared deep into Sylvain's eyes. "Welcome to the Priests of Mezzor." He gently slapped Sylvain's cheek then stood up. "Now, I must return to Paris but I will find you in the coming nights. Seek out the Comtesse LeDuijou in the grand ballroom tonight and she will begin your training." He stared at him and grinned, exposing his fangs. "Now you will be a real lady-killer, and they are going to love you!" He chuckled diabolically as he turned and strode out of the room.

"Baelaar!" Mitchell muttered to himself, clenching his fists. "And I missed him by no more than half an hour."

"Who is he?" Sylvain clutched Mitchell's jacket. His previous arrogance had drained away and his eyes were now wide with fear. "What did he do to me?"

"Have you ever heard stories of vampires?"

"Yes." Sylvain laughed nervously. "But surely…"

"Baelaar is a vampire. And now so are you."

"But… But…"

"Baelaar is the leader of the Priests of Mezzor," said

Mitchell, watching as Sylvain took in and digested the news of his transformation. "They are a satanic death cult of vampires. Whenever there is a conflict in the world – a war – they work to tip the scales and cause a massacre. They will use any method that they need to as long as it is covert: bribery, strategic assassinations, hypnosis, sabotage, whatever they think will best increase the bloodshed. They never hold positions of power for fear of being exposed, but they lurk in the shadows and manipulate those who do. They are opportunists."

"So you are not one of the Priests of Mezzor?"

"No," Mitchell scoffed. "Not all vampires follow that fool. Some go their own way, and there is a group called the Niveus Gladius, The Order of the White Sword, that oppose them. Baelaar is the vampire who turned me as well, but there are more ancient ones than him."

"Are you part of this Niveus Gladius—"

"No, I have no interest in their 'noble cause'. We share some mutual enemies, that is all. However, in return for being trained as a warrior, I have agreed to help the Niveus Gladius acquire information." Mitchell paused and stared at Sylvain who was listening with suspended breath. "Here is the most astonishing thing," he continued. "The original vampire came to Earth from another world named Magella, apparently through some magical artifact called the Well of Many Worlds. He arrived here, turned a man into a vampire then returned to his own world, and that man then turned others and spread the vampire blood."

"Another world," whispered Sylvain, eyes wide in awe. "I always suspected there was more…" His voice trailed off. Then his eyes refocused as he looked at Mitchell. "How many vampires are there?"

"I do not know. My mentor believes there are less than a hundred in the world, although even he is not sure."

"What are our powers? Can we be destroyed?"

"I cannot answer your questions now. Time is pressing. I suggest that you get as far away from the Priests of Mezzor as you can. They are a lunatic cult, deranged and deadly."

"But why did they choose me?"

"I don't know." He shrugged. "Perhaps you were in the wrong place at the wrong time."

"What should I do?"

"Fly, run and keep on running, or hide somewhere deep and dark where they cannot find you."

"If I am being hunted by supernatural beings, whether I grow wings and soar on high, or grow a fortress on my back and sink to the bottom of the ocean, I fear that I will either be plucked or shucked. Either way I am f—"

"Enough. You may come with me. But only for a night, then I will take you to the Niveus Gladius, perhaps they will help you." Mitchell stopped and stared at him.

"What?" asked Sylvain.

"That might actually be a good idea."

"What?"

"You are coming to the Royal Opera with me, posing as my manservant. I found some information reading the mind of the Comtesse LeDuijou and…"

"Reading her mind?"

"Yes, I must attend the opera to find a certain person and I must not be noticed. In order to do that I must pose as a nobleman, having a manservant will help with the illusion."

Sylvain was restless, his eyes wide and eager. "When can we hunt? I can feel the hunger already burning inside me."

"Very soon."

"Might we find someone wealthy?" asked Sylvain. "I am in desperate need of some new clothes." He tugged on his coat, still wet with blood, to show the tattered edges.

Mitchell stared at him hard and long. "Sylvain, with intense concentration you will find you may read some thoughts in the minds of mortals in order to choose your victims wisely. The Niveus Gladius only hunt the scum of society… the murderers, villains, people who are guilty of heinous crimes and who are completely unrepentant. I must warn you, if you start killing innocent people, or join the Priests of Mezzor, they will find you and destroy you."

Sylvain shrugged. "I will abide by their law. Besides, hunting the evil members of society seems a superior form of fun. More sporting."

Mitchell nodded. "Yes, and they come in all shapes, sizes and classes." He stood up and looked Sylvain up and down for a moment. "You appear to be around the same build as me. We must find you a new jacket."

"Excellent," cried Sylvain, clapping his hands together.

"Wait here."

Mitchell disappeared through a door into the palace, striding through the corridors until he found two men of approximately his size. Before they knew what was happening he had knocked both of them unconscious, dragged them into an empty room and stolen their clothes. He returned to the Mars Room a few minutes later.

Once they had both changed, Mitchell held Sylvain by the shoulders and stared into his eyes. "Now, I want something from you."

Sylvain recoiled at the ferocious look in Mitchell's eyes, reminded of his chilling encounter with Baelaar. "What is it?" he muttered.

"If you ever see Baelaar again, or hear of his whereabouts or the whereabouts of the Well of Many Worlds you will inform me. You will not stop searching for me until you find me, do you understand?" Sylvain was taken aback by the snarl in Mitchell's voice and the crimson flashing of his eyes.

"Y-yes, certainly," he stammered.

"Good, I have been hunting for them for nearly two hundred years."

"Two hundred years!"

"Yes, shortly after he turned me the Niveus Gladius destroyed many of the Priests of Mezzor. Baelaar went underground for a long time. Any time a war started I went to its battlefields in search of him, but found only rumors."

"Does he hold the secret of the Well of Many Worlds?"

"No one knows where it is. If you help me catch him or find the Well, then I will reward you with riches greater than anything you can imagine. Too many gold pieces for you to be able to count."

Sylvain stared at Mitchell as if trying to imagine that much gold. "Think of the parties I could throw with such wealth!"

Mitchell stared at him. "Just do as I say."

Three

Emily sat bolt upright, emitting a piercing scream. Brutally wakened from her struggles with the demon she was drenched with sweat. She had been clawing at its face, unable to fight free of its burning grip. Gasping for breath she stared wildly about her bedroom, trying to force the image of the demon's face from her mind.

"It was just a nightmare," she whispered to herself, running a shaky hand through her sweat-soaked hair now lying cold and lank across her fevered brow.

As her breathing slowed closer to normal she remembered the handsome young man with his hypnotic, glittering emerald eyes. How easily his eyes had overpowered her, taking total possession of her mind and body. The memory sent a hot rush of blood to her cheeks and she shook her head, stunned by the intensity and pleasure of the sensation.

A crack of morning sun was shining through the gap in her curtains, reminding her that she was now safely back from that dark place. She began to feel as though she were herself again, as though it were any other school day. She tried to think if she had any homework to finish but found she had to summon all her powers of concentration to remember what had happened the previous day.

As she forced herself to gather her thoughts, the reality of her father's murder came crashing back to her. Her stomach churned and her heart broke all over again. Waking up to this horrible reality was the real nightmare.

Pulling herself together, Emily brushed her teeth, showered, dressed and went downstairs, absent-mindedly stirring a bowl of cereal, only half listening while her mother made funeral arrangements on the phone. She could tell her mom was finding solace in the rational, her mind grasping onto the rituals and traditions society created to deal with the abyss of death. She had not mentioned the desk to her and intended to keep her promise to her father.

Emily couldn't stop thinking about the way she had behaved the last time she saw her father as she drifted through all the rituals of the following days in a trance. First there was the visitation at the funeral home. Friends and relatives arrived in a steady stream throughout the evening to pay their respects – everyone dressed in muted colors, murmuring their sympathies, looking at Emily with sad eyes as they reminisced awkwardly about special moments they had shared with her father. Their words sounded distant and empty. She smiled politely and thanked them for their kindness but she just wanted the ordeal to end.

Then came the funeral itself. It was as though the whole universe was in mourning. The heavy gray sky rained relentlessly down on them and by the time Emily got into the church her feet were cold and wet from the puddles she had been unable to avoid in the car park. Surrounded by a sea of faces she didn't bother to focus on she allowed the sermons, the hymns and the eulogy to wash over her. Then the pallbearers carried the coffin out to the hearse, which they all followed on foot to the cemetery. Then the final words: "Ashes to ashes, dust to dust." And at last, her father's body was lowered into the grave.

She tried to imagine him lying inside the casket, his hands folded over his chest; the same man who had twirled her around and around so many times when she was little, the man who had adored her. She felt as though she were all alone, with time moving inexorably forward around her. She couldn't understand how the world could keep moving forward without her father in it anymore, everything continuing as if nothing had happened, nothing had been lost. It didn't seem possible. Everything should have ceased at the same time as his heart stopped beating.

Eventually it was all over and she and her mother were alone again at home, sitting together silently in the kitchen, both staring into space.

"I want you back in school as soon as possible." Her mother's voice broke the silence, snapping Emily out of her reverie.

"Are you kidding?"

"No, I'm not, Emily. I understand what you are going through and how difficult this is. Recovering from such a shock will take a long time, but we have to move forward and focus on your future."

"What, my grades? My career? Really? Does that really seem important to you now?"

"Of course it doesn't seem important by comparison to what you are feeling. But it is. Ten years from now you will be glad that you didn't let this derail your school work."

Emily felt a ball of resentment welling up inside her. "You're sick. 'Getting on' is all you ever think about. You don't care about anything else."

"Well, that's what life is," her mother snapped. "I'm saying this for your own good."

Emily opened her mouth to retort but thought better of it. "I'm going to bed now and I'm not going to school for a couple days. You can't force me."

She ran upstairs and slammed her bedroom door, locking it behind her. Stamping into her bathroom she checked herself in the mirror. Staring into her big royal-blue eyes and pale face framed by long chestnut-brown hair she hardly recognizing the slender girl staring back. She felt like a stranger in her own life, and in her heart she knew that her mother was right and there was no option but to carry on with that life.

Over the next couple days she found that for half her waking hours she was immersed in a black cloud of sadness, pain, loss, and guilt. During the other half, however, she was able to escape into daydreams about the handsome young man from her dream. The memory of his eyes haunted her, filling her with warm feelings of pleasure and desire deep inside, making her heart race, her flesh tingle and her breath catch in her tightening throat. She would deliberately allow herself to drift into a hypnotic trance, thinking about those eyes, giving herself permission to forget her grief and to feel the pleasure and excitement.

After two days she went back to school, knowing it was what her father would have wanted, but as she set off from the house she couldn't imagine how she was going to get through the day. How could she force herself to pretend that everything was normal, when nothing was normal at all or ever would be again?

Everyone at Dawson High had seen the news reports and none of them knew how to act around her. Everywhere she went, kids either stared at her, like she was some kind of freak, or pretended she wasn't there, which she actually preferred a thousand times over the staring. Some idiots would whisper behind her back when she passed by, as though she was the one who had done something wrong.

When her best friend, Cindy, spotted her in the hallway, she ran up and threw her arms around her, hugging her so tightly she could hardly breathe.

"Oh my gosh, Emily, I've been calling you every day since the funeral."

"Thanks," she gasped when she could get in enough air. "I know. I'm sorry I didn't call back – I didn't know what to say. I just wanted to be alone to sort out my thoughts."

Cindy was the exact opposite of her. She had her whole life

planned out, from what her wedding dress would look like to how she would design her first baby's bedroom. Cindy was short with jet-black hair, wore glasses and was a straight-A student. She was entirely responsible and serious in contrast to Emily, who never even knew what she would wear the next day, much less what she wanted to do when she graduated high school.

"I understand," Cindy said, linking arms. "Listen, I gotta go to class but meet me in the caf at lunch."

"Okay."

She found it comforting to see the familiar faces of her group of lunch friends at their usual table in the cafeteria. She sat down with them, sheltering from the prying eyes everywhere else in the room. Beside Cindy was her boyfriend Chester, quiet, handsome, athletic, with his short, strawberry-blonde hair and hazel eyes. Like Cindy he was a straight-A student. On his other side was Bethany Denman, whose father owned a shipping company. As well as being from a rich family, Bethany was also beautiful and a school cheerleader. She loved spending her father's money on clothes and was very stylish, sort of high fashion with a bit of a glamorous, Gothy pin-up edge to it. She drove a nice car, had a perfect figure and perfect skin. Despite all this, she was still popular with the other kids. The only thing she was lacking was a boyfriend because she had recently broken up with the son of a wealthy banker. Everyone assumed that she would end up with Tom Price, social god of the school and also newly single.

"Have the police got any leads?" Chester asked, ignoring Cindy's scowl as she tried to silence him. "Do they know who did it?"

"No." Emily shook her head. "But his store was broken into a couple nights before his murder and…" Emily paused.

"And what?" Bethany prompted.

"The killers wrote 'The Blood Of The World Is The Blood Of The God' on the wall of the apartment in my father's blood."

"Oh my god, that is so creepy." Bethany looked genuinely shocked. They all exchanged disturbed glances.

"That is so messed up," Cindy said. "Who does that? What does that even mean?"

"Must have been some psycho," Emily said. Tears welled up in her eyes and she fought to keep control. She really didn't want to start bawling in front of the whole school.

"Makes me think it's some kind of freaky religious cult or Satan worshippers or something," said Bethany.

"The weird thing is that my father left me some old antique desk just before he was killed. I don't think it's worth any money or anything, but it had the words 'Vadas Asger' then 'demons' carved into it and my father had written 'Vadas Asger?' on the back of the purchase record. But if it's some weird cult, why would they want to kill my father?"

"Maybe they just picked him randomly," said Bethany. "I was watching that show, 'World's Most Sinister Satanic Cults' the other night, sometimes these Satan worshipper freaks just pick a random person."

"But who or what is Vadas Asger?" asked Cindy. "Is it a place or a name or what is it?"

"I don't know," Emily admitted. "I searched online and found that Asger is some old Nordic word or name that means 'spear of God' but no idea what Vadas is."

"Did you tell the cops?" asked Cindy.

"Yeah, they don't know what Vadas Asger means either."

"Are you sure the desk or something else he has isn't worth a lot of money? Like that show where people bring in old stuff that they find in the attic and have it appraised and sometimes it's worth a load of money and they had no idea it was?" Bethany said, leaning forward eagerly.

"Yeah, I was thinking that could be why, when the thieves didn't find it, they stole all his purchase and sales records, to see if he had ever had whatever it is they're looking for and if he had already sold it to someone else. But I researched the desk and it's pretty much worthless. It must have been 'Vadas Asger' they were looking for, not the desk."

"Yes, I've got it!" Bethany's eyes widened with excitement. "He probably bought some kind of evil artifact, or cursed item or something important in the Satanic Church and didn't realize it, maybe that desk is some kind of satanic artifact!"

"I guess that's possible," Emily said doubtfully.

"Yeah." Bethany lowered her voice as though confiding a dark secret. "Or maybe they wanted the desk because of what was carved in it. Maybe Vadas Asger is the name of some kind of satanic spell or ritual, or maybe it's a code or password, or maybe it's the name of someone who they're going to sacrifice!"

"Yeah, that's kinda where I was going with that," Emily said. "But not necessarily all the satanic sacrificing stuff. But maybe it's a code or a place."

"I bet it is." Bethany looked at each one of them in turn. "We should try and find out who these scumbags are."

After school Emily went by her father's store. Her mom was selling all the existing stock, having no wish to continue running the store herself. Today was the big sale and Emily was surprised at how large the turnout was. Watching the customers picking through what was left of her father's possessions, she became lost in memories when she spotted something that made her blood run cold. Three men had entered the store. As the first one strolled past her he turned to look in her direction, and she saw the scar on his face and his missing right ear. Her heart pounded in her ears and she struggled to control her breathing. It was the man from the police photo – Cady Sunner.

The three men wandered through the store, apparently examining every piece, one by one. Emily forced herself to walk slowly to the office where her mother was sifting through paperwork, looking distracted.

"Mom," she said, "call the police. Now."

"What? Why on earth would I do that?" her mother asked, distractedly.

"Because one of those men out there is that Cady Sunner guy. Detective Scannel showed me his picture at the police station… Can you please just call?"

"Hand me the phone," her mother said, shuffling through a stack of receipts.

As Emily waited, keeping her eye on the floor outside, her mother called the police, but she was put on hold and by the time she got through, the three men had left.

Without saying a word to her mother, Emily walked out after them but they had already disappeared. Not wanting to go back in she decided to go home. Arriving at the house she was surprised to find the front door was unlocked. She assumed her mother had just forgotten to lock it. She may have been doing a good job of pretending her husband's death hadn't affected her, but it must have done. She opened the door and poked her head in cautiously. Everything seemed quiet and undisturbed. Closing the door behind her, she was walking toward the stairs when something caught her eye and made her heart miss several beats. The living room had been ransacked. Furniture had been overturned, upholstery slashed and lamps and pictures lay smashed on the floor.

Was the robber still in the house? As she turned back to the door a deep, threatening voice, just a few inches away, made her jump out of her skin. She let out an involuntary scream.

"Well, look what we have here."

A tall, heavily built man wearing a black ski mask was standing in the doorway leading to the dining room. She ran to the front door, but with surprising agility he jumped in front of her, blocking her path.

"You're not going anywhere," he growled as another man, similarly dressed in black, appeared.

"Check outside and see if the mother's coming," the first one ordered.

Emily spun on her heels and ran upstairs, three steps at a time, a racehorse out of the starting gate, her heart thundering in her ears. One of the men sprang after her. As she turned onto the landing, she could sense him right behind her, so close she imagined she could feel his hot breath on the back of her neck. She felt a scream rising in her throat then heard a crash behind her. Glancing back she saw that her pursuer had hurtled sideways, head first into the wall, smashing a hole right through it.

The man cursed and stumbled as he tried to right himself, momentarily stunned. His companion charged past him but Emily was already slamming and locking her bedroom door. At the first kick from the man's boot Emily shrieked as the wood began to splinter and the metal lock buckled, a screw flying out and bouncing across the floor.

It would only be a matter of seconds before he came crashing in.

"Out the window, Emily," whispered a voice from behind her right ear. She shrieked again and spun around, but there was nobody there. Another violent kick to the door sent her running to the window. Throwing it open, she climbed out onto the ledge and jumped into the branches of the oak tree outside as the door exploded open behind her. The smaller twigs whipped her face as she plummeted through them. She grabbed onto a long branch and held fast. It swung up and down beneath her weight, smacking her head on a large knot, but didn't break.

Looking back she saw the man climbing through the window after her. What was she supposed to do from here? Drop to the ground and run? For a few vital moments she froze, searching for the quickest way down. Then, as the man reached out to grab her it was as if an invisible force pushed him from behind. Losing his balance he plunged, yelling as he went, toward the ground, landing hard. The other man appeared at the window. Seeing his companion lying below on the ground, he disappeared back into the house.

The man on the ground attempted to get to his feet, moaning in pain as the other man rushed out of the house to support him.

The two of them hobbled through the back garden and out of sight. Emily leaned her forehead against the tree trunk and took in several deep breaths before dialing 911.

Once she was sure they had gone she climbed shakily down, just as two police cars drew up, their red and white lights flashing silently.

Later, once the police had finished with their questioning and her mother was starting to clear up the mess the men had left, Emily slipped into the garage to see if the desk was still there. It was in the same place she had left it. She slumped down on the floor, leaning against it as she tried to put her thoughts into some sort of order. She thought about the strange, devilish little voice that had whispered to her to climb out the window. Was it her imagination? Some kind of audio hallucination? She could also have sworn that something had physically pushed the man out the window…

After a few minutes she went back into the house to help her mother clean up, not mentioning anything about the desk. They worked together in silence for several hours. Afterwards they had a quiet dinner and then Emily went upstairs to bed, emotionally, mentally and physically exhausted. She felt sure that Cady Sunner, and possibly his boss, were linked to the men in balaclavas and that they had murdered her father. It was possible that she and her mother would be next so it was a race against time. She was going to have to do everything she could to help bring them to justice.

Emily collapsed into bed and again plunged into the same vivid dream she'd had the other night. She found herself back in the large four-poster bed in the castle staring up at the handsome young man. She was entranced by how gorgeous he was, her eyes lingered for a moment on his chiseled abs and extraordinarily athletic physique, and then she looked into his eyes. Her heart pounded, as his glittering emerald eyes again mesmerized her.

He was close enough that she would be able to reach out and run her finger tips around the perfect angles of his chin, cheekbones and nose, if only she could move. But she couldn't move and it was because of those eyes, their stare had penetrated deep inside her, sending her into a trance, filling her with overpowering desires and a sense of excitement so intense she could not even lift a finger under her own volition.

Back in her bedroom Emily was kicking off her sheets and moaning in her sleep. Her body was wet with sweat.

When she looked into his eyes it was as though everything else in the universe disappeared and the only thing she wanted, or had ever wanted, was him.

The young man opened his mouth and spoke to her but his voice sounded distant and she couldn't make out what he was saying.

"What?" she shouted. Her own voice sounded as though she were yelling in a windstorm.

The young man spoke again but she still couldn't hear him. Emily wanted to scream with frustration she wanted so badly to hear what he was saying to her. He stopped speaking and stared at her. She could see that look of carnal hunger smoldering in his stare that sent a thrill of danger through her whole body. She saw the lightning flashing outside, as she knew it would, and heard the thunder crack and roll. The windows blew open again, hurling the vase to the floor. He moved closer and his eyes changed, blazing with a deadly, inhuman, crimson glow, flooding her body with a delicious wave of both fear and desire. She parted her lips. A moment later she found herself falling, falling, falling into darkness.

Four

As the two of them strolled toward the entrance of the Royal Opera a more striking pair of gentlemen could not be found in all of France. Every lady whose wandering eyes fell upon them must have wondered who these two handsome, wealthy young men with the pale skin and glittering eyes might be. The Royal Opera was on the other side of the palace, far from the rooms where Mitchell had caused such a commotion on the horse and it seemed as though everything was proceeding as usual as they joined the crowd filing in through the grand doors. Sylvain stared about him, high on the richness of light, color, sound and movement that his newly acquired senses now revealed to him.

"The night is beautiful, is it not?" he murmured in wonder.

"Yes," whispered Mitchell, "when you are first turned it is as though you are seeing everything for the first time; so vivid, the colors so rich, the clarity, seeing the undercurrent of life in all things."

"I have never seen colors... life itself, appear so rich and vivid. What opera is being performed?"

"It is a new one by Mozart called *Don Giovanni*."

With the hypnotic power of his eyes alone, Mitchell procured them one of the finest boxes in the house. As they waited for the opera to begin Mitchell talked in a low voice, barely moving his lips for fear of being overheard by one of the many people admiring them from below. "I have been informed that a wealthy banker is involved with the Priests of Mezzor and is helping to finance the coming revolution. When I read the Comtesse LeDuijou's thoughts I saw that he would be attending the opera tonight. I need to extract information from him."

"I know there is an uprising coming, but surely it is the people's revolution." Sylvain peered about nervously.

Mitchell shook his head. "I am not defending the monarchy. I have no sympathies for them; they have ruthlessly taxed the people of this great nation into crushing poverty."

"Then what are you saying?"

"You are still very naïve, my friend. When a violent revolution occurs and the power structure has been removed, a void is left that must be filled. Those who step in to fill it will have been involved from the very beginning and are well financed; always by the same financiers as the people they just removed from power. The new rulers and the old rulers are nothing more than puppets, controlled by the same puppet-masters who always lurk in the shadows."

As they waited for the opera to begin Sylvain told Mitchell about how he had been born into poverty in New Orleans. His parents had died when he was still young, forcing him to grow up as a servant. As soon as he was old enough he stowed away on a ship to the Old World. Hearing the story, Mitchell could understand why the experience of finding himself deep within the social circles of the wealthy and powerful of Paris was thrilling for Sylvain.

"Use your new powers," Mitchell said, "and try scanning the minds of some of these people."

Both men concentrated their powers onto mind reading and it wasn't long before Mitchell found what he was looking for in a box opposite theirs. He pointed him out to Sylvain.

"Ah yes," he murmured, "he knows the plan."

"What?" asked Sylvain.

"They are plotting a reign of terror, using a new execution device, the guillotine. They intend to chop off the heads of everyone who opposes them and create a mass slaughter."

He pointed to the middle-aged couple seated in the opposite box. "Try to read their minds. See the full horror of their crimes."

"From here?"

"Yes. You can do it."

After a few minutes of intense concentration, Sylvain shook his head in shock. "That is vile. Absolutely disgraceful!" A grin cracked through his expression of outrage. "This is entirely too much fun!"

"Wait until after the show," Mitchell said. "They will be ideal prey for your first hunt."

Sylvain was so enthralled by the splendor and emotional power of the opera that he had almost forgotten their planned hunting expedition by the time the curtain came down.

"Let's go and find them," Mitchell said as they left the box and strolled through the main lobby. They both spotted their prey simultaneously. The man was in his fifties, dressed in so much tight-fitting finery that he could hardly walk, but still managing to carry himself as if convinced of his own superiority as he pushed his way rudely through the crowd. He was short and portly, with an enormous handlebar mustache. He wore a pair of round spectacles and blinked continuously as he looked at everyone with an air of condescension. His wife was a wiry woman about ten years younger, dressed with equal finery and with a glazed, cold expression in her eyes. She might have been considered attractive once, but the cruel set of her mouth made it unlikely that anyone would approach her now.

The two vampires quickened their pace to catch up with the couple just as they stepped out of the opera house into the night.

"Excuse me, Monsieur Sangsue, might I have a word?" Mitchell called out.

The man turned, frowning at the impudence of the young stranger addressing him.

"Hmm? What is it? Do I know you, sir?"

Sylvain made eye contact with his wife and smiled without showing his teeth. At first she looked away haughtily, but she was unable to resist looking back after a few moments. Sylvain did not avert his stare and soon the lady's eyes were locked onto his and she was in a partial trance. She looked as though she had been bewitched, as if some delicious, forbidden poison had entered her system, promising both ecstasy and death.

"No, sir," said Mitchell. "We have never had the pleasure of meeting. I am Lord Gilmour. My partner and I have some business with your bank that I would very much like to discuss in private."

At the mention of business the banker's face brightened. Mitchell had found the information about Lord Gilmour, a wealthy man who was due to arrive in Paris, in Sangsue's mind. Lord Gilmour had arranged some sizeable deposits with Sangsue's bank. Mitchell also knew that Sangsue had not yet laid eyes on the young lord and had no idea what he looked like.

"Ah! Lord Gilmour!" The banker beamed, glowing pink with greed. "Yes, of course. I have made all the arrangements. Come around to the bank first thing tomorrow, if you like. I will bring the papers, and we will settle everything."

"It is really a stroke of good fortune that I found you here," Mitchell continued as if the other man had not spoken. "I have just been informed of a family emergency and will have to depart very early. I wonder if we could settle everything this evening."

"Oh." The banker was obviously, taken aback. "I am sorry to hear that. Unfortunately, all the paperwork is at my home."

"Would it be too great an imposition to go there now?" Mitchell asked.

"Well…" Sangsue hesitated. "Certainly," he said after a moment, his greed overruling his good judgment. "You are welcome to ride there with us in our carriage."

"That is very kind of you, sir. We would be delighted. Allow me to introduce my partner, Lord Sylvain DeLune."

The banker bowed as low as his large waistline and tight waistcoat would allow. "A pleasure, sir."

"Sir," replied Sylvain, raising his handkerchief to his mouth to hide the sharp points of his canines.

They followed the couple to their carriage. The footman opened the door, and the four of them climbed into the cushioned velvet interior. During the ride into Paris Mitchell and Sangsue fell into an impassioned discussion about economics, while Sylvain continued staring into the wife's eyes, pulling her deeper and deeper into a hypnotic state. Mitchell watched his new friend's progress out of the corner of his eye.

The banker's estate was a grand affair, the house surrounded by carefully manicured lawns and formal gardens lit by flaming torches; Sylvain was momentarily taken aback by its splendor. The couple led them inside to a large, formal drawing room. Mitchell requested privacy and the banker sent his servants away.

"Excuse me for a moment while I fetch the paperwork," Sangsue said, as he scurried off to retrieve the documents. Sylvain focused all his attention on the lady, sitting close to her as she glanced around self-consciously, unsure of what it was Sylvain was trying to do.

"Look deep into my eyes," he whispered and her face went blank as their eyes remained locked, their mouths just inches apart. "You will do as I command."

"Yes," she replied.

"Unbelievable. This is such fun!" Sylvain clapped his hands with excitement before leaning forward to murmur something in her ear.

The banker returned with an armful of documents and three crystal glasses full of brandy. "Well, then, here we are." He placed the papers on a table, and his wife stood up and approached him, taking a glass from his hand, and hurling the drink into his face.

"What in the hell?" he shouted, rubbing the liquid from his eyes.

"You are a bloated little truffle hunter," said his wife, slapping him across the cheek before sitting back down indignantly, looking to Sylvain for her next instruction. Sylvain roared with laughter and slapped his knee.

The banker stood motionless for a moment, his eyes wide, his face growing redder and redder.

"Candice!" he shouted. "What... What in the... What are you doing?" He looked at Mitchell helplessly, at a loss for words, while Sylvain continued whispering into the woman's ear.

"Sit down," Mitchell ordered, pointing at a chair.

The dumbstruck man immediately obeyed. "Lord Gilmour," he stammered, "I must apologize for my wife's behavior. She isn't well and..."

"I have a concern about our business arrangement," Mitchell continued. "You see, I only do business with honorable, trustworthy people, and – how can I put this? – I have doubts about your integrity. More specifically, I have heard stories about how you lure destitute young orphan girls into your basement and butcher them so that your wife can bathe in their blood to keep her youthful appearance."

"What?" The banker spluttered, shadows of guilt creeping over his face.

The sound of barking made them both turn to see Candice crawling on her hands and knees, yelping and whimpering like a dog. Sylvain was roaring with laughter once more, delighted at his newfound powers to humiliate. Mitchell frowned, annoyed at such childish pranks.

Sangsue leaped to his feet. "Candice! Have you lost your mind?"

Mitchell pushed him back down into his chair. "You and your wife are monsters! Did you think for a moment about your victims' lives? Their futures? Their hopes and dreams?"

The banker shook uncontrollably in the chair, bringing his knees up around his chest, as if wanting to crawl back into his mother's womb overwhelmed by fear and confusion.

"It was her idea!" he shouted, pointing to his wife on the floor. "Besides, they were only children, they don't matter. They're small and useless, barely able to think for themselves. Who cares? Children are annoying, the less of them the better. That's what I say!"

"You devil!" spat Mitchell, grabbing the armrests of the chair and lowering his face close to the banker's. "I should slash your throat so your words don't infect my brain with your vileness. You donkey-witted vulture. Shall we speak of the coming revolution? I see that your position is secured with France's future leaders. And I see you have a plan to create a reign of terror."

As they spoke, Candice leaped to her feet, flung open the windows of the drawing room, climbed up on the ledge, and shouted into the night air for anyone to hear, "I will eat your children! I will eat your children!"

"Candice!" the banker shouted, trying to stand up, but unable to fight free of Mitchell's restraining grip. Candice fell back into the drawing room, and Sylvain caught her in his arms. She gazed up at him adoringly.

"And what did you want with the blood of all those girls?" asked Mitchell quietly. "Were you preparing to become… vampires?"

The man's face went from flushed to deathly pale. Mitchell drew back his lips, exposing his fangs as his eyes glowed a terrifying crimson.

"God help me," muttered the banker, shaking with terror.

"You and your partners are going to be financing the future rulers of France, controlling their every move. But Baelaar and the Priests of Mezzor, in turn, will control you, from the shadows. Ah, I see in your thoughts that you are bringing in a sizable shipment of gold tomorrow, so tomorrow is the day. And what is the price? What did Baelaar offer you? Of course, immortality! The promise that you will be turned into vampires! And what is the source of your vileness? Why it's envy, of course. How utterly pathetic, you weakling," he scoffed. "And I see that ever since you were a young man you have committed any number of despicable crimes for it. You use a dagger to butter your bread. Well, hear me now" – he pushed his face into the banker's, eyes burning – "envy is born from weakness and comes creeping from its womb like the stench of rotting flesh from a newly pregnant tomb, and I smell the stench of death upon you."

"My friend has come to make a withdrawal." Sylvain joined them with Candice still in his arms, his eyes now also glowing crimson as he leered at the banker and winked at Mitchell. "He is taking out every last drop."

With those words, he sank his own fangs deep into the stringy tendons of Candice's exposed neck. She gasped in shock but didn't struggle as the blood pumped out of her throat, staining the silk of her fine dress. The banker's jaw fell open.

Mitchell tore him out of his chair. "Blow out the candle, and toll the bell," he said. "Another soul is lost to Hell."

He plunged his fangs deep into the murderer's fat neck and drank his fill. The banker tried to put up a fight, flopping around like a fish out of water until he lost consciousness and exhaled his last gulping breath. Mitchell discarded his limp body onto a chair.

"Delicious!" exclaimed Sylvain, releasing the drained body of the banker's wife onto the floor.

Mitchell glanced at him with a hint of irritation. "What foolish game were you playing?"

Sylvain smiled. "I like to play with my food. My goodness I enjoy blood! My friend, I can tell that you are very tense, even though I cannot read your mind. Which reminds me, why is it that I can read the minds of others and not yours? Can vampires not read the minds of other vampires?"

"They can, but I am older and therefore more powerful."

"Anyhow, I sense that there is something troubling you. You need to relax and enjoy yourself. I have a spectacular idea."

"Oh yes?" Mitchell peered at him skeptically. "What would that be?"

"A party to celebrate the beginning of my life as a vampire and of our friendship. Surely, we can have a little sport as we hunt."

Mitchell raised an eyebrow. "Being vampires is not something that we shout about. Secrecy is the one thing that the Niveus Gladius and the Priests of Mezzor agree upon. So, be warned, public displays will very quickly lead to your destruction. What did you have in mind?"

"Ah." Sylvain smiled mischievously. "That is my secret but I assure you it will not be in public. I will make all the arrangements and I promise not to break any rules. I will contact you in two days' time."

Noises outside the house made them both pause to listen. "Someone approaches," Mitchell whispered. Sylvain opened his mouth to reply but Mitchell motioned for him to be silent. "I'll deal with this."

He glided across to the front door of the manor just as it opened to reveal a vampire with dark-brown, ancient eyes. He was handsome in a cruel way with thick, flowing brown hair and pale skin. A wide, well-trimmed mustache stretched across a face that was thin, with a long nose, and looked as though it had witnessed endless acts of evil in both its life and its afterlife. He was immaculately dressed and groomed and accompanied by a girl of about eighteen draped in fabulous furs and jewels.

"Lord Ruthen!" exclaimed Mitchell, startled.

Lord Ruthen looked equally surprised as he paused, taking in their presence and the bodies of the two dead hosts.

The girl's scream jolted them all back to the present. "Mother! Father!" she shrieked.

In one swift movement Lord Ruthen grabbed the girl's thick, soft hair, pulled her head back to expose her smooth young throat, and sank his fangs in where he could see the beat of her pulse. As he drank the dark, rich blood from her artery, the girl gradually stopped struggling, until she finally went limp and he dropped her carelessly on the ground.

"Exquisite," he murmured, straightening up and wiping his thin lips with his handkerchief. "Mitchell, what a pleasant surprise. What brings you here? And who is your interesting-looking young friend?"

Mitchell stared at him for a moment then looked at the dead girl. "Lord Ruthen, this is Sylvain DeLune," Mitchell announced. "He was recently turned. What are you doing here, may I ask, and why did you kill that poor, pretty girl?"

"An honor to meet you, sir," Ruthen said with a gallant bow. Sylvain returned the courtesy.

"Ruthen is a knight of the Order of the Niveus Gladius."

"A pleasure to meet you," Sylvain said, stepping forward to shake Lord Ruthen's hand.

Lord Ruthen then turned to Mitchell. "I am here for the same reason you likely are, extracting information, and blood."

"But in all seriousness," Mitchell said, bending to look at the girl, "this creature does not look a day over eighteen. Surely she had nothing to do with her parents' sins."

"Yes." Ruthen gazed down at her and sighed wistfully. "So young and so very fresh. And so like her mother. You know what they say about the apple not falling far from the tree."

"You were aware of her parents' crimes and their deal with Baelaar?"

"I read it all in her mind. Her mother was emulating vampire lore in preparation to be turned. Simply diabolical! They were training their daughter in all their appalling ways. The little viper took to it with great relish. She was the lure who brought the girls to them."

"I see."

"You should have looked deeper into their minds, you would have seen."

"Outrageous!" Sylvain laughed. "What an awful family! You are so right about hunting the evil ones, Mitchell. This is truly where the fun lies."

"Indeed." Lord Ruthen smiled. "I must admit, part of me laments the fall of any innocent into evil ways, but another part rejoices. What a treat to find one so young and pretty and yet so utterly corrupt. A pleasure to drink such fresh and delicate blood. It is only natural for our kind to have a passion for the peach as well as the nectar it contains, and to desire that both should be just perfectly ripe."

"Quite right," Sylvain cried. "Well said!"

Mitchell stared, unsmiling, at Lord Ruthen. "I was referring to their dealings with Baelaar, their involvement in the coming revolution, and their plans for some sort of reign of terror with their new killing device."

"Why yes, of course. Most interesting. There will be thousands of decapitations if we do not stop them. I will be informing Fionn of everything. Speaking of which, Fionn says that you are nearly finished with your training and that your progress has been remarkable; that you are now one of the greatest warriors among us. Congratulations. Have you reconsidered? Has Fionn convinced you to join the Niveus Gladius?"

"No."

"Are you not prepared to put aside your thirst for vengeance for the greater good of humanity?"

"No."

"Once Baelaar is destroyed then will you reconsider? Or are you still determined to find the Well and follow this path of almost certain destruction into the planes of Hell, if they even exist? Will you not abandon this reckless obsession with hunting for this demon or devil or whatever?"

"No."

"What a waste." Lord Ruthen shook his head and cleared his throat. "Perhaps we will still be able to change your mind."

"Unlikely," Mitchell sneered.

"Well." Lord Ruthen sighed. "It was a delight to see you both, but I really must be on my way." He bid them goodnight and opened the front door, pausing to look down at the dead girl and then at her parents. "I do love moving in the best circles. It gives me such pleasure to seek out the places where the cream of society has curdled to poison."

47

He gave the two younger vampires a wink and swept out, leaving the door swinging behind him. Mitchell watched, frowning thoughtfully, as Ruthen climbed into a magnificent black coach and his driver thrashed the horses to a gallop.

"I like your friend," Sylvain said as the sound of hooves had faded and they stepped over the body of the dead girl and out into the night. "He definitely has a sense of style."

Later that night Mitchell was back in his apartment, one of the most luxurious in all of Paris, a penthouse fit for a king. No expense had been spared, from the finest fabrics to the hand-crafted furniture and art, he had created an atmosphere to rival the splendor of Versailles itself. There was a sharp knock at the door. Mitchell threw it open to find another tall and powerfully build vampire staring at him. His light-brown hair hung over his shoulders, framing his noble features and pale skin. He was dressed for battle as a Scottish warrior from the Highlands.

"Fionn," Mitchell greeted him, "please come in."

As they sat on two ornate thrones beneath a chandelier blazing with dozens of candles, he recounted to Fionn all that had happened since his arrival at Versailles earlier that evening.

"The guillotine, hmmmm… very interesting," Fionn mused in his deep Scottish accent. "We must do all we can to stop this coming reign of terror."

"That is your problem not mine, Fionn. It appeared strange to me though that Ruthen… well, it almost seemed as though he killed that girl as quickly as he could, so that I would not have time to read her thoughts."

Fionn shook his head and smiled. "Our friend, the banker, had his fingers in many pies. Ruthen has been following many of the different, overlapping threads that we are attempting to untangle."

"I see." Mitchell was still not convinced but decided to hold his peace for the time being.

"Mitchell, this evening there is a visitor coming who I would like you to meet. Her name is Princess Katharina. She is one of the Knights of the Niveus Gladius."

"One of the ancient ones?"

"Yes. Now she has joined us. She will be here at any moment, but first, I will ask you again. Will you not join us?"

"Remember our agreement, when we find it the Well of Many Worlds is mine to use first, once I have gone into it, you may do with it what you will."

"I still say this is madness."

"Why is it madness?" shouted Mitchell, slamming his fist on the table. "We know the Well gives access to all the realms in existence. I will use it to hunt through every devil in the nine planes of Hell and every demon in the Abyss if I must" – his eyes smoldered – "and I will destroy anyone who stands in my way."

"Will you listen to yourself? You propose to travel to the planes of Hell? To the Abyss? The realm of demons? And what if you are successful? You may very well end up trapped in Hell, or the Abyss forever. It is the height of folly."

"Then so be it." Mitchell waved his hand dismissively.

"You are obsessed."

"Yes!" he roared. "Yes I am! And it is no business of yours, so if we have nothing else to discuss…"

"At least stay for a while. Princess Katharina is only following the vaguest of rumors. Now that we are finally close to Baelaar… surely you don't want to miss this opportunity to destroy him."

Mitchell stared at Fionn for several moments before replying. "Yes, I would love vengeance. I have dreamed of that moment more times than I can count. I will help you destroy him, but if in six months we have not found him I will go after the Well."

"So be it." Fionn nodded his agreement, holding out his hand for the other man to shake.

Five

Portland, Maine, 2020

It was close to dawn and Emily was battling the demon in her dream. Lost in a cold, endless darkness the same horrific being pounced upon her. She felt the weight of it as she fought back, screaming wildly and clawing at its face while it crushed the breath from her with its burning claws.

After what seemed like an eternity Emily broke free and flew toward a bright light. Then the whole world flashed a blinding white.

She awoke with a shriek, staring frantically around her bedroom, panting and sobbing with terror. "What is going on with these dreams?" she muttered, shaking her head.

When her heartbeat had finally subsided she pulled herself out of bed, feeling dizzy, her limbs still shaking even though the sweat had now dried. She made her way to the shower, leaning on the walls to steady herself as she went, and stood beneath the warm reviving water.

Feeling better she went downstairs to find something to eat and opened her computer, continuing her search for the meaning of "Vadas Asger." When she came up with nothing she changed tack and typed in the name "Cady Sunner," scrolling through all the searches she had seen before, finding nothing new.

Out of habit, she checked her various social media sites, not that she had much interest in them anymore. A lot of students were posting photos from a hockey game the previous evening. Many of them were of the team captain, Tom Price. Every girl in the school had a crush on him, which wasn't surprising. He was tall, handsome, fit, had sparkling blue eyes and sandy blond hair and was projected to be a superstar athlete making millions by the time he was twenty. Emily had only spoken to him a couple of times and could understand why he was so popular, but like most people she assumed that he and Bethany were destined to be the power couple of their town. She knew that he'd grown up in Canada, moving to Portland a year ago, when his father was transferred for work. She knew the family lived in a house that to her looked like a mansion and that Tom had two cars – a flashy sports model and a Jeep. She flipped idly through the photos. There was certainly something about him. Like most hockey players he was a tough guy and he regularly got into fights. She had the idea that if he hadn't been a star athlete he might've been a bit of a delinquent, but the way it was, everyone let him do pretty much whatever he wanted. He was the undisputed king of Dawson High, and, until recently, had been dating the beautiful, ruthless Chanel Boxer.

Chanel Boxer was the daughter of a media mogul and her clique ran the school. They organized every major social event and party, and they were usually at the root of any vicious rumors that might start about other students. Emily had heard that Chanel had modeled for *Teen Vogue*. Cindy had nicknamed her "Cruella Macbeth".

That day, to her total surprise, Tom approached her in the hallway between classes.

"Hey, Emily, how's it going?" He flashed her a warm, easy smile.

"Okay, thanks," Emily replied, without breaking her stride.

Undeterred, he caught up with her. "So, do you have any plans this weekend?" He had all the confidence of a guy who was never turned down by the girls.

Emily glanced at him suspiciously, trying to figure out what was going on. "Uh – not really."

"I'm throwing a bit of a party the night before Halloween."

"Devil's Night."

"Yeah." Tom chuckled. "You wanna come?" He looked out from under a lock of sandy-colored hair.

Emily stared at him. Why was he inviting her to his party? She had never so much as blipped on his radar before, and now he was requesting the honor of her presence at his home? She moistened her lips with her tongue.

Emily felt something slam into her shoulder. Another student had emerged from a classroom, texting and walking, and they had collided. They both dropped their phones and when Emily squatted down to pick hers up she heard a loud tearing sound.

"You okay?" said Tom, reaching down to steady her. Emily instinctively grabbed his bicep as she stood up.

"Whoa, muscles," she murmured and blushed as her hand felt Tom's rock-hard bicep bulging under his shirt.

"What's your problem? Watch where you're going, idiot."

Emily looked up at the guy she had collided with and recognized him as Angus Keens, a football player. Before she could respond Tom punched him in the stomach. Angus grunted and doubled over and then Tom grabbed him by the throat, slamming him against the lockers. "Apologize," growled Tom, holding up his fist menacingly.

"Dude, chill!" said Angus.

"It's okay, Tom," said Emily. "I mean, thanks but it's okay."

"Apologize," said Tom, still menacing Angus.

"Okay, I'm sorry, dude."

"Not me, her."

Angus looked at Emily. "Sorry."

"That's okay," said Emily. As Tom released Angus, Emily reached around her backside and could feel that she had ripped a huge hole in the seat of her jeans.

Angus walked away muttering and Tom turned his attention back to Emily. "If anyone ever messes with you let me know and I will deal with them. Anyway, can you come to the party?"

"Thanks. Uh, I don't think I can this weekend," she lied, blushing and feeling mortified by her wardrobe malfunction as she felt how big the rip in her jeans was.

"Oh. Okay." He shrugged. "Listen, I'm sorry about your father. I know this must be a bad time for you, so if you want to just take your mind off everything for a few hours, you're welcome to come by."

"Okay, thanks," she muttered, smiling and nodding as she edged away from him, covering her bottom with her hand. She felt like a total fool.

"Are you okay?"

"Uh, yup, fine, all good here," she said, blushing even harder. He wasted only another moment of his valuable time, and then gave her one more casual smile before sauntering off down the hall.

Emily watched him go. She now understood why so many girls fell like fools at his feet. It wasn't just because of his bright-blue eyes and dimpled smile and gorgeous looks, or his easy charm, or that cocky, sexy smirk that drove all the girls wild, or the fact he was a star athlete and rich. He had such a mature, respectful manner. He was a man among boys. That was really thoughtful and sweet of him, she thought, reeling from the whole encounter as she turned and rushed off to get changed.

All morning she had been haunted by the boy in her dream. She kept thinking about how gorgeous and mysterious he was. Every time she thought about those eyes she wished she were back in the four-poster bed, staring up at him, even if it meant having to grapple with the demon afterwards. She couldn't get him out of her mind. Why was she having this recurring dream and why did she feel so helplessly attracted to someone who didn't even exist? And what was up with the demon? The awful feeling of plunging to her death and then fighting that horrific being disturbed her. She couldn't get the images out of her mind, aware that they were filling her with an intoxicating, unsettling brew of curiosity, desire and fear.

It took exactly four minutes for word to spread that Tom had asked Emily to come to his party, and that she had turned him down.

"So." Cindy grinned when Emily sat down with them for lunch. "Tell! What's up with you and Tom Price?"

Emily laughed nervously and felt herself blushing. "Uh, nothing, he just asked me to his party. It's not like he asked me on a date or anything."

"But why did you say no?"

"I don't know, I'm not really in the mood to be going to parties yet."

"Don't pressure the girl," Bethany scolded Cindy, squeezing Emily's hand. "You take as much time as you need."

Emily wondered if Bethany seemed a little too happy she had turned Tom down.

"Anyways, I'm sure he's not interested in me," she said. "The whole school thinks he should be with you." They all laughed.

"So what's the latest with your dad?" Chester changed the subject. "Haven't the cops found anything yet?"

"No, and yesterday after school some thugs broke into my house."

"What?" all three of them exclaimed.

"Yeah, and I came home when they were still there."

"Oh my god, Emily, are you okay?" Cindy was aghast.

"Yeah, thanks. I managed to get away, that's how I got these." She pointed to the scratches on her face that the branches had inflicted and which she had worked hard to cover with makeup. She proceeded to tell them everything that had happened, everything except for the strange little voice that had whispered in her ear and the dreams she had been having.

"It's driving me crazy," she concluded. "I just know that this Cady Sunner guy was involved. And now that they've broken into my house what's next? Are they going to come back to kill my mom or me? I need to do everything I can to help the police arrest Cady and his gang before they get us."

"We should all work together to bust this Devil cult," Bethany said. "That would be so cool! Could you imagine if we all got on *World's Most Sinister Satanic Cults* for helping bust them?"

"I'm all for helping you, Emily," said Cindy. "But I don't think we can just assume it was a satanic death cult, Beth."

"Whatever." Bethany gave a pretty little shrug. "Why don't you and I work on the cult stuff, finding out what Vadas Asger means, and that 'blood of the god' thing and Emily can work on finding out more about Cady Sunner. I bet he's a total Satan worshipper."

"I already spent hours looking for anything about him online but couldn't find anything," said Emily.

"Oh, I've got it," Bethany interrupted excitedly. "I was watching that show *Australia's Biggest Con Artists* the other night and all I can say is hiring a private investigator is so worth it, it's amazing the things those guys can uncover and they're good at finding people."

"That's not such a bad idea," Emily said, suddenly lost in thought.

"If you hire one, make sure you tell him to look into the satanic cult angle," said Bethany, sipping her strawberry milkshake through a straw and nodding her head solemnly.

"Okay, Beth," Emily laughed, "I will."

Emily was rushing to her car after school, hoping to get ahead of the dismissal traffic when Chanel Boxer appeared out of nowhere. She glared at Emily for a moment, her perfect, strawberry-glossed lips curled into a cupid-shaped sneer.

"Uh, hi, Chanel." Emily paused, taken by surprise. Chanel had never even acknowledged her existence before, much less spoken to her directly.

"Listen, Emily, if you think Tom has any interest in you, you're an idiot. He doesn't. He just feels sorry for you. Don't embarrass yourself." She turned and walked away without waiting for a reply.

At that moment Emily felt something snap inside of her. Her arms and legs began shaking, her heart pounded, and she felt a black rage wash over her. Taking several deep breaths she slowly turned, opened her car door and slid behind the steering wheel. Sitting very still, she tried to calm the anger that was threatening to overpower her, staring blankly through the windshield at the parking lot. She had been struggling so hard to hold herself together in the face of everything that was happening but this final, small thing triggered an avalanche of emotion. She started screaming at the top of her lungs, pounding on the steering wheel until her hands began to bruise. Some juniors getting in a car nearby stopped to stare at her with a mixture of surprise and fear, but she didn't care.

"That's it!" she shouted to no one. "As of now, the old Emily is dead. I'm not taking any more crap from anybody. The new Emily is going to kick some ass."

The moment she got home she looked up a private investigator and called the number on the screen.

"Hello, how much would it cost to locate someone?"

"Well, that all depends," replied the deep male voice at the other end of the line.

Half an hour later she was at the private investigator's office spending every penny she had saved up from babysitting the neighbors' kids, hiring a stranger to locate Cady Sunner.

Shortly after arriving home, Emily got a text from the private investigator, providing her with an address. Whoa, he wasted no time! She lay on her back, tossing a pillow into the air and catching it over and over, fearing that she might be going mad with anticipation. She was dying to drive over to Sunner's house, but she had no idea what she would do when she got there. She knew it would be foolhardy to set out on such a dangerous mission without a plan.

She ate dinner alone since her mother was working late, as usual, staring into space, going over and over things in her mind.

"Mom," she said casually when her mother finally came in. "I have to drop by Cindy's to pick up one of my textbooks. Be back soon."

She didn't wait for her mother's reply, just threw on her jacket and walked out the front door. In the car, she took in a deep breath, letting it out slowly, willing herself to remain calm. What was she hoping to accomplish? Still unable to come up with a reasonable answer, she entered the address the investigator had given her on her smartphone map app and hoped for the best.

As she drove her palms grew wet with sweat, and she had to wipe them on her jeans. The house at the address was a surprise. She didn't know what she had been expecting exactly, but not a completely ordinary house in a middle-class neighborhood. It was not the sort of place you would think a monster might live. A man guilty of such awful crimes shouldn't be living among regular citizens, leading a regular life, taking out the garbage, and walking his dog. Then again, maybe that was the exact place to find a monster… hiding in plain view.

She parked down the street from the house and sat watching it for some time. The lights were on in the downstairs room at the front of the house and after a few minutes she saw a movement behind the curtains. The silhouette of a large man stood up from where he had been seated. A chill ran down Emily's spine. Something inside her knew without a doubt that she was looking at the shape of the man who had murdered her father. She just knew. The silhouette disappeared into another room and Emily found herself sweating up a storm, hardly able to breathe. Now that she had found him, she had no idea what to do. For now, though, it was enough. Deciding she needed more time to think things through, she started up her car again and drove home. Her mother was watching television and didn't even look up as she came back in and went upstairs to her room. She began to undress for bed, even though she didn't think she would be able to sleep with all the adrenaline that was pumping through her system.

"Hello, Emily." A voice made her shriek.

Looking around the room to see who had spoken it took her a few seconds to spot the grotesque little creature sitting on her dresser, staring at her. It was about eight inches tall with bluish-green, scaly skin and a pot belly. A rat-like tail with a barbed end curled around its feet. As well as long, pointed ears and small, bat-like wings it had a large, bulbous nose. Two small black horns jutted out from above its beady, sunken eyes.

"Hello, Emily," the creature whispered again, shooting her a wicked little grin. It waved its long fingers at her, as if mocking her for being so afraid, enjoying its own ability to shock and frighten her.

It was the same voice that had told her to go out the window to escape the men. She tried to scream but nothing came out. It was as though all her senses were overloading. Her eyes lost focus and she felt the room swirling around her. Everything went black, and what felt like a minute, maybe more, later, her eyes snapped back open. For a moment, she had no memory of what had happened and couldn't figure out why she was lying on the carpet. Rubbing her eyes, she grabbed onto the bedspread to pull herself up. Then she saw it again.

"Holy crap," she said out loud, "I must be dreaming again."

The creature clapped happily. "You know that's not true. Everything you remember about me is real. I tripped the man while he chased you up the stairs. Then I gave him a little push out the window, tee-hee-hee! That was fun, yes, but it would have been much more fun if he had broken his neck, or smashed his skull and spilled his brains. Tee-hee-hee, much more fun indeed!" It rubbed its scaly little hands together.

Emily slowly got to her feet and approached the creature, never taking her eyes off it.

"What a crazy dream. Incredible how realistic everything is," she muttered as it regarded her with calm, vaguely amused interest. "This is so cool! I wonder if I jump out the window, if I could fly…"

"Er, I wouldn't advise that, Emily," the creature said, lifting its index finger in an imitation of a scholarly pose.

"Really?" Emily laughed, no longer afraid of the ridiculous looking thing. "Well, what would you advise then? And what are you supposed to be anyway?"

"I am an imp and my name is Mercurios. I was your mother's familiar, and now, I'm your guardian. Not only that, but—"

"My mother's familiar?" Emily interrupted.

"Yes, yes, quite right," Mercurios said. "A familiar is a powerful wizard's assistant. I have much to tell you, much to tell you indeed!"

Emily ignored him. "I wonder if I should start by wishing for something simple until I learn how to control the dream," she muttered, scanning around the room. "Okay, I want my whole bedroom to be purple!" She clapped her hands, but nothing happened. "Purple!" she said again, clapping her hands. Nothing happened. She put her fists on her hips and frowned.

The creature sat back and folded his arms, tiring of the game. "Emily, you must stay away from Cady Sunner. Once you are powerful, we'll kill him. We will crush him unmerciful."

"Unmerciful?"

"Yes, indeed, tee-hee-hee! But not yet, no, not yet. First you must become powerful."

She stared hard at him. "You must be some type of messenger from my subconscious. I need to take a psychology class or something." She checked her hair in the mirror and waved her reflection away.

"Emily, I know this is difficult to comprehend," Mercurios continued. "Yes, indeed. But this is not a dream. I am real. I am your guardian. I was not to reveal myself to you yet, but you have given me no choice. You are placing yourself in great danger. Great danger indeed."

"Oh, I get it," said Emily. "My subconscious is expressing its fears. Like that demon I've been dreaming about."

"Demon?" the imp asked sharply.

"Yes, well that's what I think it was, but you're not a demon, or are you?"

"Very interesting indeed. Er no, as I said, I am an imp; I am your mother's familiar. You must allow me to train you in magic, and then we will use it to find the Well of Many Worlds and return to your home planet of Magella, where you will continue your studies under the finest professors at Fengusberry Academy. We will secretly enroll you under a false identity until you are a powerful wizard indeed, and all the while we will secretly make alliances and study the weaknesses of your enemies and then when you are ready you will strike and take the throne. This is what I have been commanded. It is a great task that we must complete. Eighteen years have passed since you came through the Well to this world. Your kingdom is likely in the grip of civil war with potentially numerous factions vying for power."

"Uh, yeah, that sounds really fun." Emily could not have sounded less interested in the imp's plan as she approached him. She stared at him fascinated. "Why would my subconscious create such a freaky creature?" she muttered then poked him in the belly. "Such a cute little pot belly." She giggled.

"AACHT!" cried the imp and swatted her finger away.

"Sorry, Mr. Imp," said Emily turning away. "I made a promise to myself today, the old Emily is dead." She walked over to her bed. "And now, maybe if I go to sleep inside my dream, my subconscious will get the message that I'm not interested in going back to the way I was, so goodnight, fears. This is the new Emily, and she is going to see her father's killers rotting in jail." With that, she got into bed and turned out the light so that she could no longer see the imp.

As she drifted off to sleep, she dreamed that the voice was whispering to her that the universe was vast with many secrets — things about other worlds, something about a well, facts about darkness and evil, but she was too exhausted to remember any of it.

Six

"Princess Katharina is as ancient as Baelaar, Lord Ruthen and I," continued Fionn, speaking to Mitchell in his grand apartment. "She was born in Austria and made her two favorite handmaidens vampires as well. As a mortal, she was deeply religious, fiercely loyal to her family and country, and valued honor and integrity above all things. When she became a vampire, she retained these beliefs and sees it as her sacred duty to use her powers to battle evil." Fionn chuckled. "You can imagine her reaction when Baelaar tried to convince her that the planet Earth was a vampire god and that he was its high priest and that she should therefore serve him."

"I would imagine she was not amused."

"Not amused at all. She smiled graciously, while thrusting a dagger deep into his heart. She and her handmaidens then hacked him to pieces until he leaped out the highest window in her castle tower.

"He returned a week later and kidnapped her mother. He removed the poor lady's organs and nailed her liver to a tree outside Princess Katharina's castle, her heart to another, her stomach to another, her kidneys to another."

"Fiend." Mitchell curled his lip in disgust.

"Certainly. The princess returned home heartbroken, as one would expect, and then she began her pursuit of him. They battled

61

for many years, neither able to get the better of the other."

There was a knock on the door and Fionn raised an eyebrow, requesting permission to answer it. Mitchell nodded his assent and stood, preparing himself to meet this formidable lady. Nothing, however, could have prepared him for the embodiment of grace and beauty that Fionn escorted back across the room to greet him. She looked as though she was in her late twenties, tall and imperious with high cheekbones, long, white-blonde hair, and vibrant blue eyes. Her midnight-blue gown perfectly accentuated the color of her eyes and a fortune of exquisite pearls tumbled around her neck. Mitchell could not tear his eyes away from her.

"Princess Katharina, I would like to introduce you to Mitchell Keats."

"A pleasure," said the princess with the slightest of nods and a look of amusement in her beautiful eyes, as if she could see all too clearly the effect she was having on him.

"An honor to meet you, Princess," Mitchell said with a bow.

The princess gazed at Mitchell's handsome features for a moment, and then sat in one of the thrones, elegantly crossing her legs with a swish of fine silk.

"I shan't be staying long, Messieurs. I have been traveling all over the northlands, searching long and hard, visiting hundreds of villages in pursuit of rumors and folk tales about the first vampires and the Well of Many Worlds."

"And what have you found?" Fionn asked.

"Unfortunately, just rumors. I still have not been able to unearth any reliable information as to what happened to them in Transylvania or where they went afterwards, just some fireside stories and suggested names."

"Transylvania," Mitchell interrupted. "Is that not the land from where that legendary warrior came? The one you told me about? Vlad Tepes? He was of the Order of the Dragon, was he not?"

"Yes, Vlad the Impaler. The Dracul," Fionn replied.

"Do you think…?" Mitchell began, but the princess read his thoughts before he was able to articulate them into words.

"Yes," she said, "I believe the most ancient one changed him into a vampire. But it seems the Dracul was destroyed long ago, unfortunately, so we will learn nothing from him."

Fionn frowned. "I am confused as to why, if the original vampire was from another world and returned to that dimension, the Well of Many Worlds did not go with him."

The princess smoothed an invisible crease from the silk of her gown as she spoke, showing Mitchell the outline of her leg. "It is surmised that the Well replicates itself in whatever world it transports the user to, so that there is one in each world, acting as a bridge. Perhaps the user must somehow command it to return to the other world upon leaving, or else it will remain behind as a permanent bridge between itself and the original from which it replicated itself. So it is possible a bridge has been open between Earth and this other world, Magella, for hundreds of years…"

"So," Fionn said, "is it also possible that the one he turned before he went back to his world figured out how to command the Well of Many Worlds and decided to use it to follow him, to travel to this other world, Magella, taking it with them, thus closing the bridge?"

"Certainly. But that does not change our task. As long as the Well might still be here on Earth, we must do all that we can to find it before Baelaar does. That is the reason I wished to meet with you tonight. The only lead I have points to Russia. I am notifying you that I now intend to expand my search for the Well there."

"You must do what you feel is best," replied Fionn. "I have every faith in you."

"It was a pleasure seeing you again, Fionn, and meeting you, good sir." The princess stood, gave Mitchell a brief nod and then faced Fionn.

"One star in sight," said Fionn.

"One star in sight." The princess smiled, then left.

"What does that mean?" asked Mitchell.

"You must join the order of the Niveus Gladius to know what our secret codes are."

"At least tell me if you have shared with me the sum total of what we know of the Well of Many Worlds? Or is there something you are hiding?"

"Mitchell, all we know is that after the vampire from Magella came through the Well of Many Worlds and turned the first vampire on Earth, then went back to Magella, the first one on Earth then traveled throughout Europe. We believe he took the Well with him. He certainly went through Transylvania at some point around the year 1440, and then disappeared. That is all we know."

"I am going to Russia after the Well of Many Worlds," said Mitchell.

"We must destroy Baelaar first," Fionn reminded him.

"Only if we can find him soon. If not I will still go to Russia," said Mitchell grimly.

The next day the whole of Paris descended into a state of alarm. Riots ripped through every street and the Bastille was stormed. The gleeful mob had beaten, stabbed, and decapitated Governor Marquis Bernard-René de Launay, placing his head on the end of a pike and parading it about the city. The city was in the grip of a fully-fledged revolution. When the sun finally set on the terrible scenes Mitchell was sitting in his apartment with Sylvain and Fionn.

"I would like to train you to be a knight of the Niveus Gladius," Fionn told Sylvain.

The younger vampire laughed. "I am much obliged for the offer. However, I have no interest in being a member of any club. I prefer to go my own way and live by my own... passions. Speaking of which, I have a plan for this evening, which I think you will both find quite amusing." The other two men exchanged looks but said nothing. "I sent word out, promising a prize of one hundred thousand gold pieces for the most beautiful woman in Paris. Of course, I will be the judge, and I will be testing all of the applicants."

Mitchell looked as if he was about to interrupt.

"Do not worry," Sylvain continued, "I will abide by the rules. I won't kill any innocents or let on that I am a you-know-what. I trust you will both be attending my party for Mitchell tonight? After plundering the coffers of our friend the banker and his wife I am now in possession of wealth beyond my wildest dreams. With the promise of high-paying mercenary work and free food and wine, I have enticed fifty of the most dreadful murderers and scoundrels in Paris to come to a certain ballroom I have rented for a great feast. I neglected to inform them that they are to be the feast." Sylvain laughed and clapped his hands, obviously delighted with himself. "I promise that I will not be killing any of the lovely ladies."

"A party for me?" Mitchell scoffed. "I think not. You are throwing this thing for yourself."

"That is not true." Sylvain pretended to be affronted by the very idea. "How about you, Fionn?"

Fionn shook his head. "Unfortunately, I have pressing business."

"Mitchell?" Sylvain grew serious. "Please, I really want to do something for you to show my appreciation. You seem bitter and filled with rage. You choose not to share your personal life with me and that's fine. You would prefer to brood by yourself, that is your choice and that is also fine. You refuse to explain what this madness is about you wanting to use the Well of Many Worlds to go to the realms of devils and demons – fine again. But you have shown me such kindness and given me so much that when I see you are in some kind of inner torment I want only to bring some fun and joy into your existence. It is the least I can do. Besides, perhaps you will be able to get valuable information from some of the mercenaries who will be attending."

"That is true. I will come," Mitchell said. "I may be able to get some news on Baelaar's movements."

Two hours later Mitchell was making his way through the drunken, rampaging mobs on the streets to the address Sylvain had given him. Secreted behind anonymous-looking wooden gates, the ballroom was lavishly decorated with flowing swags of priceless black silk and hundreds of blood-red roses. Along the center of the room an enormous dining table stretched out, laid up for fifty or more people, laden with a feast fit for kings. The settings were of the finest linen and china. Crystal and silver glistened in the candlelight. Heaped dishes of every kind of meat and fish sat alongside the finest wines, interspersed with platters of exotic fruits, cakes, and pastries.

The "guests," being led in by servants were the grimiest crowd of mercenaries and cutthroats Mitchell had ever clapped eyes on. For a moment they were struck dumb by the sight of the feast. They had obviously never seen such opulence and were unsure which way to look or which succulent delicacy to lunge for first. Mitchell stood off in a corner and watched as their courage grew and they began to salivate visibly as they attacked the food and drink. He began to read their minds and found only filth and degradation. The host himself was nowhere to be seen.

Soon, the entire rabble were feasting, drinking and laughing, continually toasting the health of their "noble benefactor," as they called him, calling out for him to make himself known to them. Only once they had stuffed themselves full and drunk themselves into a stupor, however, did Sylvain make his grand entrance in velvet jacket, breeches and elegantly buckled shoes. He exuded wealth, style and power.

"Gentlemen," he declaimed, arms stretched wide. "I trust the refreshments were to your liking."

The men cheered and pounded on the table with their fists and feet.

"Tonight, you will all have the opportunity to become wealthy men."

Again the men cheered and toasted their host. Sylvain held up a large sack of gold coins and shook it, further delighting his guests. "Here is enough gold to keep you all living in luxury for the rest of your lives. All you need to do to get it is... cut off my head!"

Silence fell, as the guests looked at each other in dribbling, inebriated confusion. Sylvain dropped the sack of gold on the floor.

"In that box," he continued, gesturing to a large wooden crate in the far corner of the ballroom, which his servants were now opening, "you will find swords. There are more than enough for all of you. I command each one of you to select a weapon and attempt to cut off my head. I will fight all of you at once, using only these." He held up two daggers with exotically carved handles.

The men stared at Sylvain and then at each other. Mitchell stayed entirely still, reading their vicious, puzzled minds, waiting to see what would happen next.

"If you succeed in killing me, the survivors may divide up the gold as they see fit."

Still, the men sat motionless, assessing the situation, trying to work out if they were being tricked.

"Do you know why I am not afraid of you?" Sylvain asked as he sauntered over to the dining table, casually flipping a dagger in his right hand. "Because you are peasants, and I am a nobleman!"

Mitchell laughed at his young friend's arrogance. Some of the men were now grinding their teeth and grumbling to one another. With the social and political tensions boiling over throughout France, Sylvain was playing upon their deeply held resentments, goading them as though they were mad dogs just waiting for an excuse to attack.

"You pitiful fools dare to condemn us for our love of wealth, the finer things and sensual pleasures. You accuse us of excess, greed, and depravity. Libertinism! But I look at you – in fact, I look through you – and all I see are hypocrites."

The anger of the crowd was growing beneath the taunts. Soon, Mitchell could see, they would explode with rage and pounce. The eyes of all the scoundrels and murderers stared at him as Sylvain strutted about in an absurdly exaggerated way, taunting them.

"Every one of you would switch positions with me in an instant and you know it. Do you think that pride, covetousness, lust, anger, gluttony, envy and sloth are really that different for the rich and the poor? No, no, no my honorable and gentle friends. Riches to rags or rags to riches, it is the same man, just in different stitches."

"What is this ridiculousness?" growled Mitchell, stepping out from behind a column. "Why are you taunting them with this demonic aristocrat act? I have no time for this foolishness. When a fool plays the fool, he doesn't fool anyone."

Sylvain strolled over to him. "Except for his fellow fools, who comprise the better part of humanity. Yes, it is a sad state of affairs when the worst comprise the better part. But here we are."

"There are many good folk in this world."

"A fool that means well or a fool that means ill are still both just fools and sometimes one must play the fool to fool the fool who thinks they are fooling you."

"Ah, I cannot speak to this man," said Mitchell waving his hand dismissively. "Why do you insist on being such a clown?"

"Perhaps I am mad, what of it?"

"Some are born mad, some have madness thrust upon them and some achieve madness through self indulgence."

"Self indulgence is my favorite pastime."

"I am not referring to that kind of self indulgence."

"I am not breaking any rules, Mitchell, read their minds and you will see they are all murderers. You were absolutely correct. The reign of terror has begun. Come on, my friend. We are going to have such fun, you have no idea! First we will feast on all of these idiots in a battle royal, and then just wait until you see what I have arranged for dessert!"

Sylvain flashed Mitchell a toothy smile, strutted off and continued his speech. "We aristocrats respect ourselves in all that we do. We move through the world with grace and sophistication especially when we kill and steal. You would slash a man's throat for a handful of pennies. But we value art, education, fashion and quality workmanship for if we are going to bear the insult of birth into this crude and savage world at least we will hold our heads high and walk through it with STYLE!"

At the exact moment Sylvain shouted the world "style" he swung round and plunged a dagger through the eye of an older man sitting at the end of the table. The man let out a blood-curdling shriek and fell forward, dead, upon the table. Sylvain returned the stare of the shocked crowd, mocking them, imitating their foolish expressions.

"Well?" He laughed in their faces. "Would none of you care to kill for money?"

A brute of a man stood up, chuckling, walked over to the box, picked up a sword, and approached Sylvain. "If I kill you, I get that gold?"

"Indeed you do."

The man laughed. "I have killed for far less than that."

"I am certain that you have."

"You really believe that you can defeat even one of us?" scoffed the mercenary. "You look as soft as those fine threads that you wear. If we were in the streets I could come upon you from behind and you wouldn't know it until I had separated your soul from your body and you were looking down from above" – he glanced at the other mercenaries with a wide, rotten-toothed grin – "or more likely up from below." All the mercenaries laughed.

"Come at me from behind?" laughed Sylvain, looking the brute up and down. "Well if it were you that came at me from behind I would wager it would be a minor irritation." Sylvain roared with laughter and stumbled backward pointing at the mercenary. "Ah ha! Minor irritation!" he howled.

The man growled and lunged at Sylvain, who stepped aside with lightning speed and then did a ridiculous dance. Mitchell caught an image from the man's thoughts that made his hair stand on end. The man was thinking of how Sylvain reminded him of someone else he had met recently: he had the same pale skin and glittering eyes. His memory was of a conversation he had had a few nights earlier with Baelaar and Squire Griffith.

Mitchell probed deeper into the man's befuddled mind and saw Baelaar handing him a small sack of gold coins. He wanted to probe further.

"Sylvain!" Mitchell shouted, but Sylvain ignored him. The mercenary launched a sweeping strike at his host's neck. Sylvain easily ducked the clumsy movement and slashed his attacker's throat open. Blood gushed from the hideous wound and the man gurgled as he clutched his throat and sank to his knees and on down to the polished wooden floor.

"Yes?" Sylvain asked, turning to Mitchell, casually licking the blood off his dagger as the man writhed in his final agonies on the floor, then became still.

Mitchell looked at the dead man and shook his head. "Never mind," he said, turning his attention to the minds of the others.

"Who will be next to try and profit from murder?" Sylvain asked the group, all of whom were staring at the dark lake of blood spreading around their fallen colleague.

Three men seated at the table rose to their feet and ran from the building. Two others walked over to the box, picked up swords, and, without a word, charged at Sylvain. He dispatched them in moments, then busied himself cutting off the heads of all three slain bodies. Once their heads were off, he lifted one in each hand and pressed their lips together as though they were kissing. "Muah, muah, muah." He mocked the sounds of refined courtship. "Who would have thought one would find such tender feelings between two such villains?" He roared with laughter.

Picking up the third head he began to juggle with them, laughing with childlike glee. Becoming bored with his own show he kicked each head into the crowd. One landed in a plate of pheasant, another struck a mercenary in the face while the third landed on a dessert platter, sending strawberry, pistachio and coconut macaroons flying lightly into the air.

"Let's all get him!" bellowed one of the brutes. "He cannot fight us all!"

Having found a leader, the mob leaped up as one and ran to the box, grabbing swords. In an angry, disorganized throng, they rushed at Sylvain. Even though many of them were highly skilled swordsmen and ruthless killers, they were clumsy, slow, and foolish when pitted against the speed, focus, power and agility of a vampire.

Mitchell leaned back against the wall, watching the entire spectacle unfold before him. One man pushed an ugly, foul-smelling face into his. "You may as well try and kill him too," he leered. "Because you won't make it out of here alive."

"Thank you for your concern," Mitchell replied.

Sylvain cut through his attackers like a demonic acrobat, slashing and stabbing with pinpoint accuracy and blinding speed. Finding this too easy, he hurled both daggers into the chest of one particularly nasty-looking man and then proceeded to defend himself with his fists and feet alone, punching and kicking the rest to death, tearing out their throats with his steely fingers.

Mitchell was focused on searching the mind of a man who had left the mob and was making his way out of the building. He followed the man into the chaos of the streets. Because he was finely dressed some rioters tried to grab him, shouting "off with his noble head," but he had no trouble defending himself. As he followed the man Mitchell noticed that many buildings were now on fire. He had seen in the man's head a memory of a meeting with Baelaar, Squire Griffith, the Comtesse LeDuijou and a large group of vampires. He could see that Baelaar had indeed been very busy with turning and training new recruits, far busier than the Niveus Gladius realized. Mitchell increased his speed and came up close behind his prey, peering closely into the recent past. The next thing he saw made him gasp. This man, along with many others, had been instructed to hunt down Princess Katharina before she finds the Well.

The moment he turned into a deserted side street Mitchell grabbed the thug from behind and dragged him into a doorway.

"Where is your master?" Mitchell snarled, holding the terrified man against the wall by his throat, pressing the point of a dagger a millimeter away from his eye. "Where is Baelaar?"

"I, I don't know." The man choked and squirmed.

Inside the man's mind Mitchell saw Baelaar and a large group of young vampire Initiates standing in a spacious hall with a small band of human mercenaries. Baelaar was hiring the mercenaries to act as spies throughout the city, all tasked with searching for Katharina.

"Why is he targeting the princess?"

"I, I don't know, we were hired to be lookouts and to report to him immediately if she was sighted. I think it's something to do with Russia, some place called the Vadas Asger."

"Vadas Asger?"

"Yes, that's all I know."

Seeing nothing else of interest in the man's memory, Mitchell drew his sword and sliced off his head. "I know," he said to the body lying at his feet. "It is difficult to keep one's head when all those around you are losing theirs."

By the time Mitchell returned to the "party" the battle was over and bodies lay scattered on the floor and across the table. Sylvain was still bent over the neck of a mercenary, draining him of the last of his blood. He straightened up when he saw Mitchell, wiped his mouth and laughed.

"Now, that is what I call a party! Time for dessert! The banker's wife gave me a wonderful idea."

Sylvain's terrified servants were dragging the bodies to an enormous bathtub made of solid gold, filling it with their blood.

"The servants are all murderers too," Sylvain whispered to Mitchell. "They're next." He winked conspiratorially. "Come, follow me. In the next room I have a dozen of the most beautiful ladies in

France just as I requested. The servants will be part of the feast but not the lovely ladies, no, they are for life and love and pleasure!"

Mitchell shook his head. "You are a depraved maniac."

"Yes indeed! Isn't it fun?"

"I do not share your tastes and I am afraid I must break with you. I need to concentrate my energies on searching for the Well of Many Worlds. We can part on friendly terms, but we will likely never see each other again."

Sylvain cocked his head to one side, appearing hurt. "I am sorry to hear that. I would like you to know that I will be eternally grateful to you. You are the only man who has ever shown me any kindness in this world. Perhaps someday I will find a way to return the kindness that you have shown me. I swear, as an oath" – he held out his hand – "that if you ever need my help, I will do whatever I can for you. Thank you, Mitchell."

Mitchell shook his hand and Sylvain embraced him with what seemed like genuine affection. A sudden roaring sound made them both turn around to see that one of the walls of the ballroom was ablaze from a stray torch hurled in from the street through a high window.

"Oh no!" Sylvain shouted. "I must save my beauties!"

"I bid you adieu, Sylvain." Mitchell tipped his hat and bowed out of the ballroom.

Seven

Portland, Maine, 2020

Emily awoke from the same dream, moaning and gasping, soaked in sweat, her heart pounding. "Oh my god, why do I keep having this crazy dream?" she moaned. Yet at the same time she now looked forward to going to bed each night in hopes of seeing the mysterious young man that she was becoming more and more obsessed with. "If only I didn't have to dream about that awful demon afterwards," she muttered as she rolled out of bed. Once she was standing under the shower her mind slowly cleared and eventually turned to Chanel Boxer. Picturing Chanel's smug, sneering face she remembered her promise to herself. It was time to get tough.

In the past she had always had an intense dislike of confrontation, but she believed it was essential to change if she was going to bring her father's killers to justice. Her old life was over, destroyed. It was time to become a new person and start a new life. Before going after someone as truly dangerous as Cady Sunner, she felt it might be a good idea to sharpen her teeth on easier meat, someone like pretty, spiteful little Chanel.

She picked out a pair of tight-fitting jeans and a black tank top with a zippered jacket and then did her makeup keeping it simple but bold on the eyes. Sitting on the edge of her bed, she tied up her sneakers and chowed down a granola bar before heading off to school with a new swagger to her step.

She spotted Tom in the hallway and stopped for a moment to admire him. She thought that he looked extra gorgeous today. She then took a deep breath to calm the butterflies erupting in her stomach and walked up to him.

"Hey, you." She moistened her lips and flicked back her hair.

"Oh, hey, Emily." He seemed surprised to see her after she had so blatantly shot him down the previous day. "New jeans?" He gave her a cocky, sexy smirk that made her heart pound.

Emily blushed and laughed. "Uh, yeah."

She moved close and looked up at him through her thickened lashes. "So… it turns out I'm free this weekend. Is the party still on?"

"Yeah. Sure."

"I'd love to come. Why don't you take my number?"

She could hear the whispers all around, passing from mouth to mouth down the long hallway like a line of falling dominoes, heading inevitably toward Chanel Boxer's ears. She deliberately avoided catching anyone else's eye, keeping her gaze fixed on Tom's face.

"Sure. Hang on." He pulled out his phone and started a new contact. They exchanged numbers and Tom flashed her one of his easy smiles. "Cool, I'm excited. It'll be fun."

"I look forward to it," she said, walking away without a backward glance.

After only the slightest hesitation Tom ran after her. "Can I walk you to your next class?"

"Sure."

Now she knew for certain she would be the top gossip fodder for the rest of the day. Chanel would not be able to ignore such a blatant assault on her status.

"So, you seem to be really into biology class," Tom said, hands in his pockets, thick fringe hanging into his eyes. "You seem to know all the answers."

"Well, I don't know, I kind of like it, it's interesting."

"You're kind of a dork but that's cool, I like it." He smirked at her again.

Emily burst out laughing. "Oh good, I'm glad, my dorkiness is one of my best qualities."

Tom chuckled, and then there was a brief silence.

"So," she ventured. "It must be nice knowing exactly what you're going to be doing with your life, being practically guaranteed to be a success."

"What do you mean?"

"Everybody says you're going to go number one in the NHL draft when you decide to enter. You're going to be a big star and make millions, Tom. That must be a pretty good feeling."

"It is," he said. "It's not that, it's just... well, I love hockey. It's the toughest, fastest game in the world, and you know, growing up in Canada, hockey is everything, and I've put so much hard work in, but – well, when I was growing up, every summer I'd take a couple weeks off and go camping and fishing. I mean, I was really into that. I took all sorts of wilderness survival courses."

"Really? You? Wilderness survival stuff?" she laughed.

"Hey, don't knock it 'til you try it." He laughed too. "I could teach you enough in one afternoon to keep you alive for months if you ever got lost in the wilderness, any time of year, even if you were naked." He smirked.

Emily felt herself blushing and her heart raced. "That would be awesome!" she laughed. "Useful information."

"Yeah, I thought you'd be interested in that. You know, since you're Miss Biology and all." He bumped shoulders with her and she felt the butterflies take off again inside her.

"I'd definitely be interested." Exactly what was she interested in more, she wondered. Being naked in the wilderness with Tom? Or making Chanel Boxer pissed off as hell? Or both? She wasn't sure, but she was having fun finding out.

Tom was getting excited as he talked. "I thought if hockey

didn't work out that I would start my own business, take people for adventure trips, back to nature, eco-tourism stuff. But now between school and hockey, things are getting really busy and serious, and I haven't done any of that stuff in so long. I really miss it, you know?"

She liked that he seemed to have plans that extended beyond hockey and that his attraction to her wasn't just based on raging teenage hormones, that he felt they had a connection through similar interests.

"You could do both," she suggested. "You could play hockey and make tens of millions of dollars as a famous athlete, and then retire and open your eco-tourism business. That wouldn't be so bad."

"Yup, that would be pretty sweet," he laughed. "Thanks for the tip."

"You're welcome. I'm helpful that way." She winked at him. Winked! She was beginning to like the new Emily.

He laughed to himself. "All right, so I'll see you at my party."

"Can't wait."

Emily strutted past the shocked faces that were now lining the corridor – even some of the passing teachers seemed surprised to see Tom talking to the quiet girl whose dad had just been murdered.

"Wilderness survival courses and an eco-tours business?" Bethany raised her eyebrows across the lunch table. "Interesting. He never told me about these secret passions. Wow, Tom Price, the hockey star, super stud and social god is a simple-hearted country boy."

"I could definitely get into a guy like that," Emily admitted.

"Uh, duh," Bethany said in exaggerated tones. "Oh yeah, and the fact that he's the hottest guy in school, a gentleman, and is going to be a rich, famous hockey star."

Emily smiled awkwardly and looked at Bethany, who was now staring off into the distance. "Tom Price," Bethany said softly, smiling to herself and Emily wasn't sure she liked the look in her eye. It was as though Bethany had made the decision at that moment that she wanted Tom and Emily felt a little surge of jealousy welling up in her heart. She immediately hated herself for it.

"Any luck with the private investigator?" asked Chester.

"Yeah, did you hire one?" Bethany returned to the conversation as if nothing had passed between them.

"Yeah, I found Cady's address. I drove by his house."

"Was that a good idea?" Cindy looked doubtful. "That guy could be the murderer. What if he saw you and recognized you?"

"I know." Emily frowned, playing with the straw in her box of juice. "It's just… the police investigation isn't going anywhere and I'm afraid it's only a matter of time before they come after my mom and me."

"Just let the private investigator do the work," said Cindy. "Please, Emily, don't put yourself in danger."

"But that's the problem. I already am in danger, and I only asked the investigator to find him, which he's done already. Hiring him isn't cheap and I'm broke."

After dinner, Emily returned to Cady Sunner's house, trying to ignore the inner voices that kept plaguing her. She pulled onto his block and then drove a short way down a side street. She parked up and sat staring back at the house, wondering how to proceed.

The house looked quiet enough, so she got out of the car, scanning around to make sure no one was watching her, and crossed the street. The windows at the front were closed, the drapes tightly drawn. She found the side gate and snuck into the backyard. From there she noticed a kitchen window was open, the sounds of the TV audible from outside. She crouched down and crept up to it, peering inside.

Only three feet away someone was sitting at the kitchen table cleaning a pistol while watching a talk show. When he turned to reach for a cleaning solution, she could clearly see that it was he – Cady Sunner. A feeling of physical revulsion gripped her stomach as she ducked back, then cautiously leaned forward and peered inside again. For a few moments she just watched him, frozen with a morbid fascination, as he polished his gun with meticulous care, caressing it as though it was a beautiful woman. What exactly, she wondered, was she hoping to accomplish by being here? Maybe, if she could just watch him for a while, she would gain some much-needed insight, which would incriminate him.

Having finally reassembled the weapon, he turned it around lovingly in his hand and smiled.

"There you go, sweetheart, all clean again."

Emily remembered watching a crime drama with her dad where the police had nabbed the criminal by using a ballistics expert to prove that the bullets used to kill the victim had been fired from his gun. Looking at Cady now, Emily saw that he obviously cherished his gun, so he probably used it all the time. If it was the same one he had used to kill her father, then maybe she could get it to the police with his fingerprints all over it.

Cady got up and walked into another room, leaving the gun on the kitchen table and the television blaring music. It was now or never. Emily noticed a plastic bag lying on the ground. She picked it up then gently pushed the window further open so that the gap was wide enough for her to reach through. The hinge creaked so loudly she almost panicked and ran, but realized that no one inside the house would be able to hear such a small sound over the music. She had never been a great one for prayers, but she said one then.

Hearing no movement, she eased herself through the gap head first to her waist, her hand with the plastic bag reaching across to the table to pick up the gun. The plastic made a loud crackling sound, just as the music stopped and the audience applauded the act. She froze. They would be going back to talking in a moment and she could not afford to make another sound.

A loud knock at Cady's front door made her heart leap. She heard Cady's footsteps returning to the kitchen. Panicking, she pushed the gun back onto the table, ducked back out the window, crouched down and held her breath. Cady walked into the kitchen, picked up the gun and left again to answer the door. Emily's heart pounded in her throat. Her brain struggled with two options – one, stay hidden and try to get the gun again once he had fallen asleep for the night, but that carried considerable risk of being caught, or two, get the hell out of there. She made a decision and was just about to creep away when she heard voices in the other room. People were moving around the house. She decided to stay put, at least for the time being.

Cady was talking to another man who seemed to be growing more and more pissed off.

"You're telling me you've found nothing at all?"

"N-no!" Sunner sounded like he was choking as he tried to reply. Was he being strangled?

"We're getting very impatient!" shouted the other man.

"What about that other help you mentioned?" Sunner spluttered.

Emily wondered what kind of man could possibly bully someone as terrifying as Cady Sunner and cautiously peered inside.

"Ah yes." The other man lowered his voice. Footsteps seemed to be coming closer to the kitchen doorway. Emily glimpsed through the open kitchen door a tall pasty-faced man with shoulder-length, jet-black hair at the far end of a small dining room.

"They're scared." He chuckled. "Apparently, our reputation precedes us. They have agreed to meet with me only in public, at some place called the Sanctuary, on the evening of October 31st."

"Halloween night?"

"Yes. Fitting, don't you think?"

"Well, with their help, it should be easy."

Emily heard a sniffing noise. Through the slats she watched the pale man sniff the air, distracted by something. As he moved toward the kitchen she ducked down and held her breath, wishing she hadn't sprayed any perfume on herself that morning. Her heart was pounding so loudly in her ears she was sure he would be able to hear it. There was a splintering crash, and a baseball-sized rock smashed through the dining room window, making both men jump back, shouting assorted expletives. They ran out the front door to confront whoever had thrown it.

"Damn kids!" Cady shouted.

Emily got down on her hands and knees and crept forward, waiting until she heard the front door slam before jumping up and running to her car.

Once back in the safety of her home she went straight to her bedroom, letting out an involuntary scream when she saw the grotesque little creature from the previous night sitting on her bed, staring at her with a deranged grin on his face. Emily turned and faced the wall, breathing deeply, determined to make him vanish. Maybe he would cease to exist if she didn't look at him.

"Am I going crazy?" she murmured. She pinched herself but didn't wake up. She glanced over her shoulder, but the creature was still there, smiling and twiddling his fingers in a childish wave. This time, she dug her fingers into her forearm. "Ow!" Still nothing happened.

"Listen to what I have to say very, very carefully, Emily. You're putting yourself in terrible danger. Without me you'd probably be dead by now."

"Go away," Emily said, screwing her eyes shut.

"Who do you think threw that rock through the window to get you out of that madman's house? Guess!" He clapped excitedly. "Me! That's right! Tee-hee-hee."

How did he know about that? Had that all been part of the dream too? She took a few steps backward and sat on the edge of the bed, still staring at the wall.

"This isn't a dream," she said. "I've gone insane."

"No, you are not insane. Far, far from it. Have you never thought that just maybe there is more to the world, to the universe, than meets the eye, Emily? Yes, yes indeed, much more! That maybe all secrets have not been revealed? That the vast majority of the universe's secrets have not been revealed?"

"Yeah... sure." Emily muttered, trying to make sense of some part of the experience. "What the hell is going on here?"

"Emily, there are many worlds in existence, and what I'm about to tell you is very important, so please pay attention."

Finally she looked at him. "You're a figment of my imagination but okay. I'm listening. Talk."

"In a world somewhat like this one, a world called Magella, there is a magical artifact called the Well of Many Worlds. It enables the user to travel between worlds."

"You mean like between planets?" Emily asked, intrigued despite herself.

"Between galaxies and, more importantly, between dimensions, between the very planes of existence! When you were a baby, in a moment of great peril – a matter of life and death – your parents made an important decision. They sent you into the Well of Many Worlds." The imp paused to gauge her reaction, but Emily just stared at him, so he went on. "Now that you are almost of age it is my duty to teach you the basics of magic. Then, if possible, I will find the Well of Many Worlds and take you back to your home world of Magella to fulfill your great destiny!"

"My great destiny?" Emily burst out laughing. "Okay, now I definitely know this is a dream." She pinched herself again. "Ow! But why aren't I waking up when I pinch myself?"

"I know this is a lot to take in, Emily, but don't worry, everything you need is inside you already."

"Oh, now you're a motivational speaker? My mind has created a demented creature as a guru? Why would I create such a weird-looking thing as my guide and mentor?"

"I would prefer it if you would stop referring to me like that," Mercurios huffed, crossing his arms. "I am an imp."

"Oh, sorry. Well, since I don't seem to be able to control the dream and I can't wake up, I guess I might as well go with it. Okay, Mr. Imp, what messages from my deep subconscious do you bear?"

"The reason that you can't wake up is because you are already awake, and my name is Mercurios."

"Okay, Mercurios. Wait… the Id, that's it!" she exclaimed. "That's the psychological term. You are a monster from the Id."

"No, Emily, I am very much real. Anyhow, your parents were being violently attacked by the Lich King of Darguul who sent a group of necromancers—"

"What?"

"Necromancers are wizards that specialize in death magic. Many of them worship the demon Lord Orcus, Prince of the Undead."

"Ah, okay."

"The Lich King of Darguul sent necromancers to assassinate your parents. So in desperation, they sent you and your sister and brother into the Well… and, well… you ended up here."

"Here?" she repeated, her eyes wide.

"Yes, on Earth. Whoosh!" He made a wide arc gesture with his hands. "You just appeared here. When they put you into the Well your parents had no idea where you would end up, which world you'd fall into, whether you'd ever make it back."

"Okay, not sure how to interpret that. I need to take a psychology class, or dream interpretation or something."

"Your mother was a wizard, yes, a sorcerer. I was her familiar, and she sent me with you to be your guardian. Yes, yes, yes. And there is more. You—"

"My mom, a witch? A witch?" She chuckled. "Wait 'til she hears that. So, she put me in a well – go on…" Emily crossed her arms, challenging him to convince her with his tall tales, suppressing the tiny part of her that was growing sad to think that she might be losing her mind, imagining how her poor mother would feel when she saw her only daughter being taken away in a straitjacket.

The imp had a strained look on his face. "I was afraid of this," he muttered. "I must use the memory noodle."

"What?"

"You are not insane and you are not dreaming, this is real. There is far more to the universe than meets the eye, other worlds with intelligent life. Do you see the little trinket hanging from my necklace?"

Emily saw what looked like a tiny silver treasure chest dangling from a chain. "Yes."

"Take it off my chain, and put it on the floor." Emily did as she was told. Once the pendant was on the floor, the imp hopped off the bed and stood looking at it. "Now, since it is yours, you must speak the command words: 'Almeron sidella.'"

"What? I'm not going to say that!" she said, feeling stupid.

"Just say it, please, Emily!" the imp begged.

"Almeron…" she murmured.

"Sidella," the imp assisted her quietly.

"Sidella."

The chest began to grow. It expanded until it took up most of the open space left in her bedroom. Emily stared at it in shock. "What the…?"

"Well," said Mercurios. "Open it."

Emily opened the lid. Inside was a large, black, leather-bound book that looked ancient, a gold ring with numerous diamonds embedded in it, a blue marble, a wand and a human skull covered in runes, painted with what looked like blood. Two rubies floated in the eye sockets. There was also what looked like a wet noodle of orange pasta three inches long and one inch wide lying at the bottom of the chest.

"What is all this?" she asked.

"These are rightfully yours."

"Not sure I want them."

"Oh, yes, yes, you will want them. That is your mother's spell book; that is the Ring of Teleportation, that is the Sphere of Protection, and that is the Wand of Lightning. That," said the imp pointing at the skull, his voice lowering, "is a Skull of Monster Summoning. Very dark and dangerous indeed. And this," he said picking up the wet noodle, "is the memory noodle. Your mother was concerned that you might not believe me so she included this." He placed the noodle on his forehead, where it stuck firm, and closed his eyes.

"What are you doing?" Emily asked.

"Shhhh, I'm remembering something." After a moment the imp took the noodle off his forehead and before she could protest he clamped it to her forehead. "Say the words 'show me your memories even if they're horrible.'"

Emily curled her lip and spoke slowly. "Show me your memories even if they're horrible."

The noodle flashed a bright orange and Emily was engulfed in a vision.

She found herself in a stone chamber. A man and a woman exploded in through a heavy wooden door, both dressed in cloaks and hoods, wielding wands. The man slammed the door behind them and slid a thick steel bolt into place. He muttered some words under his breath; sparks rose out of his wand and the door glowed orange for a moment. The two wizards pulled back their hoods. The man was in his late thirties, tall and handsome with pale skin, a narrow face and piercing gray eyes beneath a head of thick, silver hair. The woman was in her late twenties, beautiful with the same pale skin, long, dark hair and eyes that were dark brown, almost black.

They exchanged a glance and strode to a large stone table upon which stood an intricately carved silver bowl, six feet in diameter and filled with a swirling mist, which was constantly forming three-dimensional worlds within worlds within worlds that continuously morphed, dissolved and formed other worlds within worlds. Beside it on the table were three babies wrapped in blankets. Beside one baby stood a white cat with one brilliant amber eye and the other a rich sapphire color, beside another child stood Mercurios and beside the third child sat a small, white owl.

"Do you all understand your instructions?" the woman asked the cat, the owl and the imp.

"Yes," they replied.

"Remember, you are not to reveal yourselves to them until they are adults," the man added. "I want them to assimilate to this…

other world, in case something goes wrong and they become trapped there. When they are of age you will give them each their magic chest and you will begin to teach them magic. Talia should be all right until then. You-know-who will not awaken until she is an adult. Once they have learned their first grade of spell casting and are able to protect themselves, you will bring them back to Magella to study at the Fengusberry Academy. You must create false identities when you return, as no one must know who they are. If word gets out they are alive they will become famous and that is not something we want until they are ready to strike. When they have completed their training they will reveal their true identities and reclaim the throne of Bravisdor."

"We understand," they all responded.

"The moment news of their return spreads everyone will be talking about them," the woman continued. "Be very careful when and to whom you give this information. First have them secretly find out who are enemies and who are possible allies and then reveal their true identities only when they are fully prepared. Gather allies first and then, when the time is right, reveal to all of Magella who they are and strike. Strike decisively and place the strongest of them on the throne."

"But what if you are killed and they come through the Well after us?" the imp asked.

"We will try and hide the Well beyond their reach, but if they do you must hide the children from them."

A deafening explosion made the door shudder, but it held firm. The wizards embraced and kissed passionately as a second explosion shattered the door into countless shards. Six cloaked figures burst through. Brightly colored balls of energy streaked from their wands and filled the air. There was another explosion and a blinding flash.

Emily came out of the vision and stared at Mercurios, stunned. "Whoa."

"You see?" he said.

"You mean to tell me I'm not of this world, that my wizard parents sent me down a well like a baby basket down a river, and these are the tools of their trade?"

"Yes. And I have been commanded to protect you as best I can, then train you in the basics of wizardry. Then, when you are ready, I will take you back to Magella to be trained properly so you may fulfill your great destiny and crush all who oppose you. Crush them unmerciful!" he shook his little fist in the air.

"You said I had a brother and sister, what about them?"

"Unfortunately they and their familiars did not make it through. We were the first into the Well and just as we were put in I was knocked unconscious by the blast of magic energy. Now, the blue marble thing there, when activated, will create a Sphere of Protection around you, a ten-foot diameter bubble of a force field to protect you from anything not magical or enchanted. It will shield you from any type of element or weather or indirect attack, such as an object thrown at you by an attacker. Unfortunately, it will not protect you against a direct physical assault by a living or undead being or a magical attack."

"Holy crap," Emily laughed, forgetting her skepticism as she picked up the beautiful, sparkling ring and inspected it more closely. "And this is a magical ring? Are you serious? If this is real this is… wow… like… I have a magic ring? And a wand? That is so cool. How can this not be a dream?"

"The Ring of Teleportation," the imp went on with his tutorial, seeing that he now had her attention, "will immediately transport you and whatever you are touching to any place in this world you can clearly and precisely visualize. Precisely. Although it does take time to activate. If the image is not detailed enough, you could end up somewhere else, or worse, you could disintegrate."

"I seeeee."

"Now, the Wand of Lightning will unleash a powerful lightning bolt at whatever you point it toward, when you speak the command words."

Emily put the ring back and stared at the wand then at the skull. "I wish I could speak to my fathers ghost and find out exactly what happened and what 'Vadas Asger' is." She reached out with both hands and picked up the skull.

"Emily, no!" the imp cried and lunged at her but it was too late.

Eight

Paris, France, 1789

When Mitchell told Fionn what he had learned from reading the memories of the thugs, Fionn ordered that the princess be notified and called an emergency meeting of all the members of the Niveus Gladius who were in or near Paris. He invited Mitchell to come to the meeting so that he could introduce him to some of the knights of the Niveus Gladius.

The following evening the two of them rode through the night, traveling deep into the countryside to the east of the city. The skies were clear and the stars shone like frozen diamonds. After several hours of hard riding, they left the dirt path they had been following to cut across open countryside. In the distance, Mitchell noticed the flickering flames of a bonfire. As they approached he could see people standing around the fire, their horses tethered nearby to a huge, fallen tree.

Steam rose off their horses' backs as they dismounted. Two vampires approached them and Fionn held up a hand in silent greeting. In all, eleven vampires were waiting around the fire, seven men and four women. Mitchell recognized Lord Ruthen, who smiled at the sight of him.

"Ah, our young friend has come to visit."

They all took seats around the fire. They came from all over Europe, all of them dressed as warriors in the style of their homelands. All had ash-pale skin, fangs and eyes that glittered with the reflected flames.

"Here is the one I have been telling you about," Fionn announced. "Mitchell Keats."

An Italian named Abrielle, rose from her seat and stood before Mitchell, so close he could smell her skin. She scanned him up and down. He returned her bold stare, admiring her shoulder-length black hair, dark eyes and full red lips.

"Well, you certainly are a handsome one," she whispered. "Welcome. I hope that you are intending on staying a while."

Some of the vampires, like Lord Ruthen and Abrielle, were friendly. Others simply stared at him, giving nothing away of what they were thinking. Fionn explained to the group how Mitchell was about to enter the final phase of his training.

"We have reason to believe that Baelaar and a large force of Initiates are going after Princess Katharina," he informed them. "I have summoned her here. But if she does not arrive tonight we will have to go after her and try to reach her before it's too late. Does anyone know of a place in Russia known as the Vadas Asger?"

The vampires all shrugged and shook their heads.

"Do those words mean anything to anyone?" Fionn pressed them.

One of the vampires held up a warning hand and they all fell entirely silent, listening intently. At first Mitchell couldn't hear anything except the crackling of the flames and the snorts of the horses as they grazed, then he made out the distinct sound of hooves approaching at speed.

"Someone is getting close but I cannot read their mind," Lord Ruthen said. "Let us hope it is the princess."

Out of the darkness rode a girl who looked no more than seventeen years old. Her long, blonde hair streamed behind her and her face looked tired from the rigors of her journey. Dressed in the white robes of a handmaiden, she was mounted on an ivory-colored stallion that glowed orange in the light of the fire.

"It's Snowdrop Windflower," Fionn told Mitchell.

"I come with news," Snowdrop announced. "My Lady sends this message for you."

She handed Fionn a wax-sealed letter. He tore the seal open and read the letter.

"My god!" he said and looked back at Snowdrop. "Do you know if any of the others are with her?"

"No," the girl replied. "She went ahead alone."

"Reckless," Fionn muttered to himself, shaking his head. He turned to the group. "It seems that the princess has discovered some documents of the first vampire. She believes she knows the location of the Well of Many Worlds. She believes it is in the Kungur Ice Caves in Russia and urgently requests our help in finding it. She is on her way there now."

For a moment the others gazed at one another uneasily, considering the implications of the news. Mitchell felt a burning excitement building inside him.

"Do you know of a place called the Vadas Asger?" Fionn asked Snowdrop.

"I have never heard of this place," she replied, handing him some ancient-looking documents. "The princess found these. They are pages from the diary of one of the ancient ones."

Fionn took the fragile documents, unfolded them carefully and started reading them out loud.

"The author's name is Selina. It says: 'The following is the account my master gave me of his transformation: One winter night, around the year 1100, somewhere in Eastern Europe he was walking in the hills, returning to his village from an unsuccessful hunt, when he saw an explosion of electrical energy on a nearby hilltop. The light from this energy illuminated the hills and valleys for miles around. Even the countless stars shimmering above seemed dim by comparison. He waded forward through the drifts of freshly fallen snow that covered the land to locate the source of the light. When he reached the top of the hill, he stumbled upon a ferocious battle between a pale-skinned man wearing black plate-mail armor of exquisite workmanship and wielding a flaming sword, and a skeletal creature with glowing green orbs in its eye sockets, wearing a golden crown and tattered royal robes, holding a black scepter that seemed to exude a terrible darkness.

"'As my master hid behind a large stone and watched in amazement as they fought, floating in the air above what appeared to be a huge, ornate silver bowl, the Well of Many Worlds. The bowl contained a magical, swirling mist, from which emanated an unearthly light. The mist formed into constantly shifting landscapes within landscapes.

"'As the two beings battled, currents of energy exploded between them and their weapons made a deep humming sound as they swung through the air. But my master was dazzled by the beauty and magic of the Well and crept forward, hoping to somehow slip away with it while the two beings above were distracted, locked in their death struggle. Even though the Well was almost six feet in diameter and looked to be made of solid silver, he believed he was strong enough to take it. As he attempted to drag it away, the skeletal being pointed a finger at him and a burst of electrical energy shot from the finger and tore through him. He screamed in pain and looked down to see two gaping wounds through his breast.

"'His blood flowed out onto the freshly fallen snow, and he knew he was on the verge of death as he sank to his knees before the Well. At that moment, he heard a terrible cry as the skeletal creature plunged into the Well, seemingly drawn like a moth by the light inside. He grabbed his adversary by his ankle, dragging him down with him. For an instant, the pale-skinned man caught the edge of the Well and clung to it, looking directly into my master's eyes. My master could see that his throat was slashed open, and there were deep gashes on his arm. But as he watched, the wounds started to heal and the man reached out and grabbed him by the throat. He lifted my master to his mouth, as though he were as light as a ghost, and plunged two sharp

92

fangs into his throat. My master struggled weakly, but he was already near death. A moment later, the pale-skinned man withdrew his fangs and pushed his still-bleeding wrist into my master's mouth.

"'With the last of his strength my master tried to break free, choking as the blood dripped into his throat. The pale-skinned man let out a diabolical laugh, then released him and disappeared into the Well, dissolving into the mist.

"'My master was instantly seized by a burning fever which devoured every cell of his body as he endured the agonizing transformation and rebirth into a vampire. When it was through, he rose to his feet, effortlessly lifting up the great silver bowl with his newfound powers, and disappeared into the wilderness to hide it.

"'Engraved upon the base of the Well were strange symbols and words written in a language not found in this world. My master spent many years trying to decipher their meaning. For more than a hundred years he lived in isolation, emerging only to hunt for living blood or to move to a new hiding spot, jealously guarding his treasure as he tried to unlock its secrets.

"'In the thirteenth century he traveled through Western Europe, searching for linguists skilled enough to help him decipher the mysterious markings. He transformed three vampires. I was one of them. He took us into the wilderness to serve him in his obsession with learning how to control the power of the Well. We worked for many decades in the Carpathian Mountains. In 1476 we traveled north and east for many months and hid in the vast labyrinth of the Kungur Ice Caves.'"

Fionn stopped reading and looked at the other vampires who were all staring at him in rapt attention.

"There is nothing more," he told them. "Ruthen, send out the messengers. The rest of you, send word far and wide – we must find the others. I will take Mitchell out on my ship. We will sail up the coast. We will all meet in Perm and set out for the Kungur Ice Caves together from there. Now go."

The other vampires sprang onto their horses and raced off in different directions. Fionn signaled to Mitchell that it was time to depart. A large raven perched on a nearby tree broke the silence with a squawk as it rose into the air and flew off northwards.

"Time for us to travel," Fionn told him.

"What do you think Baelaar will do if he finds it first?" Mitchell asked once they were riding. "Do you really think he wants to seek out the original race of vampires in their own world?"

"Baelaar is insane. I would not underestimate him. But the danger does not lie only in what he will do if he succeeds in finding it."

"What do you mean?"

"There is no telling what could happen if he gets his hands on it. In trying to use it, he might make some catastrophic mistake."

"What do you think could happen?"

"I have no idea. Anything could happen. He might open up a rift between two worlds, and creatures from another plane of existence might flood our own. Who knows how many other worlds there are, how many dimensions and how many worlds within each dimension? What sort of life forms might exist in those new realms and what would happen if they passed into this world?"

"I see."

"Or if he accidentally destroyed the Well, what might happen then? If the very fabric of the universe were to be altered, all civilization – all existence – might be annihilated. This is why we shall have to have a long discussion before you use it."

"Do not attempt to stop me," Mitchell warned darkly.

"We will cross that bridge when we come to it. For now we must locate the princess and find it. Tomorrow night, while we sail up the coast, you will complete your training. I still have one last thing to teach you. The next night, I would very much appreciate it if you would join us on the mission."

Mitchell thought for a moment before answering. "I will."

Fionn smiled. "Good. Now, vampires who have permanent dwelling places never reveal the locations of their homes to anyone, and as you know, we cannot read minds over great distances. Therefore, the Niveus Gladius communicate through a series of messengers, both vampire and mortal, who deposit letters in specific places, enabling us to retrieve news from one another. Tonight, we sent out messengers to gather the other members of the Niveus Gladius. I hope they will come swiftly. Together we may be able to end this once and for all."

Near dawn they checked into a hotel and slept all day, then rode again with the sunset. When they reached the coast they took a rowing boat out to an elegant schooner, which waited for them on the moonlit sea.

"While we sail," Fionn told him, "I will teach you the final lesson in your training as a warrior. As you know, vampires are supernatural beings. You have been a vampire now for long enough and gained enough power to control the elements that surround us. I see that you have forged a Draaken." Fionn gestured to the sword hanging at Mitchell's side. Mitchell drew it and presented it to Fionn. It was a magnificent weapon, long, hard and sharp with a double-edged blade and a hilt big enough to accommodate two hands.

"A Draaken," said Fionn. "Is the only sword in the world we can channel our supernatural powers through and make capable of severing an ancient vampire's head with one blow. Now I will teach you how to use it properly, to use your powers and supernatural control over the elements to make the blade of your sword flare into fire, turn to biting frost or crackle with electricity according to your personality, creating wounds which could prove deadly to even the most ancient and powerful of vampires. We shall learn what your personality bent is."

Mitchell took the sword with both hands and swung it through the air.

"Just as you have learned to influence the elements with your will by channeling your supernatural powers," Fionn continued, "simply channel your power through the blade."

A moment later the blade began to glow and burst into flame. Each time he swung it; it flared up, emitting the hum of an electrical surge.

"Fire, like me. Now I will show you how two or more vampires can increase their power over the elements by working together. Come, the open ocean is the best place for me to demonstrate this."

With a wave of his hand, Fionn conjured a strong gust of wind, and soon they were sailing at a good speed along the waves. When they could no longer see land he steered the ship north and resumed his instructions. First, they experimented with combining the focus of their wills. Fionn explained that to do this, one of them must envision what he wanted to accomplish in his mind, allowing the other to see it, so that they could focus together. The results were dramatic. Together they were able to raise far larger waves from the ocean and far stronger winds from the air than either of them could have done alone.

After a couple of hours, Mitchell spotted clouds appearing on the horizon, moving toward them.

"Look, a storm is coming."

"How strange," Fionn said, more to himself than to Mitchell. "The storm is coming from the east, not the west."

He peered into the distance and then spun to face Mitchell, his eyes blazing.

"Prepare yourself!" he shouted. "The enemy is upon us!"

Mitchell looked eastward as the black storm clouds, wreathed with lightning, rolled toward them, driven by gale-force winds.

"The Priests of Mezzor?"

"It must be them," said Fionn.

"We have been betrayed?"

"Apparently. I think that raven was a spy, in league with them. But if it was one of the Niveus Gladius who betrayed us they will most likely be traveling with them, so we will soon find out." Fionn stopped speaking and stared at Mitchell.

"What is it?" Mitchell asked.

"Unless of course it was you."

"What?"

"Your mind is strong. I can no longer clearly read your thoughts. But I know how obsessed you are with finding the Well and using it to go into the realm of demons and the nine planes of Hell. You could have made a deal with the Priests of Mezzor to give us up in return for being allowed to use the Well first when it is found. You could have fabricated that story, that the Priests of Mezzor are targeting Princess Katharina, knowing that we would summon our forces, go after her to protect her, drawing all the Knights of the Niveus Gladius out into the open to be destroyed." Fionn's eyes blazed in the moonlight. "And of course, I would be the first to be targeted."

Fionn drew his sword and the blade burst into flame.

Nine

There was a sound like a generator exploding into life. The rubies in the Skull of Monster Summoning's eyes flashed and a shockwave threw both Emily and Mercurios backward and Emily dropped the skull back into the chest in shock. Mercurios got back onto his feet and brushed himself off.

"What was that?" Emily asked.

There was a pounding at Emily's locked bedroom door and someone frantically rattled the handle.

"Emily?" She heard her mother's muffled shout. "Emily what was that? Are you okay? Open the door."

"The chest, Emily, remember 'Almeron sidella.'" Mercurios whispered, before disappearing.

Emily slammed shut the lid.

"Almeron sidella," she said and the chest shrunk down to its original size.

"Emily, open this door," yelled her mother.

Emily opened the door as calmly as she could manage.

"What was that sound?"

"Um, I think it was a power surge."

"Are you all right?" Emily's mother went to step inside the room but Emily blocked her path.

"Yeah, everything's fine, Mom, thanks."

"Okay," her mother looked at her doubtfully, unsure what was happening.

Emily ushered her out, shutting and re-locking the door behind her.

"Quickly, enlarge the chest," said Mercurios, re-appearing on her dresser.

Emily uttered the command words and the chest enlarged again. She opened it and they both peered in at the skull. The eyes were still glowing.

"This is very bad." Mercurios sounded worried. "You've activated the Skull of Monster Summoning. It is very unpredictable. You must use the command words and turn it off. Pick up the skull, look into its eyes and say the words 'Gorhel velsten.'"

Emily picked it up. "Gorhel velsten."

The light in the gems flickered and faded.

"Good." Mercurios relaxed. "Now, I will teach you about the other magical items: you must use both the ring and the wand sparingly. They only have energy left for a few more lightning bolts and a few more teleportations before they must be recharged, and only a powerful wizard can do that. Inside the book are many spells. You will need to learn them all. You will be able to cast spells without the use of a wand or anything else for that matter. Then, we will have a great deal of fun indeed!"

The imp grinned at her mischievously and rubbed his little hands together with glee.

Emily was only half paying attention to his words.

"Okay. What's going on here?" she whispered. "My mother heard the sound that skull made, could this actually be happening?"

The imp crept closer to her and almost laid a hand on her knee but folded his arms instead. "Emily, I have been watching over you your whole life." He leered at her with a nefarious glint in his eye.

"Ew." Emily grimaced, covering her chest with her arms as

though suddenly realizing she was naked. "Wait, you mean you're always around watching me? No matter what I'm doing?"

"Yes indeed, Emily, yes. I can become invisible at will, yes."

"Okay. Do you have any idea how unbelievably gross and creepy that is?"

"Well, I am your guardian."

"This is impossible."

"The universe is vast and ancient, Emily. Vast indeed. And that vastness is filled with mysteries beyond imagining. Yes, I have done much reading over the years. The humans of this world have some very interesting knowledge indeed: astrophysics, quantum mechanics, yes, but not as much knowledge as we have in Magella. You are getting closer with the Many Interacting Worlds theory of quantum mechanics, but you still only suspect that we are part of a multiverse and that black holes are gates between this dimension and others. The Well of Many Worlds is another such gate!"

"Okaaaaay. Well, let's just get something straight right now. You can still do your little guarding thing just as well in our living room or better yet, out on the front porch. I want privacy."

"Yes, yes, yes. We will discuss all that later. Now, if the man you are following is indeed the one who murdered your father, you are putting yourself at great risk by pursuing him. I cannot let that happen. I am commanded to protect you."

"So that woman sleeping in the other room, my mom… is a witch?"

"No. I will explain."

"And my dad was not my dad?"

"No, your father was a very powerful warlock, your mother's teacher to begin with. He taught her magic, and she was an eager student indeed and very beautiful. Soon they were wrapped in a passionate love affair."

"This is too much, I can't deal with it. What do you know about Cady Sunner?"

"I know what you know."

One by one Emily examined the wand, the sphere, and the ring, lost in thought. The imp did not interrupt her.

"Okay," she said eventually, "let's say for one second that I'm not crazy and this is all real. What about where I came from? What more do you know that you're not telling me?"

"Magella is a very similar world to this one. There are humans and animals, birds, rivers, mountains, oceans, deserts, insects, forests... even some similar languages. However, it is also very different. Magic is common there, and every type of being you could imagine, many of which exist here only in legend, walk the land. Technology is very rare and crude on Magella, but through magic we know a great many things."

"What else?"

"Your parents were rulers of a small kingdom called Bravisdor. A group of necromancers were sent to kill them. As your father held off the enemy, your mother put you in a magical Sphere of Protection, like a bubble of energy, and then into the Well. There was a terrible explosion! I lost consciousness. When I awoke, we were in this world, lying on Old Orchard Beach, and there was no sign of the Well or your siblings. I was lying on the sand, invisible, and paramedics were carrying you to an ambulance. It was October 31st. Halloween. That's why Halloween is your birthday. I followed you to the hospital and later to the adoption..."

"Whoa, whoa... hold it. But I wasn't adopted!" Emily objected.

"Yes, you were. Yes, yes, yes."

Emily's mind was spinning as she tried to grasp everything she was being told. "But my parents never said anything about me being adopted."

"They were waiting to tell you when you became an adult."

"Oh." Emily sank her head into her hands. It felt like it was going to explode. "This is all too much for me to... and how would I even go about asking my mom if I am adopted? Do I tell her that a demented little... What are you again anyway? A demon?"

"An imp!" screamed Mercurios furiously, stamping his foot and shaking his little fists in the air. "I am an imp, damn you!"

"Okay, calm down, I thought an imp was a type of demon."

"Well, we are not, thank you very much."

"Okay, uh, well, my parents here on Earth raised me as their own, and that's why I'm going after Cady Sunner. No matter what you say."

"I'll…"

She stood up and pushed her face into his. "You'll what? If you really are my guardian, then you have no choice but to help me."

"Of course I will help you." The imp wrung his hands together, looking genuinely worried. "Together, we will kill Cady Sunner and whoever else murdered your father. We will crush them unmerciful. But you must learn magic and become powerful first."

"I never said anything about killing anyone."

"Of course you didn't. Tee-hee-hee." The imp gave her a wink. "But once you are powerful enough, you will be able to destroy them without risking any harm to yourself. You could incinerate them with a firestorm spell, or blast them with a lightning bolt."

He grew increasingly excited at the thought of so much death and destruction, rubbing his belly and licking his lips, his beady eyes gleaming with fiendish delight.

"Ew, stop that. You're weirding me out."

"Or you could fill their bodies with some hideous abomination, some agonizing, disfiguring disease, yes indeed! Or drive them stark raving mad and make them kill each other!"

He was working himself into a delirious frenzy of excitement, capering about, cackling with glee. These terrible thoughts put him in a state of pure joy, and he began to sing a demented song while marching back and forth on Emily's dresser.

"Yes! Smite them! Smash them! Burn them! Blast them! Kill them! Crush them! Their blood will gush then! Incinerate them! Eviscerate them! Transform them! Violate them! Humiliate them!

Mutilate them! Skin them! Turn their eyes to boiling jelly! Fry their brains, explode their bellies! Rearrange their organs! KILL KILL KILL!" he shrieked in ecstasy, jumping up and down.

"Oh my god, will you stop doing that? My mom is going to hear you!"

The imp regained his self-control, stopped capering about, and stared at her, panting happily.

"Ah, such fun, such fun, yes indeed! But first you must learn."

"You are deranged! I'm not going to kill anyone, first of all, and let's get something straight right now, privacy is not negotiable. There is no way I'm going to live my life knowing that every moment, day and night, I'm being watched by some demented, invisible, demonic thing!"

"Oh, you hurt my feelings, Emily," the imp said, his eyes drooping sadly.

"So… why is the desk so special? Why do those people want it so badly?"

"Emily, I don't know what 'Vadas Asger' is. Perhaps those words lead to the Well's location. We must find the Well and return to Magella."

"Uh, I'm not going anywhere."

Emily paced back and forth for a moment deep in thought. "The Sanctuary," she whispered to herself, staring at the calendar on her wall. "What is the Sanctuary? Halloween is only a couple days away. Is it some kind of gangsters' meeting place? The man at Cady's house said that 'they' wanted to meet in a public place…"

Emily touched the date on the calendar with a finger and found herself recalling a time in her life when Halloween had been a joyful, magical evening for her and her family. If she closed her eyes and thought hard enough, she could still picture her father's smile the year he took her by the hand, out to the front yard to show her the freshly carved jack-o'-lantern glowing in the window. They would always have a birthday cake for her in the shape of a pumpkin or ghost or black cat. That year, her parents had dressed her in a cute little bumblebee costume. She remembered twirling around and around, showing it off to everyone, and then opening her presents while everyone watched. Gritting her teeth, she made up her mind.

"The meeting at the Sanctuary could be the only chance I have to find out for sure who killed my dad," she muttered, grabbing a red marker and circling October 31st on the calendar. "Now, all I have to do is find out what this 'Sanctuary' place is and…" She turned to Mercurios. "Is there a spell in the book that will turn me invisible? I need to be able to spy on their meeting without risking getting caught."

"Yes, there is," said Mercurios. "But it is difficult. Have patience. I promise I will teach you the beginner spells and potions."

"Before Halloween?"

"These things take time, Emily. Have patience, all in good time."

She stared at the black, leather-bound book. A chill ran down her spine as she sensed a palpable aura of dark, unsettling power emanating from it. She slowly, carefully reached into the chest and picked it up. At her touch the book almost seemed to hum with power and the pages began to glow. Emily's eyes grew wide. Was she going to be able control the mysterious force that lurked inside these pages? Part of her wanted to put it back, lock the chest and never look at it again, but a stronger part of her was completely mesmerized and she gingerly opened the covers. Inside were hundreds of pages of shimmering white parchment. It was like staring into a pool of glowing liquid. Many lines of graceful silver writing floated upon the surface of the liquid energy. It was written in a language from another world with unfamiliar symbols and diagrams in black and sometimes blood red. Emily stared at it in awe.

"That is a powerful magic item, Emily," the imp whispered over her shoulder. "The spell book of a powerful wizard is a rare and valuable thing indeed!"

"These are real spells?" whispered Emily.

"Oh yes. Yes, indeed."

"And you think I can learn them? I mean, would you really be able to help me learn them?"

"Of course. The simplest ones should be relatively easy. The more powerful spells will take a great deal of diligent work. Mastering spell-casting and becoming a wizard is no different from mastering any skill, like becoming a brain surgeon; it takes years of work and dedication. But if you can learn basic spell-casting you might be able to locate the Well. Then we can get you back to Magella, where you will study under the finest professors at the Fengusberry Academy."

"Incredible." Emily kept flipping through the pages, utterly mesmerized. The more she looked at the spell book, however, the more she felt a creeping dread growing inside her, a fear that she was meddling with incredibly dark and dangerous powers that were ultimately beyond her control. She noticed something lying at the bottom of the chest. It was a beautifully detailed tarot card. It had an image of a man dressed in robes with a long white beard, in front of him was a cup, a sword and a spell book and he was surrounded by various runes and magic symbols. With one hand he pointed down and with the other he pointed up. Across the bottom was written "The Alchemist."

"What's this?" she asked, picking up the card and inspecting it. "A tarot card?"

"A message from your parents."

"What does it mean? Is it magical?"

"No it's not magical, I suppose it means that you are meant to be a wizard."

Emily caught a glimpse of her reflection in the vanity mirror on her dresser.

"My God, who am I?" she muttered, then put the card and spell book back in the chest, shook her head as if to clear it and turned to Mercurios. "Listen, I've been having this recurring dream about a boy."

"I thought you said it was a demon."

"Yes... That too. But listen, I want to know about this boy. Do you have a magic spell that can tell me who he is or what these dreams mean?"

"Tell me about these dreams."

Emily described her dream, careful to give no hint of her feelings and desires for the mysterious young man with the glittering emerald eyes.

"It is your power awakening, Emily," Mercurios said when she was finished. "Your great destiny. Do not worry and do not fight it. You will be a great wizard and wield enormous power indeed."

"You have to help me find out who he is. Now, what should I do about the desk?"

"What do you mean?"

"I think I should find another hiding spot for it until I can figure out what's going on. I don't like it being at our house, especially since the police haven't arrested anyone, and those men are looking for it."

"I agree. Where will we hide it?"

"I don't know. It's really heavy. Hey, can you make things, like, levitate, or use some sort of spell to move it?"

"No, unfortunately, that is not one of my abilities. I will help you learn such a spell from your mother's spell book, but that will take time. We will begin with the items, the wand and ring and the sphere and the skull, and the most basic spells."

She had stopped listening to him as she took out her cell phone and dialed a number.

"Hey, Tom? Hey, it's Emily... Not much, just doing some homework, wondering what you were up to... Yeah... Listen, Tom, can you keep a secret?"

Mercurios slapped his forehead and shook his head in despair.

Emily proceeded to tell Tom everything about the package, her father's murder, the conversation with Detective Scannel, the break-in and Cady Sunner. She refrained from mentioning anything about Mercurios or her dreams. Tom agreed to come over and help her. As she waited for him, Emily searched online for a place called The Sanctuary in Portland but she couldn't find anything. Half an hour later she heard Tom driving up to her house in his Jeep.

They stood together in her garage looking down at the box containing the desk.

"It sounds like you're mixed up in something pretty dangerous," Tom said.

"I need more time to try and figure out what's going on. I have no evidence. I need to get proof that Cady Sunner is connected, but, yeah, I suppose it's dangerous, which is why I need your help. I don't want this near my mom and me anymore. It needs to go someplace else, or be hidden or buried. I don't care. Just until I get answers."

Tom thought for a second. "There's this place out of the city where I go hiking sometimes. It's pretty remote. We could bury it there."

"Perfect!" Emily grabbed two shovels leaning against the wall of her garage.

"Let's go."

"Right now?"

"Is there a better time than the present?"

Tom laughed and picked up the box with the desk in, carrying it out to the Jeep. Emily was taken aback by how strong he was. They drove out of town and after a few miles Tom turned off the highway down a dirt road into a heavily wooded area, where he pulled over and parked.

"There's a hiking trail that cuts across this road and leads to a big clearing not far into these trees," he said. "That's where we should bury it."

"Sounds good."

Emily carried the shovels while Tom carried the desk. An evening breeze floated over them, rustling the leaves on the trees and the moon soared high above, casting shadows through the trees as they headed deep into the forest. The only other sound was the creaking of branches. Emily's heart was pounding. Having Tom pay her so much attention was exhilarating. After a few minutes, the forest opened into a meadow.

"Here we are," said Tom, putting down the box. "You know, it's funny, I was planning on asking you to come hiking with me out here some time. I never imagined we'd be out here in the middle of the night burying a desk."

"Yeah, it's kinda weird." Her throat felt tight. She'd never imagined being in the middle of nowhere with Tom either. If only the school gossip squad could see them now.

Tom took one of the shovels. "Well, I guess we'd better start digging."

Emily grasped the long, hard shaft of the second shovel and pushed the blade into the damp earth. Soon she could feel her shirt growing wet with sweat, even though Tom was doing most of the work. He dug quickly and methodically, plunging the shovel into the damp earth again and again and it wasn't long before a sizeable hole had appeared. He stripped off his jacket and shirt and Emily felt her face turn hot and red at the sight of his glistening torso and chiseled abs. Tom was extremely fit and muscular.

"Work up a sweat pretty fast digging like this," he grinned.

"Uh, yeah." Emily realized she was staring at his chest and six-pack. "Yeah, thanks again for doing this."

"No problem," he said, resuming his labors.

"So, you were going to invite me out hiking?"

"Yeah."

"Maybe you can teach me some wilderness survival stuff, in case I ever find myself lost, alone and naked in the mountains."

"Of course." He laughed and stopped digging. "Although it would be much better if I were there with you in the flesh, so to speak." He smirked.

Emily stared at his strong arms and chest, at his chiseled abs and his hair streaked with sweat. Before she knew it, her animal instincts were taking over and she was moving toward him. Thrills of excitement rushed through her at the thought of what was about to happen.

"You're all hot and sweaty now. I would invite you in for a glass of lemonade if we were at home."

The old Emily would never have dared to say or do anything like this. But this wasn't the old Emily. Tom let his shovel fall to the ground, scooped her in his arms, and kissed her in a way she had never been kissed before.

Ten

France 1789

"Are you mad?" Mitchell shouted. "If you doubt me then I will let you read through my thoughts and try to find any memory of me dealing with Baelaar or his fools. I despise him!"

Fionn nodded his acceptance of this. "There is no time for that now. I can see that I have no option other than to trust you and hope that my suspicions are wrong."

Mitchell was going to protest further but thought better of it. The winds had now reached them, making it hard for them to get their breath or make themselves heard to one another.

"They are getting closer," he shouted over the roar. "What do you suggest?"

"We could try to reach some of the other knights for reinforcement. I know Abrielle and Cornelieu are on the Isle of Wight. But from the size of the storm our enemies have conjured, I'd say there are many more of them than us. They would overtake us before we could reach them." He swiped his sword through the air, sending a shower of sparks up in the wind. "Our only option is to stand and fight."

Mitchell smiled, his eyes filling with the lust for blood. He was unable to conceal his excitement at the prospect of a battle. His fangs glinted in the moonlight as a low snarl rumbled softly in his throat, mingling with the approaching thunder.

Fionn leaned in close to his ear in order to be heard over the wind. "I am beginning to fear that if Baelaar has been building his own little army he plans to instigate wars and mass slaughters all over the world, until every country on Earth is fighting. If he has heard about the discovery of the documents, he has probably shifted his focus to the Well of Many Worlds. Let's see if he is with this mob, or if he has simply sent his minions to do his dirty work."

He checked Mitchell's eyes and smiled, baring his fangs defiantly. "Now you will have the opportunity to test all that I have taught you. Be strong, no matter what happens."

"I can assure you, you do not need to remind me of that. I've been waiting for this moment for far too long. I intend to be staring into his eyes when I cut off his head."

"Remember control. Silence your thoughts and emotions and be perfectly in the moment."

Now they could see a warship at the head of the storm – a fearsome, black galleon riding a hundred-foot-tall wave, moving at the speed of an arrow. Fionn summoned every ounce of strength and created a hurricane of wind to push against the onslaught and turn their ship so that they were directly facing their enemy's vessel.

"Quickly," he cried. "Focus your will – we must counter them with a wave of our own!"

They stretched their hands before them, hauling the energy of the ocean depths beneath them up into a mighty swell. The black seas rose toward the sky as their enemies continued to bear relentlessly down upon them. The winds howled in anger as they whipped the spray high in the air. With every ounce of their will, Fionn and Mitchell called forth a wall of water that rose nearly seventy feet in the air. Faster and faster came the black galleon, the wave beneath it roaring like a leviathan, echoed by the thunder of the storm that raced across the sky above them.

"Now, roll it forward!" Fionn commanded.

With all their might, they pushed their own wave toward the

approaching enemy. The sheer size and power of the approaching wall of water was awe-inspiring. Both of them shaking with the effort, Fionn and Mitchell forced their own wall of water even higher. The two great waves met with a great crash. Peals of thunder threatened to split open the sky as millions of tons of water collided with immeasurable force. The spray whipped hundreds of feet up into the atmosphere above; colossal swells rolled out in every direction. Fionn and Mitchell were deluged by the sea rushing and pounding over them, crushing them to the deck and sweeping them this way and that, banging them into unseen obstacles. Their ship pitched wildly as if trying to throw them off, rearing like a thoroughbred horse spooked by the rattle of a venomous snake.

When the water finally drew back and their vision returned they found that the black galleon had drawn up alongside them. At least fifty vampires were manning the attacking vessel, all wearing the same black armor and bestial steel faceplates. Another dozen or more, also in full armor, wore no helmets.

"You!" Mitchell hissed under his breath, eyes flashing with hate. "Look!" he shouted to Fionn, pointing at the bare-faced vampires. Standing amongst them was Baelaar. Fionn nodded grimly.

Above the ship, the black clouds heaved and rolled. Bolts of lightning crackled between them, lighting the horror scene below.

"The ones in the masks are the Initiates," Fionn shouted. "They are the younger vampires. It is the others we should worry about."

At that moment the Priests of Mezzor unleashed the full force of their cannons into the side of the ship. Explosion after explosion, flames leaping from the gun turrets and cannon ball after cannon ball crashing into their hull. Wooden beams burst and splintered, masts crumpled and fell. From the skies above bolts of lightning rained down around them, enormous pillars of plunging blue electricity.

Even with their superhuman speed, reflexes and agility, their abilities were pushed beyond their limits as they leaped, ducked, dove, spun, somersaulted, and slid, trying to avoid either being crushed by a cannonball or incinerated by a bolt of lightning.

Every minute seemed to last forever. Then, as quickly as it had begun, it was over. The winds died down, the clouds rolled upwards and were swept away, and the ocean calmed down to barely a shiver. Mitchell stood on the wreckage of bobbing timber remains of what had so recently been their elegant ship and gazed about, immersed in a stunned, eerie calm.

"Quickly!" Fionn cried, scrambling to his feet. "They're going to board us! We'll freeze the water and bring it up beneath them."

Again, they focused their wills. The black galleon was no more than a few feet away now. With bloodthirsty war cries, dozens of the Initiates stood poised, ready to leap across the narrowing gap onto the wreckage of their ship. As the vampires crouched, ready to spring like cats, the great, black galleon pitched violently sideways, creaking and groaning as a towering spike of ice rose up beneath it, impaling its hull, lifting it into the air and plunging half the attacking Initiates into the ocean. Chaos spread through their ranks but the vampires quickly regrouped and charged with swords drawn, leaping with ease down onto the shattered schooner.

Fionn and Mitchell drew their flaming swords, two firebrands blazing in the blackness of the night, humming with power as their enemies fell upon them. First came the swarm of Initiates. They fought them five at a time, as dozens more rushed up behind them. Even though the apprentices were younger and weaker than Fionn and Mitchell, they still possessed the speed and strength of vampires. Mitchell needed to call on every moment of the obsessive training in hand-to-hand and sword combat he had received over the previous hundred and fifty years. Teacher and student stood back to back, parrying multiple razor-sharp blades as they thrust, sliced and slashed at them from every angle. At the same time, they managed to launch attacks of their own, occasionally sending an Initiate screaming into the cold black waters or a decapitated head bouncing across the splintered planks.

When they became separated, Mitchell found himself surrounded. As his attackers pressed in on him he suddenly bent over backward, arching his back into a bridge. Two of the Initiates, trying to stab him missed and impaled each other instead, while another accidentally cut off the head of one of his fellows with a badly timed swipe of his sword. Mitchell glanced up for a split second and spotted eight vampires without helmets and masks descending from above. Each held a thick, black steel pole with a cruel-looking barbed spearhead on the end. Mitchell bounded into the air, straight at them. As he hurtled past the first he slashed off his head in one clean movement, sending blood spraying through the air in a great fan as the corpse plunged into the ocean waves.

As they landed in front of Fionn he instantly killed two of them and kicked another in the chest, sending him flying into the water. Mitchell landed behind his friend and slew one as Fionn deflected the blows of another, neatly beheading him. Two more plunged their thick steel pikes through each of Fionn's shoulders and kicked his feet out from under him, pinning him to the deck, making him bellow with pain.

Mitchell ambushed the one who'd fallen as he was rising and killed him, but five more now surrounded them. One grabbed the pike which still pinned Fionn to the deck and pushed him back down as he tried to rise. Mitchell spun and killed one just as three others plunged their pikes through him, pinning him down as well. There were just too many of them. Mitchell howled and snarled as he struggled like a wild beast, but to no avail. They were trapped.

Suddenly all was quiet around them, save for the lapping of the waves against the broken hulls of the two ships. Two figures jumped on board carrying great lengths of anchor chain. It was Baelaar and Squire Griffith.

"Bind them," ordered Baelaar.

The surviving Initiates took the chains and tied Mitchell and Fionn from head to foot.

"He's a game lad he is!" shouted Squire Griffith drunkenly, rewarding himself with a swig from a bottle of Chartreuse and pointing at Mitchell. "You fought well, son, but you were outmatched. A game lad though." He jabbed Baelaar in the ribs with his elbow but the vampire ignored him. "Why don't you let this one free?" Squire Griffith turned back to Mitchell. "You should come drinking and wenching with me, lad, we'd have a fine old time!" He roared with laughter.

"These chains were forged by me, Mitchell." Baelaar spoke quietly, ignoring the blustering of the Squire. His hair was now wet and drops of blood dripped streaking down his face from his slicked-back hair. "Using the same methods we use in forging a Draaken." He held up his own sword, which glowed blue and hummed with power. It was covered in frost and clouds of icy fog rose from it. Mitchell's eyes shone crimson as he struggled furiously to get at Baelaar, desperate to tear his throat out, driven berserk with hate and rage. Mitchell's maker chuckled, sheathed his sword and turned his attention to Fionn.

"And you. I am so happy I found you."

"Tell me, Baelaar," Fionn replied. "Rumor has it that the moment your mother gave birth to you she attempted to strangle herself with the umbilical cord in despair. Is this true?"

"Oh!" laughed Squire Griffith. "He has you there."

"Be silent!" snapped Baelaar then stared hard at Fionn. "It is very foolish to try and anger me in your position." He turned and took a good look at Mitchell. "My young cub has grown into a lion. You have proven that you are ready to join us." He reached out his hand.

"Join you? Never! I intend to gut and skin you alive and fill my ears with the sound of your screams!"

Baelaar's eyes blazed. "We are vampires! We are made to rule, not serve. We are the chosen ones! Chosen by Mezzor himself! All other lives he devours, only we remain! I was guided to you, as my maker was guided to me."

"I suppose you think I should be honored that you all want me to join your little clubs?"

Baelaar grew as calm as ice, his face entirely expressionless. "I am surprised at your lack of gratitude for all that I have given you."

"Thank you for the kindness of your condescension," said Mitchell, voice dripping with sarcasm.

Fionn smiled at Mitchell. "All of the fools you see here are merely slaves who do not realize it." He turned back to Baelaar. "There are those who are even more powerful than you, are there not, Baelaar?"

The other vampires snarled behind Baelaar, eager to be unleashed on their enemies, to inflict as much suffering as possible.

"I will deal with you soon enough, Fionn," said Baelaar. "Your very existence offends me. For that, I may not make it quick." He signaled to the other vampires with a wave of his hand. "Take him away."

As the Initiates dragged him off, Fionn shouted back at Mitchell, "Remember everything I taught you."

Mitchell watched as the vampires lowered his teacher into a boat and summoned a wave to speed them away into the night.

"I can see from your abilities in battle that Fionn has taught you many skills," Baelaar continued as if nothing had interrupted their conversation. "You will be one of our finest warriors."

Mitchell spoke calmly and evenly. "I will use your skull as a door knocker."

Squire Griffith laughed. "Door knocker, haha!"

Baelaar chuckled. "That is the lion's spirit talking, but there is so much you still do not know – not just about your own powers, but about the underlying truths of the universe. Fionn has been manipulating you from the start. Planet Earth is a vampire god and we are its chosen high priests!"

"You are mistaken, Baelaar. You are its insane, deluded clown."

Baelaar laughed. "Do you really think that allowing mortals to continue existing as they have is in their best interest? They are not capable of choosing their own destinies without tearing each other apart. It is in their nature, in their blood." His boots echoed in the stillness as he paced back and forth on the remnants of the wooden deck. "Vampires, like your friend Fionn, thrive in that chaos and want things to stay as they are. But we want something better, better for all. We will bring a new order to this planet. Equality among all mortals ruled by one power. Do you really believe that Fionn cares about the fate of mortals? If he did, he would want to protect them from themselves, as we do." A hypnotic force shone in Baelaar's black eyes. "Yes," he coaxed, crouching down. "You know that what I say is true."

For a moment, Mitchell hesitated, momentarily hypnotized, then he shook himself free. "I have tasted your blood once. I am looking forward to tasting it again."

Baelaar's eyes flashed with fury. Straightening up he returned to pacing around his prisoner like a leopard.

"Why should we care about these mortals with their puny, insignificant lives? Going on and on with their infinitely tedious conversations about all the mundane, puny, pointless little details of their puny, pointless little lives. Their grotesque, ridiculous, vulgar little lives! They repulse me!" He spat into Mitchell's face. "I will smash them! They are puppets – ridiculous little flesh puppets – and I pull their strings and make them dance. If I make the merest of gestures, like killing one of their leaders, they run around in every direction losing their minds. They divide into groups, one group attacks another group, and before you know it, they are killing each other by the hundreds of thousands!" He released a peal of cackling laughter. "All that freshly spilled blood for Mezzor. Do you not understand? I am an artist. I am Mezzor's chosen playwright!"

Mitchell stared at him without a word. Baelaar was trying to read his mind. He struggled to resist him but it was no use.

"Ahhh," said Baelaar. "I see your deepest pains in your thoughts. You still think and feel as a mortal. Your mind and heart are filled with infinite wrath and infinite despair. You wish to destroy me and then…" Baelaar's eyes widened in surprise. "Then you intend to use the Well to go to the Abyss and the nine planes of Hell? And you call me mad? You are deranged, obsessed to the point of insanity. Do you not realize that you're already in the Abyss? Do you not understand you are already in Hell?" Baelaar crouched down close to him again, his fervor burning in his eyes. "You have been told that we believe planet Earth is a vampire demi-god and that we worship it, but you have not been told the rest. That is just a small part. From the knowledge we have gained from the most ancient vampire, we now know the very origin of the universe and of humanity. The great question has been answered!"

"It must be hard being you," said Mitchell.

Baelaar stared at him. "Enough sarcasm. This universe," he continued, sweeping his hand across the stars, "is Hell! We have discovered that when God cast the rebel angels out of heaven, into the Abyss, this universe is the abyss he cast them into. The stars, our sun, they are the fallen angels spoken of in all the religious texts that God cast out of heaven down into this terrible, frigid black emptiness we call the universe. When you look at the sun, or at the countless stars, you are looking at demons and devils, the fallen angels, Lucifer's mighty army! And the planets and moons that orbit them are lesser demons and evil demi-gods, worshiping their demon lords eternally as they orbit them. The planet Earth is a vampire demi-god and all the beings that live and die upon it are the souls of the damned, existing only to feed it with their blood and the sum total of their life experience. They are born here over and over, in various forms, born afresh to be beaten down and destroyed, then reborn to be beaten and destroyed again, over and over forever and ever. Do you not comprehend the unique gift I have given you? I have saved you from that terrible, pointless, miserable fate. The thought of lost happiness and everlasting pain torments you relentlessly. It has become your only reality. Let me end your pain forever! We are immortal! Embrace your new nature and you will have anything you desire!"

Mitchell stared at him for a few moments with his mouth hanging open. "I hate to imagine what your childhood was like. You are truly insane. But you are the one who still thinks like a mortal. You, existing in awe of this world, this so-called vampire god, and the universe, filled with these so-called fallen angels, the planets and stars. These things do not impress me. It is trivial compared to the power that I have touched. You think that you comprehend immortality? You understand only a mockery of it."

Baelaar raised the corner of his lip in a sneer, groaned, rolled his eyes and threw up his hands in a flourish of splenetic exasperation. He then stared at Mitchell. "You need more time," he said matter-of-factly. "I understand. Perhaps one day you will change your mind. Or perhaps, as the great Milton wrote, 'Never can true reconcilement grow where wounds of deadly hate have pierced so deep.' Either way, I will leave you to contemplate my offer." He turned to the tall, thin vampire beside him. "Ivan, drain him and send him to the bottom of the ocean."

Ivan nodded and Baelaar addressed another who wore a long black cloak and had short dark hair, high cheekbones and a small, surprisingly feminine nose. "Mephris, Celeste, help him. Then come and find me."

"It will be done," Ivan said in a thick Russian accent.

Mephris stepped forward, throwing back the cloak to reveal polished armor glittering with jewels and so did Comtesse LeDuijou.

"Comtesse LeDuijou!" Mitchell exclaimed.

"Such a waste," she said. "So, gorgeous man, my offer still stands. Stop all this foolishness and become my pet. You cannot imagine the delights that would await you."

"I'd wager she could teach you a thing or two!" Squire Griffith guffawed. "She is delightful, is she not?"

The Comtesse turned to Baelaar. "I demand that you give him to me."

Baelaar looked at her then laughed. "I do believe the Comtesse is in love."

Squire Griffith belched loudly. "Her? In love? She is incapable. She is depraved."

"Me depraved?" said the Comtesse. "Sir, the depravity of your life is only whispered in the halls of Hell."

"Love is like the guillotine," the Squire rambled on, "the first cut is the deepest and even the strongest and most cynical are likely to lose their heads." He let out a drunken guffaw at his own joke.

Baelaar placed a cold hand on the Comtesse's arm. "Once Mitchell has spent a couple centuries crushed at the bottom of the ocean his mind will break and then I will retrieve him for you."

"Cheer up, lad." Squire Griffith gave Mitchell a conspiratorial slap. "At least you've got her favors to look forward to."

"Perhaps she will be the first that I kill," said Mitchell.

"Come, we must be on our way," said Baelaar. "The blood of the world is the blood of the God."

"The blood of the world is the blood of the God," replied the others.

Baelaar and Squire Griffith sprang onto a boat floating nearby, conjured a rolling wave, and were gone.

As the Initiates chained Mitchell tightly the three older vampires turned their focus to the black ocean and within minutes a gaping whirlpool had appeared.

"Ivan," Mitchell said, "what do you think your place in the world will be if Baelaar gets what he desires? Do you really want to spend all eternity serving him?"

Ivan shrugged. "I serve my people. Order under us is the best thing for them."

"But those are Baelaar's lies! You are a fool if you believe him!"

The whirlpool was now so deep and spinning so fast that a great churning sound rose up from its depths.

"Ivan, you do not know what you are doing!" Mitchell shouted. "Stop this madness!"

"He knows exactly what he is doing," said the Comtesse.

"If you do this, I'll find you!" said Mitchell.

Ivan shrugged. "These things happen."

"Tell that to the fish, Mitchell," said the Comtesse, slashing his throat with a dagger. As the blood emptied out of Mitchell, Ivan effortlessly hoisted his weakening body high above his head.

"During the next few centuries at the bottom of the ocean," said the Comtesse. "I give you permission to dream of my beauty." She blew him a kiss.

Ivan hurled him into the center of the watery vortex. Mitchell flew through the air, walls of water spinning around him as he plunged. He fell and fell and fell until he was a thousand feet below the surface. The cold black liquid swallowed him and he continued to spin as though caught in a tornado, down into the blackest depths of the ocean. Down, down, down he sank until the darkness was complete. The pressure was unbearable. Even the body of a vampire could not withstand the crushing weight and his bones burst apart in one agonizing moment. He screamed for no one to hear and then he knew no more.

Eleven

Portland, Maine, 2020

Tom's kiss was long, deep and sensual. Their tongues, deliciously warm and wet, lazily licked and teased one another. Eventually he broke away and stared at her face, admiring her beauty, gently cupping her chin in his hand. Emily came back down to earth a few seconds later. The fact that he had broken away first, and left her wanting more, sent a hot flash of desire traveling deep down inside her. After a moment he pulled her toward him again.

"Come here," he said in a soft, low voice as his arms went around her back, his powerful hands kneading and stroking the muscles that had been aching pleasantly from the effort of digging. She sighed with pleasure, melting into his arms as he kissed her again. They floated in the bliss of each other's bodies for a few exhilarating minutes. Then once again Tom broke away. Emily opened her mouth and breathed deeply. She wanted him but she didn't want to risk rushing things. The unmistakable look of desire in his eyes, combined with his willpower and restraint, made her want him even more.

"I wonder why it took me so long to realize how beautiful you are," he mused, staring deep into her eyes.

Emily's heart surged. She forced herself to look at her watch.

"Oh man, my mom's going to kill me if I don't get home soon."

Tom stepped back and held her at arm's distance, a flash of

disappointment danced in his eyes, then his normal look of calm amusement returned. "Not a problem," he chuckled. "Let's head back then."

They hardly spoke on the way home, neither of them wanting to risk spoiling the mood. Had she blown it, she wondered. Was she even ready to start anything serious with him? What an amazing night.

As Tom walked her to her front door she was still burning with desire. She wanted to reward him for helping her. She looked at him intently for a moment, then pulled him to her and kissed him again. They took their time, savoring each other, finally breaking apart at the same time.

"Thanks for helping me."

"Any time," he said, forcing himself to move away from her and walk backward to his car, grinning mischievously at her all the way. She watched him drive away, waving breezily from the open car window as he went, and clung onto the front door frame for a few moments before trusting her legs to carry her inside. Once safely in her bedroom, the excitement became mixed with a confusing twinge of guilt. It was as though she had done something wrong.

"Hello, Emily."

She jumped, startled at the sight of Mercurios sitting on a bookshelf, biting his claws.

"Man, I don't think I'm ever going to get used to you popping up out of nowhere like that."

"A wise idea to bury the desk until we find out more, wise indeed. Yet, I wonder how wise it was to tell the boy."

"Well, who else was I going to get to help? You said you couldn't levitate it, I can't cast a levitation spell, and it's too heavy for me to carry. I needed help. Wait, you weren't watching us, were you?"

"I am your guardian."

"I told you I want privacy," she hissed at him, clenching and unclenching her fists.

"Please, don't smite me, I'm sorry! But it's your mother's spell, her command to watch and protect you, I must obey it! At home I will stay in the living room or on the porch as you have commanded, but when you go out I must accompany you."

Emily suddenly had an idea. "I feel bad that you have to do nothing but watch over me, Mercurios, but I really want to learn magic. If I set you free right now, will you still teach me? Once I'm a wizard, I won't need your protection anymore."

"You would need to become very powerful indeed in order to do that, yes. Very powerful indeed."

"What do you mean?"

"Only a wizard with more power than your mother can dispel her command. Until then I am bound to you. Either that or until you die."

"Then you better learn to walk as far away as the spell allows, stand on the other side of a wall or tree or rock or something, close your eyes, face the opposite direction, and plug your ears. I demand privacy!"

"Yes, I will obey, thank you for not punishing me." He stopped cowering and stood up straight. "No matter. What's done is done, and if he betrays you, I can teach you some spells that he might find most unpleasant indeed, tee-hee-hee. You could make his flesh rot off."

"Ew! You are truly wicked! Let's get this straight; I have no interest in ever hurting Tom. Listen, can you teach me a spell to read minds? Then, not only will I be able to find out what this Sanctuary place is and what Cady Sunner wants with the desk, but also when they have the meeting I'll be able to find out everything about them, their plans and who killed my father!"

"All in good time, Emily. That is an advanced spell."

"But I need it now!"

He hopped off the bookshelf onto her bed, making her scoot backward away from him. "I said it takes time! The plan is to teach you magic until you are powerful. Then, we will have a great deal of fun with the puny inhabitants of this ridiculous world, a great deal of fun indeed."

"Hey, I happen to like this world and its 'puny inhabitants.' Well, at least, some of them so lay off."

"I don't think you understand. Once you have been trained at the Fengusberry Academy in Magella you will be able to return to this world and rule it if you want. We can make them all slaves! Or perhaps force them all to leap into erupting volcanoes."

"What? I never asked to rule anything. And that's ridiculous!"

"I am quite serious. You have never tasted true power, and when you do and embrace your great destiny, I think you will find it to be delicious indeed. Yes, so very, very delicious!" He glanced at Emily's spell book and before she could reply, it opened to page seven. "First, though, you must promise me that you will not go after Cady Sunner again until you have learned at least the basic spells. It is foolishness to rush forward now when you are still so weak and risk almost certain death. All you need to do is to be patient, study, and in time you will have the whole world at your feet."

She shrugged. "Then, I better learn them by Halloween, because that's when I'm going after him."

"AACHT!" shrieked the imp, waving his fists in the air. "You could rule the world and you're willing to throw it all away because you are impatient? Weak and foolish indeed! Your mother would be furious at this stupidity! We must focus on finding out what this 'Vadas Asger' is and locating the Well and taking you back to Magella."

"Listen, I'm not going to another world and if we don't get Cady Sunner busted it might be only a matter of time before he kills me and my mom. So we better get started."

The imp sighed in resignation.

Emily lit some candles and sat down in front of the big book for her lesson. "Mercurios, this spell book, is it evil? I can feel the power in it every time I take it out of the chest. Is it going to, like, affect me in some way?"

"Very powerful indeed," nodded the imp. "But it is not evil, it is a neutral power, it will not control you, if that is what concerns you.

However, the longer you spend with it and the more you study it and its secrets, the more its power will absorb into your being. It has no will of its own, but yes, it is a source of great power and power is capable of influencing your nature."

They worked late into the night. The spell book was written in Elvish. Mercurios said that was what all spells were written in because the elves had been the first to discover and refine the art of spell casting. He made her spend a great deal of time learning the proper pronunciation and meanings of the words, as well as the accompanying hand gestures and mental images she was supposed to focus her mind on while casting. The first spell he wanted her to learn was a simple illumination spell, since invisibility was too advanced for her to even begin to study yet. Her first few attempts were clumsy and did not go particularly well. The first time she tried to cast the illumination spell, the light bulb in her bedside lamp exploded. It was a shocking and uncomfortable reminder that she was playing with supernatural powers that she had no understanding of, and putting her trust in a crazed imp. However, after considerable effort she finally managed to create a fairly effective illumination spell. It was one of the most exhilarating moments of her life. The room glowed with a haunting, silvery-blue light that didn't seem to have any particular point of origin. Emily danced about and squealed with joy at this sign that she was soon going to be able to do things she had never before dreamed possible.

Mercurios also taught her the command words to activate her Sphere of Protection, Ring of Teleportation and Wand of Lightning, although she didn't actually use the ring or wand, not wanting to waste any of their energy. By the time she went to bed at one o'clock she was exhausted and plunged straight into a deep sleep.

A couple of hours later she found herself awake, staring into space. She could see the stars shimmering in the sky through her bedroom window and only gradually realized that there was an eerie, glowing mist approaching. She sat up, rubbing her eyes. The mist grew thick outside her window and Emily stared at it as it swirled. She drew in her breath. Outside her window a ghostly apparition was forming in the mist. She sat bolt upright and stared in horror, eyes wide and mouth hanging open. The corpse of her father appeared out of the mist, floating outside her window. His face was deathly pale and his eyes were milky white. He was grinning grotesquely at her and she saw to her disgust that all of his teeth ended in sharpened points. He clawed at her window and his long, sharp, rotting nails made a sickening, light screeching sound as if being drawn along a blackboard. Emily was paralyzed with a mixture of terror and fascination.

"Daddy?" She choked on the word.

"Open the window, honey," came an eerie, otherworldly, distant voice from her father's mouth.

Mercurios appeared beside her. "Look!" He pointed at the chain hanging around her neck as he danced about waving his other hand frantically. "Take it off and put it on the ground and say the magic words. We must send your father back to his grave. The skull has raised him. Your father is undead, he is a ghoul."

"A what?"

Mercurios snatched the charm from around Emily's neck and threw it onto the floor. The miniature chest was glowing.

"A ghoul, your father's corpse reanimated. Undead."

"Emily," moaned her father as he floated before them. "You are in great danger and I am here to tell you... that you have no hope. You will die." The ghoul cackled and clawed at the window.

"Say the words," insisted Mercurios.

"Go to Sammy and offer yourself to the cult, Emily!" the ghoul cackled again. "You know the old saying, with friends like these..."

"Emily, ghouls eat dead human flesh," shouted Mercurios. "Say the words!"

"Almeron Sidella," muttered Emily in a daze, staring at her father, shivering uncontrollably.

The chest expanded to its full size and Mercurios flipped the top open. "Look!" he exclaimed, pointing inside. The ruby eyes of the Skull of Monster Summoning were pulsing with a red light. Emily stared at them, her own eyes wide in fear, and then looked back at her father.

"Say 'Gorhel velsten!'" shouted Mercurios. "The Skull summoned him when you wished to speak to his ghost! Pick up the Skull and say the words, Emily, we must deactivate it. Who knows what other undead beings or monsters it might summon. It is quite temperamental and very unpredictable."

Emily slid off her bed and knelt down beside the chest. As though in a trance she reached in and picked up the skull. She held it in front of her and looked into its glowing eyes. Then glanced up at her father.

"Who were all the people involved in killing you?" she asked.

"The real question, Emily, is who will kill you?" The ghoul tore the windows open and bared its teeth.

"Gorhel velsten," she said. The lights in the gems flickered out and with a wail the ghoul disappeared and then the mist dispersed.

"Daddy!" Emily called after him, but he had vanished into the night.

The next morning when she awoke she felt groggy. She had cried herself to sleep after the disturbing encounter with her father, haunted by the horrible look on his face. She thought about what he had said. Then her mind went to her recurring dream about the gorgeous, mysterious boy with the glittering eyes. She was shocked to find that in her waking hours she longed for him as though a part of her was missing and he was in possession of it.

"Mercurios?"

The imp appeared a few moments later. "At your service."

"My father had a friend named Sammy who works at one of the shipping warehouses. He occasionally picked up antiques there that had been shipped in from various places. Could it have been Sammy who told Cady Sunner my father had that desk?"

"Quite possibly. They must not find out about 'Vadas Asger,' until we know what it is. Stay away from them."

Just then her mom pushed open the door to her bedroom. Mercurios disappeared.

"You know you could knock, Mom," Emily said.

"Don't be silly, dear." Her mother looked her up and down. "Honey, I think it's time you started dressing like a lady. Those clothes are just terrible. How do you ever expect to be taken seriously dressed like that?"

"Thanks, Mom," Emily snapped. "By the way, your hair looks like you had it done at the dog groomers."

"Emily! What's gotten into you?"

"What's gotten into me? Why don't you just go back to work and focus on your great career. These random attempts to act like a mother every few months are a waste of your time and mine."

"Excuse me?" Her mother pushed the door all the way open, and Emily groaned. "It's my hard work that has allowed you to live in such a nice house. You're a grown woman now. It's time you started acting like one."

"Okay, fine. So stop telling me what to do then, since I'm a grown woman and all."

"Emily, this is my house and there are still certain rules—"

"Oh, so I get it. When it's convenient for you, I'm a grown woman, and when it isn't, I'm a child. Is that how it works?"

"I don't have time for this." Her mother turned and walked away. "I'm late for work. Clean up this room and get to school." She headed downstairs, and Emily slammed the door shut behind her.

"Go back to living in the office, Mom," she shouted through the door. "So when you die you'll be able to look back proudly and think, instead of spending time with my family, I wasted every waking hour of my life working so I could purchase the most expensive kitchen appliances available." She gave the door a kick.

At school, the halls were alive with an expectant buzz about

Tom's party that night. At lunch Emily and her friends sat talking in the cafeteria.

"So, uh," Emily said to her friends. "I broke into Cady Sunner's place last night."

"What?" the others exclaimed simultaneously.

"Are you insane?" Cindy demanded, leaning forward and grabbing her friend's hands, looking into her eyes. "What were you thinking? I know you're devastated by your father's death and you aren't thinking clearly but this is getting out of control."

"If Cady Sunner and his gang aren't busted soon they might kill my mom and me. I have to do everything I can. I mean, we'll only be safe if they are all in jail."

"Oh my god," said Cindy, wringing her hands in anguish.

"Really, Emily," said Bethany. "That's nuts, what do you think he would have done if he'd caught you? He's a killer. He would probably have you tied up in his basement right now and be torturing you just like in that TV show *I Was Kidnapped by a Freak*."

"Yeah, Emily," said Chester. "Listen to us, that's crazy."

"I need to get some kind of evidence."

"The first step to getting evidence," said Bethany, "is gathering information. Just like on that show *World's Most Deranged Drug Lords*. You gather intel and that will hopefully give you leads to find hard evidence."

"Emily, please," implored Cindy. "You're my best friend and you have me really scared, what you did was really stupid, please stop this."

"You could set up a camera to automatically film his house, or maybe set up a microphone," said Bethany. "You should buy some spy surveillance stuff."

"Spy stuff?" Emily laughed. "Where would I get that and… wait… Cindy, your dad's got an electronics store…"

"Oh no! Now you're talking about wire-tapping Cady's house?" said Cindy, exasperated. "No, Emily."

"Not necessarily. The kitchen window is always open. He has a big backyard and there are bushes at the far end, I might be able to hide a shotgun microphone in those bushes and just leave it there and record everything. I wouldn't have to go near him."

Cindy looked thoughtful. "I don't know, Emily."

"Please, Cindy, help me out."

"But what are we going to tell my father?"

"We'll say I'm doing a biology report on birdsong and I need to record them."

"Ohhhh, this is so exciting," said Bethany. "We're going to expose a killer satanic cult."

"Yeah, or get murdered," said Chester. "I don't want you going near that man's house, Cindy."

"I won't, babe. Okay, Emily, if this will keep you from breaking into his house I'll help you but you have to promise me you won't go back inside."

"I promise."

As Cindy and Emily left school that afternoon, Chanel Boxer and her minions walked by.

"Nice outfit, rhinoceros nose," Chanel taunted Cindy. "Shouldn't you be selling Girl Scout cookies or something?" Her minions giggled obediently.

"Hey, Chanel," Emily said. "Just shut it."

"Oh yeah? Or what?" Chanel shot her an insolent sneer.

Mercurios appeared on Emily's shoulder. "You dislike this one a great deal, don't you, Emily? One day, we'll prepare something of exceeding nastiness for her, won't we? Oh yes, indeed!" Emily looked around to see if anyone else could see or hear him. "Don't worry, no one but you can see me."

"You'll find out soon enough," she said, ignoring the imp and staring directly at Chanel.

Chanel laughed. "Wow, original comeback. Well, once you and Cathy Cupcakes here figure it out, let me know." She gave Cindy another dirty look and stalked off.

"See you at the party tonight, Chanel," Emily called after her.

Chanel glanced over her shoulder, angry eyes blazing, not breaking her stride, obviously unsettled by Emily's new show of confidence. As she should be, Emily thought.

"How I hate her," Cindy said as they walked out of the school.

"Yeah," Emily agreed, her mind already on other matters.

"So, tell me honestly what's up with you and Tom?" Cindy asked as they climbed into Emily's car. Emily frowned, a little uncomfortable. She wasn't ready to share what had happened between her and Tom last night. "A lot of people are saying that you are together. Is it true?"

"No, we've just hung out a bit that's all."

"Oh." She sounded disappointed.

"What?"

"Nothing. He seems like such a great guy, though. And it would be so much fun to double-date…"

"Double-date? That's what this is about?"

Cindy blushed. "Yeah."

"Okay, well, we'll see."

First they went by Cindy's father's electronics store, picked up the shotgun mic and a wireless recording device and got a tutorial on how to use them. Then they stopped at a Halloween store called Marabar's to buy some costumes. Emily decided to dress up as an eighteenth-century vampire. It would be classic gothic all the way. Cindy found a hilarious bunny rabbit outfit. She leaped out of the changing room.

"My true nature revealed!" she cried.

"Whoa, you look hot."

Cindy laughed.

After some searching, Emily found a gorgeous midnight-blue ball gown that was perfect. She had some fake jewelry at home she could add for effect, and for the final touch she bought an amazingly realistic-looking pair of fangs. As they were walking out of the store they noticed a flyer stapled to a telephone pole, advertising an all-ages bash at a rock club called the Sanctuary, which was opening on Halloween. The blood drained from Emily's face as she slowly reached out to tear off the flyer. As she read it over again, she shuddered. Could this be the same Sanctuary? It would explain why she hadn't been able to find it online. It was a brand-new club that didn't even have a website yet. But why in the world would those men be interested in meeting at a Halloween party in a club?

"This must be it though," she muttered to herself. He had said the people they were meeting were scared, so they wanted to meet in a public place.

"What? What is it?" Cindy asked.

"I know where we're going for Halloween." Emily passed her the flyer.

"No admittance without costume," read Cindy. "I like it!"

After dropping Cindy off, Emily drove home. When she was in her bedroom Mercurios was waiting on her desk.

"You dislike the Chanel girl intensely don't you? Perhaps some day you should give her a taste of your Wand of Lightning. We could very easily make her head explode and turn her into a pile of ashes, tee-hee-hee."

"Listen, I just want to make something clear. Just because I don't like Chanel doesn't mean I want to blast her with a lightning bolt."

"Of course you don't, Emily, tee-hee-hee," he chuckled, giving her a knowing wink. "Oh, and that reminds me, your name isn't Emily."

"What?"

"Your real name is Talia."

"Okay, stop right there. My name is Emily, got it? I'm Emily Bliss. That's who I am."

"Whatever you say. But I don't like this plan of yours. Focus your energies on learning magic, that is what's important, forget about everything else."

"Listen, Mercurios, I promise to be safe, I won't go into Cady's house again or anything like that. But I need to find out as much as possible. I'm going to record him from a safe distance. It's a compromise. I get to do what I want and be safe at the same time."

"Foolish."

She drove by Cady Sunner's house, parked her car just up the street, snuck into Cady's backyard and hid the mic in his bushes, pointing it at the open kitchen window. Then she went home, made sure the signal was being recorded onto her computer and started getting ready for Tom's party.

Twelve

For more than two centuries Mitchell remained trapped, crushed in the depths of the watery, black abyss. During that time, his body was barely able to regenerate itself. For decade after decade he existed in an almost comatose nightmare. Every hour of those years, however, his hunger for blood grew stronger, the pain becoming so great it eventually hauled his mind out of the blackness and into a full, agonizing consciousness when a shark tore open a large fish nearby and a cloud of blood engulfed him. He was barely able to move, but he could sense the life forms moving around him in the darkness. The faint, enticing scent of the blood drove his body to start the long process of healing.

With what little strength returned he fed upon whatever creatures of the deep found their way to him, but their feeble life forces did not provide the same power as human blood. It took forever for them to provide enough strength for him start moving, inch by painful inch, to escape his chains until eventually he was able to break free of them and the weight of water above him and haul his crushed body up toward the surface of the ocean.

As he came closer to the surface Mitchell could hear the thoughts of humans on a ship crossing far above him. When he finally broke through the waves, under cover of darkness, he was able to grasp onto the side of the hull with his bony fingers, hanging there, dragged in the ship's wake, until he could muster the strength to lift his own weight out of the water and throw himself onto the deck. There he sprawled in the dark for several hours before crawling to a hatch and dropping into a dark corner of the hold, where he remained for the next few weeks, feeding on the blood of rats.

Like the creatures of the deep the rats' blood was also weak, but it kept him alive as his body fought to regenerate itself. Occasionally he would catch the thoughts and voices of sailors and smell the blood coursing through their strong veins as they worked. He learned that the ship was headed far north to Sweden. When it finally docked, he waited until nightfall and slithered from the hold, crawling silently to the shore, unseen and unheard by the slumbering population. He lay in wait on the rocks beneath a pier, exhausted by his efforts, kept alive by the force of his will.

"Wherever you are," he whispered to the stars above, "I will find you."

After a few hours he mustered the strength to crawl into a cave and for many months he lay there, feeding on the blood of any birds of animals that scurried too close to his waiting fingers. When he had healed enough to stand upright, he stepped out into the world of humans once more, ready to hunt. Now he was not only one of the most ancient vampires on earth, but his power had grown well beyond his years, the centuries spent crushed by the ocean having accelerated his development.

He was not prepared, however, for the profound changes that had taken place in the world of mortals and his eyes were wide in amazement as he moved silently amongst people who barely noticed his existence. He stole modern clothes from a traveler's suitcase then crossed by boat to England, stole a horse from a farm and rode southward, passing landscapes populated by gleaming towers. He saw machines that flew across the sky and at night he saw the people inside staring at boxes with moving pictures projected onto glass.

Everything was so shiny and hard.

He needed to learn how to blend into this new reality. It was essential that he master his new environment if he was going to thrive. In the two hundred years he had existed as a vampire before being crushed in the depths of the ocean, Mitchell had amassed a fortune and had buried his treasures in various spots in the English countryside. His first task was to locate those stashes that had not been covered in concrete and dig up belongings that he hoped would now be worth the fortune he needed.

Leaving the countryside for the city he started to acquaint himself with the survival skills needed for the modern world. He learned how to use a computer and drive a car, while all the time searching for information about the movements of the Priests of Mezzor and for any of the Knights of the Niveus Gladius. Once he had turned his treasures into cash he purchased some real estate, cars and a private jet and hired his own personal pilot.

He developed a taste for the raw, primal power of rock music. One night he was out at a rock club in London. He was dressed simply but stylishly and wore a long black trench coat to cover the fact they he was carrying his sword. Getting it past bouncers had been easy, using the hypnotic power of his eyes. While observing the mortals as they danced and played endless games of seduction, he fleetingly caught the thoughts of a young man sitting alone in a dark corner of the club. Mitchell froze. For a moment, he had seen a clear image of Baelaar standing in some sort of temple and he realized that he had stumbled upon a recently turned Initiate of the Priests of Mezzor.

As Mitchell edged closer, the young vampire's thoughts grew darker. He recalled sneaking into a hospital earlier that evening and feeding on infants and children as though they were rodents. Mitchell was disgusted but his face showed no expression as he pulled up a seat at the same table. The Initiate looked at him in surprise. When Mitchell smiled, exposing his teeth, the young man drew back suspiciously.

"Who are you?"

"Baelaar sends his greetings. There is a situation that must be dealt with immediately. Mephris has gone rogue."

"What?"

"He is a traitor. He is working with the Niveus Gladius."

"That's impossible!"

"That is exactly what I said, but unfortunately it is possible. I will explain how, but we must go somewhere more private. Shall we step outside?"

The Initiate hesitated before nodding. Mitchell led him out of the club into an alley between two buildings.

"We are telling everyone to keep their eyes open for him and to report any sightings immediately," Mitchell said. "Have you seen him?"

"The last I heard, he was in America working on… but don't you know that?"

The Initiate frowned, realizing something was wrong. Mitchell was standing too close to him, making him shiver involuntarily.

"Of course," Mitchell replied. From the vampire's thoughts he could see that Mephris was his maker and that he had gone to a place in America called Portland, Maine. The Initiate had accompanied him and then returned to England. Mitchell saw jumbled images of a warehouse on the waterfront. The Initiate had also overheard a conversation in which Mephris mentioned the Well of Many Worlds, although the boy had no idea what it was. All he knew was that Mephris was seeking it, and that was why he had gone to Portland. He also knew that there was a meeting with a group of American vampires planned there in a couple nights at a place called the Sanctuary on Halloween.

"What did you say your name was again?" asked the Initiate, slowly backing away.

"My name?" Mitchell smiled, his canines gleaming in the lamplight. "My name… is Vengeance."

With one swift movement, Mitchell drew his sword of flame and sliced off the young man's head. Stepping over the bleeding corpse, kicking the head to the side, he sheathed his sword and walked away.

"Portland, Maine," he muttered to himself. "The Sanctuary, October 31st, All Hallows Eve. Hmmm... it's a full moon on Halloween this year."

Behind him the body disintegrated into a pile of ash that was then scattered by a gust of wind.

Thirteen

Emily sat in her bedroom staring at the palm of her right hand. "Mercurios?"

"Yes." The imp appeared on her dresser.

"You've been around my whole life, do you know how I got this scar?" She held up her hand. There was a scar running down the lifeline. "I've had it ever since I can remember and I don't know how I got it and my mom doesn't remember."

The imp jumped off the dresser, ran over and leaped onto Emily's lap and stared intently at her hand. "No, Emily, I don't remember."

There was a pounding on Emily's bedroom door and she nearly jumped out of her skin. Mercurios vanished. When she opened the door Emily found her mother standing, arms crossed and frowning.

"What, Mom?"

"I got a call from the school earlier. Apparently, you're failing math! Do you want to tell me what's going on?"

"Mom, I don't want to talk about it now," Emily said quietly.

"Apparently all your grades are falling. What's going on?"

"Other than my father dying?" Emily said, unable to keep her sarcasm in check.

"Other than that. I know it's been very hard for you, dear, but I'm just concerned. Do you need a tutor?"

"No. Listen, I can deal with this myself. Just give me time!"

"Well, it certainly doesn't seem like it! You can't let your grades slip like this!"

"Yeah, because achieving good grades is everything and nothing else matters. Listen, Mom, why don't you just go back to work, since that's the most important thing in the world and let me deal with my life."

"Emily, I work very hard to provide this life for you – a life that you obviously take for granted – so I have the right to know what's going on."

"I don't take it for granted, Mom, I'm grateful for it, but there's more to life." Emily thought for a moment. Maybe a half-truth would get her out of this situation. "Look, I've just been doing a lot of socializing, that's all. That's a good thing, isn't it?"

"What, with Cindy? But she's a straight-A student."

"Not just Cindy."

"Do you mean a boy?"

"Uh… yeah. And you need to respect that this is my personal life and have confidence in me that, even though I won't be getting a hundred per cent on every exam because I want to actually spend some time enjoying my life while I'm young, I will pull through."

She waited before adding any more, unsure how her mother would react. She had never spoken to her about this kind of stuff before. She had a bad feeling in the pit of her stomach that she might just have made a big mistake.

"Oh… I see. That makes sense." Her mother nodded. "Well, it's wonderful that you've found a boy you like, but I expect you to be responsible about this. You've got to keep up with your studies." Emily could feel herself blushing angrily. "You have to think about your future, your career."

"Okay, I will worry about my life and you can worry about yours. Are we done?"

"For now." Her mother headed off downstairs.

Whew! Emily thought. I got out of that one!

"Em?" her mother called up the stairs.

Emily stopped halfway closing her door and poked her head back out. "Yes, Mom?"

"Why don't we cook dinner together tonight?"

She had a sneaking suspicion that this invitation was just a cover for the dreaded "sex ed" conversation. She knew she couldn't avoid it forever. It was programmed into every parent's DNA – "the talk." She groaned inwardly at the thought of it, but she also knew she had to get it out of the way.

"Um, okay."

"Okay, great. Come on then."

Emily walked downstairs as though she was on her way to her own execution. As expected, her mother began discussing male-female stuff as they prepared dinner, and it was just as awkward and embarrassing for both of them as expected.

"Now, honey, at your age, there are these things called hormones."

"Yes, I know, Mom. And they're present at any age."

"Let me finish, please. Now, hormones can affect young people in strange ways. They're like a chemical reaction that can create an imbalance in your brain. It can almost be like a mild form of insanity. You might find yourself thinking and acting a little crazy and getting impulses, thinking and feeling things—"

"Gee, Mom, I know."

"Oh, you know so much, do you?"

"Mom, I know about hormones and puberty and all that stuff. I'm nearly eighteen!"

"Oh, you do!" her mother exclaimed. "Well, just imagine for a moment that despite your vast experience, there might just be a couple things that I have a little more experience with than you." She banged down an empty pot and fished inside of the cutlery drawer.

"Okay, okay, look, I'm sorry."

"Does he respect you?"

"Yes, Mom."

"Oh, so you haven't…"

"No, Mom, listen, to put a quick end to this conversation, I'm a virgin, okay?"

"Oh, well, good dear, I'm glad you've been so mature about this. Always remember: The best way to find out if a boy really loves you is to see if he'll wait for marriage. It really is just that simple."

"Okay, thanks, Mom, can we talk about something else now?"

"No, Emily!"

Emily spent the next hour helping her mother in silence, letting her do all the talking. When dinner was finally over, and all the dishes had been washed, she retreated to her bedroom to finish getting ready for the party while listening to rock and roll on her stereo at full volume. It was her favorite style of music and always transported her to another place.

When she arrived outside Tom's mansion she could hear the dull thudding of rock music coming through the closed front door. Just as she was about to let herself in Cindy arrived with Chester and a second later Chanel, Tyler, and the rest of Chanel's squad pulled into the driveway and got out of their cars in their various costumes.

Chanel was dressed in an expensive-looking dress, real jewelry and designer shoes, as if she had just stepped off a New York runway. She wore a "Miss Universe" sash and looked like a movie star. Emily hated her even more for it. She wondered if Tom would be more attracted to her or Chanel, then hated herself for even caring.

As Chanel's squad approached in their super-sexy Halloween costumes, Chanel looked at Cindy's costume and spoke loudly to Tyler, "Ugh. Cupcakes has the fashion sense of a clam."

"Hey, take that back!" Chester, dressed as a Viking, glared at her.

"Shut up, Chanel." Cindy, glowered. "It's personality that counts, and yours sucks."

"It's personality that counts!" Chanel held her flat stomach to indicate how hard she was faking a laugh. Her friends laughed with her.

"Don't even bother," Emily murmured to Cindy, taking her friend's arm. "C'mon. Let's just go in."

Chanel turned her attention to Emily. "Do your parents – oops! I mean, does your mother still dress you for Halloween?"

Emily stopped and slowly turned back toward Chanel, chin up, her hands on her hips. Chanel and her friends all waited for her response, their eyebrows raised expectantly.

"You know, Chanel, I've always wanted to ask you – doesn't the fact you have to spend so much money just to look good enough to walk outside each day make you insecure?"

"Is that it?" scoffed Chanel. "That's all you got?" She turned to her friends and laughed.

"Is that what went wrong with Tom?" continued Emily. "Is that why he dumped you? He finally realized that under all those designer clothes, there was nothing worth looking at?"

The other girls exchanged nervous and amused glances. Chanel clenched her jaw, her eyes blazing as Emily turned and opened the front door, her head still held high.

There was a packed crowd of dancing bodies, all waving their hands in the air as they bounced to the rock music that was shaking the walls of the house. Even in the excitement of the party Emily could not seem to calm her fury. Every nasty remark Chanel had ever made raced through her mind. She was buzzing with adrenaline and didn't know what to do with herself.

Bethany arrived, looking amazing in a skimpy little dark angel costume, and Emily felt a surge of insecurity well up. How could she possibly compete with Bethany? She was gorgeous, rich and a total sweetheart. She fought to bury her feelings of jealousy and insecurity.

"Hey, guys."

"Wow, Beth you look hot," Cindy exclaimed with genuine awe.

"You too!"

Emily spotted Tom in the living room. He was talking with some of his hockey buddies. Just seeing him made her feel better, and yet there it was again, a strange twinge of guilt mixed in with the other feelings she was experiencing. He smiled across the room and she waved back. Far away, she spotted Chanel cutting a swathe through the party, followed by her posse. A mid-tempo rock anthem came on.

Everyone cheered and began singing along as they danced. Someone bumped into Emily, their drink sloshing over her hand.

"How's it going?" Tom asked.

"Great. Thanks so much for inviting me."

"Aw, yeah, I'm glad you came. You want to dance?"

Emily's eyes widened and for a moment, she was a little taken aback. "Dance? Uh, yeah, sure."

Tom smiled his easy smile and wrapped his arms around her. As much as she tried to avoid glancing in Chanel's direction, she couldn't help it and found her looking back at them, thunderstruck. In fact, all of her posse was staring. Emily looked up at Tom and a part of her felt a dark thrill of triumph. Tom held her around the waist with his strong hands and her fingers glided over his broad shoulders as he pulled her closer. She practically swooned, then tilted her face up to allow Tom to kiss her.

Emily could feel the eyes of a hundred jealous girls watching them, thought maybe she even heard a few jeers from the guys as well, the sound of trouble approaching.

A surge of excitement and desire burst through her and she felt incredibly alive. The moment was shattered as someone grabbed her by the shoulder and spun her roughly around. An enraged Chanel faced her, seething. Emily was pretty sure Chanel was not the type of girl who would risk getting into an actual physical fight. That would be utterly beneath her. But she was certainly willing to wage war in her own way.

"Do you have some kind of death wish?"

"What?" Emily said. "I didn't know you wrote your name on his forehead in Sharpie."

"Hey, girls, calm down!" Tom stepped between them.

"You calm down!" Chanel shouted, shoving Tom's hands away from her.

A crowd of onlookers was forming in a circle around them.

"Maybe I should leave," Emily said quietly, touching Tom's sleeve.

"Yes, leave," Chanel said.

"What? No. Why? I mean…" Tom stammered, ignoring Chanel.

"What do you mean 'no?'" demanded Chanel. "Of course she should leave!" Chanel crossed her arms and glowered at Emily. "Go. Now."

Tom turned to face Chanel. "Listen," he said, loud enough for the whole room to hear, "Enough! Like I told you; it's over, just move on."

Chanel looked as though she was about to have a stroke. "You seriously mean to say," she whispered, "you're choosing her… over me?"

"Chanel, I broke up with you, it wasn't working out. Why can't you accept that?"

"Fine," she said, holding the palm of her hand up to Tom's face. She turned her attention to Emily as if she'd reached some sort of decision. "That's the way it is. But so you know… your life is over."

"Ooohh, melodramatic," some guy said above the silence and a couple of people laughed. Chanel spun on her heel and strode out of the room.

"Wow, Tom," Emily said. "I'm really sorry…"

"No. That wasn't your fault." He took her hands in his.

"Well, regardless, I'm gonna go find Cindy…"

"You don't have to go, Emily."

"No, I think I do. It's okay." As she walked away, Emily had a strange feeling, thinking about the pleasure she had taken in hurting Chanel. How well do I know myself? she wondered. She had only walked a few feet when Cindy ran up to her, eyes wide with excitement.

"Okay, what just happened?"

Emily sighed. "Tom and I were dancing and…"

"Uh, yeah, I think everyone in the whole party noticed that."

Emily rolled her eyes. "Anyway, Chanel basically threatened to kill me. That was pretty much it."

"You are so my hero!"

Emily laughed. "Why?"

"What do you mean, why?" Cindy shook her head in awe. "Seriously. All the girls in school will be worshipping you."

Something about that statement made Emily uncomfortable. It reminded her of what Mercurios had said about her being able to conquer and enslave the world when she became a powerful wizard. At just that moment, Chanel strode back in, turned off the music and addressed the suddenly silent room.

"Everyone, listen up. I wasn't sure if I was going to hand out these party favors, but our good friend, Emily, has actually informed me that this is the perfect time." She pulled a pile of something out of her shoulder bag. Squinting for a better look, Emily realized they were photos. "Here are some photos a photographer that works for my father's newspaper took. Everyone knows that Emily's father was murdered, but nobody knows why. Well, the reason is because he was a criminal. He was mixed up with the mafia, and I guess he must have ripped the wrong people off, because this is what they did to him."

She began handing out the pictures. Emily's heart stopped for a moment and her stomach churned. Cindy looked at her, confused.

"No. That's not true," Emily said.

Chanel walked up to her and handed her a photo. "Here – just one more dead criminal."

Emily yanked the picture from her hand. It was a reporter's photograph of her father's badly beaten, bloody corpse. Her eyes filled with tears and the photo vibrated in her shaking hands. The sight of the bloody and lifeless body of her father, the man whom she loved so dearly and who had loved her and been so tender and caring with her since she was a child, horrified her. Her eyes stayed glued to the photo. There he was, brutalized and murdered. She felt all the blood drain from her face. Her head spun. She stumbled forward and Tom caught her. She looked at him, not understanding what was going on, unable to grasp how someone could be so cruel, wondering where she was…

"It's okay, I have you." Tom looked over his shoulder. "Hey, Chanel," he said, as Emily's world spun around her. "Get the hell out of my house."

"But why? The fun was just getting started."

"Leave now!" he shouted, struggling to keep control of the rage welling up inside him.

Cindy strode up to Chanel, bristling with fury. "You sick, twisted, evil… You think you're going to get away with this? You're going to pay. You're going to pay for this, Chanel. I'm gonna do something to you that you'll never forget!"

"I have to go home," Emily murmured.

"Do you want me to take you home?" Tom asked.

"No, I just – I just need to go. I need to be alone."

"Listen to me, Emily," Tom was saying, "I want you to know I am never going to let anyone hurt you like this again. I promise."

Emily nodded and walked to the front door, numb from shock, the photo falling from her fingers to the floor.

As she stumbled down the steps, Cindy caught up with her. "Emily, wait, I'll take you home."

"No. Please, I need to be alone right now."

"Are you sure?"

"Really, Cindy, it's okay."

"I'm going to get her for this, I swear."

"Don't. She's a sad case who just needs help."

"No, she's a horrible person who needs her ass kicked."

Emily walked outside in a daze and the door shut behind her, muffling the noise of the party. She was just about to get into her car when she spotted Chanel's new sports car parked under an ancient oak tree. She opened the door of her car, reached into her glove compartment and took out the wand Mercurios had given her. The little imp appeared on her shoulder.

"The Wand of Lightning, Emily, yes, yes indeed!" he whispered excitedly. "She is merely a foolish girl and poses no threat, and there are some dark clouds in the sky, tee-hee. Yes indeed, your first kill will be regarded as an unfortunate accident. You will wait until she comes outside, then blast her into oblivion!" Mercurios clapped his hands with demonic glee. "Hurray!"

"Will you please stop saying that!" yelled Emily then lowered her voice to a whisper. "I'm not going to electrocute anyone!"

The imp went silent, as Emily glanced up and down the street. When she was sure the coast was clear, she raised the wand and pointed it at an enormous branch about twenty feet above Chanel's car.

"Vaza bel thlemin," she commanded.

A great bolt of lightning leaped from the wand and blasted the base of the branch, immediately followed by a second bolt that exploded into a distribution transformer on a lamppost. The huge branch fell with an ear-splitting crack and crushed Chanel's car. Seconds later the power went out along the whole street as the transformer exploded like a firework. The mansion went totally dark and silent for a few seconds before the cheering and laughing replaced the music.

"Uh oh," muttered Emily as the imp cackled with glee.

"Good shot, Emily! But you lost control. Use only one lightning bolt at a time."

Emily jumped in her car and started the engine. As she drove away her heart pounded. "I could have killed someone, that second lightning bolt could have gone in any direction."

She was filled with self-doubt. Who was she to be playing with these powers? She wasn't a wizard or witch or whatever, she was just some nobody high school girl.

"Do not worry, Emily, with practice you will gain complete control over your spells and magic items. Patience and hard work. Everyone knows that's the key to success in anything in life. Magic is no different."

When she got home, Emily told Mercurios she wanted privacy and ran straight to her bedroom, her mind racing. The voices of different people kept spinning around her brain – Chanel's, the detective's, Tom's, Mercurios's, the bizarre encounter with her dead father. But mostly, she kept thinking about Cady Sunner. Seeing those awful photographs had made her even more determined to help the police catch her father's killers. She turned on her computer and checked the recordings coming in from the shotgun mic. She spent several hours going through long periods of nothing, occasionally broken up with phone calls that were about mundane, every day things and the sound of Cady's television. But then she came across a conversation that had just occurred.

"Yeah, what?" She heard Cady's voice. "Oh, it's you." Emily thought she detected a trace of fear in his voice. "Yes, everything is being arranged at the warehouse in two nights… No, I asked him, he hasn't found out anything more about it."

Was this the warehouse that Sammy runs? she wondered. It? Was "it" the desk?

Emily heard Cady get up and his footsteps scuffled as he walked across the kitchen floor. A moment later a door slammed. He must have left his house, she thought.

Her mind was whirling.

"Mercurios," she said and the imp appeared a moment later.

"At your service."

She played him what she had just heard. "My father mentioned Sammy when he was a ghoul and now I hear them mention a warehouse. It must be the warehouse my father's friend Sammy runs."

"Indeed," said Mercurios. "I am certain that you are correct."

"And what did he mean when he said that they hadn't found out anything more? Since he specifically said the word 'more,' that must mean they found out some information… I think I'm going to have to have a talk with Sammy."

Fourteen

Emily awoke the next day with a scream. Her tangled sheets were wet with sweat. Once again she had dreamed of the mysterious boy and then the demon, experiencing exactly the same heady mixture of desire and terror. She wanted to ask Mercurios about him again but she had slept late and had to rush if she was going to make it to school on time. It would have to wait until later. She quickly showered and brushed her teeth. Looking at herself in the mirror, she sighed.

"Well, you're eighteen, Emily, Happy Birthday," she said quietly, then walked into her bedroom and got dressed.

Arriving at school she spotted Tom standing near the doors talking to a couple of his hockey buddies.

"Hey, Tom."

"Oh, hey. Listen, I'm really sorry about Chanel…"

"You don't have to apologize for her. It wasn't your fault."

"Yeah, well, anyway, I'd like to make it up to you."

Emily smiled. "That's not necessary."

They walked into the school together as Tom's friends took the hint and went their separate ways.

"So, are you going to let me take you out on a date?"

"Sure." Emily grinned.

During the day various friends wished her happy birthday. Cindy and Chester gave her a couple gift certificates to some of her favorite stores. Everyone was talking about how the tree outside Tom's house got struck by lightning, crushing Chanel's car, and about what they were going to do for Halloween. The day seemed to last forever. Emily's mind swirled with thoughts of Tom, her father, the mysterious boy in her dreams, the Sanctuary, and what she was going to find there.

After school, Emily and Cindy stopped at the salon to get their hair done together. When they were leaving Cindy nudged her friend.

"You know, Em, after you left Tom's party Bethany kinda moved in on him."

"What?" Emily frowned, not liking the feeling of jealousy she could feel surging within her. "What happened?"

"Well, nothing major, but she was being super flirty and Tom spent most of the rest of the night talking to her, that's all."

"Well, I can't control who he talks to," she snapped.

"Okay, chill, just thought I should let you know."

After the hair salon Cindy's cousin, a film makeup artist, came over with her makeup bag. She made Emily look like a real vampire, complete with very pale skin, blue veins along her neck and hairline and blood-red lips. Emily pulled on the blue ball gown. With her hair pinned up and falling in ringlets over the side of her face, lace gloves and faux pearl necklace she peered at herself in the mirror and wished that every day could be Halloween.

The night air was crisp and clear and the autumn leaves glowed in the twilight. The sunset painted the scattered clouds on the western horizon in lurid colors, as the full moon rose, yellow in the east. The dry leaves crunched under their feet and all around them fairies, goblins, ghosts, ghouls, werewolves, princesses, aliens, superheroes and super-villains raced with bags of candy from house to house while jack-o'-lanterns glowed and grinned from every window and porch.

The Sanctuary was already packed when they arrived. The atmosphere was electric. The venue was much larger than she had imagined. There looked to be about four hundred people there and whoever had put the club together had done an incredible job. It had a great sound and light set-up.

"I will definitely be coming back here," Emily said, her eyes wide in excitement.

Everyone was in full costume. The whole tea party from Alice in Wonderland were there; Alice, the Mad Hatter, the White Rabbit, and the Dormouse. There was also Tweety Bird, Cinderella and the Tin Man. Every type of costume imaginable was on display. A thick, eerie, dry ice mist covered the dance floor while strobes and beams of blue and red lit the witch trees and tombstones and other Halloween decorations scattered about the club. The music was primal rock; hard, driving, relentless beats pounding deep inside her, filling her with excitement. The dance floor was rocking.

She felt as if the beat possessed her, as though it were one with her heart, pumping hot blood through her veins. The bass, drums and guitars drove their steady pulses into her, while the singer alternated between deep, melodic crooning and snarling intensity. The lyrics were dark and passionate, rising at points to an unearthly howl.

Emily scanned the crowd for Cady Sunner and the pale-faced man but saw them nowhere. She and Cindy ordered a couple of sodas, found a table near the dance floor and sat down. Emily was never much of a dancer, but Cindy could never resist the lure of the beat. She bounced in her seat, unable to resist the rhythm any longer and Emily watched her friend join the mass of gyrating bodies on the misty shrouded floor, happy just to watch the party unfold. She felt as if she were on another planet, a club at the far edge of the universe where alien beings congregated to party.

Her heart gave a sudden jolt as she spotted the pale-faced man from Sunner's house. Everything about him unnerved her. Now that she could see him clearly, if intermittently, in the flashing lights, she noticed he was actually handsome, but his features were marred by the condescending sneer on his lips and the deadly coldness in his eyes, as though everything he saw around him filled him with contempt.

The three young men behind him all looked to be in their early twenties. They too were good-looking but had the same pallor to their faces. Two were tall and narrowly built and the third was short and noticeably muscular with shiny black hair that fell over his face in sharp spikes. He was also immaculately groomed, wearing a tailored suit, dressed as a gangster. Emily kept her face toward the dance floor, following them with her peripheral vision as they pushed through the crowd and took over a table in the back corner, the muscular man shooing other people away to make room.

After a few moments, once they had settled, she got up and casually walked over to the other side of the dance floor, leaning against a wall near to their table. In such a big crowd she was pretty sure she wasn't being too conspicuous as she eavesdropped on their conversation. The man who had terrified Cady Sunner was doing all the talking, the others leaning in to listen with rapt attention, but the music was too loud for Emily to properly make out what he was saying. She wondered if she should get Mercurios to go invisible and sit by them and listen.

∗

Mitchell had taken a night flight on his private jet to get to America and when he stepped off the plane his eyes were sparkling with exhilaration. Over the previous months he had fully returned to the world and was now ready to play a part in the story of a new age. He checked into the Royal Suite of the best hotel in Portland and slept through the day. At sunset he rose and went out into the back streets, scouring the thoughts of all the seedy nighttime characters skulking around in the bars and alleys until he found a young man sitting with a drink, thinking about a robbery he had just committed, where he had left the victim bleeding to death from a savage beating. He showed no remorse for what he had done, so Mitchell engaged him in conversation, suggesting that he might have a job for him.

As they talked he read the young man's thoughts and knew that he was planning to beat him and rob him as soon as there was an opportunity. When Mitchell suggested they should go somewhere quieter to talk the young man saw his opportunity and readily agreed. Amongst the trashcans behind the bar Mitchell drained him of every last drop of his blood. Once he had fed he hailed a cab and gave the driver the address he had found for The Sanctuary.

As he walked through the front doors his senses were bombarded by the thundering rock music he had grown to love in London. He smiled to himself. It was as though the raw, vibrant energy of the music, the lights and the gyrating bodies of the young dancers filled him with a sense of belonging. He chose an inconspicuous spot along one of the walls to stand and survey his surroundings.

He scanned the room again and froze as his eyes fell on Mephris, with three younger vampires sitting at a table on the other side of the dance floor. Mitchell tried to read the minds of the younger, weaker vampires before making a move. With some intense concentration he was able to isolate their thoughts from the other three hundred clubbers and follow their conversation.

"Well, you're going to get a chance to prove yourselves very soon," Mephris was saying. "Tomorrow night the transaction will take place at the warehouse. We can eliminate a large portion of their gang. Then we will be able to take total control of the ports."

*

Emily was walking toward the doors of the club, looking for a spot where she would be able to speak privately with Mercurios, when Cindy came shimmying over. She grabbed Emily's hand, dragging her onto the dance floor.

"Come on!"

"Uh, Cindy, I don't really want to."

Cindy ignored her, dragging her through the crowd, dancing as she went. Emily broke away from her friend, laughing. "Listen, I'm going to grab a soda – you want one?"

"No. Make sure you come back though."

Emily headed back toward the exit. As she walked she turned her head to her right and it was as though the whole world went into slow motion. That was when she saw him…

Emily staggered, as if struck by a bolt of lightning. Steadying herself, she looked again and saw the boy from her dreams standing on the opposite side of the club. He was leaning casually against a wall, scanning the scene just as she had been doing. For a moment time and reality seemed suspended. It felt as though her heart had stopped beating, everything had frozen and the wall between dreams and reality had collapsed. She sucked in a deep breath and felt her heart begin to pound in her chest once more, hot blood pumping through her veins, bringing a flush to her cheeks, hidden beneath her makeup.

She knew without a doubt that this was not a dream and that it was the most monumental moment of her life. She was frozen to the spot, her eyes locked on him, her feet rooted to the floor. He had the same commanding presence as the man who'd been intimidating Cady Sunner, but he was far more powerful and attractive. There was an otherworldly quality about him. He seemed so magnetic, even just standing there doing nothing. Emily was absolutely dazzled. She felt that he was even more gorgeous in real life than in her dream, if that was possible. She couldn't have torn her eyes away even if she had wanted to. To see the mysterious young man of her dreams, who had been haunting her thoughts, and had filled her with such a powerful longing and desire, standing across the room in the flesh, was overwhelming. A force more powerful than any she had experienced before drew Emily to him. She was certain to the core of her soul that this was destiny.

She noticed he was alone, but he didn't look self-conscious about it. For some reason she couldn't decipher, he seemed out of place.

Then she realized he wasn't wearing a costume. He was stylishly dressed and it all fitted him perfectly, even though it seemed he had thrown it together without any effort. She wondered how he had managed to get into the club without a costume.

He looked to be about a year older than her, but he definitely seemed mature far beyond his years. His skin was pale like the others, and there were shadows of darkness under his eyes. Then there were those sparkling emerald eyes that had transfixed her so often in her dreams. She could see them glittering even from across the room. When he made even the smallest of movements he had a lithe, animal grace, effortless and powerful. Emily found it indescribably attractive. There was something else about him, about the way he carried himself, about his presence even as he just leaned against the wall… She couldn't quite put her finger on it. Then she had it. Never had she seen a person in possession of such total self-confidence.

She had seen confident men and reckless men and arrogant men, but this was something else. He had a sense of self that needed no explanation, made no excuses, and didn't try to impress. His confidence was so strong it created an aura around him. It was silent, total and unshakable. He seemed a wolf among sheep. Emily was so mesmerized by him that she completely forgot why she had come to the club in the first place.

As she stood staring at him, a shiver cascaded down her spine. The magnetic force that was drawing her to him was overpowering. She had an irresistible urge to speak to him, to stand face-to-face with him, to touch him. What could this possibly mean? she wondered. The stranger from her dreams was actually real! Had she tapped into some sort of psychic powers through her dreams? And if so what did it mean? She couldn't just walk up and tell him she had been having dreams about him. He'd think she was a psycho. Then again, who knows, maybe he'd had the same dream. She told herself that none of that mattered. This was destiny and it would not be denied.

As she watched, unable to move, a beautiful brunette wearing a skimpy, sexy cat costume sidled up to him. Emily's heart sank. The girl had a perfect body and knew exactly how to show it off.

I could never compete with that, she thought, feeling a wave of intense jealousy wash over her. The scar on Emily's palm burned and itched and she rubbed it with her thumb. The girl was obviously interested in him. She smiled and batted her eyelashes as she talked, trying to get him to crack a smile. He must have said something funny, because she laughed and casually put her hand on his chest, letting her fingers glide suggestively down over his stomach. Emily was impressed by the girl's nerve and, at the same time, envious.

She remembered what he looked like with his shirt off and thought of her fingers gliding over his perfect abs and her heart pounded even faster and her flesh become hot. She couldn't hear what the girl was saying, but the boy smiled and laughed a little, flashing perfect white teeth and… fangs.

Ah, so that's it, thought Emily. He's dressed as a modern-day vampire! That would go with the long black coat he was wearing. His makeup and teeth looked professionally done. They were even better than hers, subtle but extremely convincing.

Throughout his conversation with the girl, the young man remained leaning away from her, casually against the wall. Sometimes he looked at the girl but more often he let his eyes drift around the room. If Emily wasn't crazy, he almost seemed bored with the girl and her flirtations. During the few minutes she spoke with him he seemed to remain friendly but detached.

Well, Emily thought, if he's not interested in her, then he must have some even more perfect girlfriend somewhere. She felt another surge of jealousy and wanted him more than anything in the world. She shook her head, half in a daze, amazed at the power of the emotions he always awakened in her. She felt incredibly nervous about approaching him and desperately tried to regain her composure.

Please don't look at me, she thought, please don't look at me… then a moment later… please look at me!

Just then the boy's eyes slowly turned and looked directly into hers. As he calmly held her gaze, Emily could feel her heart beating so fast she was afraid she wouldn't be able to breathe. She felt dazed. Seeing his face and looking into the eyes that had so hypnotized her, possessed her, haunted her, this moment in her life hit her so hard, so profoundly, Emily knew that it would be etched in her soul for all eternity.

Overwhelmed, Emily looked away, gasping for air. A second later she looked back as though the gravitational pull of his being was unstoppable. He was still calmly staring at her. Realizing she was being ignored, the other girl shrugged and walked away. He didn't give her a second glance. Even though her heart was pounding and her mouth was dry, Emily found herself walking toward him, drawn to him by something that she could not resist. The image of Tom flashed through her mind and she felt a twinge of guilt. She bumped into a table, spilling a girl's drink all over her. The girl let out a cry.

"Hey, watch where you're going!"

"I am so sorry."

Emily continued toward him, but didn't dare look back into his eyes. She did not want to fall over another table like a complete idiot. When she reached him, she leaned against the wall, breathing in the deliciously subtle scent of his cologne and trying to look as casual as him. She felt him lean away from her almost imperceptibly.

Emily's eyes paused on his designer black leather boots, then on the thick gold, diamond-encrusted watch on his wrist and the big gold ring on his right hand with a massive, glittering emerald in it that matched his eyes.

Well, whoever he is, she thought, this guy is seriously rich. That watch is probably worth more than my mom's car. She had a feeling like the time when she'd gone cliff-diving into a lake as a child, when, after working up the courage to jump, she'd stepped forward to leap. As soon as his emerald eyes came to rest on her, she knew there was no turning back because she was already halfway down the cliff and still falling.

Fifteen

"So," Emily said when she felt able to talk, "which one will we have for dinner?"

Mitchell looked puzzled and she smiled, giving him a glimpse of her fangs, so he would get her joke. He returned her smile but remained aloof, going back to scanning the club, taking in the table of four men. He looked liked some kind of fierce angel. She found his confidence, charisma and raw masculinity intoxicating. Her body was tingling all over. Emily could imagine armies blindly following a man like this into war, willing to face certain death for him. She felt a fool for even thinking such a man might be interested in talking to her.

Why would he ever want me? she thought. He's obviously totally superior to me in every way. You are way out of your league, Emily.

"Hmm," he said eventually. "That will require a great deal of thought." His voice was low, sexy and hypnotic and sent a shiver down her spine. He spoke with an English accent, frowning and pretending to contemplate the question seriously. Then he pointed at the kid in the Tweety costume. "How about that one?"

Emily giggled. "I was thinking the whole Mad Hatter's tea party. Or is that too greedy?"

He looked at her again and unleashed the full magnetic force of his smile. His green eyes glinted and Emily's confidence skyrocketed.

"Hmm... I would avoid the Hatter," he said. "I think there is something seriously wrong with that bloke."

Emily pretended to weigh his words with deep concern. "Yeah, you may have a point there. Well, how about just Alice?"

He glanced at her with mock disapproval. "Alice? You would kill Alice? After everything she's been through?"

"I guess I'm just a very bad person." Emily winked at him. She couldn't believe she did that! She felt the rush of adrenaline course through her. She was flirting with him and he wasn't turning her away as he'd done with the brunette.

"How about the hippie?" he suggested, pointing at a kid approaching the dance floor.

"Definitely!"

"Or the giant bagel with cream cheese?" He gestured toward a girl struggling to dance in her absurd costume.

Emily pointed at a Grim Reaper leaning against a wall. "How about Death?"

"Killing Death... now that would be interesting."

His eyes glowed with an inner light that made her gasp. It was as though he was trying to look deep inside her and Emily could feel herself going into the same hypnotic trance she had experienced so many times looking into his eyes in her dreams. She opened her mind and heart to him, wanting his gaze to come all the way inside her and fill her with his enormous presence. She began to salivate. She licked her lips and swallowed. Someone walked up to them wearing a Crimson Ghost costume. Emily snapped out of her trance. It took her a moment to realize who it was.

"Tom? Is that you?"

"Hey, what's up, Emily?" he spoke casually, but stared at her long and hard.

"Cool costume," she said, feeling kind of awkward.

"Thanks, and you look amazing. You wear that look well."

"Oh, thanks." Emily felt herself blushing a little.

"Who's your friend?" Tom asked, nodding in the direction of

Mitchell. Though he seemed relaxed, Emily sensed tension in his voice. Her heart hurt. It struck her at that moment how much she cared for Tom. Images of their shared moments flashed through her mind and she felt as if two powerful internal forces were pulling her in different directions.

"Just a random partygoer," Mitchell said, moving to leave. "If you'll excuse me…"

"No wait…" Emily held up a hand, then glanced at Tom as if to tell him she was busy before he came to say hello. She turned to the boy she'd just met. "I mean, there's something I wanted to ask you."

"Hey." Tom touched Emily's elbow gently. "Just come find me when you two are done talking."

He walked off through the writhing, costumed crowd. Emily stared after him for a moment, impressed. That was pretty mature of him. She then turned back to the boy from her dreams and noticed he was wearing a gold pendant in the shape of a large teardrop, engraved with what looked like runes. It hung from a thick gold chain around his neck.

"That's a really cool pendant."

"Thanks," he said distantly, still surveying the club.

"Was that a gift from your girlfriend?"

He paused to look at her, raising an eyebrow, and then returned to watching the table of pale men. He seemed vaguely amused.

"You're not very good at that, are you?"

"At what?" she asked, the self-conscious Emily creeping back in.

"Fishing for information. You're not very subtle." He glanced at her sideways and gave her a cocky, sexy smirk.

She laughed awkwardly, feeling like she had just fallen off the cloud she'd been floating on. "Oh… uh, yeah, I guess I'm not."

He laughed gently at her social ineptitude and she was absurdly happy that she was amusing him. Suddenly, he tensed, and his expression grew stern. She followed his gaze toward the four men who had stood up from their table and were heading for the exit. She wondered now if he was somehow connected with them. He gave her a cold, hard look.

"I have to leave. Don't follow me."

In shock she watched him turn and glide off through the crowd after the four men.

Oh my god, this is so humiliating, she thought, I totally blew it. And, to think that I believed he might be interested in me. Why did I have to say that and sound like such a fool? He obviously thinks I'm a total loser.

She stared after him, stunned, confused, and deeply disappointed. She could feel her skin growing hot and prickly with humiliation. Or was it exhilaration? Either way, she was filled with curiosity as to what his connection with those men was. Did he know they were dangerous? Maybe that's why he left so abruptly. Maybe he was trying to protect her. Part of her was severely disappointed that he might be associated with such lowlifes, but part of her wanted to go after him.

*

Outside the club, Mitchell followed the four vampires behind the building into a parking lot and through an empty construction site. No one else was around.

Mitchell threw back his coat and unsheathed the sword that it had been covering. The cold, cruel blade glinted then burst into flame as he leaped thirty feet through the air and landed directly in front of the startled vampires.

"You!" Mephris whispered in horror.

"I've been looking forward to catching up with you for a long, long time, Mephris."

Mephris nodded to his companions. "Time to prove yourselves," he snapped, then turned and ran into the night. The three young vampires watched as he disappeared into the darkness, then turned to face Mitchell and sprang into action. The two tall ones drew their swords, which shone the cold, pale, bluish-white of frost. The third tore a metal bar from a nearby fire escape. All three came at him at once.

He stepped smoothly aside as the first lunged forward, thrusting his sword at Mitchell's throat. With a quick slash of his Draaken, his assailant's arm was severed, and the vampire fell to the ground with a shriek. A moment later the second one's head lay beside the first one's arm. With one final swipe to the throat, Mitchell dispatched the third vampire.

As the three bodies turned to dust, Mitchell sheathed his sword and stared in the direction that Mephris had disappeared.

"Ashes to ashes, dust to dust," he muttered. He started after him with the speed of a racehorse then stopped. Something was approaching on the street. He turned to see a truck hauling a large trailer, the type used to transport animals. He stepped into the road in front of it and held up his hands. The truck slowed to a stop.

✱

Emily was just about to follow the young man out of the club when Mercurios appeared on her shoulder. "No, Emily, not yet," he whispered in her ear. "It's too dangerous! You're not powerful enough yet."

"Well then, you'd better figure out a way to help because I'm going," she replied, heading for the door.

Outside she scanned the area, the parking lot, the nearby buildings, but the boy and the four men were nowhere to be seen.

"Where did they go, Mercurios?"

"I do not know."

"And you wouldn't tell me even if you did."

"I must protect you, Emily. That is my command."

"Mercurios, that was the boy I've been telling you about, the one from my dreams."

"Very curious indeed."

Emily's heart sank as she walked across the parking lot and

climbed into her car. She wondered how everything could have been so exciting and magical one moment and so depressing the next. She checked the time and realized that she had to get home soon or her mother would start to worry. She found it incredibly frustrating that she had been unable to gather any more useful information from the sinister-looking men and even more frustrating that she had no idea how to find the boy again.

She had been driving for a while when her car died on a side street right by Baxter Woods.

"Ugh! I forgot to put gas in it!" she said, tapping the fuel dial.

She switched on her hazard lights and pulled out her cell phone but the battery was completely dead.

"Perfect," she muttered. "I don't suppose you're carrying a can of gas?" she asked the imp.

"No, Emily." He sounded as though he was sulking at her disobedience but she ignored him.

"Okay, well if you can't help, then could you give me some time alone? Please don't pop up out of nowhere until I call you. Or summon you, or whatever."

"As you wish." The imp disappeared.

Emily remembered there was a gas station not far away if she cut through the woods so she took her wand and got out. She went to lock the car door, but then didn't bother. "No one in their right mind would want to steal this piece of crap, and it's out of gas anyways," she thought as she walked down the side of the road.

It was a beautiful night, lit silver by the full moon and stars above. With a night like this it was impossible to be angry for long. Normally she would not have been foolish enough to go wandering through a patch of forest at night where potential lunatics could be lurking, but she had her wand and knew that Mercurios was somewhere close by. It wasn't like she was out in the wilderness. The gas station was probably only a ten-minute walk away.

She stepped off the road and onto the damp, soft ground. There was a wide path blanketed in newly fallen leaves and she was grateful that her heels weren't too high.

The crunching of leaves and twigs beneath her shoes echoed through the trees, a lonely sound that sent a chill down her arms. Every few steps she would slip, snagging her foot on a root or a fallen branch. What a strange sight she must be, she thought, stumbling about in the woods in her ball gown and vampire makeup.

After a few minutes she could no longer see the road behind her. In fact, there was no sign of civilization at all. She could imagine that she could've been hundreds of miles from the modern world, and it would've looked the same. The center of town seemed to have ceased to exist. A slight breeze blew and the nearly naked branches of the trees creaked overhead, their silhouettes dark against the stars and moon, their branches like the arms and hands of skeletons reaching out across the sky. She paused for a moment to try and get her bearings as a few leaves fluttered down from above. It was so beautiful and peaceful, yet spooky at the same time. Even here, in this little clump of trees between the city and suburbia, she felt the beauty, magic and mystery of a forest at night. A long, haunting howl sounded in the night air. She froze, spellbound by the lonely, soulful beauty of it. She shivered. That was no dog. A howl so deep, so wild could only be… a wolf.

*

Mitchell read the truck driver's mind and saw that he was making a delivery for York's Wild Kingdom Zoo. Having used his hypnotic powers to force the driver to stop, he sent him into a deep sleep. Walking around to the back of the trailer he opened it up. Inside were five fully-grown white Arctic wolves. Upon seeing Mitchell, and understanding his silent, psychic command, they leaped out of the back of the trailer and crowded around him like excited puppies welcoming home their beloved master.

*

Wait a minute, Emily thought. There aren't any wolves around here... are there? To hear that sound at night, in the forest, under the full moon on Halloween was strangely thrilling, as though she was on some secret adventure deep in the wilderness. At the same time, it was unnerving. She stood still, holding her breath and listening for a few minutes before continuing.

She emerged into a small clearing. The trees cast long shadows across it in the silvery-blue light. She spent a moment or two listening intently for any other sounds nearby. She was wearing her Ring of Teleportation in case of an emergency, but was afraid to use it for the first time in case she messed up and ended up disintegrating. Although, she guessed that would be better than being eaten by wolves. Or would it?

"Mercurios," she whispered fiercely. "Was that an actual wolf?"

"I don't know," she heard his familiar, insidious little whisper. "I think you should run, Emily. Prepare your wand and run back! Lock yourself in the car!"

"Yeah," she said as another howl rose up, louder and closer. "I think you're right."

She drew her wand and was about to start back toward the car, when she heard a rustling nearby. It sounded as though a light breeze had sprung up, but she couldn't feel any wind. She sucked in a breath as five huge white wolves loped into the clearing like ghosts.

Sixteen

For a moment, Emily couldn't tell if what she was seeing was real. Her eyes and ears delivered the message to her mind, but her mind refused to accept the package. The wolves drifted into the clearing, their eyes like shining amber, their tongues lolling out across their fearsome teeth. The leader of the pack saw Emily and came toward her, sniffing the air. She readied her wand as he emitted a low growl and crouched back on his haunches, preparing to jump.

Halfway across the clearing a dark shadow materialized in front of her out of the night air, just as the wolf launched itself at her with a blood-curdling snarl. The animal crashed into the shadow and was thrown backward as though it had hit a wall. She could see now that the dark shape between them looked human. A commanding voice said what sounded like "Stregoya!" and the shocked wolf immediately lay down, submitting to the authority of the dark shape standing above it. The figure knelt down beside the wolf, petting it and whispering in its ear. The wolf licked at his hands and face, whimpering happily.

As his face turned toward the moonlight, Emily gasped. The dark figure was the boy from the club. Her mind reeled, trying to absorb what had just happened while she watched in wonder as the wolf, which had looked so ferocious a few moments before, rolled onto its back to be petted.

He stood up. "What are you doing out here?" he demanded, glaring at her.

Emily shrank back. She observed that when angered he was fearsome and ferocious like a wild beast. The wolf slunk back to join the others as they formed a circle around her and the young man. She stood there, mute, returning his glare with wide eyes feeling totally intimidated by him.

"I told you not to follow me."

"I-I…" Emily's mouth hung open.

"You are a very unusual girl." His tone had softened slightly as he gazed intently into her eyes. "Is this normal for you? Are your parents aware of your… habits?"

"M-my what?"

"Well, most girls your age, or any age for that matter, don't dress up as vampires and go wandering around the forest alone in the middle of the night for entertainment."

"The wolves…" she stammered, recovering a little of her composure. "Did you…"

He looked at them as if he had forgotten they were there. "I helped them reclaim their freedom."

Emily tried to look at anything but his eyes. They were just as powerful as in her dreams and the memory made her feel hot all over, filling her with fear and desire. She couldn't think straight when she looked into them. They hypnotized her. She felt that after a few moments of gazing into them, he could have complete power over her, which was a thought that scared and at the same time excited her.

She cleared her throat, staring at the ground. "Assuming you aren't some kind of disgruntled zookeeper…" His chuckle made her glance up and she was lost again in his gaze, like she was floating toward him. With enormous effort, she lowered her eyes again and continued, "Then why did you…"

"I don't believe that wild things should be caged."

"Oh."

"Especially when they are my brothers and sisters."

"Excuse me?"

"In a spiritual sense." He smirked.

Okay, she thought. Is he kidding or is he a nutcase?

"This poses an interesting problem," he went on, thoughtfully.

"What's that?"

"What to do with you."

Emily realized that she had no idea who this guy really was. She didn't know anything about him, only that she dreamed about him, and that he was somehow associated with some very dangerous people. Now, here she was, alone with him in the middle of the night with a pack of wolves he seemed to somehow have control over. He obviously had superhuman powers. Could he also be from Magella? Was he an actual real-life vampire? Is that why his eyes hypnotize me? she thought, and then felt foolish. She wondered if her wand would even work on him if he turned out to be from Magella. She tried to think of how to escape if he survived one of her lightning bolts.

Her car was only a few hundred yards away, yet it was as if she had stepped out of it and into another world. It might as well have been a million light years away.

Whether or not he was a vampire, the young man was obviously much faster and stronger than she was, so running away was out of the question. If she started screaming he might just kill her immediately. The only chance she had was to try and befriend him. If he thought she was on his side, maybe he'd let her go…

She thought of the ring again. Maybe it was her only hope. She desperately tried to remember the command words to activate it, but her mind was blank. If she were going to use magic it would have to be her wand. Most disconcerting of all, however, was the way he kept staring at her.

"Do you always do that?"

"What?" he asked.

"Stare right through people. It's almost as if you can see through my dress," she said.

He said nothing. Her heart pounded and it took all her willpower not to run away.

He gently reached out and took her by the chin, lifting her face to stare into her eyes. "Your eyes, they're…" he said.

For a moment Emily stared back into his eyes. She inhaled softly as the hypnotic power of his eyes engulfed her. It was intoxicating. She wanted to give in to it, open herself and give herself to him completely. But then, after a moment of bliss, her instinct for survival shot adrenaline through her veins and she broke his gaze.

She cleared her throat and tried to speak evenly, but her words tumbled out in a confused rush as she slowly backed away from him, looking up at the full moon.

"Um, well, yeah, I agree, yes," she gasped, "all wild animals should be free. And wolves are really important to the health of the herd and the whole ecosystem and all that stuff. They keep the populations balanced and healthy. Did you know they even change the landscape they live in through affecting the course of rivers? I saw this awesome five-minute clip on YouTube the other day called, 'How Wolves Change Rivers.' It was one of the most interesting things I've ever seen."

Oh my god, she thought, what am I talking about? Please someone stop me! She abruptly stopped her babbling and bit her fingernails.

"Don't bite your fingernails," he ordered.

Emily dropped her hand to her side. "Sorry."

They stared at each other in silence. His presence was as intimidating as it was exciting and Emily could feel her heart pounding in her ears. The first wolf broke the silence with a howl, prowling back and forth impatiently. Then they all followed suit.

"You're quite right," he said eventually. "Are you a biology student?"

"Um, no, I mean yes. Also, I watch a lot of nature programs in bed, like National Geographic and Planet Earth… but yeah,

I'll definitely probably be pursuing biology in college…" She was babbling again and felt like a complete fool.

Mitchell continued to watch her, his head cocked to the side. "Everything you said is true. But wolves are much more than that. Many cultures believe they are a link to the spirit world."

"Oh? I didn't know that. They don't teach stuff like that in biology."

"I can assure you… they are."

She looked up into his eyes and he gave her a penetrating look. Another shiver ran down her spine. Again she felt as though he had opened her up and was looking into her mind and heart, entering her through her eyes and coming deep inside her. She glanced at the circle of wolves and wondered if she should tell him about her dreams. She decided against it. The memory of his eyes turning crimson and then the sickening feeling of plunging to her death and encountering that terrifying demon shot through her mind. Her throat was tight as she tried to swallow. The wolves paced about, restless, their eyes never leaving the two of them.

"So, what are you doing out here?"

"I ran out of gas and my cell is dead and I have to call my mom."

Mitchell tried to read her mind. A dazed expression came over her face. She squinted her eyes and clutched her head. Her mind had automatically erected a defensive wall, and after learning that her name was Emily he stopped.

"What are you doing to me?" she moaned, but her words weren't really meant for him.

"Emily, I…"

"How did you know my name?" She pulled away from him.

He drew closer. "Shh. Don't be afraid," he whispered as he took her hand. He felt her palm warm against his. "I hear your heart pounding. You're frightened, but we won't harm you. You'll have to excuse them." He nodded toward the wolves. "They've never been on a real hunt and they are very, very eager. We have a long way to go tonight."

Emily was close to hyperventilating now, but only partially out of fear. His proximity and the feeling of his hand in hers were overwhelming sensations. Her brain was on overload. Even though his flesh was cool the place where he had touched her felt like it was on fire. She didn't know why but it seemed as though his touch spoke to her, it told her "I want to protect you and take care of you. You are the most precious thing in the world." How had he known her name? She was almost sure she had never mentioned it at the club.

"Look into my eyes," he coaxed her in the same low, velvet voice. "Don't be afraid."

"Who are you?" Emily parted her lips and drew a deep breath into her lungs, looking directly into his eyes. He gazed back at her, and once more she was transported into that beautiful, emerald world, as the full moon soared high above, like a great, silver peach, pouring its pale nectar down upon them.

"I won't harm you," he said softly.

"Okay," she murmured, in a trance, feeling calm and tranquil. When she was fifteen she had badly broken her ankle playing soccer. The doctor had injected her with a painkiller and it had felt kind of like this. Her breathing slowed as her heart rate returned to normal.

"That's better." He peered at her. "There's something about you, I can't quite…"

His voice trailed off.

Emily emerged from her trance and returned to her normal state. "What?"

"Never mind."

"You think you recognize me from somewhere? Like a dream?"

"I don't think so… but… possibly. Why?"

She wanted to tell him everything but the intensity of her desire for him in her dreams made her blush and she felt too embarrassed to talk about it. She was mesmerized and dazzled by him. Biting her lower lip and brushing her hair back over her shoulder, she revealed her neck…

Mitchell gasped involuntarily at the beauty of her throat. Primal desire and hunger flashed in his eyes. He inhaled deeply, savoring the scent of her hair and skin. He bared his teeth and bent closer to the soft flesh. But then, with a supreme effort of will, he looked away.

"There's a dangerous man on the loose in this area. It's time for you to go home. It's incredibly foolish for you to be walking around in the middle of the night out here alone. You should have locked yourself in your car. Didn't your parents teach you anything?" he scolded, looming over her, big and intimidating. The severity of his tone and the displeasure in his eyes surprised her, making her want to win back his approval.

"Yeah, um," she stammered.

"Next time try not to be so foolish," he snapped, like a father scolding his teenage daughter. "Try thinking before you act."

"Okay, sorry."

"Which way would you be going?" His tone was kinder. "We will escort you."

Emily spotted Mercurios above them on a branch, frantically motioning to her, dancing about, and waving his hands in the air. She ignored the imp and lowered her wand. He noticed it for the first time.

"What is that? Part of your costume? What are you? A vampire wizard?" he chuckled. "Just being a vampire wasn't good enough?"

"Uh, yeah, kind of." Emily blushed and laughed and felt like a goof. Then she cleared her throat and stepped up to Mitchell. "Why were you so rude to me earlier in the club? And how do you know those four men? What happened when you left? Are you following them?"

"I apologize if I appeared rude – it was nothing personal. Unfortunately, I don't have time to explain everything now, so if you don't mind…"

"I was trying to find the gas station over there." She pointed vaguely off in another direction. He held out his arm to her and she took it, walking through the trees as if on air.

As they walked Emily felt totally safe and protected with him. Her mind swirled with a thousand questions and her heart was brimming with emotion, but she remained silent, too intimidated and filled with wonder and confusion to even speak. When they reached the gas station she turned and looked at him. Her hair had fallen over her face. He reached out and tucked it gently behind her ear.

"Let's keep this between us," he said, winking at her.

She nodded. "But who are you? What's your name? Why do the wolves listen to you?"

"Come." He gestured to one of the wolves and it ran over to them. "Don't be afraid, it won't harm you." The wolf stood before them with its tongue lolling out. "Here." Mitchell took her hand and placed it on the animal's head. "Sweet dreams, Emily," he said, releasing her hand and giving a gallant bow, never taking his eyes off hers.

He and the wolves moved so swiftly, they seemed to dissolve into the shadows of the forest. For a moment, Emily stood rooted to the spot, staring into the trees, her eyes wide with wonder and her mouth hanging open. Finally, she returned to reality and wandered in a daze over to the gas station, where she called her mother on the pay phone.

"Mom, I..." Where could she even begin? How could she describe what had just happened without sounding like she'd lost her mind? "I ran out of gas and I don't have any money. Could you come meet me?"

What had he meant by "sweet dreams?" She wondered. Did he know about her dreams? When she got home she pestered Mercurios to tell her more about the boy.

"I am telling you I don't know who he is," he insisted. "It is very strange that you have been having dreams about him."

"The way he controlled those wolves, do you think he could be from Magella too?"

The imp stared at her for several moments before nodding. "That's what I was thinking. He seems to possess supernatural powers."

"Are there vampires in Magella? I thought it was a costume, but the way he controlled those wolves… Do you think that's why the word 'demons' was carved under 'Vadas Asger'? Did vampires come over and they thought they were demons?"

"Vampires are very rare in Magella, the Paladin, Rangers and Wizards Guild have destroyed most of them. But it is possible. He is more likely a wizard or necromancer."

"What about the other part of the dream that I've been having? That… That demon? And what did you mean by this recurring dream being my power awakening inside me or whatever?"

"It's your great destiny, Emily." Mercurios's eyes flashed with mischievous excitement.

"Why do you keep saying that? What do you mean by my 'great destiny?' You just mean you think I can become a powerful wizard and reclaim the throne in my parents kingdom, right?"

"You know it's much more than that! The demon is awakening inside you Emily, tee-hee-hee. Do not fight it."

"What… demon?"

"It is your great destiny, or at least it was meant to be. When you were conceived, the Lich King of Darguul forced your parents to summon a demon into you. Once you were born you were to be sent to Darguul to be trained by the Necromancers Guild until you became an adult and a powerful necromancer, and then the demon inside you would awaken and possess you and through you it would rule your parents' kingdom and turn all the people into slaves and worshippers of the demon lord, Orcus, and then conquer all of Magella. But something unexpected happened. The Well of Many Worlds had been lost for nearly a thousand years, and then it inexplicably appeared in your parents' castle one day. The Lich King realized that a demon would be able to use the Well to tear a permanent rift, to open a permanent gate between the Abyss, the realm of the demon lords, and the worlds of the living. He decided that that would be your great destiny. But your parents were having none of that. They decided to flee the Lich King and conduct an exorcism ceremony on you and banish the demon inside you back to the Abyss and save the worlds of the living. They wanted to escape, but the Lich King found out and sent a group of necromancers to kill your parents and if possible bring you and the Well of Many Worlds back to Darguul. That is when your parents sent you and your brother and sister into the Well with instructions that the familiars let you all assimilate, then bring you back to Magella when you were adults to get you an exorcism before the demon fully awakens, and be trained at the Fengusberry Academy so you could reclaim the throne."

The imp stopped talking to allow time for this lengthy explanation to sink in. Emily thought about all the times she had had her dream and battled the demon.

"You're telling me that that demon I've been dreaming about is not only real... but it's inside me?"

"Yes."

"INSIDE ME?" Her voice was rising toward hysteria.

"Yes. And soon it will possess you completely."

Seventeen

"Why didn't you tell me this before?" Emily shouted. "First you tell me I'm a wizard from another world and my name is Talia and now you're saying I'm possessed by a demon? A demon? Who or what the hell am I?"

"I thought you knew and were just pretending. Hasn't it been whispering to you in your mind your whole life?"

"Whispering to me? What? No! Oh my god, I can't take this." Emily put her head in her hands, her breathing fast and shallow. She looked up, her face was pale. "I feel light-headed. I can't breathe."

"It's anxiety, calm down," said Mercurios. "Lie down, catch your breath. Perhaps the demon's slumber has been very deep and only now that it is beginning to awaken and gain power is it communicating with you."

Emily did as he suggested and lay down on her bed. "Oh my god, I'm possessed. I need an exorcism!" She sat bolt upright again, filled with terror. "How do I get it out of me?" she screamed. "Please get it out of me! I've seen what happens to those people in horror movies! Get me a priest!"

"Please calm down! Yes, the only way is through an exorcism. But that is very advanced magic indeed, might be years before you are powerful enough. Would be too late by then. The only way is to take you to Magella to the Fengusberry Academy. There are some of the most powerful wizards in Magella there. They will be able to do the exorcism and then you can begin your advanced training in wizardry."

"But what if we can't find the Well? We still have no idea who, what or where this Vadas Asger is." Emily stared at Mercurios. "Wait a second, are you just saying this to trick me into going to Magella?"

"No, I swear!"

"Then why didn't you tell me earlier?"

"Oh, don't worry, if we can never return to Magella the demon will awaken and I will teach you magic and you will conquer and enslave this world. That's why I was telling you to just go with it. It is very likely that we will not be able to ever find the Well and get back to Magella."

"Don't worry? JUST GO WITH IT?" Emily shouted. "You're saying you didn't tell me because you think we're stuck here anyways so it's inevitable and… Wait a minute, you don't seem concerned, I get the feeling you want this demon to awaken. Are you insane? I don't want to turn into a demon and enslave the world!"

"Well, that won't be your decision. I am quite sure the demon will want to enslave the world, so just relax and go with it. It will be useless to fight it."

"Stop saying that!"

"I cannot believe that you didn't know," said Mercurios. "Please, you did know. Admit it. Don't play games. All those times I laughed and winked after you'd say 'Oh no, Mercurios, I don't want to slay my enemies, I don't want to enslave the world,'" he did an absurd impression of her voice, "'Oh no, Mercurios I wouldn't want to do that, I would never want to crush my enemies unmerciful.'" The imp burst out laughing. "I knew you were just playing games, deep down you want to but you haven't accepted yourself fully yet." He put a hand on her knee, his eyes concerned, supportive and sincere. "And there's nothing wrong with that, Emily, it's the most natural thing in the world. You have to accept yourself for who you are, you have a demon inside you. Just enjoy it, go with it, dare to be different. You want to enslave the world and crush your enemies and that's okay. Accept it, you need to be more inclusive."

"Inclusive?" she shrieked.

"Besides, imagine how fun it will be to be a powerful demon terrorizing this ridiculous world, haha! Power is such fun!" The imp clapped his hands and capered about with glee. "Ah, such fun such fun indeed. We shall terrorize them all!"

"Okay listen, you are my familiar, right?" said Emily, grabbing the imp and holding him up as he squirmed to be free.

"Yes, please put me down."

"And you must obey my commands?"

"Yes, unless they contradict your mother's commands."

She grabbed him by his throat, staring into his eyes. "Well, I command you to do everything in your power to help me get this demon out of me!"

"Yes, I will obey" – the imp cringed – "please do not smite me!"

That night Emily had trouble sleeping. She tossed and turned, horrified by the revelation that she was possessed by a demon. She also couldn't stop thinking about the young man from her dreams, wondering who he was. She was now totally obsessed with him. Her bedroom seemed unbearably hot and she kicked off her bed sheets. She found it difficult to concentrate on anything other than him for more than a few minutes, and then her thoughts would inevitably return to him. Part of her wanted to just give in and think of nothing but him. Maybe I have a fever, she thought, though she didn't feel as though she was getting sick. She thought about how she longed for him, how she was filled with a terrible aching and emptiness in her heart for him, how she felt such a desperate need for him in every fiber of her being, and how she was willing to say or do anything to be with him. She rolled over, obsessively replaying every word he had said to her over and over in her mind, searching for hidden meanings, answers. She loved how calm and confident he was, how he radiated confidence and raw, primal masculine power like a magnetic field. Beautiful like an angel and ferocious like a beast. Finally, just before dawn, she fell asleep.

When she awoke a few hours later her body was filled with a soft, voluptuous languor instead of the usual terror. Her lips spread into a delicious smile as she remembered her dream from the night before. She thought of the two of them standing in the moonlit glade surrounded by wolves. Her whole body felt relaxed, as if all her muscles had melted into happiness.

"Wow," she sighed. "What a hot dream, so crazy." Then she remembered the conversation with the imp, "and disturbing."

Downstairs, she sat eating at the breakfast table with her mother, who was flipping through a newspaper, glancing up at her every so often.

Emily's eyes fell on the front headline in her mother's hands: "Wolves Escape from Transport Trailer." She let out a gasp.

Her mother looked at her questioningly. "What?"

"The wolves that escaped," Emily stammered. "Could I read that?"

Her mother stared at the newspaper a moment, and then handed it to her. Emily read aloud: "Last night at approximately 11:00 p.m., five Arctic wolves escaped from a trailer transporting them to York's Wild Kingdom Zoo. The driver of the trailer, who has requested that his name be withheld, reported stopping for a man who was standing in the middle of the road. The next thing he remembers was waking up in the driver's seat of the truck. When he searched the trailer, he found that the animals were gone. The driver was not injured."

"Apparently there were a couple of terrible fires last night too," her mother said.

"Hmm?" murmured Emily, barely hearing her mother. She couldn't read any more. Could it be true that what she had experienced last night at the club and in the forest was not a dream? Was it real? Was he real?

She finished breakfast and rushed up to her bedroom. "Mercurios," she whispered fiercely.

The imp appeared on her dressing table. "At your service."

"Who was that boy last night? I thought it must have been another dream. But, but it wasn't."

"I know. He is different, and so are those other men. There is something otherworldly about them. I've been thinking about this all night, yes indeed, thinking long and hard. Emily, I am certain that you are correct, they are from Magella. They are not of this world. That is what I believe. It is possible that they came through the Well of Many Worlds, as we did. Though who they are and for what purpose, I do not know. They may be after you, either to bring you back to the Lich King in Darguul, or to kill you. Or their being here may have nothing to do with you at all."

"I can't believe that he's actually real. What does it mean? And there was something so powerful about his presence," she said, gazing off into the distance dreamily. "And his eyes were… hypnotizing, just like in my dreams."

"Yes, there is a spell that will help you resist any form of hypnosis. Perhaps that is the next one you should learn," Mercurios said, holding up a gnarly finger.

"But what if I don't want to resist it?"

"Foolish!" he cried, jumping up. "Do you not understand? They may very well be necromancers from Magella, or working for them. They may be associated with the ones who attacked your parents and may have used the Well specifically to come to Earth to hunt you. For all you know, if he had found out your real identity he might have killed or kidnapped you."

Emily frowned but said nothing.

"Your mother would never be so foolish and reckless as to put herself under the power of anyone, much less a complete stranger."

"Wait, if the boy and the wolves weren't a dream then what you told me wasn't either. Is it true? Am I possessed by a demon?"

"Yes."

"Well, then you remember what I told you."

"Yes, but the only way to get an exorcism is to find the Well."

Emily stared into the dressing table mirror.

"My god, who am I? Or what am I? It's about time to get the wheels of justice rolling and at the same time try to find out anything we can about the Well. I have to get this thing outta me. Tonight, I'm going down to the warehouse to have a talk with Sammy. Whatever is happening there they said it was going to be tonight."

"No, no, no, foolish girl! You need to learn the spells! Patience."

"Patience? That's the last thing I need. Either I'll turn into a demon or Cady Sunner and his goons will kill my mom and me. What we need is information."

Mercurios was about to say more but Emily cut him off with a hand over his mouth.

"Don't waste your breath. Either help me or go away."

"I will help you, but your mother would be very disappointed at your lack of discipline, yes, very disappointed indeed, Emily."

"Well, she isn't here, is she?"

"No, she is probably dead, killed protecting and saving you." He stared at her with his beady eyes.

She hadn't considered this and felt a wave of guilt for someone she couldn't even remember. She brushed it aside. "I get the feeling that you actually want me to become a demon. Well, you have to obey me and, guess what, I'm not after a day of vengeance, I'm after a day of justice."

At school, Emily couldn't concentrate. Twice her teachers asked if she was living in a dream world when she failed to respond to a question, and the other kids laughed at her. Her mind reeled back and forth between nervous anticipation at confronting Sammy, the fear of the dark power growing inside her, and her obsession with the young man from her dreams who she now knew was real. She had so many questions. She knew she had to find him again. Who was he?

Was he really from Magella, or just a ridiculously hot animal-rights activist? And how did he know those men who seemed to be working with Sunner? Were they all from a different world? And if so, why were they here? She couldn't stop thinking about the young man's eyes and the effect they had on her.

When she thought back to their encounter in the forest, she remembered how it had felt as if the past and the future had disappeared for a few minutes. Every ounce of her being had been present in those moments, exploding with life. She had to find him again. The natural place to start looking for him was at the club. But the all-ages night only happened there once a week, no one would be there now. Seven days seemed like an eternity to wait for her chance to go search for him. She prayed she would dream of him that night and find herself back in that silvery night in the forest, standing with him under the full moon.

Walking through the halls between classes, Emily turned a corner and ran into Chanel.

"Oh, hey!" Chanel said in her singsong voice. "Haven't seen you around. Working on your family photo album?"

Emily felt a flash of rage blaze through her. She had an idea. "Chanel, can I speak to you in private for a moment?"

"What could you possibly have to say to me?"

"It's about Tom, and it's private."

"Okay, but make it quick."

Emily led her into an empty classroom and as she turned to face her Mercurios appeared on her shoulder.

"Yes, Emily," whispered the imp, rubbing his little belly and licking his lips. "Time to try your charm spell on a living victim. Then perhaps you can make her drink acid. Now, remember the correct pronunciation."

"Well, Chanel, it's like this. Valerun daia karmellun." Emily spoke the words while looking deep into Chanel's eyes and making a series of simple gestures with her hands. As she spoke she focused on feeling and channeling the energy of the world all around her, like Mercurios had taught her. In a moment her hands were glowing with blue, magical energy and she directed it at Chanel. Chanel's eyes glazed over before she could protest, and Emily wondered if the charm spell had worked already.

"Chanel?"

"Very good, Emily," giggled Mercurios. "Well done, indeed! Will you make her drink poison?"

"No!"

"Yes, I'm Chanel." A big, happy, brainless smile spread across Chanel's pretty, pouting lips.

Wow! Emily couldn't believe her own magical powers.

"Chanel, it's extremely hot in the school, and you have an intense desire to strip naked and run through the halls shouting, 'I am Chanel Boxer, Queen of the Idiots!'"

The imp cackled with devilish glee. "Yes, Emily! Brilliant. I cannot wait until you learn spells of power and destruction, then we will really have such fun! Crush them unmerciful!" He shook his little fist in the air.

Chanel gave another broad, vacant smile. "Yes, that's exactly what I want to do!"

As she began getting undressed Emily hurried out of the classroom, walked a few yards down the hall and then stopped, leaning against a wall, trying to look casual.

A couple of moments later, Chanel came running and skipping out of the classroom, stark naked, crying at the top of her lungs with glee, "I am Chanel Boxer, Queen of the Idiots! Welcome, all idiots! I am your queen!"

All the students walking to and from their classes stood and stared in utter astonishment at the sight. The sound of laughter and cheering spread through the corridors as people called their friends out to enjoy the spectacle and, best of all, pulling out their cell phones to take pictures. Chanel continued on her happy way, proclaiming again and again her idiotic rulership. As she disappeared down another corridor, the halls behind her remained alive with chatter and laughter. Emily burst out laughing and followed after her.

A couple of minutes later Chanel had slowed down to a walk. Emily wondered if maybe the spell was already wearing off. Chanel then stopped and stood in the middle of the hallway surrounded by dozens of shocked and delighted students. The smile faded from her face as she returned to the real world and looked down at her naked body. There was a moment of nearly complete silence, and then an earth-shattering shriek erupted from deep inside her.

Down the hall, Emily spotted Mr. North, the assistant principal, making his way toward them. "I found her," his deep voice reported into his walkie-talkie.

Chanel frantically tried to cover herself with her elegant, fluttering hands as she looked in every direction at the laughing faces, lost in a state of utter confusion and horror. Finally, she turned and ran screaming down the hall, straight into Mr. North's waiting arms.

"Gotcha," he crowed. "All right, miss, your streaking days are over. Come with me."

Emily stumbled into the bathroom, laughing so hard the tears streamed down her face. The imp rolled around on the counter, rubbing his belly and cackling with delight.

"Yes! So much like your mother indeed!"

Emily stopped laughing. "What did you say?"

He continued to cackle. "Ah, what fun! Yes, you are so like your mother – she had a wonderfully wicked sense of humor too, dark and deadly indeed. That is what I liked most about her."

"What did I just do?" Emily asked her reflection in the mirror in a whisper. "Am I becoming just like Chanel? Or... am I becoming like my real mother? Or is it the demon waking up?"

The thought disturbed and disgusted her. "I am Emily Bliss, that is who I am."

Shaken, she turned on the tap and ran the water until it was as cold as possible, then washed her face off in the sink. Suddenly, she longed for her mother, whoever she was. She wished she could've known the woman who actually gave birth to her.

But there was a nagging fear in the back of her mind that her mother was evil and that the spell book itself was changing her, turning her into someone who wouldn't even recognize her former self. Was it helping to awaken the demon? The desire to learn magic and the fear of what she might become if she spent too much time with that spell book was starting to torment her.

"I will be using magic to do good though," she told herself for the hundredth time.

"Yes," continued Mercurios, looking at her. "So much like your mother, you look like her too, your hair, your body, your cheekbones… but not your eyes, no," he whispered at her ominously.

Emily stood in a daze, staring into space, water dripping down her face, contemplating the magnitude of what the imp was saying. Then she snapped out of it.

"Enough, Mercurios!" she shouted. "My name is Emily Bliss and my father was the kind, decent, gentle, loving, honorable man who raised me and showed me love, and my mother is the woman who I've known all my life and they would be ashamed if I turned into some kind of petty tyrant or vengeful psycho!"

"Fair enough," tittered Mercurios. "But once you have a delicious taste of power——"

"I will still remain true to who I am," she cut him off. "End of discussion." She turned and left without waiting for a reply. As she walked out of the bathroom, she ran into Tom.

"Hey, Emily – what's up?"

"Oh, hey, Tom." Emily smiled, but the sight of him stirred a number of conflicting emotions inside her. She still really liked him and found him incredibly attractive in so many ways, and the fact that he was a regular human being from Earth was somehow very comforting. Being near him made her feel as if she had her feet on the ground, that she was still the Emily Bliss she had always known, living in a familiar world, and she liked that. Yet at the same time, when she thought about the other boy a very different level of desire rose inside her, raging through every square inch of her body.

"Did you see what Chanel just did?" Tom said, a puzzled look crossing his handsome face.

"No," she lied, "what's going on?"

"I think she must be wasted or something. She was running through the school naked."

"No way!" Emily feigned surprise. "Uh, listen, I have to go – my mom's expecting me."

She knew Tom was watching her go, probably wondering what was going on with her, whether or not she was still interested in him, but she couldn't think abut him at the moment. She was obsessed with the young man from her dreams. She would have loved to hang out with Tom, and have him close to her right now, but what bubbled deep inside was a cauldron of confusion.

When Emily got home she sat down glumly in a chair in her bedroom looking at a picture of her father. She knew he'd be disappointed in her if he'd seen her be so cruel to another person, even Chanel Boxer. Since Emily was little, he'd taught her to feel empathy for the pain and struggles of other people, even when those people seemed unworthy of it. He had taught her that it was better to try to understand why they hurt you than to hurt them back. But even as she remembered that and hung her head in shame, she felt herself growing angry again. Wasn't it that same compassion that let people like Sammy to betray people like her father? If instead of standing up to the Chanel Boxers of the world she spent her time trying to understand "their pain," wasn't she in danger of letting them win? Had her father's kindness and trust been what ultimately led to his death? Was it kindness or was it… cowardice?

She felt terrible even thinking such a thing. She knew it wasn't really her father she was angry at. It was Sammy. She was convinced that he had betrayed her father, and she had to go and confront him. Sammy was supposed to be her father's friend. It enraged her that her father's trust had been betrayed so cruelly. She was outraged at the thought of Sammy and the killers getting away with what they had done.

"Maybe I can shame him into confessing to the police that Cady killed my father," she thought. "Or maybe if I use my charm spell on him, I can force him to tell them everything he knows. At least then I'd be using my power for good."

At dinner with her mother that night, Emily was quiet and thoughtful. Then she said, "Mom, can I ask you something?"

"Of course, dear."

"If someone was pushing you around, would you, you know, push back?"

"What do you mean?"

"Just in general, if someone pushed you, I mean really pushed you... would you fight back, or just take it?"

Her mother sighed and put down her fork. "Emily, I know that life as a teenager can seem very... dramatic, and these things seem really important to you right now. But when you grow up, you won't even remember this, whatever it is."

"I'm not talking about the future. I'm talking about now."

"But, darling, what's important is your future, your career. The things that are going to be important to you later on are whether you got good grades and—"

Emily pushed her chair back hard so that it screeched along the tile floor. "So you're saying that the only thing that matters is the future, and the stuff that happens now isn't important?"

"No, no, not at all. What I'm saying is: the things that are important now are the things that create a solid foundation for your future."

"So everything I do now is only important if it works out ten years from now?"

"Well, in a way—"

"What if it's the same way in ten years?"

"What?"

"What if in ten years I'm thinking that whatever I'm doing then is only important if it provides a solid future ten years from then, and then ten years after that, I'm thinking that whatever I'm doing then is only important if it works out ten years after that? Does the 'now' ever matter?"

Her mother shook her head, frustrated. "Listen, honey, trust me. When you grow up, you'll laugh at all these things that seem so important to you right now. You just don't understand."

Emily suddenly felt furious. "You know what, Mom? Maybe this family wouldn't have turned out to be such a disaster if Dad had stood up to you!"

"What?" Her mother's eyes narrowed.

"You heard me. Nothing he ever did was good enough for you. You knew he was a simple-hearted man when you married him. But you relentlessly drove him to make more money, more money, more money, and it was never enough; a bigger car, a nicer house, that's all you ever cared about. He wanted so much to make you happy – he tried his best but the more he tried, the more you made him feel he wasn't good enough, that he would never be good enough." Tears welled up in Emily's eyes and her voice quavered.

She stormed out the front door. Her mother shouted after her but Emily didn't hesitate as she got in her car and backed out of the driveway. She knew exactly where she was going.

"This may be a very bad idea, Emily." Mercurios appeared in the passenger seat.

"I have to do this." As she paused at a red light her phone rang. It was Tom.

"Hey, let's get together tonight," he said.

"Actually, I'm on my way to confront my dad's so-called friend, Sammy, at the warehouse where he works. I think he was involved in his murder."

"Let me help you then."

"What?" Emily was caught off guard by this offer. "No. Thanks, but I really don't want to lay my problems on someone else's shoulders."

"Emily, I want to make sure nobody hurts you."

"No, really, I'll be fine."

"My offer is just as much for myself as it is for you. I'll worry about you a lot less if I'm there with you."

She liked the idea of seeing him but her conflicting desires made her feel it was impossible right now.

"Thanks, Tom, but really, you don't have to worry. I have to go." She hung up.

She left her car in a parking lot just down the road from the warehouse and walked across the two empty lots, giving herself time to gather her thoughts and gain some courage.

"Emily, I must insist you reconsider," said Mercurios from her shoulder.

"I have to do this. I have to confront him. If it goes wrong, I'll use my wand and my ring."

The sun was setting and the clouds on the horizon were lit up as though they had been set on fire. She walked toward the warehouse side entrance, shivering a bit from the cold breeze blowing in off the water. She felt uneasy, but her anger propelled her forward. She pushed open the heavy steel door. Inside was a huge, empty, brightly lit warehouse.

"Sammy!" she shouted, trying to sound fearless.

Nobody answered, but she could see a figure in the upstairs office standing with his back to the window that overlooked the warehouse floor, having an animated conversation on the phone. Her heart thumped in her chest and her adrenal glands told her that she should be afraid, that she should turn around, run out to her car and drive home, but she ignored them and climbed the stairs to the office. A far stronger emotion than fear took over. She was gripped by rage as the memory of her father's photos, of his corpse, filled her mind.

When she reached the top of the stairs, she flung the office door open. The man was just hanging up the phone. He spun around and gaped at her. "Emily! What are you doing here?"

The office was a mess. A big desk against the far wall was covered in stacks of paper. Boxes were piled haphazardly under the window. Crumpled pieces of paper littered the floor. High above the big desk was another, smaller window overlooking the parking lot. It was open and letting in the chilly night air. Glancing out through the window Emily was momentarily stunned to see Tom's Jeep pull up.

"Emily!" said Sammy, a look of worry crossing his face. "You gotta get out of here!"

"I want to know why you aren't helping the police put Cady Sunner in jail, especially since it was you who betrayed my father!" Emily cried, her fists clenched and tears streaming down her face. She hated that she always cried when she was furious. It was so humiliating. "He's dead because of you, isn't he?"

Sammy held his hands up. "Emily, I swear I had no idea they would, but" – he glanced furtively through the window to the warehouse floor – "listen, you have to get out of here!"

"So it was Cady who killed him." She strode up to Sammy and slapped him across the face as hard as she could. "Do you know what they did to him?" she shouted. "Did you see what they did to my father?"

He stared at her, too shocked to speak.

"You were supposed to be his friend! My father never hurt anyone. He was…"

Emily's voice caught in her throat. Sammy grabbed her by the shoulders.

"I swear, I didn't know they would kill him. I only just met them, and now I'm trapped too. I… I have a family—"

She whipped out her wand and, hearing the sound of feet on the steps, swung round just as Tom appeared at the door.

"Tom, I told you to stay away!"

"I made you a promise. I'm not going to let anyone hurt you again."

"Who is this?" Sammy asked.

"Is this guy bothering you?" Tom looked menacingly at the older man.

"What is 'Vadas Asger'?" asked Emily turning back to face Sammy.

The sound of the main door of the warehouse rolling back made them all turn. A convoy of five SUVs and six forklifts carrying huge crates drove inside and parked. About twenty-five men emerged from the SUVs and began helping the forklift drivers unload the crates and break them open with crowbars while six more vans drove in.

Sammy's face turned pale. He grabbed Emily again, shaking her. "You have to hide! If they find you here, they'll kill you!"

Eighteen

Sammy pushed Emily roughly behind the pile of boxes under the window.

"Keep quiet and keep your head down!" he hissed before straightening up to meet the visitors coming up the steps to the office.

Tom crouched down beside her. "What's going on?" he whispered.

"I don't know," she said, peeping cautiously through the window that overlooked the warehouse floor. The men absorbed in opening up the crates looked East Asian, while the men who'd poured out of the vans were all white and seemed to be speaking to one another in Russian. It was impossible to do an accurate headcount but there now seemed to be about fifty Russians and thirty of the East Asians. A number of the men in each group were carrying guns.

Emily remembered Detective Scannel talking about the Russian mob and Chinese Triads moving into the Portland area. Two men, who appeared to be their leaders, burst into the office, talking together in low voices as the others kept working below. Sammy stood waiting for them to address him, obviously terrified. A side door Emily hadn't seen before opened and a tall, well-dressed man entered and headed for the office steps.

"Mr. Denman!" Emily whispered.

"Bethany's father?" said Tom. "What's he doing here?"

"I don't know."

There were more men running up the steps to the office. One was Cady Sunner and another the pale-faced man from Cady Sunner's house, and who she had seen at the club, followed close behind, carrying a briefcase. There was also a third man. Emily recognized him from the picture Detective Scannel had shown her. He was the man known as Commander Claw. The pale-faced man with the briefcase was speaking to Cady.

"We are wasting a lot of time here. Just remember, none of this would be necessary if you had exercised more self control."

Emily strained her ears to catch every word.

"This whole mess is on your head," he continued. "It would've been easy for me to extract the information, but not once he was dead."

Emily felt sick to her stomach and had to exercise intense self-control not to throw up right there. Her head was swimming with a million thoughts.

"If you had come sooner," Cady snarled, "things might have been different. I couldn't wait forever."

"We were following hundreds of other leads, you fool."

"Okay, okay, but I told you a hundred times, I didn't mean to kill him. We were just roughing him up a bit, trying to get him to talk, and he died."

The man stared at him. "Just roughing him up? You beat him to a pulp, then you shot him five times!"

"Yeah." There was a pathetic whine to Cady's voice now. "But I didn't mean to hit any major organs. It was bad luck, that's all."

"Bad luck?"

"If you had left him to me," Commander Claw growled, "I would have burned him with the alcohol claw."

The pale-faced man turned to Mr. Denman. "Here's your first payment," he said placing the briefcase on the table and opening it. Mr. Denman flicked quickly through the contents, snapped it shut and picked it up.

"Very good."

"And here is the itemized list." He handed Mr. Denman a large, thick envelope. "Once everything is sold and turned into gold, burn the list."

Mr. Denman dropped the envelope on the table in front of Sammy. "Go through this, when the shipments come in every piece and every ounce of gold must be accounted for."

"Okay sure, no problem." Sammy was sweating like a pig and blotting his terrified face with a pocket-handkerchief. He lit a cigarette with trembling fingers.

"Mr. Denman has arranged for two of his ships to crash," the pale-faced man was explaining. "That will distract the coast guard while Commander Claw brings in the shipment with his submarines." He suddenly stopped speaking, stiffened and seemed to sniff the air. He slowly turned and looked directly at the boxes, behind which Emily and Tom were hiding. They both held their breaths and then Emily heard another voice, which made her heart leap into her throat.

"Well, well, well, if it isn't Mephris."

She would have recognized that haunting, velvety voice anywhere. Along with everyone in the office she looked up to a window high above the desk. There he was, perched casually on the windowsill, looking down with a mocking smile on his lips. Emily's mouth grew wet. She opened her lips but stopped herself from speaking. Tom looked from Mitchell to her and saw the expression on her face. Across Mitchell's lap lay a sword, still in its sheath.

"What little scheme are we working on this evening, gentlemen?" asked Mitchell.

"You."

Emily turned and saw that it was the pale-faced man she had seen at Cady Sunner's house and then at the Sanctuary who spoke.

A mixture of fear and anger flooded Mephris's face as he fought visibly to control himself, a sneer forming on his lips.

"How nice to see you again, Mitchell. Nothing for over two hundred years and now twice in a week."

His name is Mitchell! Emily thought it was the most wonderful name she had ever heard. What did Mephris's mean by "nothing for two hundred years?"

Mitchell, paused, sniffing the air and looking around, for a split second his eyes rested on Emily and Tom, then turned back to Mephris as if he had seen nothing.

"When you ran away from me the other night, it made me feel a little sad for you," he teased. "It reminded me of old times. You haven't changed at all, Mephris. You're still a coward. Still the bumbling, infantile buffoon you always were."

Mephris clenched his fist. "Buffoon! You call me a buffoon? You are the fool!"

"And a slave to a silly cult." Mitchell continued. "Tell me, how is Baelaar? You're still his errand boy, I see."

"Soon the Niveus Gladius will be nothing more than an embarrassing memory!"

Mitchell narrowed his eyes at Mephris and tried to read his mind, but the vampire mustered all his strength to push him out. Mephris was shaking with the effort and Mitchell laughed at him.

"You're going to have to get used to disappointment. I am now more powerful than you, Mephris. And I intend to make you and your master scream before I destroy you."

Mitchell was distracted for a second as another man burst through the door.

"Ruthen!"

Lord Ruthen glanced up in surprise. "Mitchell!"

As always Lord Ruthen was impeccably dressed and wore a fortune in antique jewelry. Before anyone else could speak a roaring sound like an approaching hurricane rose up outside the warehouse. Mitchell turned in the window to see at least a hundred motorcycles approaching. Realizing what the noise was, the Russian and Chinese gang members on the floor below ran to their vehicles, pulling out weapons as they went. If ever there was a time to use the Ring of Teleportation, Emily thought, this might very well be it, but she forced herself to wait. It had to be a last resort. She was still terrified of what would happen if she made a mistake.

"Come with me," Mr. Denman shouted to Cady Sunner and Commander Claw and they ran down the steps, vanishing through the same side door they had entered through.

Mitchell dropped lightly down from his perch to the floor as Mephris reached into his coat and withdrew a bottle of liquid with a rag stuffed in the top. He snatched the cigarette from Sammy's lips and held the burning tip against the rag before hurling it at Mitchell. Sammy shrieked in fear and stumbled backward as Ruthen unsheathed his sword. Emily was stunned by the agility with which both Mephris and Mitchell moved. No human was that fast. But of course she understood now, they were not from Earth.

As Mephris fled down the stairs, Mitchell vaulted over the flying bottle and landed in a crouch as it exploded against the wall behind him, setting the office ablaze. A machine gun sent a stream of bullets through the window above where Emily and Tom were still crouching. Mitchell heard Emily cry out in shock. Some of the bullets smacked into Sammy and with a long scream he spun round under the impact and fell to the floor dead as shattered glass rained down over Tom and Emily.

Emily cried out again, a sound Mitchell couldn't ignore. "What are you doing here? Are you hurt?"

"No, I'm okay." She and Tom crawled out from behind the boxes.

"This guy again?" Tom shoved a thumb in Mitchell's direction.

"I'll get Mephris." Ruthen shouted at Mitchell. "Meet me in Eastern Cemetery at midnight."

Without waiting for a reply, Ruthen disappeared after Mephris. Below them, in the main warehouse, at least a hundred leather-clad, tattooed bikers had charged in wielding knives, chains, baseball bats, axe handles and guns. It was a barbarian army, an awe-inspiring collection of some of the biggest, toughest, wildest men on the planet in full battle frenzy.

The Russian and Chinese gang members were equally well-armed and had joined ranks to face the vicious onslaught. Within seconds, it was a battle scene of epic proportions, the roar of gunfire and the bloodcurdling battle cries echoing off the roof high above as the combatants came face-to-face. Bats and axe handles smashed skulls, arms, shoulders, and teeth. Those wielding knives ducked, dodged, sliced and stabbed in every direction. One huge biker, armed only with a set of brass knuckles on each fist, pummeled his way through the very center of the battle like a crazed gladiator, roaring his defiance of all those around him.

"We need to get you two out of here," Mitchell said, sheathing his sword and slinging it over his back.

"Who is he?" asked Tom again.

Emily snatched up the envelope Mephris had put on Sammy's desk.

"Come with me," Mitchell ordered her.

"But—"

"Do as I say!" He lifted her in his arms and she immediately felt more safe and protected than she ever had before. Mercurios appeared on her shoulder.

"Your Sphere of Protection, Emily… use it," he whispered urgently, then disappeared.

Emily pulled the sphere out of her pocket and whispered the command word. As it glowed blue she immediately had the sensation that a bubble of almost liquid-like translucent energy surrounded her. Nobody else seemed to notice it.

"Hold tight," Mitchell whispered in her ear, sending a shiver of pleasure rippling deep inside her. To Tom, he said, "Follow us."

As they flew down the stairs into the madness below, Emily caught a glimpse of some of the Chinese gang members who had broken away from the fight, jumping into an SUV. The engine revved and they raced toward the far exit, where other gang members were frantically trying to pull open a door that seemed to have been welded shut.

"Get that door open!" shouted a burly Russian man.

"It's sealed!" shouted one of the men desperately trying to tear it open. "We're trapped!"

Seeing their panic a huge biker picked up a rocket launcher, aimed, and fired it at the SUV. The rocket flew the length of the building and collided with the SUV with a deafening blast. The vehicle exploded. Burning bodies came crawling and shrieking out of the wreckage.

Mitchell carefully put Emily down and punched and kicked his way through the battle with superhuman focus, strength, speed and precision, making a path for Emily and Tom to follow.

"Yes!" shouted Mercurios, dancing with glee at the carnage Mitchell was wreaking. "Crush them unmerciful!"

Emily screamed as a blinding flash of light appeared directly in front of Tom, along with what looked like a large, black doorway that immediately vanished. Shielding his eyes, Tom ran at full speed into what looked to the half-blinded Emily like some kind of massive man who had stepped out of the black doorway. Like an oncoming freight train, the man knocked Tom to the floor. As he struggled to get back to his feet, the figure bent over and plunged something long and sharp into his chest. Tom screamed in agony.

"Tom!" cried Emily.

Mitchell spun around, and, without hesitation, strode toward Tom and his attacker. Now her vision was clearing Emily could see that it was a hideous being, at least twelve feet tall. Its skin was horribly withered, it had enormous black holes where its eyes should have been, its tusks protruded from its lower jaw, and atop its ugly head were a pair of horns. Without breaking his stride, Mitchell swept out his sword. His supernatural powers sent a surge of energy through the blade and it erupted into flames. With one mighty strike, he decapitated the creature where it stood and thick, black ooze spewed from the body as it fell to the floor in horrible, jerking spasms.

Seeing Tom was still alive, Mitchell sheathed his sword and

reached down to help him to his feet, just as the monster's body dissolved into a viscous, black puddle.

Tom looked at Mitchell in a daze.

"What are you?" he asked. With his strength and awareness returning, he shouted louder, "I said, what are you?"

Mitchell noticed that Tom's shirt was ripped across his chest and a red light was glowing underneath it. Tom followed his gaze down and staggered backward with a look of horror on his face.

"Tom!" Emily screamed as he turned and ran off around the side of the warehouse into the crowd.

One of the Chinese gang members grabbed Emily by the throat and held the point of a jagged knife to her eye, using her as a human shield. Emily dropped the envelope and stealthily drew her wand. Before she could use it Mitchell leaped across and plunged his sword through the man's torso.

Emily screamed as the thug's eyes bulged, his face contorting in agony. He released his grip on Emily's throat and she slid her wand back into her inside jacket pocket, picking up the envelope as Mitchell grabbed her and took off. As they sped toward the side door, Cady Sunner jumped on top of one of the parked vans, drew two pistols out of his jacket, and began firing randomly into the crowd, laughing like a maniac.

As Mitchell and Emily ran past him he fired after them, but the bullets bounced off Emily's invisible Sphere of Protection. They flew through the parking lot and hurtled up the street, leaving the battle behind them. Emily heard police sirens approaching. She buried her face in Mitchell's powerful chest and breathed deeply. The horror of the carnage she had witnessed only moments before abated with the rhythmical rise and fall of his powerful stride.

"Where do you live?" he asked.

She told him where her mother's house was. He said nothing, just tore through the streets and parks with the speed and power of a galloping horse. It was like a dream, the way he ran at such speed, bounding over fences and navigating between buildings and around trees. When they arrived in her mother's backyard he set her down on her feet.

"What were you doing there?" he demanded angrily, looming intimidatingly over her. "You could've gotten killed!"

"I went there to confront Sammy."

"You're a fool!" he bellowed and Emily shrank back. "Do you have any idea how dangerous those people are?"

"They murdered my father," she said in a weak voice.

"So you know they are killers!"

"You wouldn't understand!" she yelled back, tears brimming in her eyes, "That was Cady Sunner in there, and he was the one who did it. Please, Mitchell."

Just speaking his name sent a shiver down Emily's spine. Mitchell ignored her and she chewed angrily on her fingernails.

"Don't do it again," he ordered. "You'll be killed. You think throwing your life away is going to help anyone or anything? And I told you not to bite your fingernails."

She pulled her fingers out of her mouth and crossed her arms defiantly. "You can't tell me what to do, you're not my father."

"I have to leave." He walked away. "Just obey me and don't go near those people again. You are a naïve little girl meddling with people who could crush you in an instant."

"What do you care anyway?"

He stopped and stared at her. "I don't know," he muttered. "For some reason I feel very protective of you." He shook his head. "But I have to go."

It started to rain and Emily felt her face getting wet. Mitchell simply turned away and leaped on top of the fence like a big cat.

"Oh!" Emily moaned in frustration and clenched her fists. He infuriated her. "No wait!" she cried, running toward him as he stood on the fence. Her heart began to race, her stomach was full of butterflies, and adrenaline coursed through her blood.

"Wait! Please, I'm sorry. I'm just… Thank you. I owe you my life. You must think I'm incredibly ungrateful. Please, will I ever see you again?" She was willing to say or do anything to keep him there. "I know your secret," she blurted out, gambling that Mercurios was right.

Mitchell jumped back down off the fence. His face was calm but deadly serious and he stared at her long and hard. He stepped close to her, looming over her. "And what secret would that be?"

"Don't worry, I'm also from Magella."

"Excuse me?"

"Magella, aren't you from Magella?"

"How do you know of Magella?" he asked, grabbing her roughly by the shoulders.

"Mitchell." Emily shrank back, reaching for her wand. He noticed the fear he was causing and released her.

"So, you are from Magella?" she said.

"No, I was born in England." He stared deep into her eyes and Emily felt her mind begin to float. Her body grew hot like it always did when looking into his hypnotic, glittering emerald eyes. "In the year 1546."

Her mouth fell open and she could feel hot sweat forming on her flesh from the excitement of having her suspicions confirmed. "I knew it," she whispered, her eyes wide.

"The dark fairy tales are true, Emily; vampires do exist."

"I knew it. I thought you were either a vampire or a necromancer from Magella, or maybe even a vampire necromancer. But you're not from Magella?"

"What do you know about Magella?"

"Not much, only that I'm not from this world."

Mitchell looked at her for a moment. "I knew there was something different about you…" he whispered. "But how…"

"I was a baby. I don't remember anything. Apparently, my parents were wizards who sent me through some magical artifact called the Well of Many Worlds, and here I am."

His eyes widened. "Do you know where the Well is?"

"I have no idea."

"I sensed something about you. Both our blood is from Magella. And that's why the wolves led me to you."

"What?"

"In the forest, that is why the wolves led me to you and why one leaped at you. Wolves almost never attack humans, what you see in the movies are lies. Wolf attacks on humans are incredibly rare. But I instructed them to hunt for a vampire, a being with blood like mine, blood from another world. Blood from Magella. Wolves are proficient at tracking vampires. I used them to track Mephris to that warehouse. Just as the old legends say, wolves are the guardians of the spirit world, acutely aware of beings that are crossing or caught between the worlds of the living and the worlds of the dead, like ghosts, ghouls and vampires. Since the original vampire came from Magella, all vampires have otherworldly blood and wolves are extremely aware of them. When they came across you they sensed that your blood was from the same world as mine and the way you appeared, your vampire costume… it was you they thought I was after."

"Sorry, you instructed them? But wait, I thought you said you weren't from Magella."

"I'm not, but the first vampire was and we all carry his blood. I have to go." Mitchell turned to leave.

"No! Wait!"

"Return to your life, Emily," he said, his eyes now cold. "Leave this to me. I will get your revenge for you. And after that, pretend that I was just a dream."

He turned and leaped over the fence, disappearing into the night.

"Mitchell wait!" she cried, but he was gone.

Nineteen

Mitchell arrived at the cemetery at exactly midnight. Lord Ruthen materialized out of the darkness a moment later.

"Mitchell." He smiled and grasped the other vampire's hand. "I never thought I'd see you again. Have you been in hiding all this time?"

"Why were you at the warehouse, Ruthen?" Mitchell responded coldly.

"Hunting Mephris, of course."

"Really?"

"Yes, why else?"

"Do you remember the last time you saw Fionn?"

"Yes, that terrible night of the meeting about the princess."

"Are you aware of what happened after?"

"No."

After a moment's pause, Mitchell told him about the battle at sea, his ordeal at the bottom of the ocean and his recovery in the wilderness. He observed Ruthen intently as he spoke, but Ruthen's face remained expressionless. He listened carefully and finally shook his head.

"It was a great loss. Fionn was the best of us. How much do you know about what the Priests of Mezzor are up to here in America?"

"Not much," Mitchell said.

"What about the location of the Well? Do you know anything?"

"No. Do you?"

Ruthen shook his head. "I have no knowledge of its whereabouts. However, they recently caught up with Princess Katharina."

"The princess!" exclaimed Mitchell, excited. "She still exists?"

"As far as I know."

"And the others?"

"Most were hunted down and destroyed around the time that you and Fionn were attacked. Some escaped and are in hiding, but I have not been able to find them. I was hoping to get help before attempting to rescue the princess. She is hiding in the Kungur Ice Caves. I alone can do nothing, but the two of us together might be successful."

"The Kungur Ice Caves? She has been there ever since the night when Fionn read the ancient documents that Snowdrop Windflower brought him?"

"I don't know but apparently she is there now."

"I didn't even think of going there, that was so long ago."

During a brief silence, Mitchell realized Ruthen was trying to read his mind. He pushed him out and his hand went to the hilt of his sword. Ruthen laughed. "Please excuse me, Mitchell. I merely wanted to test your strength for the battle ahead. I see your time crushed in the depths of the ocean has made you very strong."

"I am ready. There probably isn't a single vampire in existence that I cannot now destroy." He smiled menacingly.

Lord Ruthen didn't flinch. "Good."

Mitchell tried to read Lord Ruthen's mind and the two vampires struggled in silence for a full minute before Mitchell stopped. They both looked fatigued from the effort.

"Yes," Ruthen said. "Very strong indeed."

"I still cannot quite read your mind… yet. Have you told me everything you know about what the Priests of Mezzor are doing here in Portland?"

"I have. I only recently arrived here and have not had time to collect much information. All I know is that they've been searching all along this stretch of the coast. They're using criminal gangs to collect knowledge and gain control of the ports. They know something."

"With all due respect, it seems as though you have accomplished absolutely nothing over the last two hundred years. I find that surprising."

"I was in hiding," Ruthen said. "The Priests have large gangs of vampires searching all over the world for the remnants of the Niveus Gladius. I had to be cautious."

"We have to get to the princess."

"Yes, meet me outside the Belogorsky Monastery two nights from tonight. I will be there shortly after sunset. It's not far from the caves. If you arrive later and I'm not there, then you will know that I have gone ahead."

"Good." Mitchell nodded his approval of the plan. "I'll meet you there."

Ruthen nodded and vanished back into the darkness. Mitchell stood in deep contemplation for a long time, as still and silent as the surrounding gravestones; then he too vanished into the night.

"Very foolish! If it wasn't for the Sphere of Protection you would have been killed and all your work would have been wasted!"

Emily sat in her bedroom with Mercurios. The imp was beside himself with frustration while Emily was doing her best to ignore him. She was thinking of Mitchell, experiencing a deep, physical longing to see him again as soon as possible.

"Why did Mitchell say 'pretend I was just a dream?' Does he know about my dreams? And did you see Cady Sunner shooting into that crowd? I'm sure he must have killed somebody in that fight, so if the cops showed up and got him maybe he'll be put away for that. As long as he gets jailed forever, I don't care who he's charged with killing, that's all that matters." She remembered Tom and grabbed her cell. There was no answer.

"Tom, it's me, Emily," she told his voicemail. "Please call me." She hung up and looked at Mercurios. "What was that massive… thing at the warehouse that came out of that black door?"

"I think it was a Cambion demon."

"Which is what?"

"A type of lesser demon."

"There are demons like that wandering around Magella? And you want me to go there? I thought you were supposed to protect me!"

"No, it is from a different dimension – the Abyss, the realm of demons."

"But how did it get here?"

"I have been trying to figure that out. I suspect that the bridge created by the Well of Many Worlds between Earth and Magella has been left wide open for a very long time, since the first vampire came here probably. It is creating an imbalance in the universes and gates between various worlds are beginning to open and close at random, especially when beings who are not from this world—"

"But Mitchell said he was born here, that he's not from Magella," Emily interrupted.

Just the thought of him made her heart pound with nervous excitement. She had never been obsessed with anyone or anything before and it made her feel incredibly alive while at the same time filling her stomach uncomfortably with butterflies. She found it difficult to think of anything but him.

"Then, when those whose blood is not from this world gather together," continued Mercurios. "Along with your powerful magic items… it seems that it's causing random dimension doors to open to random realms. Magic is alien to this world, your learning and using it here could be contributing to the imbalance."

"What do we do?" asked Emily. She went to chew her fingernails then stopped herself.

"We continue your training and search for the Well of Many Worlds like we planned."

"But what about Cady Sunner? What if he avoided getting caught last night?"

"You should forget about him and focus on what is most important."

"How on Earth am I going to tell Bethany that her father is involved with the gangsters that murdered my father? I have to tell Detective Scannel everything, well, everything except the stuff that will make him think I'm crazy."

Emily picked up the envelope that she had taken from Sammy's desk and tore it open. It contained hundreds of pages that appeared to be lists of tens of thousands of works of art and various quantities of gold.

"Mercurios, I want you to go through this and work out what this is."

"As you wish."

"Do charm spells work on vampires?"

He looked at her in surprise and then realized what she was thinking. A mischievous grin appeared on his face. "Naughty girl!" he said and laughed as Emily threw a pillow at him.

"Come on, I'm serious! I have to do something."

"No, I'm sorry, charm spells are useless against vampires."

"Darn." Emily walked into her bathroom and stared at her reflection in the mirror. "Talia… Talia…" she murmured, reaching out and touching her reflection. "Who am I?"

As she lay awake in bed that night she wondered what Mitchell was doing at that exact moment. She wondered if he was thinking about her too. She wished he would magically appear at her window, open it and come inside her bedroom. She bit her lip and moaned in frustration, wondering how long she would have to wait until she saw him again or if indeed she ever would. She was mortified that he thought she was just a foolish, naïve little girl and had been so cold toward her just before he left. It drove her crazy that she had no idea how to find him. It all created a longing inside her that was so strong it was taking complete control of all her thoughts and emotions. She felt like she was drowning.

The next morning, she summoned Mercurios the moment her eyes opened, curious to find out what he might have discovered about the list.

"Very interesting indeed," said the imp. "I was awake all night on the computer." He held up the list. "These are all missing works of art, paintings, sculptures, as well as gold and jewelry. The magnitude of this treasure horde is massive beyond imagination."

"What do you mean?"

"They are shipping plunder worth well over a trillion dollars into America."

"A trillion? That's impossible."

"It's plunder from every major war for the last six hundred years!"

"What?"

"Over a trillion dollars worth of gold and black market works of art and antiques from all the great lootings in history. Imagine all the treasure the Nazis stole during World War Two when they looted Europe. A lot of it was recovered but hundreds of billions of dollars worth of art and gold is still missing. It's all in this list!"

"Oh my god."

"And that's just part of it. After the Nazis were defeated the Soviets looted them and over two million pieces of art still haven't been found from that horde, trillions of dollars worth of art and gold and jewelry are still missing. But not anymore! And that is just two lootings. Over the last six hundred years there have been many wars, each involving the looting of at least one country, often multiple countries. They are shipping in the greatest store of treasure the world has ever seen. There is treasure in this list from the Russian revolution, valuables that the Bolsheviks first looted from the churches, not to mention the imperial family's crowns, jewels and Faberge eggs and the Old Masters hanging in the Hermitage museum, paintings by Rembrandt, Botticelli, Cranach the Elder, Cezanne, Van Gogh, Poussin and Degas and icons from the fifteenth and sixteenth centuries. The Communists sold off Russia's cultural inheritance for pennies and much of it is here!" He waved the list in the air.

"This is incredible." Emily took the list from him and flicked through the pages as he continued.

"They also have much from the plundering of Cyprus by the Turks, and many pieces from the sacking of Italy by Napoleon, many wars, many lootings, most incredibly they have The Amber Room, an achievement so spectacular it is hailed as the eighth wonder of the world. This is the greatest treasure the world has ever seen!"

"And Commander Claw will be transporting it all to America in his submarines," said Emily. "What should we do? Should I take this to the police? But what should I tell them?" Emily sat down on the edge of her bed, staring into space. "So that's why my father's records were stolen and why they killed him!" She looked at Mercurios. "But my father would never be involved with something like this... unless he was so crushed by feelings of failure that he resorted to crime. Or maybe he found out what they were up to and was gathering evidence to take to the police and that's why they killed him."

Her mother burst into her room and Mercurios vanished.

"Mom! Can't you knock? It's called common courtesy! I thought my bedroom was the one place in this house that was mine!"

Her mother ignored her. "We have to talk. What exactly did you mean by what you said?"

"What did I say?"

"About how if your father had stood up to me, maybe things wouldn't have turned out like this? About my concern with building a future for us – for you – somehow wrecking our family?"

"Ugh, now is when you're thinking about this?" Emily sighed. "Just forget about it."

"No, I won't forget about it. I work tirelessly to provide a good home for you. How can you be so ungrateful?"

Emily felt the resentments she'd been harboring for so long well up inside her. "Because, Mom, you pushed Dad, just like you push me. You pushed him and pushed him and pushed him – and for what?"

"What are you talking about?"

"Nothing he could do was ever good enough. He ran an antique store, Mom. What did you expect from him? A mansion? A Rolls Royce? Come on."

"Emily, your father was terrible with money. I was trying to help him…"

"He tried his best, and you didn't care!" Emily shouted. Tears were now streaking her cheeks but she didn't try to wipe them away. "All that time over the years that we could have spent together as a family, all those fun, happy memories we could have created together, wasted because all you cared about was work and making money and you made him feel like a failure and drove him away and now he's dead and we can never get that time back and we'll never see him again!" Emily sobbed uncontrollably.

Emily's mother turned white with horror. "Emily," she gasped.

"You have a bunch of things – great!" Emily yelled. "A bunch of stuff! The best fridge and stove money can buy. A bigger house with one more bedroom than the last place we lived in. But what worth do they have compared to our lives? How much time have you spent at work compared to the amount of time you spend with me? I feel like I barely know you. Or that you spent with Dad? He loved us! I mean, you go on and on about 'being successful.' What does that even mean to you? A list of stuff that you bought? I'll tell you, for me, it's love and friendship and fun and family and creating great memories with the people you love and now he's dead."

Her mother pounded on the doorframe with her fist. "When my father died, he left my mother and sisters and me with nothing. Nothing!" she shouted. "Can you understand that? You have no idea what that's like! I was never going to let that happen to you!"

Emily calmed herself and sniffled as she tried to wipe away her tears. "But you had each other, didn't you? And things turned out all right, didn't they?"

"Yes, but you have no idea how hard it was growing up like that."

"Tell me about Grandma. What was she like? Were you close with her? Or was she a stranger to you?"

Her mother sighed and lowered herself into the chair at Emily's desk.

"No, Emily, she wasn't a stranger to us. We spent a lot of time together."

"Well, tell me about her then. You never talk about her. We never talk about anything real. All we ever talk about are my stupid grades and what you think my future career should be."

Her mother sighed, rubbing her forehead. "My mother got odd jobs here and there. Every month, it was the same thing. We were always broke, but somehow we would make it through. Just barely. It was because of her that we survived. She was a funny lady, loved to tell stories. She was always making up fairy tales to keep us entertained, because we couldn't afford anything else. No TV, no trips to the movies… or anywhere else for that matter. But her stories were better than any TV show." She smiled as she remembered. "As I grew up, I worked really hard at school and had two part-time jobs. I didn't do anything but work. I'm sure that doesn't surprise you. My mother would laugh – she was so proud of me – but she also always told me that a woman only has a limited time to find a good man and have children and once that time is gone, it's gone forever.

"She thought I should find more balance, raise a big family and enjoy life. She told me that having children was the most amazing and fulfilling experience imaginable and so special because it's only for women. But I never listened to her. I resented both my parents. You have to understand, we were always looked down at and bullied by the other kids because we were so poor… it was humiliating."

Her mom took a deep breath and stared at Emily, as if mustering the courage she needed to continue.

"So I never had any children of my own."

Emily was shocked. She had assumed her mother never meant to tell her.

Her mother shrugged and smiled sadly.

"I guess it's time I told you. You're old enough to know. You were adopted. Your father desperately wanted children, but I didn't want to take the time off work, so we adopted you. I want you to know that having you has been wonderful, and I regret not having given you some brothers and sisters.

"Spending all my time on my career and not having children is the biggest regret of my life. I thought I had to choose between a career and having a big family, which is silly, and I chose the career. Big mistake. I chose a life of toil and you're right, all that time I sacrificed on work and for what? I could have been spending it with friends and family, having fun and creating beautiful memories, like you say, instead I spent it working and what has it given me? As you say, a house with extra bedrooms, but no children to use them, and some nice appliances for my kitchen and an expensive car. Empty bedrooms are the saddest things. They're each a missing child that you could have shared your life with and all the joy they would have brought."

Tears started in her eyes. "It doesn't mean anything and I sure won't be able to take any of it with me when I die."

Emily, wanting to console her, moved to her side, sitting on the armrest of the chair and holding her hand, then leaning over and hugging her.

"Please don't think I don't appreciate everything you've given me, but really, I'd rather have a mother who I actually have a relationship with. Why don't we spend some time together and get to know each other and talk about something other than school?"

Emily's mother chuckled and wiped away the tears.

"You're absolutely right. That would be wonderful. It's just been so hard for me to face the fact that I made the wrong choice in life, so I buried myself in my work instead of simply changing course."

Emily noticed the clock. She stood up and kissed her mother on the cheek. "Well, let's arrange to spend some more time together. Right now, though, I actually do have to get to school."

"So, you mean you're okay with it?"

"With what?"

"Finding out you were adopted? I really had no idea how you would react. I've been nervous about this moment for years."

Emily smiled. "You and Dad will always be my parents."

On her way to school she couldn't stop thinking about Mitchell. She wanted to tell him about the treasure before going to the police. She still hadn't heard from Tom and was feeling deeply guilty and worried. She couldn't find him at lunchtime either.

She told herself he was probably just recovering from the shock of all that had happened.

At lunch Emily was quiet, not sure what to say to any of her friends, especially to Bethany, who she assumed knew nothing of her father's activities. Thankfully, Chanel's surprise performance was still all anyone was talking about and, not surprisingly, Chanel was also not at school. Apparently, she had sat in the Main Office for some time, wearing nothing but Mr. North's jacket, until her father came to pick her up. There were conflicting rumors about the cause of her bizarre behavior, and speculation ran rampant, but most people assumed she must have been drunk or on some kind of drugs.

"Has anyone seen Tom?" Emily asked the group.

"No," Bethany said. "And I haven't been able to get in touch with him."

"Oh yeah?" Emily felt a twinge of jealousy at the thought of Bethany and Tom talking to each other.

"Yeah," said Bethany. "Why? Haven't you been in touch with him? I thought you two were a thing." She smiled sweetly and Emily wondered if she was gloating, or was she just being paranoid?

"No, uh, I mean, we're friends, but, yeah, not sure where he is. Listen, I was with him last night, we went to this warehouse where a friend of my father's works who I think was involved in his murder. He was there with some gangsters."

"Oh my god, I saw it on the news," Bethany exclaimed. "There was a huge explosion and fire at a warehouse in some kind of gang warfare."

"You were there?" exclaimed Cindy.

"Yeah." Emily looked at Bethany. "Your father was there too."

"What?" Bethany burst out laughing.

"I'm not joking, Beth, your father is mixed up with some really dangerous people."

"Shut your mouth," Bethany snapped. "Don't blame me if Tom likes me more than you. It's really pathetic that you'd stoop so low to go after my family. I thought you were better than that." She stormed off, leaving her lunch unfinished.

"Bethany!" Emily shouted after her, but she was gone.

"What the hell is going on, Emily?" demanded Cindy just as the bell rang.

"I swear Mr. Denman was at that warehouse!" Emily glanced at the time. "I gotta go to class. We'll talk later."

Walking into biology, Emily was surprised to see Tom at his desk as usual. She approached him slowly.

"Hey, what's up? I was trying to get in touch with you."

He looked up at her and shrugged. "Yeah, I meant to call but I was busy with some stuff." He gave her an easy smile, but when Emily looked into his eyes she saw that his pupils were so dilated they had completely consumed his blue irises. She stepped back in shock, stumbling on a classmate's backpack.

"Sorry," she said, still staring at Tom's eyes.

Tom reached down and unzipped his gym bag, taking out his Halloween costume, the Crimson Ghost. He placed the mask up to his face.

"I... I," she stammered, "Just wanted to make sure you were all right."

"Never better."

"What's up with your eyes?"

"Class, please take your seats." The teacher, Mrs. Toth, bustled into the classroom.

"Why are you putting on your Halloween costume?" Emily whispered.

"Why don't we get together tonight and pay Mr. Sunner a visit? I'll knock him out and we can tie him up and torture him to death. I bet that would turn you on..."

"Mr. Price, Ms. Bliss – please continue your conversation after class."

"Excuse me?" Emily asked in shock, ignoring Mrs. Toth's instruction.

"Okay, you two, enough socializing!" The teacher raised her voice.

"Hey!" Tom shouted back angrily. "I'm talking to my girl!"

"What the hell?" Emily stumbled backward, nearly tripping over more bags on the floor. Their classmates laughed, as Tom turned his attention back to Emily.

"Tom!" Mrs. Toth slammed her books down on her desk. "How dare you! Get out of my class!" She pointed at the door.

Tom spun around in his seat, completely transformed by rage. It appeared to everyone in the room that he had lost his mind. He stood and roared at Mrs. Toth. "How dare you even speak to me, you bloated imbecile! You, you, you stupid idiot!"

He screamed in pain and grabbed his left hand and struggled with it, as though it were about to attack him. Every eye in the classroom was on him as he struggled to master himself. Pulling on his costume, he strode toward Mrs. Toth. A boy with thick glasses caught Tom's eye as he passed and Tom spun around.

"What are you looking at, nerdlinger?" he bellowed.

Before the student could react, Tom slapped him across the face so hard he sent the boy flying out of his chair and into a wall. The force of the impact smashed in a section of the dry wall and the boy fell unconscious. Students started to scream and run for the door. Mrs. Toth tried to join the rush to get out but with one powerful leap, Tom cleared the twenty feet that separated them and grabbed her by the throat with one hand. Everyone froze and watched in horror.

"I am the Crimson Ghost!" he screamed in her face, tightening his grip and lifting her off the ground as she kicked and struggled helplessly for breath.

"Tom, stop!" Emily cried.

Tom's eyes changed into glowing green orbs and two beams of eerie green light shot from them into Mrs. Toth's. Her face went blank, her body limp. After a moment, Tom cast her on the floor like a bag of trash. Mrs. Toth came out of her trance a few seconds later and looked blankly around the room, as though she had no idea where she was. She began writhing around on the ground, clawing at the air, babbling incoherently as green rot appeared on her neck, eating away the flesh where Tom's fingers had been.

Tom burst out laughing, then turned to the classroom door and walked out. "I'll call you later, Emily," he said, without looking back.

Emily snapped out of her shocked trance. "Tom!" she shouted, running after him. The other kids crowded around their fallen teacher, pulling out their cell phones to dial 911.

Mercurios appeared on Emily's shoulder. "No, Emily, you mustn't! Very dangerous indeed!" he whispered. "Stay where you are."

"He's my friend."

"He's not your friend anymore. I don't think he's even human now."

Mercurios disappeared, just as she caught up with Tom in the hallway.

"Tom, wait!"

He turned to look at her. "You know, Emily, you're the only one in this whole place I've got any respect for. I'll pick you up later and we'll go after Cady. I know that skinning him alive is guaranteed to get you all hot and bothered. Oh, and by the way, if I ever see you talking to that guy again, I'll kill you both."

"What?"

"You heard me. I saw you with him, the guy from the club and the warehouse. I went to your place after and I saw you two talking in your backyard last night. You're never seeing him again. You're mine now."

Twenty

Before Emily could reply, a student named Spencer Scott walked by them, fiddling nervously with his cell phone.

"Hey, Emily."

He clumsily dropped the phone on the floor. As he bent down to pick it up, Tom stepped on it, grinding it to powder with his heel.

"Hey!" Spencer protested. "That's my phone!" He straightened up and faced Tom.

"Hey, nerdlinger." Tom smiled maliciously. "If you ever even look at my girl again, I'll be crushing your skull, not just your phone."

"Dude," Spencer muttered, holding his hands up in surrender.

Tom grabbed him, spun him around and picked him up by the back of his boxer shorts.

"AAAARRRRRGGGHH!" screamed Spencer. "Stop!"

"Tom, what are you doing?" shouted Emily, grabbing his arm.

"Giving this nerdlinger a wedgie," laughed Tom.

"Stop it!"

"Yeah," laughed Tom. "I guess so, for now." He hurled the kid across the hallway, skidding him along the polished floor.

Emily knew Tom was strong, but this was something else entirely. Spencer smashed through a classroom door, splintering the wood. She heard people inside the classroom crying out in alarm as they surrounded Spencer's prone body and yelled for someone to call an ambulance.

"Stop it right now!" Emily shouted.

He turned to her. "If you know what's good for you, you'll stop talking to all these losers. I wouldn't want to have to take you out on a hike and throw you off a cliff or something." He chuckled, striding toward the school exit as though nothing had happened.

Emily stood frozen to the spot, not knowing what to say or do. Obviously, something had happened to him at the warehouse when he was attacked by that demon. What had Mercurios said? That he wasn't even human anymore? She followed him outside. In front of the school, a student in a wheelchair was just about to go down the ramp. As Tom walked by he grabbed the back of the boy's chair and pointed it toward the stairs.

"Hey, Crazylegs, why don't you take the stairs?" He laughed and shoved the wheelchair straight down the cement steps. The kid screeched and Tom burst out laughing as he watched him tumbling out of his wheelchair and crashing to the ground.

An elderly woman witnessed the attack and ran up to the fallen boy, crouching to help.

"Oh, my goodness!" She looked up at Tom in revulsion. "You animal!"

"Tom, you need to stop!" Emily cried before rushing down the stairs to help the shocked, bruised kid back into his wheelchair. Once the kid was settled the old lady stormed up to Tom and pummeled at his chest with arthritic hands.

"You terrible, terrible man! To hurt that poor boy!"

Tom laughed in her face. "You think that's pain? I'll show you pain!" He grabbed her brittle arm and began slapping her face again and again, yelling at the top of his lungs in a crazed, sadistic fury. "Yeah! Yeah! Granny gets it good!"

The old lady's screams alerted passing kids who ran for help. Emily knew what she had to do. As she took out her wand Mercurios appeared on her shoulder. "No, no, you mustn't reveal yourself! You're not powerful enough yet. If you kill him, they will know you have magic and take you away and conduct experiments on you. Better to run away and call the police."

Emily hesitated, then put away her wand, and quickly pulled out her cell phone, dialing 911.

"You're right, I couldn't kill him anyways. What's happened to him?"

"Demonic possession."

Tom stopped slapping the old lady and grabbed her wrist tightly. "You've got a rotten personality, old lady," he chuckled. The old woman cried out as a sickly green glow emanated from her flesh where Tom was holding her. He threw her violently on the ground and smiled at Emily.

"Tonight's gonna be fun."

With that, he turned and walked away. Emily's attention snapped back to the old lady as she let out an agonized wail. She was holding up the wrist that Tom had grabbed. It was still glowing green. The flesh rotting like a corpse.

"Tom!" Emily shouted. "We have to get her to a hospital!"

"Whoa, whoa, whoa," he said, turning back. "You're going waaaaay too fast in this relationship, babe! Since when did your problems become my problems?" He laughed and walked away. "Pick you up at eight, Princess."

All the calls from other students' cell phones had finally produced an ambulance, which came careening into the school parking lot, followed a moment later by a police car. The paramedics attended to the old woman while police talked to various witnesses of the assaults. Not wanting to be interviewed, having no idea how she would explain what she knew, Emily hurried home. The moment she got into her bedroom, she slammed the door.

"Mercurios!" she whispered frantically.

The imp appeared. "At your service, my lady."

"What's going on? He's possessed?"

Mercurios thought for a moment. "Did you notice the glow

coming from Tom's chest after Mitchell killed the demon at the warehouse?"

"Yes?"

"I am almost certain it was caused by a Cambion stone, a most unpleasant weapon indeed. Those demons take small amounts of molten rock from a volcano that stands at the center of their world and, using dark magic, they turn it into a magical weapon. Oh yes, a nasty weapon indeed."

"What did it do to Tom?"

"If they manage to pierce a human's heart with it, the Cambion stone has the power to transform the person and dominate his mind. It is a demonic possession from within the stone. This possession can also give them… demonic abilities and powers. Yes, Emily, dark powers indeed."

"Is that what's going to happen to me?" Her eyes were wide with horror.

"Oh no, that's just Tom's Id being magnified by the evil magic of the stone until it takes control of his mind. But you are going to be fully possessed by a demon. Far more powerful."

"Oh great! Well how do we get it out of him?"

"Taking out the stone now would surely kill him. Like you he needs an exorcism. We would have to find the Well and go to Magella."

For hours Emily wracked her brain, trying to figure out how they could locate either the Well or Mitchell or both. As she climbed into bed, she felt as though her heart was being torn out. She lay there, exhausted but unable to sleep, late into the night. Her mind and emotions were in turmoil. A light tapping on her bedroom window made her heart miss a beat. She sat bolt upright. In the quiet of the night, it sounded disturbingly loud and eerie. What if it was Cady Sunner? Or Tom? This was the kind of thing that happened in horror movies. What if it was the corpse of her father again reanimated as an undead ghoul? A shiver went down her spine. The curtains were closed, and she couldn't see who, or what, was outside her window.

She picked up her wand and held it at the ready as she crept toward the window.

"Mercurios," she whispered.

"Yes," the imp appeared on her dresser.

"Did you hear that?"

"Yes."

"Okay go invisible and get ready."

The imp disappeared as the knock came again, softly.

It's probably just a branch in the wind, Emily thought. With one swift movement she hurled the curtains aside. There was no one there. She leaned forward a little. A face appeared out of the darkness and she jumped back, letting out a shriek before slapping her hand over her mouth. Looking back at her through the window was the face she had been dreaming and obsessing about. Her heart exploded with excitement and she threw her window wide open.

"It's you! Am I dreaming?"

"I thought it might be too late for the front door. May I come in?" Mitchell gave her an irresistibly charming smile.

"Of course!"

Emily beamed as he came all the way inside her room and shut the window behind him.

"How did you get up to my—" She stopped short. Of course, climbing straight up the side of a house was probably nothing for him.

"There are advantages to being undead," he said. He looked at her for a moment then looked at her wand. Emily glanced at it and put it down on her desk. "I didn't know who it was."

"So that's a real wand?"

"Yes."

"Fascinating."

Just the sight of him in her bedroom made Emily's entire body feel hot. Her mouth opened slightly and her throat felt tight as she drew in a deep breath. Her stomach whirled with butterflies. She was so excited and nervous and at the same time a little afraid. She found him incredibly intimidating. But deep down inside a part of her was certain that he would never harm her; that he wanted to protect her and take care of her. She blushed and glanced down and noticed her clothes were strewn all about the room.

"Ummmm, oh…" She began awkwardly grabbing piles of clothing from the floor. "Sorry about the mess. It's not usually like this…"

"Don't change your habits on my account," he gave her a cocky, sexy smirk.

Now she was even more embarrassed and excited. She ran to her closet with her armload of dirty clothes, flung everything inside and shut the door before they could come tumbling back out. She then spun around breathlessly.

"Please… sit down."

She pulled up her most comfortable chair and grabbed his hand for a split second to guide him into it. To her surprise, his hand wasn't all that cold; not as warm as a human's, but close. Her heart pounded with exhilaration that he was actually sitting in her bedroom.

"Can I get you anything to eat or drink?" She paused. "Oh wait… vampires drink blood. Never mind."

Mitchell crossed his legs and donned a "guilty as charged" smile.

"So…" Emily sat on the edge of her bed. "Do you raid blood banks?"

"Don't worry, I've already fed tonight," he said matter-of-factly.

A shiver ran through her. She realized that in her infatuation, she had failed to take into account the fact that he murdered people for meals. "So… you raided a blood bank?"

"Occasionally I raid blood banks or hunt animals when I am starving and desperate, but that only keeps me barely alive, usually I feed on living humans. Emily, you must understand, I only hunt people who repeatedly commit horrendous crimes and are totally unrepentant; murderers, rapists, psychopaths—"

"But how do you know they're guilty? How can you just go around judging and condemning and then killing people?"

"I read minds. I hunt for psychos. I find them. I feed on them. It's that simple."

"Wait, what?" Emily craned her neck forward. Do you mean to tell me that you've been reading my mind this whole time?" She was utterly mortified. "Oh no," she moaned. "Oh no, I can't believe this…"

She slapped her hand on her forehead. "The other night, in my mother's garden… the things I was thinking… Oh, no," she whispered, remembering the less-than-pure thoughts about Mitchell that had raced through her mind that night. He had probably seen all the fantasies she'd had about him. Could he see what she had just been thinking? She groaned as these thoughts pounded into her, dropping her head into her hands, burning with embarrassment.

"Emily, listen to me," he said patiently.

But she was in no mood to calm down. "Do you have any idea how humiliating this is? Is this some kind of joke to you?"

"What? No, of course not," he said, covering a smile with his hand. "I have never read your mind, Emily." His eyes were calm and clear. This caught her off guard.

"Huh? You haven't?"

"No. I respect your privacy and would never intrude upon it unless it was for something important. When I met you in the woods, I felt you were different somehow. It was important to me that I gain a clear understanding of what was going on. I tried to read your mind, but it was very hard. I tried to push deep into your thoughts and memories but to my amazement, you noticed and you resisted, so I stopped. I didn't want to hurt you."

"In the forest?" asked Emily, recalling the night. "Oh wow, I do remember feeling a little light headed for a minute, but I didn't know why."

"Other mortals don't notice when I read their minds. It must either be because you are from Magella, or perhaps it has something to do with your parents being wizards or your study of magic."

So many questions burned in her mind. She wanted to ask him everything but was too nervous to think straight.

"Is it getting hot in here?" she murmured, getting up to crack open the window.

When she turned back their eyes locked. He stared at her intently and she had the feeling she was floating into a tranquil, emerald heaven. She could feel her breathing slowing and her heart rate returning to normal. After a moment, she felt like herself again.

"Did you just hypnotize me?"

"Only a little bit," he said. "My eyes naturally have that effect, but if I concentrate, I can make the effect much more powerful."

"Oh." She thought about other effects he might have on her and blushed. She found it very arousing and unsettling that he could gain such power over her so easily and even more unsettling that she liked and desired it. Like every other time she looked into his eyes a part of her wanted to open her mind to him completely and let him come all the way inside her and totally possess her, mind, body and soul.

"I have so many questions I want to ask you," she said. "I have no idea where to begin. Why are you here?"

"Actually, I've come to see the documents that you took from the warehouse."

"Oh." Emily's heart dropped at the realization he hadn't come to see her, then she felt ashamed. At the same time she was excited by what she and Mercurios had discovered.

"Oh my gosh, this is incredible." She picked the pile of documents up off her desk and handed Mitchell the list. She told him everything that Mercurios had told her. Mitchell's eyes grew wide with wonder as he scanned the pages.

"So that's it!" he whispered. "My god. That has been Baelaar and the Priests of Mezzor's master plan from the beginning!" He stood up and paced back and forth.

"What?"

"Of course," he continued, ignoring her. "They not only act as shadow governments to instigate wars and mass slaughters as blood sacrifices, but they are the ones in control of the looting of the conquered countries! They have instigated wars for six hundred years so they could loot the world's treasures. They took everything they could and stashed it, knowing that with the passage of time the value would increase vastly. They were waiting, waiting for some predetermined time or event. And now, they are finally making their move, they are going to liquidate the whole of it, over a trillion dollars of looted treasure. And what are they going to use all that money for? Perhaps to instigate the greatest slaughter, the greatest blood sacrifice, in history?" Mitchell stopped pacing and looked at Emily. "And they're going to start here in America."

Twenty-One

"Does it have the date the treasure is supposed to be shipped into Portland?" Mitchell asked.

"I couldn't find any shipping timetable in these documents."

"No matter."

"What do you mean 'no matter?' We have to stop them!"

"Not my concern."

"What? Why?" Emily stared at him. "This is the most important thing ever and you don't care?"

"I have more important things to deal with."

"More important? What could possibly be more important than this?"

"I must find the Well of Many Worlds."

"But why do you want the Well so badly?"

"That's my business."

"Who are these Priests of Mezzor?"

"A satanic death cult of vampires."

"I can't believe that Bethany's father is mixed up with them."

"Who?"

"Mr. Denman, the guy who owns a shipping company and is going to arrange for two of his ships to crash to distract the coast guard so Commander Claw can bring the treasure in in his submarines. He's the father of one of my friends."

"That's unfortunate."

"Does Vadas Asger mean anything to you?"

Mitchell looked shocked. "Where did you hear that?"

"It was carved into an antique desk my father left me, why?"

"I heard those words many years ago, we thought it was a place in Russia where the Well was hidden, but I could never find anywhere with that name. And now the princess is in the Kungur Ice Caves… it must have something to do with Russia but I have no idea what."

"We are pretty sure Cady Sunner is after the desk because of that. We think 'Vadas Asger' is a place or code or person that will lead to the Well. So I hid it so they wouldn't find out. Who is this princess?" Emily felt a twinge of jealousy.

"It's crucial that I find out what it means and find the Well. I must go to Russia."

"Well, I'm going to courier this list to the police with an anonymous note saying where it was found and what their plan is."

"Good for you."

"Then I'm going to help you find the Well. I need to find it too. I… uh need the Well to save my friend Tom. Since we're looking for the same thing, I think it would make sense to team up and work together. We should probably stay close together until we find it."

She told him what Mercurios had said about Tom, but said nothing about the fact that she was possessed by a demon, not knowing how Mitchell would react to that.

"Don't be a fool," he growled waving his hand dismissively. "It is far too great a risk. I promise to tell you when I have found it and you are welcome to use it when I am done with it."

His tone made Emily feel like a silly little girl but she stood her ground, determined not to lose him again. "The risk is irrelevant, because I'll be looking for the Well with the help of Mercurios and the spell book. I'm going after it with or without you, so it might as well be with. Right? With magic we may be able to help you find it faster."

"Hmmmm, I have a lot of questions I would like to ask this imp of yours about the Well of Many Worlds."

"Unless you agree to take me with you I will command him not to answer any of your questions."

He stared at her long and hard. "Okay fine," he sighed.

"Amazing!" She couldn't hide her excitement. "What now?"

"What now is; I should give you some background information."

Mitchell explained everything that had happened in Paris with Sylvain and the French Revolution, followed by the events that took place after his return from the depths of the ocean, including what Lord Ruthen had told him in the cemetery. Emily just sat there staring at him, mouth open wide in awe.

"So you see, I must go to Russia to try to find the princess, she and the words 'Vadas Asger' are the only leads I have to find the Well. If you insist on coming I suggest you bring clothes for very cold weather."

Emily felt another rush of jealousy as she tried to imagine this princess and wondered if she were beautiful, then immediately hated herself for it.

"But how are we going to get there?"

"In my jet."

"Your jet?"

"Yes."

"Whoa. What do you do for a living? Oh, wait, yeah, I guess you don't really need a job if you are immortal and have superhuman powers."

"No." Mitchell chuckled. "Over the ages I have accumulated more wealth than I could have dreamed of. Prepare for the trip," he ordered, taking out his cell phone. "James, we need to be ready to leave immediately. Very good." He hung up his phone and looked at Emily. "Now I would very much like to meet this imp of whom you speak." He glanced around her room.

"Mercurios," said Emily. Nothing happened. "He really doesn't want to reveal himself to anyone else," she explained with embarrassment, wondering what might happen if Mercurios refused to appear and Mitchell thought she was just imagining him. "Mercurios, I'm going to Russia. It would be a lot safer for both of us if you came along. Hello?"

Mercurios appeared on her dresser.

"Ah, there you are. Don't answer any of his questions until we are on the plane and if he tries to read your mind, disappear." She turned to face Mitchell. "Mitchell, I'd like you to meet Mercurios. Mercurios, I'd like you to meet Mitchell."

"So very pleased to meet you," Mitchell said after a moment, obviously surprised.

"He's cute, isn't he?" Emily laughed.

"Adorable," Mitchell mumbled.

"Ahem," Mercurios interjected, not appreciating being talked about like he wasn't there. "I suppose I should thank you, Mitchell. You've done an excellent job helping to protect Emily. Yes, an excellent job indeed."

Mitchell stepped forward and stared more closely at Mercurios. "How fascinating," he said. "Well, after four hundred years, I thought I had seen pretty much everything there was to see… but this…"

As Mitchell continued to stare at Mercurios, Emily shoved some things into a backpack, including her warmest parka, readying herself for the chill of northern Russia. She then wrote a note telling her mother she was going to have a sleepover at Cindy's and texted Cindy, asking her to cover for her. When she was ready Mitchell told her to climb on his back and they went out of her window, into the tree. She could feel the muscles of his shoulders and back moving beneath her as he descended nimbly through the branches as if she were no weight at all. She clung to him tighter than was strictly necessary. They then ran to the street where Mitchell had a new cherry-red Lamborghini parked.

"Whoa, is this your car?" Emily's eyes widened.

"One of them."

"Wow." She climbed into the passenger seat. She had never been in a car this expensive and was soaking it all in. "I could get used to this," she murmured.

Roaring into the airport, they turned into the private jet section and drove straight out onto the tarmac, parking beside the steps to the plane.

"Mr. Keats," the pilot greeted them. "Everything is ready."

"Good. This is Emily Bliss, she'll be joining us. Emily, this is my pilot, James."

Emily shook his hand. "Pleased to meet you."

The plane was massive for a private jet and no luxury had been spared. The seats were buttery soft beige leather and the carpet was thick wool. There was a bar, a kitchen, a movie screen and a huge bathroom equipped with a hot tub.

"Wow," Emily said, looking about her. "Nice jet! This is nicer than most people's houses! By the way, where do you live?"

"I have a number of places but I would call my estate in England my home."

Emily turned to Mercurios, who had appeared when the pilot shut the door of the cockpit. "Um, would you mind giving us some alone time?"

"If you insist, I'll wait in the—"

"Closet," Emily said, giving him the evil eye, "I insist."

Mercurios took the hint and disappeared.

Oh, crap," Emily exclaimed slapping her forehead. "I totally forgot my passport!"

"Don't worry." Mitchell smiled. "I will take care of that."

"Oh, okay. Oh, crap!" Emily exclaimed again as another thought struck her. "I forgot to send the list of treasure and a note to the police."

"It will have to wait."

"Okay. Look, I promise Mercurios will answer all your questions," Emily said as she and Mitchell buckled their seat belts for takeoff. "But I want to talk with you first." As the jet taxied out to the runway

Emily stared at Mitchell, her heart pounding hard. "I have so many questions to ask."

Mitchell uncrossed his legs and reclined his chair. "Ask away."

"Who are you? I mean, I know what you've told me but what happened before? How did you become… what you are?"

As the plane lifted sharply into the sky Mitchell took a deep breath and stared at the ceiling as if his memories were hanging there, waiting to be plucked. "The sixteenth century, when I was human, was a time of amazing change. It was the beginning of the modern era. The New World had been discovered. The Renaissance in Italy was peaking and spreading north. The printing press had created a revolution. Some of the greatest minds in history were achieving their most masterful triumphs: Copernicus, Galileo, Shakespeare, Sir Frances Bacon, Christopher Marlowe, Michelangelo, Leonardo da Vinci… Like I said… an amazing time."

Emily listened enraptured as Mitchell spoke, however he described his life before his transformation into a vampire only in vague brush strokes. She wanted more details and had so many questions but she didn't want to interrupt him. He told her that when he was a little older than she was now he had been turned into a vampire. He explained that shortly after his transformation he had met Fionn, the leader of a group of vampires called the Niveus Gladius and had been trained by him as a warrior but had rejected the offer to join them. He did not explain why. He told her that he had then spent ages hunting for the Well of Many worlds but again refused to explain why. That brought them up to what he had already told her about Sylvain and the French Revolution.

"Did you ever see that vampire Sylvain again?" she asked. "Or Fionn?"

"No, Fionn was destroyed. I have no idea what became of Sylvain. Now I would be very interested in asking Mercurios some questions if I may, you did promise."

Emily was less than satisfied with what Mitchell had told her and still had a million questions, but she relented. "Um okay sure, Mercurios come here."

The imp stepped out of the closet. "Yes?"

Mitchell wanted to learn all that he could about Magella and the Well of Many Worlds. Emily watched and listened as he grilled the imp for information on how to use the Well and what other dimensions he knew existed, particularly the nine planes of Hell and the Abyss. The imp explained that as far as he knew those dimensions, along with many others, did indeed exist and could potentially be accessed using the Well, but he had no idea how to operate it. Mitchell stood up and paced for a long while, deep in thought. Emily didn't interrupt him. As usual she found him deeply intimidating. Although he was inhumanly gorgeous, he was also a beast, both powerful and deadly. She didn't want to annoy him. They made a couple of stops to refuel and change pilots and eventually arrived in Perm, Russia.

When the customs official boarded the plane Mitchell hypnotized her with his eyes and she did not ask to see any passports. Emily felt another surge of jealousy at how attracted the customs official obviously was to him. She didn't like the thought that any woman in the world would probably fall on her knees at the sight of him. A stretch SUV limousine was waiting for them on the tarmac and carried them to the Belogorsky Monastery.

The ancient monastery was a magnificent building, its golden domes frosted in snow, making it look like a giant magical gingerbread house covered in confectioner's sugar. The same snow was hard and crunchy underfoot as Mitchell searched the area for Lord Ruthen. More snowflakes began to fall and Emily felt them wet on her face and lips. She stuck out her tongue to catch them.

"Look!" Mitchell pointed at some footprints. "They're leading toward the Kungur Ice Caves. He must have already gone on. Unless this is a trap. Either way, I feel we should leave for the caves immediately."

Climbing back into the limousine they set off on the hundred-mile trip. As they drove, Mitchell talked. "In answer to your earlier question, vampires are, in a sense, inorganic beings. Rather, we are not governed by the same rules that organic beings are. The inorganic blood of a vampire enters a mortal like a conquering army, eliminating all that is organic life. It feels like being burned alive from the inside out. The mortal, physical body dies, and only the vampire body remains, yet we maintain our individual characters, minds, and spirits."

It had been hard enough for Emily to wrap her mind around the revelation that he was more than four hundred years old. Understanding that he was immortal was more than she could fully comprehend. Then again, she still hadn't entirely digested the news that she was from another world either.

"We are beyond death," Mitchell continued. "In that our blood is inorganic and enables our cells to regenerate perfectly forever. The vampire's genetic coding replaces the human genetic coding, and that new DNA sends out commands to the tissue of the body to continually regenerate as that of a young adult in prime physical health. Regardless of the person's age at the time they are turned, they will always appear as if in their prime, unless they go without blood for too long, in which case they will soon look like a withered corpse."

"Why?"

"In the DNA of all mortal beings, there is essentially a self-destruct mechanism, commonly known as aging. We don't have that – I suspect, for hunting prowess, yet, we aren't really alive either. We are not alive, we are not dead, we are undead, but why?" He shook his head. "Who knows? We carry on existing, balancing between two worlds. Perhaps that is why we have supernatural powers over the base elements of this world. Being an eternally regenerating undead being has obvious benefits. Any injury quickly heals, any poison or illness we are immune to. We also have superhuman strength and hypnotic eyes to seduce our prey."

"I've… um… noticed," Emily felt her blood burn hot in her cheeks. Mitchell chuckled.

"The pale skin and the fangs are obviously common to all vampires."

Emily blushed as she thought of what this would mean when Mitchell was ever with a woman. Would his heightened awareness and ability to read someone's mind make him an incredible lover? She bit her lip as a burst of excitement exploded deep inside her. Not being able to stop thinking about him in this way was driving her insane. Once again she lowered her guard, opened herself up to her desires and fantasized about the delicious pleasure of abandoning herself to him.

As they approached the mouth of the cave the sky had cleared and the stars above shone with an incandescent clarity in the wintry northern night. Their light glinted off the freshly fallen snow that crunched beneath their feet. A light breeze creaked in the pines above. Emily felt the vastness of the nighttime wilderness surrounding them. It was both beautiful and spooky. Looking at the gaping black maw of the cave opening up in front of her, she was overwhelmed by a rush of dread and exhilaration at the thought of venturing inside and following its winding veins deep into the heart of a mystery.

Mitchell scanned the area. "Strange – I cannot sense the presence of any other vampires."

Emily held up her Sphere of Protection, muttered a magical incantation, and gestured with her other hand. A silvery-blue light spread across the area around them. Mitchell looked at her in wonder.

"An illumination spell." She grinned. "I know you don't need it, but I do. Mercurios told me a trick that all wizards in Magella use. They cast it on a portable object, like the sphere, so they can carry it with them. It'll last for hours. And if I ever need to turn it off, I just pop it in my pocket."

"Brilliant," said Mitchell.

"Yes, very good indeed," said the imp, clapping his hands.

Emily smiled proudly, relishing Mitchell's approval. Drawing out her wand, she prepared to enter the caves. She was making her first steps toward becoming a wizard, and there was nothing in this world, she reasoned, that could be more shocking to her than that.

"We could potentially spend weeks in here," Mitchell warned as they slid inside. "It's an enormous labyrinth."

A long tunnel led to the first big grotto. It was about two hundred feet in diameter and over sixty feet high but Emily's spell illuminated every inch of it, causing beautiful crystals to sparkle on the walls. Long stalactites of ice hung from the ceiling like frozen spears, and stalagmites grew over six feet high from the floor like strange translucent mushrooms.

They continued onward through this frozen world, entranced by its otherworldly beauty. In one grotto, they found hundreds of crystallized snowflakes the size of their hands covering the floor. In another they found a frozen lake as big as a football field. But they saw no sign of the princess or any other vampire. They were about to travel deeper into the labyrinth, when they heard a sound. At first, it was so quiet that Emily wasn't sure if she had heard it or just sensed a presence, but Mitchell spun around and she then saw a dark shape standing in the opening of the passage.

Mitchell drew his sword, while Emily pointed her wand at the shape. She couldn't see the face of the person silently gazing at them because it was shrouded by a heavy cloak with the hood pulled low.

"Who are you?" Mitchell demanded.

"I owe you deep apology. I ask for forgiveness," said a low, calm voice, thick with a Russian accent. The figure stepped forward and pushed back his hood.

"You!"

Twenty-Two

Ivan, the other vampire, who, along with Mephris and the Comtesse LeDuijou, had hurled Mitchell into the depths of that terrible whirlpool so many years earlier, stood before them. Mitchell leaped forward, his sword bursting into flames as he raised it to swing at Ivan's neck. As he landed, he froze. Ivan watched him, unmoving, hands hanging by his sides, unarmed. Mitchell checked his swing curious as to why he was not defending himself.

"Who is he, Mitchell?" Emily asked.

"Why are you here?" Mitchell snarled, ignoring her. "Defend yourself!"

Ivan's voice remained cool and controlled. "This right, it is yours – to destroy me. However, I would like an opportunity to explain myself."

Mitchell slowly lowered his sword and sheathed it. "What is it?"

"Will we sit?" Ivan gestured to two large rocks on the cave floor.

Mitchell nodded curtly and took a seat on one of them, while Emily and Mercurios hovered nervously in the background. Mitchell tried to read Ivan's mind, but Ivan was nearly his match in age and strength, and he couldn't grasp his thoughts.

"I was born in Perm, in 1579," Ivan began, "and joined the military at a young age. When I was twenty-two, a vampire made me. I remember a dream, like suffering a fever, then the agonizing pain of awakening. I existed for two hundred years alone, stalking blood, filled with hunger. Then Baelaar and others found me in Moscow. Baelaar told me that by joining the Priests, I would serve a greater good for mankind. I was grateful. You know the power an older vampire can have over a young one."

Mitchell nodded and Ivan continued, "My job from the beginning was to seek the Well of Many Worlds. Baelaar wanted it. We learned that the princess had information that might lead to the Well, that she was leaving Paris for Russia, so we sent spies to watch her. That is why we hunted you and Fionn and other Niveus Gladius knights. Baelaar hoped that the princess would lead us straight to the Well, and when she did, he wanted her to be alone, isolated."

"What are Baelaar's plans, if he gets his hands on the Well? And what are his plans once they sell the trillion dollars worth of looted treasures they are shipping to America?" Mitchell asked.

"You know about that?"

"Yes."

"The truth is the opposite of what he told me when he first brought me into the Priests of Mezzor. He hates humans. The Priests of Mezzor will use the money to enslave the world, I don't know how but that is Baelaar's goal, then he hopes for a gateway to a world where the first vampire came from."

"What happened to the princess?"

"We chased her, but she escaped. For a very long time we chased, but every time she escaped… until…"

"What happened?"

"We captured her a little while ago. Baelaar drained her of nearly all her blood, so she is weak and he read her mind. She fought, but they found and read the diary in her mind."

"Who's diary?" Mitchell asked grabbing Ivan by the shoulder.

"One of the first vampires turned on Earth."

"The rest of the diary that Snowdrop brought to us!" whispered Mitchell, eyes glazing over as he contemplated this revelation. Then he focused again on Ivan. "What happened to the princess?"

"Baelaar killed her."

"And the others? How many knights were killed?"

Ivan sighed. "Many. But me, I only saw the attack on you and Fionn."

"And did you kill Fionn?"

"Baelaar killed him."

Mitchell lowered his head into his hands. "Where is Baelaar's main fortress?"

"There are three, maybe more. I know only one. It is in Iceland."

"Iceland?" Mitchell's eyes narrowed. "Of all the places I've studied and believed Baelaar's lair to be, Iceland never crossed my mind."

"Yes, a couple hours from Reykjavik. I will show you. They never told me where the others are."

"What is in this diary? Does it say where the well is?"

"I don't know."

"How many of the Priests of Mezzor are there?"

Ivan shrugged. "Now... hundreds."

"Hundreds?"

"Yes. This is why Baelaar disappeared for so long. He was creating and training new initiates. Of course, most of them are relatively young and weak. Baelaar doesn't care. He made far too many. They have armies of human slaves there too, in huge underground caverns. They have collected human skulls for centuries and have hundreds of thousands of them that they have used to build an underground temple to Mezzor, including Baelaar's throne, which is also made of human skulls." Ivan smiled. "I was sent here to trick you."

"What do you mean?"

"They know you are here, Mitchell," Ivan said, his eyes watching carefully, waiting for this news to sink in. "Baelaar sent me to tell you that the princess is held captive in an abandoned village close by. I'm supposed to convince you that I am on your side. Then I'm supposed to bring you there, where an ambush awaits you."

"But how does anyone know I'm here?" Mitchell's eyes grew cold. He looked away. "Of course, as I always suspected... Ruthen."

"Yes, I heard last night Lord Ruthen arrived and they caught him. Baelaar told me he drained him, got information, and then killed him himself."

"What? I thought he was a traitor."

"Not that I know of."

"Damn!" Mitchell strode a few paces away, trying to control his emotions.

"I am sorry."

"Why not just ambush me here then?"

"Baelaar has a plan for you. In a village close to here, there is mineshaft, hundreds of feet down into the earth, an easier place for an ambush. I'm to bring you into the basement of the building where the shaft is, then we attack you, drain you of nearly all of your blood, and throw you into the shaft. Before you have a chance to heal, we melt the rock walls of the shaft and then make them hard again, filling the shaft. Then you are completely imprisoned by solid rock, buried alive."

"Weakened by loss of blood and unable to feed, I wouldn't be able to escape and I would exist there forever..." he concluded grimly. "Or until my mind broke, at which point Baelaar could bring me back and make me a mindless slave." He ground his teeth with rage. "So what made you change your mind? Why are you trying to help me?"

"Baelaar decided to put me in charge of the fortress in Iceland. It was the first time I saw the true nature of his plans. I had a clear understanding. They are trying to create an ultimate blood sacrifice, and I, like a fool, helped them. I believed what they told me. I was brainwashed by them. But now I know."

"What happened?" Mitchell asked.

"They laugh and speak of how such a big population of humans on Earth is hard to control. They talk of killing all humans except for a few hundred thousand, who they will make into slaves. After that, I buried my thoughts deep inside and watched and waited. I will do anything to make up for my mistake."

"Who is waiting for me?"

"He sent the strongest."

"Of course," Mitchell said with a bitter chuckle. "Who?"

"They are very tough. Five of them… and me."

After a moment, Mitchell turned around, determination blazing in his eyes. "Well, let's not keep them waiting."

"What do you mean? I just told you—"

"Ivan—"

"No, I will deal with them. I owe you," Ivan implored.

"You're going to take all five by yourself? You're not going to be good to anyone dead."

Ivan shrugged. "These things happen. No matter. I will take them with me or I will survive and return in a couple of hours," he said, standing up and turning to leave.

Mitchell nodded. "I understand," he said. "You are an honorable man. By the way, what do the words Vadas Asger mean to you?"

"Nothing."

"All right, thanks for your help."

Ivan smiled and swiftly left the grotto.

"What are you going to do?" Emily's voice broke the stillness.

"We will follow him. You'll need to get rid of that light, though. We cannot trust him."

Emily put the sphere in her pocket, and everything went dark except for a faint glow from her jeans.

"I don't like bringing you," muttered Mitchell. "But leaving you here alone could be much worse."

They waited a few moments before following. He had gone cross-country so they left the limousine. Ivan traveled quickly, but Mitchell had no trouble keeping up with him, even with Emily on his back and Mercurios on hers.

As they entered the town, they passed buildings covered with vines, with roads and sidewalks under a light, powdery snow buckling after many summers of grass growing through them. It was a ghost town, which nature had reclaimed. A light breeze blew and loose shutters from a nearby house creaked mournfully as snow-laden currents of air eddied and dissipated. No sign of life. The three of them kept to the shadows and watched as Ivan walked into the center of the main street.

"Gillings," Ivan called out, his voice echoing off the abandoned walls.

He was met by silence apart from the night wind rattling the doors of the dilapidated buildings. Then Emily noticed a pair of glowing red eyes staring out through an empty window across the road. Mitchell lowered her from his back and she took out her wand. The eyes disappeared and a moment later a figure strode out of the doorway.

"Where is he? Did you lose him?" the vampire asked Ivan gruffly.

"Gillings," Ivan said calmly, "I never liked you."

"Is that so?" Gillings sneered.

In one smooth movement, Ivan drew his sword. It shone the cold, pale bluish-white of a frost brand, and wisps of ice fog rose from it. He aimed a fatal strike at Gillings's neck, but Mitchell was faster. As soon as Ivan had uttered those words, Mitchell leaped out of the shadows and slew Gillings himself, his sword blazing with fire. Ivan checked his swing and looked at Mitchell in surprise.

"I had to make sure you had the guts," Mitchell said with a smile.

They grinned at each other like schoolboys, then walked up the main street, their swords drawn and humming with power. Emily and Mercurios followed close behind, Mercurios giggling and muttering in her ear, "Yes, that one had a lot of blood in him, a lot of blood indeed!"

Emily rolled her eyes. "Man," she whispered, "you're an incredibly violent imp!"

"I am! I am tee-hee-hee! Crush them unmerciful!" he shouted with glee, shaking his little fist in the air.

They were nearing the center of town before the other vampires attacked. One leaped from an upper balcony on the left side of the street, hurtling down upon Mitchell, while the other three burst from a building on the right and swarmed over Ivan. They were no Initiates, they were full-fledged vampires, strong and deadly, and their swords glowed with bursts of electricity.

The vampire who had attacked Mitchell seemed to momentarily catch him by surprise. He was thrown to the ground, his shoulder badly gashed. Recovering, Mitchell swept the vampire's legs out from under him with one kick, and, once back on his feet, kicked him in the chest, sending him flying through the brick wall of an abandoned house. Ivan slashed the arm off one of his attackers, the biting frost from his sword searing the vampire's flesh. The vampire shrieked at the top of his lungs and leaped about in a frenzy as he frantically tried to reattach the severed limb.

Emily was desperate to help. She cried out, "Vaza bel thlemin."

A great bolt of lightning shot from her wand and exploded into the vampire Mitchell had kicked, just as he was crawling to his feet, blowing him backward through the wall again. He screamed and writhed in pain, convulsing on the ground.

"Whoa!" Emily said, staring at her wand.

Mitchell glanced at her. "Shocking," he smiled.

At that moment there was a thunderclap so loud it made their ears ring, followed by a blaze of lightning a thousand times greater than the one from Emily's wand. Everyone was knocked to the ground by the force of the electricity.

What looked like a great black doorway opened up in the middle of the road and a huge man-like creature appeared, just as the doorway disappeared. The creature was about twelve feet tall with a moss-green and gray hide. It glanced about with emotionless, black eyes.

The vampire Emily had blown through the wall stumbled to his feet just in time to receive the creature's fist right in his face, hurling him back through the wall again. The creature charged forward and crushed another member of the Priests of Mezzor beneath its enormous fists before tearing his head off. Mercurios cheered and cackled.

Emily heard Ivan roar with pain and turned to see that one of the vampires had put a sword through his side. A vampire, which Ivan must have killed while they were all distracted, lay on the ground beside him, crumbling into ash. Ivan destroyed the one who had stabbed him.

Another vampire went for the creature, attempting to decapitate it, but the creature dodged the sword and punched the vampire in the chest, sending him cartwheeling through the air. Mitchell bounded across the street and, in one swift movement, beheaded the vampire who was about to deliver a lethal blow to Ivan from behind.

Emily felt the crushing grip of a huge hand snatching her up. She dropped her wand and screamed, "Mitchell!" The creature waved her above his head and bellowed in fury. The vampire that had been hurled three times through the wall crawled to his feet and came reeling across the street, swinging his sword blindly at Mitchell, who was now looking in horror at Emily.

"Emily!" he cried.

At that moment, Ivan plunged his sword into the vampire's heart before slicing off his head, which tumbled to the ground, its eyes wide open and staring at Ivan. Ivan kicked it through a window like a soccer ball.

Mercurios hovered in front of the creature's face, spitting a large blob of disgusting goo into its eye. It bellowed loudly, took a poorly aimed swipe at Mercurios, and then tried wiping its eye with its free hand. Mercurios then spat in its other eye, blinding it completely.

The creature roared again, and to free its other hand, hurled Emily aside. She flew through the air toward one of the buildings, screaming at the top of her lungs. Mitchell jumped into the air, thrusting himself off the wall with one leg, and caught Emily just before she hit the stone. He spun and landed, setting Emily safely down on the ground.

"Thanks," she whispered in awe.

Mitchell rushed back into the battle.

The blinded beast stumbled about, waving its great hands in the air and howling. Mercurios appeared near its feet, snapped his fingers, and the creature tripped, crashing to the ground just as Mitchell rushed up and hacked off its head with three fast swipes from his sword. Mitchell, Emily, Mercurios and Ivan stood for a moment, surveying the corpses turning to ash and contemplating the great man-like creature as it dissolved into a pool of green-and-gray ooze.

Emily sank to the ground and drew in a long, deep breath. "Whoa!"

"Mercurios," said Mitchell, "what was that creature?"

"A troll, sir," replied Mercurios.

"From the Abyss? Like the demon?" asked Emily.

"No, trolls live in parts of Magella."

"Lovely," she muttered.

"And what sort of creature are you?" asked Ivan, staring at Mercurios.

"An imp," said Mercurios, obviously offended.

"Do you mean to say that was some kind of dimension door it came through?" asked Mitchell.

"Yes, indeed."

"But… how?" Mitchell asked. "Is it the Well? What's happening?"

"I can't say for certain," Mercurios said. "However, I believe that the Well of Many Worlds has kept a bridge open between Magella and Earth for so long that the divisions between these worlds are blurring, yes indeed. This bringing together of a large group of beings, whose blood is from Magella and who are using powerful magic, has destabilized the delicate balance of the various worlds, which is resulting in the brief opening of random inter-dimensional doorways, like the one at the warehouse."

Mitchell contemplated this. "So the more destabilized the barriers between the worlds become, the greater the chance for catastrophe and chaos." He turned to Emily and Ivan. "Ivan, take me to this mineshaft. I want to see it for myself."

They followed Ivan into the building that the four vampires had emerged from and came upon a wide, round shaft that descended straight into the earth.

"So this was intended to be my tomb," mused Mitchell. They stood staring into the dark hole in silence for a moment, and then Mitchell glanced at Ivan. "Did you hear that?"

"What?"

"I thought I sensed a whisper of a thought."

They stood concentrating intently.

"It's Princess Katharina!" Mitchell cried.

"What?" Ivan gasped.

Without replying, Mitchell leaped into the mineshaft.

Twenty-Three

"Mitchell!" He heard Emily's scream coming from far above him.

Ivan followed him into the mineshaft. They plummeted together through the blackness for what seemed like an eternity. Finally they landed, hundreds of feet below the Earth's surface, standing either side of a rectangular steel box, bound with heavy chains.

"Hurry!" shouted Mitchell. "Grab one end."

Together they lifted the box and began the seemingly endless climb back out of the mineshaft to where Emily was anxiously waiting. When they reached the surface, Mitchell tore the chains apart with his bare hands and ripped the lid off the box, revealing what looked like a mummy.

"I had no idea," Ivan stammered. "They keep secrets in case we are captured."

Mitchell stared at the desiccated corpse, trying to think what it could mean. "Baelaar must have meant this to be a tomb for both of us. It's not your fault, Ivan. Listen, I know a place we can take her to heal. She needs blood, but it might take a few days until we can communicate with her or I can read her mind."

Mitchell pulled out his cell phone, barking instructions. "We need to be ready to fly within two hours... Very good."

They closed the box and carried it to the closest road, where Mitchell had arranged for the limo to meet them. Emily and Mercurios followed.

"Thank you for everything, Ivan," Mitchell said as they reached the car. "I cannot have any other vampire know the whereabouts of my home so I will bid you adieu here. I will keep you updated by text as to the recovery of the princess."

They exchanged numbers and Ivan vanished into the night. The limousine sped Mitchell, Emily and Mercurios to the airport where they loaded the box onto the jet. As they flew Emily watched in a turmoil of mixed emotions as, every half hour, Mitchell sliced open his wrist and allowed thick drops of ruby-colored blood to fall into the dry mouth of the mummy. With every new cut she would wince as if she could feel the pain herself, but every time Emily was elated to see how fast the wound on his wrist would heal. The mummy seemed not to change. Although Emily shared Mitchell's wish to restore the princess, she also dreaded meeting someone who might be her rival for his affections.

"As I thought," Mitchell said after a couple of hours had passed, "it looks like it will be a few days before she has recovered enough for us to get the information we need."

"Where are we going?" Emily asked.

"To my place in England. We should be safe there."

Once the adrenaline had slowed down in her system, Emily realized that she was famished and she started to eat from the array of fresh fruit and hors d'oeuvres that had been laid out for her, holding in the many questions she wanted to ask. Mitchell sat, frowning, deep in thought, and she was too intimidated to speak.

When they landed in Newcastle upon Tyne there was a silver Rolls Royce Phantom waiting on the tarmac. After putting the still shriveled corpse of the princess in the back, Emily enjoyed the feel of the expensive leather as they slid into their seats. She took a deep breath, pleased to be alive and excited to be able to breathe in the scent of luxury, unlike the princess in the back.

Mitchell was still silent and brooding. Twice she was about to break the silence but couldn't think of anything to say that wouldn't sound like she was pestering him for information. She was afraid of annoying him. As they roared northwards Emily could see through the window the moon illuminating the lush rolling hills of the English countryside. After about an hour they veered off down a side road, driving for another twenty minutes.

As Mitchell slowed down, Emily leaned forward in her seat and peered through the windshield. She could see an ancient cemetery at the base of a hill to the right. They approached the main gates, defended by two round towers, each crowned by overhanging turrets covered in wild plants that had taken root among the stones. Mitchell pushed a button on his keychain and the gates swung open to allow them through.

"Um… Mitchell," Emily said as the building came into view, "you live in a castle?"

"Yes, this is my home."

"Whoa."

Even in the moonlight she could distinguish little more than a part of the dark outline of massive walls and ramparts, but she could see that it was vast, and ancient. Silent and lonely it seemed to be frowning on all who dared to awaken it from its brooding slumber.

Another gate delivered them into a courtyard where a grove of ancient oaks had taken root and flourished over centuries. Climbing out of the car Emily looked up at the high Gothic windows above and breathed the damp night air.

"Wow," she murmured. "It's beautiful."

Mitchell gently lifted the desiccated corpse out of the car and carried it to a set of double doors. Emily grabbed her backpack as Mitchell took out a large key and opened the doors. She and Mercurios followed him inside.

They passed through the entrance foyer into the great hall and Emily gasped as she looked down the long room. She had never seen such grandeur and luxury. It made her feel like a princess.

"Oh, Mitchell, this is amazing," she said, staring at the works of art hanging from the walls.

He said nothing as he led them through another set of double doors into a second chamber of equal splendor. Above the couches and tables, the soaring Gothic windows had been preserved with reverential care, a complete contrast to the overgrown exterior. Along the wall to her left was an opening and a broad staircase of shining oak and red carpet ascended into the darkness.

The centerpiece to the room was the biggest fireplace Emily had ever seen. It was built with slabs of marble, and there were ornaments over it of the prettiest English china. Above the fireplace, hanging on the enormous chimney made of granite was a large painting. It was about ten feet in height and six feet in width. Emily stared at it. The canvas had been burned so only about a third of the painting remained on the bottom right side. Emily could make out what looked like the lower section of a flowing gown and guessed that it was a portrait.

She slowly lowered her backpack to the ground as she gazed around. Mitchell laid the corpse of the princess on a table in front of the fireplace and then knelt to light the fire. As the flames licked over the dry logs he straightened up, rolled back his cuff and once again slit his wrist and dripped his thick blood into the dry mouth of the princess.

"It's very late," he said once he had finished. "I expect you're exhausted. Come, I will show you to your room."

"Uh, thanks." She felt self-conscious and out of place. She gestured to the picture. "Is that a portrait of someone? Was there a fire?"

Mitchell looked up at the charred painting. "Yes, there was a fire here long ago in one of the wings when my family was attacked. That was all that could be salvaged."

"Attacked? Who attacked you?"

"It's a long story."

"Who is the portrait of?"

"I'd rather not…" He stared at her long and hard, then looked up at the portrait and then back at Emily. He gave her a quizzical look. "I'd rather not discuss it," he said. "Follow me."

He walked off before Emily could say anything else. They ascended the broad staircase of shining oak and red carpet.

"Wow, this staircase is incredible, right out of *Gone With The Wind*!" said Emily. Mitchell didn't respond.

After many flights and many landings, it brought them onto a long, wide gallery. On one side it had a line of doors and on the other side were windows. Emily looked through one and discovered that it overlooked the quadrangle, looking down on the oak trees.

"How long have you owned this place?"

"I grew up here in the 1500s and then eventually purchased it back in the early 1700s."

"You grew up here? Tell me about it."

"Here is your room," he said, ignoring her question and opening a door.

Emily walked into a large, ornate bedroom. It was beautiful. There was a huge, four-poster bed. Thick velvet curtains covered high windows and in the corner an old-fashioned black cabinet stood, at least twelve feet tall. On the floor was a Persian rug that glowed with a thousand different-colored threads as Mitchell lit the fire, which had already been laid in the fireplace.

"Make yourself at home," he said. "Sleep well."

Emily opened her mouth to speak but Mitchell strode out of the room and shut the door behind him. She stared around the room in silence for a moment. "Mercurios, this bedroom is like the one from that dream I've been having."

"Your dream took place in this room? Are you sure?"

She slowly turned around in a circle, inspecting her surroundings. "I think so, it's similar, yet different, I mean I was lying in a four-poster bed like this in a bedroom in a castle, bit of a different setup though, but… I don't know, it's kinda freaking me out."

"What do you want to do?"

"I don't know."

Emily shook her head then thought of something and pulled out her cell phone. She texted Cindy, asking her to cover for her for one more evening.

"I guess that's a bonus of having a workaholic mom who lives at the office, Mercurios," she mumbled. "Probably won't notice I'm gone, but just in case I'm gonna get Cindy to cover for me again."

The imp appeared, sitting on the edge of the bed. "Good thinking."

"I guess I'll go to bed now, privacy please."

"As you wish." The imp disappeared.

As Emily slid under the sheets the touch of the silk on her skin made her sigh with pleasure. She quickly fell into a deep sleep.

A couple of hours later she awoke with a start and sat bolt upright in bed. For a moment her heart was gripped with fear as she looked around at the unfamiliar surroundings. The fire had died and the embers barely illuminated the room with a soft orange glow. She stared about and the events of the previous day came flooding back. The castle was silent except for the wind outside the windows. Emily lay back down and was about to close her eyes and go back to sleep when she heard what sounded like a muffled shout. She sat back up again and concentrated, trying to hear more clearly.

"Mercurios?" she whispered. There was no response. Emily heard the sound again and she slid out of bed and started putting on her clothes. "Mercurios," she hissed again.

The bedroom door opened and the imp appeared. "Yes, Emily?"

"Did you hear that?"

"Yes, it sounded like it was coming from the west wing of the castle, where the chapel is."

Emily crept out of her bedroom, followed by the imp. Her heart pounded as she descended the giant staircase one step at a time. She heard another muffled shout in the night.

"That is so creepy, um, maybe I should go back to bed."

"Yes, a good idea," the imp agreed. "No business of yours."

"Do you think the castle is haunted? Or what if it's the princess? If she's awake Mitchell will want to know."

Emily made her way down to the hall. Crossing to the table before the still flickering fire, she leaned over the corpse and put her ear close to its mouth. She could hear nothing. The fire gave a loud crack and pop, making her shriek and jump back. Without saying a word, she and Mercurios continued over to the doors they had originally arrived through. They walked down the hall and crossed over to another set of double doors with a huge white wooden crucifix hanging upon them, signaling it was the entrance to the chapel. Emily stood staring at the door handle for a moment before tentatively reaching out to open it. The door was locked.

"Do you want me to try to pick the lock?" whispered Mercurios.

"No," Emily whispered, backing away.

She turned and ran back through the great hall and up to her bedroom, keen to get back to the safety of her warm silk sheets. As her fingers touched the door handle she heard the sound of footsteps coming up the stairs. Looking around her she spotted a tall potted plant and dodged behind it, peering through the thick foliage. A moment later Mitchell walked across the landing and continued up the stairs to the next floor. He was covered in blood.

Once the sound of his footsteps had died away she went back into her bedroom, pacing back and forth in front of the fire as Mercurios watched, sitting on the edge of the bed amongst the rumpled silk sheets.

"Do you think he's into some kind of satanic stuff?" she asked. "Was he in the chapel with the door locked? Why was he covered in blood? What is that all about? Human sacrifice? Like, I know he's a vampire and everything, but a chapel? I mean, you say that the nine planes of Hell actually exist and the Abyss and all that; so what if he worships some kind of demon? What if he's been lying all along and is involved with the Priests of Mezzor? The blood of the world is the blood of the god…"

255

"I don't know Emily, these are all possibilities. Perhaps you should use your ring of teleportation and get out of here right now."

"No. No, I need to find out what is going on. We need to find the Well so I can get an exorcism, remember?"

Once back in the bed she slept only fitfully. When she eventually rose and opened the curtains she was struck by the beauty of the castle's surroundings and felt foolish for all the black thoughts she had allowed to disturb her night. The sun was high and she was excited at the prospect of exploring.

"Mercurios," she said.

"Yes?"

"I want privacy when I'm with Mitchell."

"As you wish."

She found her way downstairs and noticed that the mummified body of the princess was now gone. She heard noises from behind a door on the opposite side of the room and when she entered she discovered it was the dining hall. The long table of polished oak could easily seat twenty people and the most spectacular chandelier Emily had ever seen hung above it. The chairs and the ornate sideboard were also made of polished oak. A distinguished-looking gentleman wearing a tuxedo entered through a doorway, which she guessed led to the kitchen.

"Ah, Miss Emily," he purred, "you are awake. Master Keats has instructed us to have the chef prepare whatever you desire for breakfast and to assist you with anything you may need. I am the butler. My name is Willard."

"Nice to meet you." Emily blushed slightly.

"And for breakfast is there anything that you particularly like?"

"Well, anything really, thanks, I mean what does the cook have?"

"Pretty much anything you wish, Madam. What would you normally order at a restaurant if you went out for brunch?"

"Ummm, not sure." Emily laughed and shifted on her feet, feeling self-conscious. "Maybe French toast or an omelet?"

"Excellent, Madam, any particular type of omelet?"

"Uh, I guess the cook can surprise me."

"Excellent."

"Can I ask where Mitchell is?"

"He will not be available until later."

"Okay, um, is it okay if I look around the castle? I'd love to see what it looks like from outside now that it's daylight."

"Of course, just give me one moment to place your order with the cook and I shall show you around."

Willard disappeared into the kitchen and returned a few moments later. "If you will follow me, Madam," he said and led her through the great hall into an enormous library, through another set of doors and out into the courtyard. He opened a gate onto a lawn, which looked out to wild countryside all around.

"How big is the property?"

"Around eight hundred acres."

"Wow!"

To her left the rolling hills below were dark with woods that swept down to a narrow valley at the bottom of which a stream foamed over boulders and disappeared into a grove of ancient oaks. A herd of sheep grazed on the side of a hill in the distance creating a scene of pastoral beauty. Turning around she could see that the fortifications of the castle spread out to cover the whole crown of the hill, and were now partly in a state of decay. She stared at the grandeur of the ramparts, towers and battlements. Her eyes drifted over to a shrubbery a dozen yards away and she saw that there was a dead rabbit lying under it, its throat ripped out. Emily stared at it a moment then looked at Willard. He seemed not to have noticed.

"If you would like a view of the countryside from a higher vantage point I can take you up to the ramparts," he said.

"Uh, yeah, that would be great, thanks."

The butler led her back inside and up the great staircase past the floor her bedroom was located on and out onto the ramparts. They extended around three sides of the edifice; the fourth was guarded by high walls and by the main gateway. Walking out onto the large terraces a big smile spread across Emily's face.

"It's so beautiful."

"Indeed. Your breakfast should be ready momentarily and you have a busy day ahead, so we should be returning to the dining parlor." With that he turned and led her back inside.

"Busy day?" asked Emily as she almost ran to keep up. "What's going on?"

"Master Keats has given instructions for you to be properly attired for dinner."

"We're going shopping?"

"I believe the shopping has been done for you."

The chef not only made her an omelet, there was French toast, a bowl of fresh fruit and berries, coffee, various freshly squeezed juices and a basket of freshly baked pastries, all displayed on the finest china, crystal and silverware. Emily imagined it was like staying at a five-star resort, not that she had ever been to one. When she was finished Willard returned.

"Was everything to your liking, Miss Emily?"

"Yes, thanks, it was wonderful. I was wondering, could you show me the chapel?"

"Unfortunately I cannot, the door is always locked and that is the one room in the castle that the servants are forbidden from entering."

"Oh, okay." Emily's mind was burning with curiosity as to what was in the chapel and what Mitchell was doing in there in the middle of the night.

"Now," said Willard. "Before we get to the fitting and the hair and makeup, Master Keats has asked me to help you with any etiquette questions you may have. He wants you to feel confident to dine in the finest of company."

"Ah, um okay."

For the next hour Willard instructed Emily in etiquette and Emily enjoyed the thought that she could now dine with royalty and fit right in. When they were finished two impeccably dressed ladies entered the dining room.

"Miss Bliss," said one. "My name is Alexandra and this is Kitty."

"Hello, nice to meet you," Emily said, standing up and shaking their hands, resisting the urge to drop a curtsy.

"Please come with us," said Kitty. "We want to do a fitting for the gown and then get started on your hair and makeup."

They led her back into the main room with the huge fireplace. There was a magnificent yellow gown spread out on one of the couches. It looked as if it had come from another time. Then she saw the jewelry laid out on the table in front of the gown.

"What is all this?"

"Master Keats wanted you to be properly attired for dinner."

"Uh, okay, ummm…"

The lady named Kitty took Emily by the hand and guided her over to the gown. It was a glorious, old-fashioned-style yellow ball gown with gold hand stitching and a low neckline that accentuated her décolletage. Kitty took all Emily's measurements and then disappeared with the gown while Alexandra took Emily upstairs into a bathroom on the second floor that was prepared like a beauty salon. She bleached and toned Emily's hair until it was platinum blonde, then dressed it in a style of Hollywood curls, half pinned to the side. Kitty returned and got to work on her nails and makeup, creating a delicate, smoky eye and a ballet-pink lip with a dewy finish. Her nails were done light pink with a French tip. Emily felt like she was at the ultimate spa, being prepared for a marriage ceremony. As they worked she asked the two ladies what they knew about Mitchell but both said that they had been contacted and hired by Willard and had never met his Master. The gown was returned, altered to fit her exactly and she slipped it on with their help.

When they were finished they took her back downstairs to the jewelry. There was a white gold ring with a spectacular 25 carat canary diamond surrounded by smaller diamonds, a dazzling necklace with hundreds of diamonds, earrings with large canary diamonds as the centerpieces and a thick diamond bracelet.

"This can't be real," she said.

"Oh, I assure you all the pieces are real," said Kitty. "Beautiful, aren't they?"

"Are you kidding? They're fit for a princess."

They helped her put on all the jewelry, then Emily noticed there were five boxes of luxury-brand shoes to pick from. She chose a pair of strappy champagne pumps that sparkled and shone. When they were finished the two ladies rolled in a heavy antique mirror.

Emily was speechless. She had been totally transformed. Her thick platinum hair cascaded down over her shoulders in glamorous waves, the gown was the most beautiful thing she had ever seen and the jewels sparkled and shone. She felt like a fairy-tale princess.

Alexandra and Kitty said their goodbyes as Emily thanked them profusely.

"Wait," she said nervously. "What do I do now?"

"The photographer will be in shortly," said Alexandra.

"Uh, photographer?"

As the two ladies disappeared through a door Emily glanced out of one of the windows and saw that the sky had grown dark with swollen storm clouds and the wind was bending the trees with powerful gusts. Her gaze returned to her reflection in the mirror just as a man with a camera and lighting equipment entered the room.

"Hello, my name is Peter, I'm the photographer."

Emily turned around. "Hello, nice to meet you."

"You look spectacular," he said as he set up his light with a reflector.

"Thanks, uh, what's all this for?"

He looked up at the charred portrait on the wall and then at Emily. "I've been hired to try and recreate that portrait in a photograph, so that an artist can then paint another one. Now, would you please take a seat on that chair?"

He pointed to a large leather chair. Emily looked up at the portrait and for the first time realized that the gown she was wearing resembled what she could see of the one in the painting. He's dressing me up to look like another girl, she thought and her heart plunged. She felt like a fool for thinking that this was all for her. She obediently sat down and the photographer arranged her position and arms.

"Who is she?" Emily asked, feeling sad, jealous and embarrassed all at the same time.

"I don't know. I was hired to try and recreate what's left of that painting in photographs, that's all I know."

"Oh. Do you know Mitchell?"

"Mr. Keats? No, I was contacted and hired by the butler, Willard."

As he adjusted the lighting, clicked some shots and then adjusted the lighting some more, he instructed her on precisely how she should sit, where to place her hands and how high her chin should be, Emily was filled with conflicting emotions. On the one hand she was horrified that Mitchell was dressing her as another girl, but at the same time she was thrilled by the experience of such a spectacular makeover. Never in a million years had she imagined looking so glamorous and beautiful and she loved it. After two hours he was finished and left the room.

Thunder rumbled and Emily glanced through the windows. It was now pitch dark outside between the flashes of lightning. The wind had been rising at intervals the whole afternoon and now a torrential rainstorm began. Willard entered the room and re-lit the fire, informing her that the master of the house would be in shortly before disappearing once more. A few moments later she was startled by the sound of Mitchell's voice.

"You look wonderful. Perfect!"

Emily turned to see him standing at the bottom of the stairs in a perfectly tailored tuxedo.

"Thanks." She blushed. Her heart surged at the thought that he was pleased with her. It was as though she desired his approval more than anything in the world and it filled her with joy, then her smile faded. "What is this all about?" she asked. "Why are you dressing me up like whoever was in that portrait?"

"It was very precious to me," said Mitchell walking over and reaching up to touch the edge of the frame. "I am going to hire an artist to use the photographs and what I can salvage from my memory to recreate it."

"Who is she?"

Mitchell hesitated for a moment. "Someone I knew long ago. You really do look lovely."

"Thanks."

Classical music began playing from hidden speakers. "Would you care to dance?" he asked.

Emily burst out laughing and blushed, feeling goofy. Then she regained her composure, realizing this was an opportunity to be in his arms. "I'd love to," she said.

She felt protected in his powerful embrace as he guided her effortlessly around the room. His confidence was intoxicating and the feeling that she was a fairy-tale princess with her prince once again flooded Emily. She wanted it to last forever.

"I know that this is going to sound incredibly cliché," he said. "But you have wonderful, beautiful eyes."

Emily laughed and blushed. "Thanks."

Lightning flashed outside and the rain beat in torrents upon the windows.

"I noticed them the first time I saw you."

Emily smiled, filled with joy and excitement that he was attracted to something about her. A few moments later, however, he released her.

"Come," he said. "Dinner awaits."

"But I thought you didn't…"

"I don't. I will be content to watch you eat."

He led her into the dining room and Emily sat down in the seat of honor. Mitchell sat next to her. Only her place was set.

"What's happening with the princess? Any luck reviving her?"

"Nothing yet. I hope it will take only a few more feedings. I expect you are eager to get home. I can have my jet fly you whenever you like. Perhaps when you have finished dinner?"

"Uh. Yeah, I mean, no, not at all, I'm not in any major rush." Her heart plunged to see that he seemed to be fine about getting rid of her so soon.

"Oh, good then, well, just let me know."

"Does Willard know that you are a vampire?" she whispered.

"No, none of them do. I only hired them a couple years ago to help with the upkeep as I travel a lot. Depending on how long I have to stay in this world I want this place to be well taken care of."

"What do you mean by 'how long you have to stay in this world?' You're planning on going to Magella if we find the Well? Is that why you offered to have me flown home alone? But what about the looted treasure? We have to stop them."

"No, I'm not going to Magella and the treasure is really no concern of mine. I would love to get revenge and destroy Baelaar, but the Well is more important."

"Then where are you going? And what do you mean you don't care? You said yourself that they are probably going to use those trillions to create the biggest slaughter ever and enslave the survivors."

"If you must know I'm going to Hell. I'm sorry, but that is more important."

"What?" Emily burst out laughing.

"Make whatever choice you make," he said with a dismissive wave of his hand, "It matters not. All roads lead to the grave."

Mitchell stared at her evenly and her laughter faded. She felt a chill run through her. She opened her mouth to speak just as Willard entered the room with a silver pot containing soup. He carefully ladled it into the bowl at Emily's place.

"Lobster bisque," he announced.

"Thank you."

"You're welcome," he said and disappeared back into the kitchen.

Emily sat looking at Mitchell for a moment as the thunderstorm raged outside. A million questions were racing around in her head. She wondered if she should tell him of her dreams but was afraid to let him know that she was possessed by a demon. Then again what if he's a demon worshipper? she wondered with a shiver.

"Please eat," Mitchell said.

She picked up her spoon and tried her soup. "Mmmmm that is soooo good! What do you mean you are going to Hell?"

"I am going to use the Well of Many Worlds to travel to the nine planes of Hell and the Abyss if necessary."

"But why?"

"That's a long and complicated story. I'd rather talk about other things."

"I saw you last night." She glanced up nervously, wondering how he would react. He didn't seem concerned so she continued. "I heard noises coming from the chapel so I got up and then I saw you come upstairs covered in blood. What were you doing in the chapel?"

"I was in the chapel but afterwards I went outside to hunt. When you saw me I had just returned."

"You killed a rabbit."

"Yes, how did you know?"

"I saw it outside today."

"Yes, enough blood to keep me alive, but I must do some real hunting again soon or I will start to grow weak."

"What were you doing in the chapel? May I see it?"

"No, that is off limits. Tell me about yourself. Tell me more about your magical training."

"Well, Mercurios appeared one night and told me I was from another world and my parents were wizards and then he gave me this pendant." She held up the chest on the chain around her neck.

"It's a magical chest that grows into a big chest. It had my mother's spell book in it as well as a Skull of Monster Summoning, a Sphere of Protection, a Ring of Teleportation and a Wand of Lightning."

"Can I see them?"

"Sure." Emily put down her spoon.

"Hold on," said Mitchell, standing up and walking toward the kitchen door. "I'm going to send Willard home."

Mitchell went into the kitchen. Emily heard some muffled conversation as she continued to eat her soup. A flash of light and a crash of thunder outside startled her. The storm was raging. Mitchell came back into the dining room and sat down.

"We are now alone."

The thought that she had Mitchell all to herself sent thrills of pleasure and desire through her. "I'll show you the chest, but first you have to tell me who the girl in the picture is."

Mitchell stared intently at her and she could see that his glorious emerald eyes were tortured and flashing crimson.

"Do you believe in true love?" he asked.

A lightning bolt struck near the castle and was instantly followed by a deafening crack of thunder.

"I-I guess so."

"Her name was Marigold. She was the most beautiful, radiant woman in all the kingdoms of the world."

Emily flushed with jealousy and she clutched her spoon tightly.

"She was like an angel," continued Mitchell, his eyes glazing over as he stared off into space, lost in memories. "Everyone loved her. She was kind, smart, witty, tender and beautiful, the most beautiful woman in creation. It would be impossible to meet her and not love her. She was so gentle and lovely... insightful. But she also had such a fun, adventurous side, so much spirit, passion, such a love of life. We used to climb trees together by the river, or pick berries and lie about in the long grass talking and joking for hours. Or sneak out at night and go for walks in the meadows, picking wild flowers by moonlight, or sitting by the river and looking at the stars. She was always filled with joy and wonder at the beauty and majesty of nature, and she held in her spirit a wild and free naturalness. Every time she entered a room, everywhere she went, everyone would turn their heads and even the dourest of countenances would brighten. She created beautiful gardens, danced upon the dew as the sun rose, and walked the fields barefoot in moonbeams. She was a light of pure loveliness. No matter how bleak and gray the world seemed, just her presence would fill it with color and beauty and magic and splendor."

The more he spoke the more Emily burned with jealousy and the more she hated herself for it.

"From the moment we met it was obsession," he continued, "As though we had always been lovers. The more time we spent together the more we wanted; it was a hunger for each other that could never be satiated, increasing with every feast. A few months after we met, Marigold came to me the day before All Hallows Eve, Halloween. She told me that any blood oath sworn under a full moon on All Hallows Eve, when the barriers between this world and the world of magic were at their weakest, would last forever and that year it was a full moon. I guess she was right. I often think, with most people love burns brightly at first but eventually fades, but not with me. Just as my body became frozen in time when I was turned into a vampire, eternally young, so did my love for Marigold. It burns just as brightly inside me now as it did all those years ago, an eternal flame that will continue on until the end of time."

He looked at Emily for a moment then stared off into space, his eyes growing distant.

"And so will the pain of her loss. The horrors we see in life haunt our steps all the way to our graves, clinging to us like a chilling mist." He looked at Emily again. "They change the colors of the world, leaving it forever darkened."

"Was, uh… Was she your wife?" she asked, trying to look and

sound casual, putting another spoonful of the hot, creamy soup into her mouth.

"No. Her father opposed the match. We had plans to marry… but we never got the chance."

Emily swallowed and looked down at her soup. Mitchell glanced at her and then stared off into space again, lost in memories. There was an awkward silence.

"You know, um… my birthday is on Halloween." Emily felt pathetic trying to get his attention and she blushed.

"That's nice," he said but only seemed to be half listening.

"And, um," she muttered. "It was a full moon this Halloween when I met you. Maybe we were meant to meet."

"Hmm?" said Mitchell, snapping out of his trance. "Now show me that magical chest."

Emily put down her spoon and took the chest from around her neck. She placed it on the ground. "Almeron sidella."

The chest grew to its full size and she opened it. She was wearing her Ring of Teleportation but the sphere, wand, spell book and skull were all still in the chest.

"Amazing," said Mitchell, leaning forward. "This is a real spell book?"

"Yes, Mercurios is using it to teach me spell-casting."

"That's amazing, Emily," Mitchell looked at her and smiled. Emily's heart soared once more beneath his approval. Whoever this Marigold was, she could bet that she wasn't a wizard. She felt a surge of pride and hoped that Mitchell found it exciting and attractive that she was studying magic.

"Yes, it's so exciting," she gushed. "Learning magic is so much fun. Although I've only learned two spells I can imagine what it will be like when I can cast the advanced ones."

"And this," he said, pointing to the Skull of Monster Summoning. "How does it work?"

"Simple, you just draw a circle on the ground where you want the monster to appear and then stand back, hold up the skull, look in its eyes and say the command words. Then, when it's activated, you say the name of whatever being you want to summon."

"The same words you said to make the chest enlarge?"

"No the command words for the skull are Gorhel velsten."

Lightning flashed and thunder exploded outside. Mitchell seized the skull, leaped to his feet and charged out of the dining room, back into the main room with the fireplace.

"Mitchell!" cried Emily, jumping to her feet. "What are you doing?"

Twenty-Four

Emily shrunk the chest, snatched it up and started to run after Mitchell. After a few stumbling steps she stopped to throw off her shoes. Mercurios was in the other room, standing on the couch.

"What's going on? Why does he have the skull?" he shouted, dancing about frantically.

"Mitchell!" she yelled. "That thing is really dangerous! Stop!"

She came into the great hall in time to see Mitchell enter the chapel and slam the door behind him. She grabbed the handle and tried to open it but it was locked.

"Mercurios, unlock it."

The imp grabbed the doorknob and stuck one of his claws into the lock. He fiddled with it, squishing up his face with concentration. After a moment the door swung open. Emily rushed through and stopped dead in her tracks. The ceiling soared high above and huge, intricate stained-glass windows covered the walls, depicting exquisitely rendered scenes from the bible. Hundreds of thick white beeswax candles illuminated the building, reflecting in the polished oak of the pews. At the far end was a white marble altar, surrounded by hundreds of red roses. Mitchell was in front of the altar. He had slashed his wrist open with a dagger and was finishing drawing a circle on the white marble with his blood. She could see articles of clothing and jewelry lying on the surface.

"Oh my god," Emily whispered. "It's a shrine for his dead girlfriend."

Mitchell held up the skull and stared into its eyes. "Gorhel velsten!" he said.

"Mitchell, no!" she screamed.

There was a sound like a giant generator igniting. The rubies in the skull's eyes glowed, releasing a shockwave that knocked Emily off her feet and sent Mercurios cartwheeling through the air. Emily pulled herself back onto her feet and rushed forward.

"Marigold Bonneville," said Mitchell.

Another shockwave was released and Emily was on the ground again, screaming and writhing in pain, momentarily engulfed in crackling red energy.

"Get your hands away from the Skull of Monster Summoning, you damn vampire!" shrieked Mercurios, beside himself with rage, standing on a pew shaking his tiny fist in the air.

The crackling red energy disappeared and Emily crawled to her feet. "Oh my god," she moaned in a daze. "He's using the skull to bring his ex-girlfriend back from the dead!"

"Use your wand, Emily!" shrieked the imp. "Blast him unmerciful!"

Mitchell put down the skull and stood staring at the circle of blood on the altar. His eyes were blazing, his face contorted in a frenzy.

"Where is she?" he roared, then spun around and strode toward Emily. "Why isn't it working?" he bellowed and Emily shrank back in fear. He was crazed and out of control. Mitchell glanced at Mercurios and snatched him up in his fist. "Why isn't it working?"

"P-please calm down," whined Mercurios as he squirmed to get free. "Put me down!"

Mitchell dropped the imp, stumbled back to the altar and collapsed on it with his head in his hands. Emily rushed over to him and put her hands on his back. "Mitchell..."

"If you are trying to summon the ghost of this Marigold," said Mercurios. "It likely won't work. She's been dead far too long, her spirit is in another dimension by now and it is a tricky thing indeed to summon beings from other dimensions. The skull works best summoning monsters that are in the same world it is located in."

"Not her ghost," Mitchell moaned, his eyes were tortured, haunted. "Not her ghost. She is in Hell, or the Abyss. She is a demon."

"Gorhel velsten," said Emily, picking up the skull. The eyes stopped glowing and the hum of power fell silent.

"A demon?" said Mercurios. "The skull could have summoned it, yes indeed. However, demons are difficult, they are from another dimension, anything from another plane will only come for a brief time, if at all, before they are pulled back to their own dimension."

"What do you mean she's a demon?" asked Emily, horrified.

"When my mortal self died" – Mitchell struggled to get the words out – "she sold her soul to bring me back from the dead." A bitter, pained look glazed over his eyes. "Now that I know the Abyss and the nine planes of Hell actually exist I must go to her. If I can't bring her back here I must go to her."

Emily felt as though a knife had been thrust through her heart. "What?" she whispered.

"I will go into the Well and hunt for her through all the demons and devils in all the planes of Hell and the Abyss if I must," he snarled.

Emily stared at him in horror.

"Perhaps Baelaar is right," he continued. "What is in this world but grief and woe?" His eyes became distant as he stared into space. "The world is like some evil wizard that inverts all he touches, turning dreams to nightmares. We are all ensnared in its diabolical spell as it works its reverse alchemy, turning life and love to dust and despair."

"No, no, no!" Emily murmured. "Are you telling me that you've been given all these powers and immortality and all you want to do with it is destroy yourself? Or be trapped in the Abyss or the Planes of Hell?"

"You obviously understand nothing of what I have told you," he snapped, standing up to leave.

Emily was furious and blocked his path. "I don't understand? I don't understand? In all these hundreds of years, did you ever stop to think of all the amazing experiences you could have been having? All the incredible things you could have achieved for this world?"

Mitchell all but spat at her words. "I will not abandon her! We are one. To lose her is to lose myself. Ah!" He waved her away. "You could never imagine such loyalty."

"My father was murdered, Mitchell. My father was murdered and I am hunting his killers, but that will not stop me from living life!"

His face darkened, his eyes were haunted. "I dream of her, out there, lost and alone, or worse…" His eyes focused again and he looked at Emily. "She is everything to me. We are one; we are each other… as one, forever. That is true immortality. I could never leave her in the outer darkness alone! Without the best of me who am I? I am a non-entity, an apparition, a voice on the wind from another age, a figment of a dream, a shadow in the night, gazing across a chasm at the world of the living, at its warmth and humanity."

Fierce jealousy surged through Emily and she immediately felt a twinge of shame at feeling such animosity for a girl who had done nothing to her, who had lived and died over four hundred years before her, but there it was.

"You believe that, but what if there is no Hell? Or no afterlife? You believe there is but Mercurios has never been there, he doesn't know for sure. Or what if there is and she's not there? Then you'll be throwing everything away for nothing!"

"I do not claim to know what lies beyond this world, but I cannot take the risk that her soul is out there somewhere, alone in torment. She and I are one! Can you not understand that?" Mitchell's eyes blazed. "This vampire body seems immortal, but it is nothing. I have touched true immortality through her. Our souls are one. We will always find each other, beyond life and death… beyond everything!" he shouted, then regained his composure and stared at Emily, his eyes smoldering. "I feed upon hot blood each night, but I have been starved for nearly five hundred years. My past and my future are a crimson tempest. But I will never grow from this devil's rain. I could drink oceans of blood and find no nourishment. The only nourishment that can bring life into me is in Marigold's eyes, in her hair, her laughter, in her heart, her body, her joy, her pleasure, her safety, her health, the love in her eyes and the sugar touch of her lips. I have been banished from my home; it is gilded banishment, but still banishment.

"I am in exile from my native land, for my true home is wherever Marigold is. For nearly five hundred years, the chessboard of kingdoms has shifted around me and I remain a rock in the middle of this stormy sea. Only my love can bring life back to me, for there is witchcraft in her eyes, in her lips. She cast her spell on me the first moment I saw her. This world does not exist to me. All I have are my memories. I live in a world of ghosts. It is a world of phantoms that are born and live and die like shadows in the night. She is the only thing that is real. Ah." He waved his hand dismissively. "You can never understand."

Mitchell's face softened. He stepped closer, gazing deep into Emily's eyes as he gently took her by the waist. He inhaled the scent of her hair, savoring it as he spoke into her ear, their bodies barely touching, sending delicious thrills of pleasure and excitement deep inside her.

"I want you to know that meeting you has been the only light in my existence of over four hundred years of darkness. With you, for the first time in over four hundred years I felt alive again. I am deeply grateful for that and I will hold it in my heart and cherish it for all time."

Emily's heart surged. She pressed her body against his.

"I will never forget you," he said, his voice low and sensual in her ear. The words he spoke, the proximity of his body, aroused a need and desire in Emily unlike anything she had ever imagined. It was as though a power had taken complete control of her mind and body and the only thing that existed was him and the all-consuming need to be with him drove her wild. Her love and longing for him was like a physical sickness, mixed with elation. She loved the way he looked at her sideways and curled his lip into a smile, she loved his voice, his pale skin and bright eyes, the sweet smell of his body, his golden, slightly mussed hair, she loved the way he looked at her when she spoke. She thought he was so loyal and perfect that she didn't deserve him. But she had to have him. The thought of losing him made her feel like she was going to go mad. She wanted to scream with frustration. Her mind reeled with all he had told her and she needed to calm down and think clearly, to make some sort of plan.

Her heart was exploding with the words he had just spoken. She barely dared to consider it, but it sounded like he was falling in love with her, and if it wasn't for Marigold... Bitter jealousy of the dead Marigold surged once again within her.

I wish he had never met her! she thought fiercely. She hated Marigold. She absolutely despised her. Emily tortured herself by imagining how beautiful she must have been, but even worse, she tortured herself by imagining all the little things they must have shared, the things that were theirs and theirs alone, their little inside jokes, the shared moments of fun and laughter and passion and tenderness, the love letters they wrote to one another, their touches, caresses, their kisses. Emily wanted to scream. No, no, calm down, it's okay that he's still obsessed with his ex who's been dead for four hundred years. No, it wasn't okay. She wanted to dig up Marigold's bones and set them on fire. She wished she could somehow learn a spell that would make him forget that she ever existed. She was determined to find a way, any way, to dissuade Mitchell from completing his dark mission of self-destruction. Then she noticed something on the altar. Mitchell had indeed turned the chapel into a shrine for his dead love. On the altar were some ancient pieces of women's clothing and jewelry and among them was the beautiful pearl necklace with the ruby and diamond pendant Emily recognized from her recurring dream. Her heart stopped.

"My dream," she murmured and stepped away from Mitchell.

"What?" he demanded.

She pointed to the necklace. "I've been having this recurring dream and that necklace was in it."

"What dream?"

There was a wailing cry from another part of the castle. "Shh," ordered Mitchell. "The princess is awake!"

All the stained-glass windows in the chapel shattered simultaneously. Emily shrieked as through them leaped dozens of hideously disfigured people.

"Zombies!" screamed Mercurios. "Ghouls! The skull has summoned them from the graveyard."

Emily snatched the necklace from the altar and held up her wand. Mitchell drew his sword and it burst into flame. Dozens of zombies and ghouls in various stages of putrefaction came charging at them.

"Run!" shouted Mitchell.

As they ran for the doors he hacked through the undead beings that rushed at them with deranged moans and shrieks.

"Vaza bel thlemin!" shouted Emily and a massive bolt of electricity leaped from her wand, blasting four ghouls out of their way.

They charged through the doors and Mitchell slammed and locked them. They ran through the great hall as more zombies came crashing through the windows of other parts of the castle. Mitchell hacked through more of them and Emily unleashed another blast from her wand, sending two zombies hurtling back out of the window they had come through. Mitchell tore open a set of double doors and pushed her inside.

"They won't be able to get in here, lock the door and stay in the dungeon until I get back," he ordered and slammed the door before she could reply.

Emily locked the door. Everything was pitch black so she pulled out her Sphere of Protection and cast an illumination spell on it. In the bluish-silver light she could see an ancient stone stairwell descending in front of her. Slowly she walked down the stairs. Mercurios sat on her shoulder muttering, "This is not good, not good indeed."

Emily reached the bottom of the stairs. She stood in the middle of an enormous stone storage room, panting for breath. Everywhere about her were hundreds of boxes and old pieces of dusty furniture piled about. She could hear the sound of thunder crashing and rolling above as the storm reached a higher pitch. Her heart pounded in her chest. Outside, the bursts of lightning lit up the whole landscape and were as dazzling and beautiful as they were terrifying in their destructive power.

"Mercurios," she said, holding up the pearl-and-ruby necklace. "This is from my dream."

"What?"

"That recurring dream, the dream I've been telling you about. I was in the room of a castle lying in bed and Mitchell was standing in front of me and I was wearing this necklace. It's Marigold's."

"What are you saying?"

"I-I don't know." Emily's heart was racing and her breathing was fast and shallow. She caught a glimpse of her reflection in a large, full-length, dusty, antique mirror and stopped and stared. "Oh my god, what's going on?"

Her heart beat faster, her head grew hotter; a ringing sound filled her ears, she felt oppressed, suffocated. She was on the verge of hysteria.

"Oh my god, Mercurios, it wasn't a recurring dream…" She stared at the imp, her eyes wide in horror. "It was a memory!"

She stumbled backward with the impact of this shattering realization and put her head in her hands.

"What do you mean?"

"That's the demon I'm possessed with and I'm having her memories! Don't you see? It's Marigold's demon that I'm possessed with and she's waking up!" She looked back at the reflection. "He said she was a demon. Am I possessed with the demon of Marigold Bonneville? Was it her all along? Trying to get back to Mitchell she traveled back to the worlds of the living into me, possessing me when I was in Magella, and then she came through the Well of Many Worlds inside me, to find him. Oh my god, and he even dressed me up and did my hair to look like her."

A new crashing rose above the thunder as dozens of zombies pounded at the door at the top of the stairs and fought to tear it down. Thunder crashed and split the air in the night above. Emily looked at herself in the mirror and let out a blood-curdling scream of terror. "IT'S THE DEMON OF MITCHELL'S EX-GIRLFRIEND. SHE'S COME BACK FROM HELL TO KILL ME AND POSSESS MY BODY SO SHE CAN HAVE HIM AGAIN!" Lightning and thunder flashed and exploded again and again above the castle as she started hyperventilating. Her body shook uncontrollably as tears streamed from her eyes. "Who am I?" her voice quavered. She stared at her reflection for a moment then let out a piercing scream and hurled the necklace at her reflection in the mirror. As the mirror shattered Emily stumbled backward and collapsed on the ground, unconscious.

Mitchell hacked and slashed his way through a group of zombies back to the door of the dungeon, holding the corpse of the princess in one hand. He pounded at the door with the hilt of his sword. "It's Mitchell, open the door."

Emily came to, crawled to her feet in a daze then ran up the stairs to the door, throwing it open. Headless bodies of zombies and ghouls were strewn about the great hall as Mitchell entered carrying the still-withered corpse of the princess. She was moaning and Emily looked at her with a mixture of revulsion and fascination as Mitchell slammed the doors behind him and locked them. He then carried her down the stairs and laid her on the cold stone floor.

"If I can revive her even the tiniest bit more I will be able to read her mind and see what she knows." He slashed a gash in his wrist and squeezed drops of blood into her mouth.

"Yes, her mind has not been destroyed," he whispered excitedly, closing his eyes to concentrate. He focused intently, searching for thoughts. "She found the rest of the diary – the records of one of the first vampires on Earth – in the Kungur Ice Caves." He looked at Emily. "I see the rest of the diary in her memories." He closed his eyes to concentrate harder. "An old, tattered book. Much is badly damaged, illegible, but there are still some readable parts. The year is 1781, and the author's name is… Yes, it's her, Selina – I can't make out her last name."

Emily leaned closer to hear Mitchell's voice, which had grown dimmer from the effort of concentrating.

"It says: 'I have come to hate these accursed caves. We have been hiding here for an eternity…' Then it says, 'We are making good progress… nearly figured out… words of command… written in a strange tongue. These words are alien to this world… I fear our Master has gone mad.' There are pages torn out here. The next page reads, 'I think of my children and wonder what their fate will be. Those nights when I slipped away in secret to make my children… yes, without a doubt the most exciting and fulfilling experience I have had since my birth into immortality. I will escape this madman and return to them someday, my children of the night…'" Mitchell paused and opened his eyes, staring into space. "So she was the one, Selina! She must mean the vampires she made – Fionn, Baelaar, Prince Vlad the Dracul, Squire Griffith and Princess Katharina… and who knows who else."

"I wonder who she was in life," Emily said quietly. "What she was like when she was human."

"We'll probably never know." Mitchell sighed, then closed his eyes and continued to focus. "'Our Master knows not that I have created them, nor do the others. I will never tell them about my children. They are my secret and I am confident they will remain my secret as our dark Master thinks of nothing save the artifact and no longer concerns himself with reading our thoughts. When we arrive in America, I will find a way to escape and then return to Europe to find my children. I fear nothing in this world save the loneliness of eternal night... We are to travel from London to New York on a passenger ship called the *Pinalute*. I look forward to the new world.'"

Mitchell stopped. "There is no more."

Emily felt her face turn pale. "The *Pinalute*?"

"Yes, why?" asked Mitchell, opening his eyes and looking at her curiously.

"Well, the antique desk my father left for me, hidden in my mom's garage, that had Vadas Asger carved in it. There was a plaque on the side that said *Pinalute*..."

Emily trailed off, taken aback by the ferocious look in Mitchell's eyes.

"The *Pinalute*? Where is it? Where is this desk?" He lunged forward, grabbing her arm, shaking her. Frightened, Emily shrank back, and Mercurios appeared in front of her, staring warily up at Mitchell. Realizing that he was scaring her, Mitchell released his grip and stepped back. "I apologize, Emily. You must understand – this is of the gravest importance. Where is it?"

"Buried outside Portland. It's just an empty desk, I already searched it."

"That must be the captain's desk. Thank you, Emily," he said softly, kissing her cheek. "This changes everything."

He began pacing as he tried to piece his thoughts together. "Once Baelaar finally managed to capture the princess and read the diary in her mind, he would have assumed the Well was aboard the *Pinalute* when it crossed and would have searched the shipping records in New York to track the ship down. But they obviously couldn't find what they were looking for. Reading the minds of the Initiates I dispatched in Portland, I learned that they have been hunting for something up and down the eastern coast of the US for several years now, but they didn't know what it was." He paused. "I don't understand. The shipping records should have given them all the information they needed about any ship that arrived to the New York port..."

"Unless it never arrived," Emily whispered.

A look of revelation crossed Mitchell's face. "Yes. Yes, that's it. That's it! That's why Baelaar has recruited everyone he can, even humans – the crime gangs, the drug traffickers, your friend's father that owns the shipping company, Mr. Denman – anyone connected with the eastern ports, eliminating anyone that refused to work for him. If there was no record of the ship's arrival, he'd assume the ship either sank or was blown off course by a storm and forced to land somewhere else. And all this time it was you – you – who had the captain's desk. It must have been washed ashore somewhere, probably containing the captain's log, which would have the last coordinates, the last location of the ship before it sank or went off course! If I can find those coordinates, I might be able to find the Well of Many Worlds." Mitchell's eyes were delirious with excitement.

"That's why they killed my father," Emily murmured to herself. Stunned, horrified. All along, it was the artifact that had brought her to this world that had cost her father – the most important part of her world – his life. At last she understood. "The desk must have been sent through Sammy's warehouse when my father bought it from whoever had found and restored it. When Cady came looking for it, Sammy must have told him that my father had a desk from a ship called the *Pinalute*. Cady contacted my father but was so aggressive and rude that he suspected something and denied having it, hiding it away in the garage so that he could do more research on it and find out why Cady wanted it so badly. Why it was so valuable to him. Dad must have thought it was an important historical artifact, worth a lot of money, and that maybe this was going to be his big financial break, and that he would be able to get his family back. But he never found out why they wanted it." Emily came back to the present and looked at Mitchell. "But what is Vadas Asger?"

"I don't know."

"Remember how at the warehouse they said they are going to liquidate all the works of art for gold?" said Mercurios. "Gold is valuable in Magella too. Perhaps it is the common currency in all the worlds. Indeed they are not just planning slaughter and enslavement here. They are also planning on traveling to Magella and perhaps beyond, with their gold, conquering and enslaving and slaughtering all mortals. They conquer one world, turn all its wealth to gold, take the gold to the next world where they use it to gain total power and loot and slaughter that world, then turn all the valuables of that world to gold, then take that gold to the next world and so on…"

"Yes, that's it!" exclaimed Mitchell. "They will have mountains of gold when they are finished selling everything, trillions of dollars worth. They are not just going to enslave and slaughter here, they are going to use the Well to systematically conquer all the worlds they can, looting each to finance the conquering of the next!"

"But I'm telling you, the desk is empty," said Emily. "There's nothing in it."

"Do you think you can teleport us back? Every second counts."

Emily nodded. "I-I think so."

"Your bedroom," said Mercurios. 'You know every inch of it, you should be able to visualize it very clearly."

"Are you sure? If I mess up we could be disintegrated."

"You can do it, Emily," Mercurios assured her.

She forced herself to concentrate as best she could. The fear of disintegration actually helped her focus.

"Take your time, Emily," Mercurios said, taking her hand as if protecting her from Mitchell's pressuring. He eyed Mitchell, and then squeezed Emily's hand again. "Yes, there is no need to rush. Just concentrate."

Emily struggled to block everything out, as she took Mitchell's hand and Mercurios hopped up onto her shoulder. She pictured her bedroom as clearly as she possibly could, felt the energy of the universe flowing all around and through her, and began channeling it. When she spoke the command words, there was a rushing sound all around them, and everything went black. Emily felt as though she was floating in the emptiness. Then they were back in the bedroom.

She let out a gasp of relief. "Yes, it worked!" she cried, as Mitchell embraced her.

"Amazing, Emily!"

The excitement faded as quickly as it came. There, sitting in her bedroom chair, casually flipping through a very old, battered book was Tom, still in his Crimson Ghost costume.

Twenty-Five

"What's he doing here?" Mitchell demanded.

For a moment Emily thought she saw a flicker of jealousy in his eyes. The thought thrilled her.

"Tom," she said nervously. "What are you doing here?"

Tom looked at Mitchell with utter disdain. "Jealous, buddy? I've been in her bedroom lots of times."

Mitchell gripped the hilt of his sword but Emily placed her hand on his.

"No, please don't hurt him," she whispered. "He's a really good person when he's not possessed." She turned back to Tom. "Tom, that's a lie and you know it."

"This is an interesting read," said Tom, tapping on the book. "Near the end, there are some particularly interesting entries. A lot of it's still legible. Shall I read it?"

"The captain's log!" Emily's eyes widened. "But where…?"

Tom stared back at the book, running his fingers over the pages. "I knew there must be something important in that desk, so I dug it up and smashed it. There was a hidden compartment."

Mitchell tried to read Tom's mind but saw nothing but darkness.

Emily took a few careful steps toward him. "Tom, that log is incredibly important.

Give it to me, please, and…"

"Stop," Tom snarled. He held up a hand and green flames burst from his palm, swirling around his fingers. "Unless you want me to incinerate it, you'll stay right there, shut your sweet little mouth, and listen like a good girl."

Emily froze. Mitchell's eyes blazed and he stepped forward but Tom moved his hand even closer to the book, his eyes challenging Mitchell to come closer. Mitchell stopped. He dared not risk the flames reaching the ancient, dried-out pages. Tom cleared his throat dramatically and began reading.

"There has been another murder. A young girl was found dead early this morning. Many of the passengers have locked themselves in their cabins... Blah, blah... Ah, here we go... A storm seems to have arisen out of nowhere. It is growing in fury by the minute."

"Tom?" Emily ventured carefully.

"Ah, ah... Shh..." Tom wagged his finger at her then turned to the final page of the book. "One of the passengers has lost his mind. He appeared on deck holding the decapitated heads of his companions, two men and one woman, by their hair. In his other hand he held a long, blood-streaked blade. As he faced us the storm seemed to heighten. The wind howled like a demon beast. His eyes were glowing crimson. I am now certain that he and his companions are responsible for the mysterious deaths on board. They are not human. I believe they are demons from the pits of Hell. May God save us! The crazed man hurled the heads overboard and screamed into the sky, 'I, Vadas Asger'"

"Vadas Asger!" Emily and Mitchell repeated in unison.

Tom looked at them. "You know him?"

"No," said Emily. "Never mind."

"So Vadas Asger was the first human on Earth to be turned into a vampire," muttered Mitchell.

Tom resumed reading. "'I, Vadas Asger, say that we are a blasphemy against God! Do you hear me? But no longer! When I am gone, this curse will be wiped from the Earth and the dead and damned will no longer walk with the living!' Then, he slashed his own throat so violently that his head was nearly severed from his shoulders, and he plunged into the seething waves." Tom burst out laughing. "Man, I wish I could have seen that, that would have been hilarious!" He shut the book and gave Emily a penetrating stare.

"So that's what happened to them," said Emily quietly, glancing at Mitchell.

"Vadas killed them then destroyed himself, thinking he was ridding the world of vampires, not realizing that Selina had made others."

Tom chuckled. "Pfft, and your boyfriend here is descended from those bloodsucking freaks."

"Tom," said Emily, trying to stay calm. "Mercurios knows what happened to you. He's figured a way to cure you. Right, Mercurios?"

Mercurios appeared on her desk. "Yes, I believe I have."

"What is that disgusting little thing?"

The imp glared angrily at him. "Very foolish words, yes, very foolish indeed."

"What a hideous little toad creature!"

"I'm an imp, damn you!" shrieked Mercurios shaking his little fists.

"Once I'm finished with smart guy here" – Tom gestured at Mitchell – "I'm going to squash that repulsive little toad head of yours, you freak." He stood up and faced Mitchell. "I don't like you hanging around my girlfriend, she's my pretty little pet, get it?"

"Tom!" Emily was frustrated beyond endurance. "Please just give me that book. We don't have time for this!"

He pushed his Crimson Ghost face into hers and screamed, "Don't you understand? I love you!"

Mitchell moved to protect Emily but Tom grabbed him with superhuman speed and Mitchell burst into green flames. He howled in pain and rage and his whole body thrashed violently about as he burned. Tom spun and hurled him backward with such force that he launched Mitchell like a cannonball through the window, glass shattering as he flew through the branches of the tree outside.

"Mitchell!" Emily screamed.

Never had Emily imagined that her death would come like this. Not that she had given the subject much thought. But nothing that had happened in her life previously could have prepared her for the events of the last two weeks.

Tom tore off his mask, revealing the crazed obsession that burned in his eyes. He advanced upon her and gave her an almost friendly smile and a wink.

Emily felt a terrible sadness that she would never be able to avenge the murder of her father. She then thought of her love. Had he been destroyed? Her fear vanished and was replaced with a feeling of overwhelming gratitude for having been able to experience something so transcendental. She loved him unconditionally, irrevocably and eternally. The thought filled her with courage.

Tom's eyes had turned into glowing green orbs, inhuman and demonic. Emily raised her chin and stared into them defiantly, daring him to kill her.

"You're mine now forever," Tom whispered fiercely.

Mitchell came leaping back in through the window, the flames extinguished, and threw himself on Tom. They both crashed clean through the wall and across the guest bedroom next door. Emily spotted the book on the floor between Tom's feet and remembered her Ring of Teleportation. Taking a picture in her mind of the scene that lay before her, she closed her eyes and spoke the command. A split second later, she was right beside them. As she reached for the book she was hit by Tom's elbow as he drew it back to punch Mitchell. She tumbled over the bed and hit the dresser.

"Emily!" Mitchell shouted, but Tom kicked him in the chest, sending him flying through a large, standing mirror. Tom snatched up the book.

"You hit my elbow, you idiot!" he shouted at the unconscious Emily.

Tom was creating orbs of green fire in his hand and hurling them like fastballs with superhuman speed and agility. Mitchell dodged three and swept out his sword, using it to deflect them in every direction. As they hit the walls, ceiling and floor the orbs burst into flame.

Coming to and shaking the stars out of her head, Emily grabbed her wand from where it had fallen on the floor. Tom was throwing five fire orbs every second. Mitchell had got his eye in and was now batting them back straight at Tom, sending him stumbling backward, momentarily stunned.

Seizing his opportunity, Mitchell leaped across the room into a diving roll while sheathing his sword, rose up from the floor in front of Tom, grabbed him by his jacket and pulled him into a back somersault, using his feet to launch him, upside down, through another wall.

Flames rushed up the walls, burning in waves across a section of the ceiling and consumed a chair in the corner.

"You all right?" Mitchell shouted and Emily nodded. "Good. Get out of the house!"

"Mitchell, please don't kill him, we can still save him!" she screamed.

He nodded and charged after Tom, rocketing across the room through the hole in the wall as Emily ran out of the burning bedroom and down the stairs. Mitchell jabbed Tom in the face as he was getting up. Tom tried to swing back but Mitchell was faster and hit him with a couple of body shots and a thundering uppercut.

"Emily is mine!" Tom screamed, catching Mitchell with a right hook and pushing him back through the hole into the guest bedroom. Mitchell swiveled, grabbing Tom in a bear hug, powering right through the window, crashing together through glass and branches.

As Emily ran for the front door, Mitchell and Tom plummeted past the window and she stopped to watch what would happen next. They hit the ground hard and continued their struggle. Mitchell swung at Tom, who ducked at the last moment. His fist smashed into the trunk of the tree and splintered a section of it. Tom caught Mitchell with a straight left that sent him sprawling across the lawn. He was back on his feet in a flash, kicking Tom in the knee and sending him backward toward the street. Mitchell pounced on him, viciously pummeling his face. The book soared out of Tom's hand and skidded onto the street.

"Well, well, well. Delivered right into my hands. You truly have outdone yourself, Mitchell."

The powerful voice stopped the fighters in their tracks and they looked up to see Mephris, Lord Ruthen, the Comtesse LeDuijou, and three other vampires standing in the street, along with Cady Sunner. To Emily's utter shock and horror, her mother and Mr. Denman were with them.

Mitchell snarled at the vampire who had spoken and who now bent to pick up the book. "Baelaar." There was a look of utter hate and bloodlust in his eyes, a wicked smile forming on his lips as he rose to his feet. "Finally, after all these years."

Emily stared at the vampire Mitchell had called Baelaar. So he was the one. His hair was professionally dyed blood red and he wore it slicked back. His skin was pale and he wore black eyeliner smoked out. Across his shoulders was a bright-green crocodile-skin cloak with fur trim that hung down past his knees. Crocodile-skin boots and black pants along with a skull belt and black dress shirt completed his outfit. In his right hand he held a black cane with a gold skull with diamond eyes on the end. On his fingers were bejeweled gold rings. Wrapped around the fingers of his left hand was a tiny, bright-green snake. On his left shoulder sat a large raven.

"See?" Cady Sunner crowed. "I told you we would find him here. I saw him in the warehouse that night with the girl."

Mitchell glanced at Lord Ruthen with seething hatred.

"Hello, Mitchell," Ruthen purred.

"Once I'm finished with Baelaar, you're next."

"Hey, Freakshow, give me that book," Tom snarled at Baelaar.

Mephris looked him up and down, amazed at his audacity. "Who is this bit of meat in the clown costume?"

"Pipe down, pig face. I wasn't talking to you." Tom strode over to Mephris and stood before him, hands at his hips. "What? You some kind of tough guy?"

Mephris lunged for him but Tom pulled the vampire's coat over his head and began punching. The others watched in shock, trying to figure out how a human could possess such strength and speed.

Emily watched in disbelief from the window, her face deathly pale and her bottom lip trembling. "Mom?" she muttered. She stared at her mother and Mr. Denman standing by Cady Sunner, the man who had murdered her father, as though they were friends. She vaguely realized that the person in Tom's grasp was the vampire named Mephris. She didn't recognize the rest, but they all had the inhumanly pale skin of vampires. She couldn't tear her eyes off her mother; there was something about her that wasn't right; she looked like the others. Had her mother been turned into a vampire? Had she been in league with them all along? It was too horrifying to imagine.

"Is that why dad didn't trust her?" muttered Emily as she held up her wand and opened the front door.

"Run, Mom!" she shouted. "Get away from them! I have you covered. If any of them come after you I'll blast them with a lightning bolt."

"What on Earth are you talking about, dear?" her mother asked. "And why are you pointing that stick at us? Please, please listen to me. I know this is a terrible shock to you but let me explain. Mr. Denman and I have been together for a little over a year. A little while ago Cady Sunner and Mephris contacted Mr. Denman about shipping some things over from Europe. They were offering a huge amount of money. They were also looking for an antique captain's desk from a ship. By the time I understood what was going on and that your father was involved, they had killed him." Her eyes grew wide and wet as she pleaded with her daughter. "You have to believe me. Then they said they would kill us if I told the police. I didn't know what to do. Then late last night they, they turned us into vampires."

She glanced nervously at Mephris and Tom fighting. Then she looked back at Emily who was slowly shaking her head as tears ran down her cheeks.

"No, no, no, no, no," Emily muttered.

"Come to mommy, they've promised they won't harm us if we turn you into a vampire and they promised to make us rich." Her eyes brightened. "We'll be able to live together as a happy family. There are a lot worse fates in this world than being rich and immortal, Emily."

Tom shoved Mephris away and burst out laughing. "Your mother is one of those blood-sucking freaks!" He pointed at Emily. "What a burn! You just got totally burned! Ah ha your life sucks, you loser!" Mephris pounced on him and they continued fighting.

"Come and live with you and Mr. Denman and the people who murdered Dad?" Emily screamed. "As a family? Oh my god, you are psycho! That's why Dad didn't want you to know about it; even back then he didn't trust you."

"What?" her mother asked.

"You are a psycho!" Emily screamed.

Baelaar finished flipping through the captain's log and closed it, pulling out a cell phone and punching some numbers into it.

"Mmmm delicious delectable Mitchell," murmured the Comtesse LeDuijou. "Still looking sooooo gorgeous!"

Emily pointed her wand at Comtesse LeDuijou, filled with fierce jealousy. "Who the hell are you?"

"Thank you for the coordinates, Mitchell," said Baelaar. "Now we will be on our way."

As fast as lightning Mitchell kicked Baelaar in the chest, sending him flying backward into a parked car. The impact crushed the side of the car and the windows exploded. The raven let out a squawk of fright and frantically flapped its wings as it rose into the air.

"Mephris!" Baelaar shouted as he got to his feet. "Stop fooling around! Everyone, follow me, leave the girl for later."

Mephris managed to struggle free of Tom. His eyes blazed red with rage, and he growled like an animal. A split second later, Baelaar was gone, racing down the street like the wind, followed by his raven and the other vampires. Mitchell sprang after them.

Cady Sunner stared at the demolished car in horror. "My car!" he cried, drawing his gun and pointing it at Tom. Emily aimed her wand at Cady, but Tom was faster. He knocked the gun out of Cady's hand and punched him in the jaw, sending him crashing into another parked car. Then Tom spread his hands wide and an area of glowing green swirling vapor appeared all around him until it was as if his whole body, except for his eyes, had disappeared into it. The cloud of green vapor then flew after the vampires, leaving Cady Sunner lying unconscious in the street.

Emily took out her phone and dialed.

"Detective Scannel? Cady Sunner is smashing up parked cars in front of my house, waving around a gun… Great, thanks… I think it might be the same gun as the one he used to kill my father… Thanks, oh also, my house is on fire."

She hung up and turned to Mercurios, who had appeared on her shoulder, gawking at the spectacle. "Mercurios, I think the vampires are going to use their power over the elements to go to the bottom of the ocean after the Well. Is the Sphere of Protection strong enough to keep the water away from me if we follow them?"

"Yes."

"Good, then let's go."

"But, Emily, you have Cady lying unconscious in the street! He is helpless, perfect for your first kill. Blast him unmerciful, Emily!"

"It's not my right. I am not the judge, jury, and executioner. That is not how a civilized society works. It's not how my father raised me."

"Ah, but our good friend Mitchell would not hesitate to kill him, Emily. Cady is a murderer, you know he is, and Mitchell hunts murderers. If it's okay for him to kill, then why not you? You know for certain that Sunner is guilty."

Emily looked down at the unconscious body of her father's murderer.

"Yes," continued the imp. "Surely, there is nothing wrong with killing a killer, Emily. He rightfully deserves it."

"My father… My father would be ashamed, and besides, Mitchell is a vampire and…"

She paused, remembering something Mitchell had told her.

"What?" asked Mercurios. "That makes it okay?"

"No. You just gave me an idea."

*

Mitchell flew like a bullet through the night after the other vampires with Tom close behind. As they barreled toward the shore he could see dozens of other vampires joining the group up ahead.

*

Emily plucked her pendant from around her neck, placed it on the ground, and spoke the words of command. The chest swelled to full size. She opened it and took out the Skull of Monster Summoning.

"What are you doing?" asked Mercurios. "The Skull of Summoning is only for summoning beings of darkness, Emily. Monsters!"

"I know."

"Well then, what are you doing? Very curious, what monster might you be intending to summon?"

"Just trust me."

Emily found a stone lying in the grass and used it to trace a circle on the ground in front of her. Then, she held the skull and spoke the command words, channeling the magical energy. Soon, the skull's eyes began to glow. It sent out a shockwave that made Emily stumble but she was prepared for it this time. Emily spoke a name in a firm, clear voice.

"Who, in the burning bogs of Caeltrethon, is Sylvain DeLune?" Mercurios asked.

Twenty-Six

Mitchell hurtled past the warehouses and down to the shore. Reaching the water, he used his control over the elements to freeze an icy path beneath him as he ran. Dark clouds massed overhead and he could hear thunder rumbling in the distance. An area of darkness, blacker than the surrounding night, gathered ahead of him, stretching out over the ocean as he rushed toward it.

With a final crackle of energy, Emily stumbled backward, gasping for air. The summoning had taken so much concentration and effort that for a moment she thought she might faint. But it had been worth it. Standing before her, wreathed in ruby mist, was Sylvain DeLune, exactly as Mitchell had described him. He looked as though he had just stepped out of a party thrown by Marie Antoinette herself. He carried a sword by his side and held a crystal glass filled with what looked like blood. He was in the middle of uttering something when he appeared.

"And that my friends is why I never— WHAT ON EARTH?" Dropping the glass, Sylvain looked around in wild confusion. "What the… Where… What is happening?"

"Technically vampires are beings of darkness," Emily told a stunned Mercurios. "Monsters." She then spoke the command words to turn off the skull. She put it back in the chest, shrunk the chest and snatched it up before turning her attention to Sylvain. "Hello, Sylvain. I'm a wizard and I summoned you."

He looked her up and down and one eyebrow rose suggestively.

Emily could feel herself blush a little. "I'm a wizard from another world. I used a magical skull to summon you."

"Are you mad, woman?"

"No. There's no time to explain. Your friend, Mitchell Keats, is in trouble. The Priests of Mezzor are after him. If we don't help him, they will enslave the whole world!"

"Mitchell? Where? I haven't seen Mitchell in ages!"

"He told me you swore an oath to repay him for the kindness he showed you."

"I did."

"Then hold my hand!"

Sylvain hesitated for a moment and then clasped Emily's outstretched fingers. Visualizing the waterfront area clearly in her mind, she activated her Ring of Teleportation. Just as the sound of approaching police sirens grew louder, they were gone.

*

Mitchell watched the group of vampires stop. Bursts of lightning exploded between the ominous clouds and thunder rolled all around him. The vampires disappeared into the ocean. Mitchell summoned all of his supernatural power and drew his sword; the water in front of him parted as he plunged into it. It felt like he'd jumped off a cliff as he fell. He had surrounded himself with a bubble of air about fifteen feet in diameter, using the strength of his will to keep the millions of tons of water from caving in and crushing him.

*

The command words were barely out of Emily's mouth before she and Sylvain materialized on the waterfront.

"Impressive!" said Sylvain. "How on earth...?"

"Shh. There's no time to explain." Emily stared into the distance. Ahead, across the water, she saw the storm brewing. Lightning flashed in the clouds and the distant rumbling of thunder was almost continuous. "There they are." She pointed. "They're under those storm clouds – I'm sure of it."

"Let the vampire deal with this," said Mercurios, appearing on her shoulder. "Very dangerous indeed."

Sylvain stared at the imp in amazement. "What on earth is that… thing?"

"Never mind. Sylvain, Mitchell is out there, at the bottom of the ocean. I can't get us there, because I don't know exactly what it looks like. Can you get us there?"

Sylvain looked out at the water and then back at her. "My dear, I can make my own road to walk on as I please."

"Okay, then don't mind me. Just go." Emily climbed onto the vampire's back.

Sylvain leaped forward. He ran, freezing the water beneath him into an icy pathway, just as he'd boasted he could. As they sped over the waves, Emily prayed that they weren't too late.

*

Mitchell plunged into the abyss, the flames from his sword flickering and dancing on the walls of water that rushed by, plummeting hundreds of feet each second. He saw the dim shapes of the large group of vampires submerged below him. Down, down, down he fell. The pressure was mounting every minute, but Mitchell was strong. He had gained a great command over the elements. As he plunged deeper and deeper he was able to keep the crushing weight of the water at bay, falling faster and faster. Tom was close behind him.

One by one Mitchell overtook the Initiates. One young vampire appeared out of his depth. As Mitchell hurtled by, he slashed him brutally with his flaming sword. The young vampire screamed in agony, lost control and was swallowed by the ocean, the pressure crushing him and bursting his bones into millions of pieces, as it had done to Mitchell so many years before.

More Initiates appeared out of the darkness. He passed a dozen more in his plunge and one after another they each met the same fate as their companion. The immensity of the ocean around and above him felt all too familiar. At last, he landed on the bottom. The flames running up and down the blade of his sword illuminated the surrounding area. Lying on its side on the ocean floor before him, like the skeleton of a long-dead whale, was the sunken ship they were after. As Mitchell approached it his feet sank into the wet sand. He entered the hull, still surrounded by a bubble of air. He walked through a couple of cabins on what was once the starboard side of the ship but was now little more than rotted timbers interspersed with rocks and sand. Ahead of him in the liquid darkness, he saw a glow.

Emerging from what had once been the main storage area, carrying a magnificent silver bowl covered in strange-looking runes, was Baelaar with his raven once again perched upon his shoulder, surrounded by the gang of vampires. A magical, swirling mist filled the silver bowl, emanating an unearthly light. That's it, Mitchell thought in awe. The Well of Many Worlds.

*

When they reached the spot where Emily had seen the vampires disappear underwater, she activated her Sphere of Protection, and Sylvain drew his sword, plunging straight down through the waves. Emily held on for dear life as they dove through pitch-black darkness. She cast an illumination spell on Mercurios, making his gray skin glow with a bright, silvery-blue light that lit the ocean around them for a hundred feet.

*

Mitchell hesitated momentarily, entranced by the artifact's beauty. Baelaar, Mephris, Lord Ruthen, the Comtesse LeDuijou and six other elders saw him and drew their swords. They were joined by a large group of Initiates. Their combined power created a dome of air at least forty feet across. It rose twenty feet above them, as though they were all standing in an immense glass room. He set his gaze firmly upon his archenemy, while Baelaar focused on the Well. His eyes glowed with lust as he caught glimpses of other worlds materializing and dissolving again and again in the mist inside.

"Well, Mitchell," he said eventually, his voice filled with awe. "You truly have outdone yourself. I thank you. With this offering, you have repaid me for my gift of immortality to you."

"If you join us, Mitchell," the Comtesse LeDuijou coaxed, "you can be my master." She winked at him.

Mitchell ignored her.

"Baelaar, I may not be able to out-fight all of you. But I can assure you that I'll be taking you with me to the gates of Hell. I am no longer that reckless youth you sent to the bottom of the ocean all those years ago. Every ounce of my being has been focused to a dagger's point. There is nothing that will save you from me. No power in existence will stand in my way. You are utterly doomed."

"Well said, Mitchell." Lord Ruthen spoke up, slowly turning to Baelaar. "All right, Baelaar. Give me the Well."

Baelaar tore his eyes away from his prize. "What?"

"You heard me."

Mitchell was staring in shock at Lord Ruthen when Tom fell from the ocean above, landing in the middle of the group. The vampires stared at him, confused, trying again to comprehend how a human could possess such power.

"What is this?" Tom looked around. "Some kind of underwater freak convention? You." He pointed at Mitchell. "I'm going to make something very clear to you, so you never forget it."

"Who is this bucket of blood," Baelaar demanded, "and how does he have these powers?"

Tom spun around, leaping at Baelaar and punching him in the face. Baelaar flew backward, slamming into an enormous wooden beam, splintering it and dropping the Well. The raven squawked and flew about. There was a blinding flash and a bolt of energy leaped out of the Well, exploding into Lord Ruthen's chest. The vampire was blasted backward with such speed and force he shot hundreds of yards into the black, crushing water that surrounded them. While two of the other vampires attacked Tom, Mephris rushed at Mitchell, who vaulted over him to face Baelaar, aiming a deadly strike at his head. Baelaar dodged the deathblow by inches and Mitchell sliced a deep wound through his arm. Baelaar let out a shriek. Mephris, the Comtesse LeDuijou and more than a dozen of Baelaar's minions turned to attack Mitchell together, leaving one to brawl with Tom.

Mitchell fought like a man possessed, slashing, kicking, punching with superhuman speed, focus and acrobatic precision, but battling all of them at once was too much even for him.

"I don't want to be that psycho chick who says 'If I can't have him no one will,'" the Comtesse LeDuijou announced. "But, if I can't have you, no one will!"

Her sword flashed with bursts of electricity as she attacked Mitchell. Mitchell felt every bite of every blade from each of their weapons. He slashed, spun, kicked, flipped, dodged, dove, rolled and stabbed with such mad ferocity that the spraying blood became a thick mist in the air. Mephris caught him with a well-placed thrust, plunging his blade through Mitchell's side, while another slashed him across the back. Mitchell howled in pain and barely dodged a sweeping strike from the Comtesse LeDuijou that would have taken his head clean off.

Baelaar rushed past him and seized the Well with his good arm as his raven landed on his shoulder. He was about to charge into the ocean through a hole in the wreck and start the long journey to the surface, when he looked up and paused, astonished at what he saw. Following his gaze, the vampires all looked up to see a globe of bright, silvery-blue light descending upon them, as though the moon had fallen from the sky into the depths of the ocean. As the light drew closer, they saw a vampire with a girl on his back, who carried some sort of glowing, grinning creature on her shoulder, descending from above.

"Crush them unmerciful!" cried Mercurios with delight, shaking his little fist in the air.

"Vaza bel thlemin," Emily shouted and a bolt of lightning leaped from her wand, striking the astonished Comtesse LeDuijou square in the chest and sending her hurtling into the dark water that surrounded them. "Vaza bel thlemin," she cried again and another bolt blasted into Baelaar. The raven exploded in a cloud of feathers as Baelaar dropped the Well and was hurled to one side, smashing back through the rotten timbers of the ship. As soon as Sylvain landed on the ocean floor, Emily jumped off his back. She looked around for her mother and Mr. Denman but they had disappeared.

"You!" Baelaar spluttered, recognizing Sylvain, the young man he had turned into a vampire all those years ago. "I turned you into a debauched maniac."

"And I thank you for it." Sylvain gave a roguish grin.

With that Sylvain attacked Mephris and two other vampires. Mitchell seized the opportunity to renew his attack, slashing one vampire across his chest and then parrying an attack from another, just as another lightning bolt leaped from Emily's wand. It struck the vampire full in the face, electrocuting him. His body went into hideous, jerking spasms, and smoke rose from it. A clap of thunder shook the ocean around them. Great bursts of electricity shot out in every direction from the Well and beside it a huge black gate opened up. Out of it emerged a beast unlike anything any of them had ever seen. Its body was that of an enormous green turtle, twice the size of an elephant, with the head of a dragon and a great fin that ran down the back of its long, thick neck. Its teeth were the size of butcher knives.

The monster crashed into the middle of the battle, roaring in rage and confusion, sending up a great spray of wet sand and splintering numerous beams as it thrashed. Everyone leaped, dived or rolled out of the way except Mephris. He had been so intensely focused on Sylvain that he was the last to see the creature that had appeared behind him. He spun around just in time to see the monster's jaws gaping wide. He let out a brief, piercing shriek before the teeth closed around him, tearing him in half.

Tom grabbed Emily, snarling like a deranged animal, "You're mine!" Just as the creature's tail swung around and knocked them both flying into the Well. Tom's scream abruptly ended as he disappeared into the magical mist. Emily managed to catch hold of the rim of the Well. As she struggled not to get sucked in she felt as though her body was being pulled in two. Mercurios tugged frantically at her arm.

"Mitchell!" she screamed.

"Just let go," Mercurios shouted. "We will go through the Well to Magella. Just let go!"

"No! Stop it!" she screamed. "Not without Mitchell!"

Distracted by the horror of seeing Tom vanish into another world and by the effort of trying to pull herself out of the Well, she didn't notice the dragon turtle had now turned its attention to her. The beast opened its jaws and lunged. Mitchell hewed off the head of the last remaining vampire and sprang onto the back of the monster's shell. The great beast lunged and thrashed, its long neck striking like a snake. Emily screamed and desperately tried to pull herself out of the Well as Mitchell, with three swift, perfectly placed strikes, beheaded the beast. He leaped off its back as the creature's head writhed on the ocean floor, kicking up a sand storm, its gargantuan body collapsing onto Baelaar as he struggled to reach the Well.

Trapped beneath tons of dead flesh and shell, with only his head and shoulders sticking out, Baelaar was unable to free himself before Mitchell pounced upon him. At long last, he had his archenemy within his clutches. Mitchell's eyes burned with vengeful fury as he raised his sword for the kill.

To her horror, Emily saw that her whole body was beginning to turn into the magical mist. She was caught halfway between two worlds and was beginning to transform into pure energy. She was disintegrating and the pain was excruciating. She screamed in agony.

"I'm dying, Mitchell, help!"

Mitchell had a split second to choose between fulfilling the dream of revenge he had pursued for so long and saving Emily's life. He flew across the space between them and began to drag her out of the Well. Baelaar managed to struggle out from under the carcass of the dragon turtle. He rushed up behind Mitchell and kicked him in the back, sending him over the edge, into the Well. Like Emily he managed to grab onto the rim to stop himself from plunging all the way in. He too began to disintegrate into a mist of pure energy. He and Emily were merging into one, engulfed by the mist, becoming one being of pure energy that blazed forth, lighting up the ocean around them for hundreds of meters.

Baelaar positioned himself to push them further into the Well when the light and power generated by them merging into one, blinded him and his flesh burst into flame. Baelaar rushed, shrieking into the vast, dark ocean as Sylvain dove behind the dragon turtle carcass to avoid meeting the same fate.

Emily's whole being was engulfed by the brightest light that she had ever imagined and she knew that her physical form had transformed into pure energy. She could feel Mitchell's presence and could feel the two of them merging into one. An incredible cascade of memories flashed through her mind and what she saw shook her being to its core.

Twenty-Seven

South of England May 1563

The blinding flash of light disappeared, then, as if waking from a dream, Emily found herself in another time and place. She was aware that it was late spring in England in the year 1563. Mitchell was still human. He had gone hunting, riding out from his family's castle far into the countryside. A violent thunderstorm had passed through a few hours before but now everything was calm as evening fell and the full moon rose in the east. Mitchell inhaled the fresh, fragrant scent of the forest and meadows, filled with joy. He tethered his horse to a tree and crept up a ridge beside a cliff face, stalking a magnificent stag.

At the top of the ridge Mitchell crouched down and silently stretched his bow. He had a perfect shot as the beast stood silhouetted in front of the full moon. Just as he was ready to let the arrow fly, something spooked the animal and it bounded away into the forest. A moment later Mitchell saw what looked like a woman appear where the stag had been only a moment before, silhouetted in front of the moon. He was convinced he must be experiencing a mystical vision. He was far from any town or village, so to see a woman in an elegant dress wandering out here in the wilderness at night was beyond bizarre.

"What is this?" he hissed as he lowered his bow. "Is it a ghost?" A shiver went down Mitchell's spine as he stared transfixed. The apparition moved toward him and he slowly stood up as if pulled by some outside force.

When the figure collapsed on the ground he rushed forward to see who or what it was.

He knelt down and turned the woman over to see a beautiful girl about the same age as him. Her hair and dress were wet and disheveled. She had a fresh cut above her temple, surrounded by a purple bruise, and her hands were covered with dirt. For a moment Mitchell could only stare at the girl in wonder.

"Has some sorcery transformed the stag into a lady?" he wondered aloud. "After all Artemis turned Acteon into a stag for seeing her virginal modesty and ravishing beauty. But now the stag has transformed into Artemis, for this is no mere lady, this is a goddess whose lustrous beauty shines so radiantly that all the stars in their burning spheres are sick with envy and weep silver tears." He glanced up at the sky then back at Marigold. "But the night grows dark, come, I will protect her and take care of her until I find out the name of this bright angel and from which of the heavens she fell to earth to grace this crude, rough, shoddy world with her glorious perfection."

He picked her up in his arms and carried her to his horse, Sunalus.

Watching this scene unfold, Emily realized that the girl was Marigold and she now found herself entering into Marigold's memories of the event. The night before she had fallen into an argument with her father and had woken up early that morning still angry with him. She decided to go for a ride to clear her head. It was a beautiful day so she continued riding for hours, getting further and further away from the familiar lands that surrounded her father's castle. In the early afternoon a thunderstorm had blown up out of nowhere. Marigold was just about to turn back when a lightning bolt struck a tree only a few yards away. Her terrified horse reared and threw her to the ground as a burning branch cracked away from the tree above and crashed down on top of them. Marigold hit her head on a rock, rendering her unconscious.

Some time later she had awoken, dazed and soaking wet from the rain. Her horse was nowhere to be seen. She began the long walk home, but grew disoriented. Scared, lost, wet and cold, she wandered in circles for hours until, exhausted and still delirious from the blow to her head, she finally collapsed. When she opened her eyes she found herself staring up into the face of a handsome young man.

"Are you an angel?" she asked in a weak voice.

The young man smiled. "You are safe now."

She smiled and nodded, slipping back into unconsciousness and holding tightly onto him.

Emily's memories shifted. It was five months later, October 31st 1563, All Hallows Eve. Mitchell and Marigold were standing on the top of a hill. The full moon was rising in the east, bathing the beautiful countryside with a magical, silvery-blue light. The hill overlooked a small cemetery and areas of forest and rolling hills that lay around Mitchell's father's castle. Marigold had made a circle of freshly picked wildflowers and they stood within the circle facing each other, staring into each other's eyes.

"It is said that a blood oath sworn under a full moon on All Hallows Eve, when the barriers between this world and the world of magic are at their weakest, will last forever," said Marigold, then laughed.

Mitchell smiled and said nothing.

"We will bind our souls together forever," Marigold whispered.

"I would love nothing more," Mitchell murmured.

"Then here underneath the twilight skies in the glow of a wild cat's eyes, I invoke Queen Mab," laughed Marigold. "And all the faerie kings and queens as they sit on their foxglove thrones, and all other mystical powers, to witness and bless our blood oath and our love and intertwine our two souls and destinies into one thread forever until the end of all things. Beneath the inconstant, ever changing moon, our love will remain changeless and will burn as an eternal flame. We invoke the powers of magic to bind our souls together for eternity. Hear our oath!"

She drew out a dagger and cut a gash in her right palm down her lifeline. She winced in pain and then took Mitchell's left hand and did the same along his lifeline. Then she held up her hand, her bleeding palm facing him. He did the same and their fingers entwined and their palms met and their blood mingled and Marigold wrapped their hands together with a thick red silk thread.

"I hereby join my spirit with yours forever," she said. "In this life and in all lives to come until the end of time."

"I hereby join my spirit with yours forever," said Mitchell. "In this life and in all lives to come until the end of time."

A breeze rustled the leaves of the trees and bent the blades of grass as the two lovers kissed.

Emily's memories shifted again. It was eight months later, now mid-summer of the next year. Mitchell was standing in the great hall of his family's castle in the midst of an argument with his father, the duke.

"I make no apologies for what I have done."

"But you will be hanged!" the duke shouted, slamming his fist upon the table and rising to his feet.

"I know!" Mitchell shouted back.

"What good will that do anyone? Will you throw your life away?"

"I will fight and slay every last one of his men if I must! If I have to die to save our people, our country, then so be it. Throughout the lands the revolt is brewing and I will lead them."

"Are you foolish enough to think that I was not aware, ever since the arrival of this new advisor, that the Lord Protector is a changed man? Are you fool enough to think that I have not spent weeks now planning the most effective way to remove this advisor without raising the suspicions of the Lord Protector and risking a civil war?"

Mitchell hesitated. What new advisor? Had he sabotaged his father's plans? His heart plummeted.

"You are impetuous!" thundered the duke. "Impulsive! Reckless! You think you grasp the scope of all that occurs here, yet you understand nothing! And because of that, all my carefully laid planning is for naught! Politics is a game of chess, son, a game of patience and strategy, and you... you've come along and kicked over all the pieces like a blundering fool!"

"Surely you can understand," Mitchell responded, less angry now, "that I cannot stand by for a single day more, seeing starved corpses in the fields, families being destroyed all across our country! He is literally taxing our people to death. How many more families must be destroyed before you take action? The people are against him. The time has come. He will be overthrown! Father please" – he approached the duke – "if I have made a shambles of your plans with my hot-headedness then I will earn back my honor with my sword or with my blood."

The duke stared at him for a moment then smiled and waved his hand. "Ah, it would have come to this sooner or later." He stared out of the window. "I had simply hoped for more time..." He looked back at Mitchell and placed a hand upon his shoulder and smiled. "Your courage and your love for your people is repayment enough, my son."

One of their servants entered the room and bowed. "Sire, Marigold Bonneville..."

"Marigold!" exclaimed Mitchell, swinging around.

"The daughter of the Lord Protector?" the duke growled.

"Show her in," Mitchell ordered before his father could turn her away. The woman hurried from the room.

The duke peered at his son. "I see there is more to this than I thought."

Marigold entered the room with the servant and curtsied gracefully. She appeared to be distressed.

"Marigold, welcome," said the duke, calming his irritation with difficulty. "What brings you here?"

Her gaze shifted between father and son, then settled on the duke. "Sir," she began nervously, "I have grave tidings. My father is sending a large armed force here. You and both of your sons are to be tried and hanged for high treason and the rest of your family banished. He believes that you have been plotting against him. He is sending all his men in the hope this will provoke the rebellion he knows is coming, that all the traitors will rally around you when he strikes. That way he believes it will be easy for him to crush the revolution before it has been properly organized."

"This is outrageous!" roared the duke. "How dare he threaten me? And why would you betray your father to come here and warn us of this atrocity, young miss?"

"Please," she implored him, "you have only a few hours."

"MY ARMOR!" shouted the duke as he strode out of the room. A few moments later trumpets blared outside and a knot hardened in Mitchell's stomach. Marigold rushed forward and embraced him.

"Why on earth did you have to challenge my father like that, in front of everyone?"

"I could not stand for it any longer. He is destroying our country, our people, everything we love! I had to do something!"

"Someday you will be a strong leader, Mitchell. Your people love you. I can easily imagine you becoming king one day." She took his hands in hers. "Please do not hate him. You do not know him like I do. He is not himself lately. Dark changes have come over him ever since his new advisor arrived. Everything seems..." She struggled for a moment to find the words. "Like a waking nightmare."

"Who is this man everyone is blaming?"

"He arrived one evening, just after sunset. His name is Baelaar – that is all that I know. When I look into his eyes, I feel despair pierce the core of my being." She shivered at the recollection. "It is as if the world I knew has disappeared, and I am alone in a vast, dark wilderness. It is as if my father has become a different person. He scarcely remembers me anymore."

"I had to stand up for our country, our people! Can you not see that?"

Marigold gazed at Mitchell. "Yes," she said. "I do understand. And I love you for it."

Mitchell stared at her for a moment. Then, he took her in his arms and pressed her body against his. His desire for her, ignited by her beauty and the warmth of her flesh, so close to his, pulsed through his blood. They kissed luxuriantly.

"And with your father removed from power, nothing will stand between us," Mitchell said after a few moments of bliss.

"Is that what this is really about?"

"You are mine!" He grabbed her by her shoulders. "I promise I will not harm your father, but he must be removed from power, and then you will be my wife. I will let nothing stand in the way of that."

Marigold gasped with excitement at this display of all-consuming passion. Mitchell reached over to an ornate wooden box on a nearby table. He opened it and took out the pearl necklace with the ruby-and-diamond pendant Emily remembered from her dream and from the chapel.

"Happy Birthday, my love. I wish your eighteenth birthday could come under better circumstances."

As Mitchell secured it around her delicate neck, tears rolled down Marigold's cheeks.

"It's beautiful!"

The danger that Mitchell was about to walk into was suddenly agonizingly clear to both of them, and the possibility that this might be the last time they would see each other in this life filled them with terrible dread.

"I love you more than life itself," he said. "You are my heart and my soul and my everything, just as we swore, in this world and in all worlds, forever... and time and death cannot touch that."

He took her in his arms and she reached up to him for one last kiss.

Emily's memories changed again. It was a few hours later and she could see a large group of knights gathered in front of Mitchell's castle, their brightly colored banners waving in the breeze. The late-afternoon sun shone down on the meadows that spread out from the castle in gently rolling waves, a golden light shining upon green hills. Along the edge of the nearby wood, a fox crept past, its tail swishing above the long midsummer grass as bees buzzed dreamily among the wild flowers, blissfully unaware that within hours, those peaceful hills would be drenched in the blood of dying men. Behind the force of knights were hundreds of peasants, equally ready for battle, armed with their axes, hammers and pitchforks.

Mitchell was wearing armor and sat, grim and motionless, upon his white stallion, Sunalus. The blare of trumpets broke the silence as a great force of knights appeared, marching up the main road toward the castle. Leading the group was the captain of the guard. Emily could see that these troops outnumbered the castle's forces by at least three to one. When they were a few hundred yards away the trumpets blew again and the knights halted.

"Throw down your weapons. Surrender and the Lord Protector will be merciful upon you!" cried the captain of the guard.

The men did not move from their positions. From up the road, behind the Lord Protector's ranks, a dark, cloaked figure rode into the empty field between the two forces. The captain of the guard looked on, surprised. No one spoke or stirred. For a moment, only the chirping of birds could be heard, the hum of insects, the breeze through the grass. Then a slim, white hand emerged from the cloak and drew back the hood to reveal the fair face of Marigold.

"Stop!" she cried out.

Mitchell's heart surged at the sight of her. The silence continued as warriors from both sides stared at her and exchanged confused looks. She sat up proudly in her saddle, her chin held high. Mitchell had never seen her look so beautiful. She was an angel, parting a glittering ocean of swords and spears. She faced the captain of the guard, holding up an official-looking scroll.

"My father commands you to return to the palace at once. There will be no battle here today."

The captain considered her for a moment. "And why, may I ask, are we being called back to the palace? Why did your father not send his official messengers?"

"You may ask him yourself when you return. Here, read his command," she held out the scroll and stared at him with a calm, steady gaze.

The captain approached her slowly and took the scroll, breaking the wax seal and reading it. He thought for a moment, and then burst out laughing.

"She is lying! A pretty forgery though, Milady."

"How dare you!"

"How dare I?" His eyebrows were raised, smug. "Well, Milady, I searched your bedchambers and found love letters from the son of our enemy." He pointed at Mitchell, as gasps and grunts of disapproval spread through the warriors. "She is a traitor! Seize her! I will bring her before her father myself."

Two guards dragged her from her horse, carrying her to the rear of the army.

"Marigold!" Mitchell shouted, moving his horse forward, but the knights on either side of him held him back.

At that moment Mitchell's father swept out his sword, rose up in his stirrups and thrust it high into the air.

"FOR OUR PEOPLE!" he shouted in a voice filled with the pride and power of his lineage.

With a great cry, the heavy cavalry charged straight at their foes. Mitchell led the right flank, sweeping off to the side of the main force, but his eyes never left the spot where they had taken Marigold. With each enemy he ran through with his sword, he was fighting his way closer to her. Hundreds of riders, led by the duke, crashed into the ranks of their enemy. Many were impaled upon the gleaming spears. Shields dented and broke, men shrieked and died, horses reared and fell, swords stabbed, hacked and slashed. Arrows whistled overhead. The duke charged through a breach in the wall of shields and, with a mighty shout and sweep of his sword, he slew the captain of the guard, his strength fueled by anger.

Mitchell was leading his men in their charge when he heard a terrible cry. Instantly he knew what had happened. Dread sank into the pit of his stomach as he located the source of the sound. He saw his father clutching his neck as he continued to fight valiantly, a well-aimed arrow had pierced his throat. His father's horse collapsed to the earth a moment later.

"Father!"

The duke's elite guard tried to reach him in order to drag him out of the fray, but they were overwhelmed and surrounded by more enemies. A whirlwind of fury rose inside Mitchell and he broke ranks, galloping headlong into the thick of the battle like a comet streaking across the battlefield to his father's rescue. He descended upon the enemy, as though summoned from the pits of Hell, breaking through their ranks, hurling their warriors back. His magnificent horse, Sunalus, used his powerful chest as a battering ram, smashing aside the enemy's horses and bursting through a wall of shields, as Mitchell cut their soldiers down, one after another. His sword sang as he brought it down upon them again and again, sending their blood spraying into the sky. Fourteen soldiers he slew before his beautiful steed was killed beneath him. As Sunalus fell, Mitchell sprang from his back and landed beside his father's body. To the west, the sun sank in a bloody bath of clouds.

Mitchell rose to his feet and saw a strange storm rising. It seemed to emanate from a dark figure standing on the hilltop where they had taken Marigold. All around this figure the air turned an ugly brownish hue, and ominous rolls of thunder pealed across the land.

A massive soldier wielded his sword down upon him. Mitchell raised his shield to block it, but the force of the blow broke the shield in two, the blade opening up his chest just below his collarbone. He cried out in pain. The soldier raised his sword again for the kill. Air as dark as a murky swamp turned the skies black. From the swollen clouds, a great bolt of lightning shot out, bursting between the spears of two nearby soldiers. A blinding flash ripped through the atmosphere, and a booming sound crashed as if the very molecules of air around the soldiers had burst asunder. The two soldiers fell to the ground and Mitchell seized the moment to thrust his sword through the heart of the soldier attacking him. "For my father!" he cried.

The soldier fell onto Mitchell, blood gushing from his wound. The skies opened up, clouds like enormous black sacks of water slashed apart and a torrent of rain poured down. With a great shout, the duke's men charged and fought to reach Mitchell and his father. Lightning crashed in different spots all around them, explosions of thunder became so numerous and deafening it seemed as though the whole world had fallen into the maw of some massive, roaring beast.

Mitchell shoved the body off him and struggled to stand, covered in his enemy's blood. He turned to the lifeless body of his father. Everywhere around him were the bodies of the dead and dying.

"Father!" he cried, rising to his feet, but four more of the enemy soldiers were immediately upon him. One thrust his sword through Mitchell's side, and he cried out with blinding pain. Another tried to bring his axe down on his skull, but he parried the blow with his sword and the axe merely grazed his brow, knocking off his helmet and cutting his forehead open. The third stabbed him through the thigh and punched him in the back of the head. Mitchell howled again and was knocked violently backward onto the sword of another who had crept up from behind. In a burst of ferocity Mitchell killed them all but suddenly, out of nowhere, a dagger hurled with superhuman strength plunged into his chest and he sank to his knees. His eyes rose to the small, grassy hill overlooking the battle.

"Marigold..." he muttered. He glimpsed her watching him in horror, hands covering her mouth. She had seen her father's soldiers cut Mitchell down. Her terrible, piercing wail echoed over the battlefield. Mitchell tried to rise but fell back down to his knees.

Marigold did the same, collapsing unconscious to the ground, her world destroyed.

As the battle continued to rage around him, Mitchell was blinded by the streams of blood flowing into his eyes from the gash on his forehead. All was confusion and chaos. As he knelt in the mud beside his father's body someone appeared over him. It was the strange, dark figure from the hilltop peering down at him. It must be an apparition, he thought, for the man wasn't dressed as a soldier of any kind, nor did he resemble any of the local peasants. He wore a long black cloak made of the fine threads of a nobleman and superior black leather riding boots. His hair was brownish red and slicked back, his skin was deathly pale, and his eyes were like burning Hell.

It's the Angel of Death, it has to be, Mitchell thought. Peace washed over him, knowing he would see his father, brother, mother, sisters and Marigold again one day in the afterlife. He only wished he could hold his beloved in his arms and look into her royal-blue eyes one last time. He prayed silently for her soul, for his family, to be granted eternity in paradise, and that they should all be reunited there. The wind picked up and the rain now fell in great horizontal sheets, washing the blood from his face. The storm reached a new intensity, with a renewed frenzy of thunder and lightning, as he blinked through the rain pelting his eyes. The strange man smiled down at him. His voice was filled with malevolent pleasure.

"Well, my brave warrior, you truly have the heart of a lion!" He gave a low, mirthless chuckle as he pulled the dagger from Mitchell's chest and sheathed it. "Now, you will feed that lion's heart on the blood of the world!"

The dark figure looked up at the clouds and slowly raised his hands as though embracing the whole sky. He spoke strange words that Mitchell did not understand. Twin bolts of lightning burst from the clouds, as if the man was commanding them, and he laughed triumphantly.

"Isn't it magnificent!" he cried, staring at Mitchell with crimson, glowing eyes. "The glorious blood of thousands of brave men pouring onto the earth! And these rich and fertile lands drinking it up! Mezzor drinking his fill, drinking all that is rightfully his!" He cackled with devilish glee, abnormally long and sharp canines exposed as he threw his head back.

Mitchell slumped sideways, lying on his back, feeling the life force weakening inside him, draining out through his wounds. He stared at the being before him and understood now that it was not the Angel of Death – at least, none he had ever learned about from the holy books. But what it was he could not imagine. Then, so quickly he didn't even see the man move, the dark figure was upon him. Sharp fangs sank deep into Mitchell's neck, piercing his jugular vein. Mitchell cried out in burning agony and tried to struggle, but the man's grip was like an iron vice. Mitchell felt the last waves of blood pumping out with each heartbeat and knew that this pale man was gulping them down in a frenzy. The world around him seemed to grow steadily quieter – no more shouts of soldiers, no more thunder crashing. Mitchell felt himself floating, rising up above the carnage. He was dying, he knew, and everything felt both distant and tranquil. Below him, he saw his body lying on the ground as he hovered above. The strange being ended its blood-drinking feast and gazed down at him. When it spoke, Mitchell heard nothing but its words. No sounds of trumpets, no swords striking cold metal shields, no screams of agony. Nothing. The rest of the world ceased to exist. He closed his eyes.

"Now drink. Drink deep, and you will truly walk with the kings. It is the Feast of the Gods of which you will partake!"

With that, the creature slit its own wrist with his dagger and pressed the wound to Mitchell's lips. At first Mitchell resisted but then the blood filled his mouth, running down his throat. Trying not to choke, he instinctively swallowed and felt a wave of power and life rush through him like an electric current. He drank deeper.

"Yes, already so thirsty," the creature chuckled.

With each gulp of blood, a wave of renewed strength rolled through Mitchell's body and the whole world about him transformed. It appeared as though everything was made of blood and he had a burning thirst for more. He felt like he could drink the whole world.

After a few more moments the being pushed him away. Mitchell felt the droplets of blood streaming from his mouth, bubbling out over his lips and his mind reeled as if waking from a terrible dream. He had been drinking this creature's blood! He recoiled in disgust. Then a series of shocks convulsed his body and he began writhing and howling.

"Enough!" smiled the pale being. "More than enough." He stood and laughed, gazing down at Mitchell as if he were his own child. "Now, young lion, I have broken the chains of your mortality. I unleash you on an unsuspecting world! Yes, yes! THE BLOOD OF THE WORLD IS THE BLOOD OF THE GOD!" he shouted. To Mitchell, his voice boomed louder than the thunder that rattled the ground. It split his ears like bolts of lightning exploding through the sky.

Twenty-Eight

South of England July 1564

Marigold was carried off unconscious to the castle of her father, the Lord Protector. She came to as she was being taken through the main gates. "Her father has given orders that she be hung at dawn for treason," she overheard one of the soldiers say.

Marigold screamed and struggled until she broke free of the soldiers who were carrying her. She rushed through the doors of the tallest tower, slamming and locking them behind her. Up the stairs she flew and a few minutes later emerged at the top of the tower overlooking the battlements and surrounding countryside. Thunder boomed and rolled above. The winds bent the trees and rain pelted down. Marigold stood looking out over the landscape, tears mixing with the raindrops as the wind blew her hair. Her looks were pale and wild.

"Hell, vengeance, death, madness!" she cried. "All is cursed! Rise tempests, rage and blast this wicked world with your thunderbolts!"

Lightning flashed and thunder crashed all around.

"Unleash your dreadful wrath and burn all with Hellfire! Smite this loathsome earth with its serpent heart that feasts upon the doom of all that live and love!"

Eyes blazing, she spread her arms and shouted with strength and authority. "Let my voice travel upon the gale. Hear me all powers of

317

darkness and of light. I conjure you and any who would take up my offer. Bring my Mitchell back to me!"

There was another blinding flash of lightning and thunder exploded a split second later. "I challenge the angels above and all the fiends of Hell's dismal deeps; if any of you dare to bring back my love to me I will pay the price!"

There was another flash of lightning and blast of thunder.

Meanwhile, back on the battlefield Mitchell was racked by agonizing pain, like being devoured from the inside. It was as if every cell, every fiber that had been human was now dying, and his body was expelling its past self like toxic waste. He writhed in the mud as the battle swept over him, until, finally, it was all over, and he felt completely transformed.

When he sat up he found that most of his father's forces had retreated inside the castle walls, which were now surrounded by the enemy. The rain had abated but sheet lightning still flashed among the clouds and every few moments ominous thunder rumbled overhead. Great fires had sprung up all about the castle and the Lord Protector's army was rolling up catapults, battering rams and other siege engines. Corpses lay everywhere, but his father's body had been removed from the battlefield.

Mitchell pulled off his armor and undershirt to inspect his wounds. To his utter astonishment there wasn't a mark on him. Not a scratch.

"Is this some sort of dream?" he murmured to himself. "Or am I dead? Yet, if I am dead, why am I still here? Am I a ghost?"

He moved his tongue around the inside of his mouth and gasped when it grazed against something long and sharp – his own canines. Crawling to his feet he gazed around at what should have been a familiar world but now felt completely alien to him. What a darkly magnificent world it had become. It was like he was seeing it for the first time. The fires, the sheet lightning, everything seemed so vivid, the colors so rich, the indescribable beauty and magic of the night. His eyes captured it all with a clarity never before dreamed of. He could see the undercurrent of life in all things as a vibrant energy field. Not just in organic, living beings, but in everything. He detected the life force in the rocks, the wind, water and fire. He could perceive the intense uniqueness of each individual thing. Every pebble, tree, plant… Each object was unlike any other. Each seemed to have its own awareness.

Mitchell left his amour where it was and made his way, shirtless, toward his fathers castle, which was now his, past the bodies of warriors that lay scattered on the battlefield like fallen autumn leaves. The skirmishing continued in places and as he approached the rear of the enemy forces, he drew his sword. Coming up behind an enormous catapult with a speed and dexterity he had never achieved before, he slashed at the soldiers manning the machinery. They were about to ignite a large ball of pitch, a mixture of sulphur, ground limestone and pine tar that would explode on impact, setting practically anything ablaze, its fiery resin clinging to everything it touched, flaring even more fiercely when doused with water.

Mitchell lifted the ball of pitch, which was nearly four feet in diameter, and attached it around the end of a ten-foot length of chain, which he tore with ease from the catapult.

A mounted soldier rode up. Upon seeing Mitchell returned from the dead, the man's face contorted in horror. His eyes widened, and he screamed as his horse reared. Mitchell slew the soldier as he fell and leaped onto the back of the horse, hoisting the chain over his shoulder. He marveled at how he was able to pick up something this heavy as easily as lifting a tankard of ale.

The fires that had sprung up around the castle were so immense that the clouds overhead glowed orange. His people were defending the walls well, raining arrows down upon their foes, but the enemy was relentless. Using a torch that an infantryman had left plunged in the ground, Mitchell ignited the pitch. Once it was fully ablaze, he swung it above his head and spurred his horse into a gallop, crying out, "Hell has come to claim your souls!"

The enemy soldiers in the rear whirled around as he thundered down on them, the great, flaming ball of pitch circling high above his head. Spurring his horse into their midst, Mitchell released the chain, hurling the burning orb straight at the new captain of the guard, who sat astride an enormous, chestnut-colored stallion in the center of his troops. The captain was turning to see what the commotion was about when the ball of flame hit him square in the face. The force of the blow tore his head off. The pitch exploded on impact and as the chestnut stallion bucked wildly, with the captain's headless corpse still in the saddle, dozens of the surrounding soldiers were ignited in liquid fire. They dove to the ground, screaming and rolling on the grass, desperately battling to put out the flames.

As his stolen steed crashed through the ranks of foot soldiers, Mitchell swept out his sword and killed them by the dozens. Chaos spread through the enemy ranks. Many recognized him, crying out, "The dead have risen, the dead have risen! Run, this is a cursed land!"

Many threw down their weapons and ran in every direction as Mitchell continued to hack his way through them. Within minutes the entire enemy force was fleeing the castle. Mitchell pursued them, slaying the soldiers at will, until he had chased every one of them past the borders of his land. He then turned and rode back to the castle.

The soldiers upon the battlements could not tell who was terrorizing the enemy forces below but they shouted in joy at the sight of them fleeing. As the battle ended the storm clouds disappeared, leaving behind an eerie calm. Some soldiers had come out to help the last remaining injured back into the castle, and Mitchell found he could actually smell the blood congealing on their wounds.

He heard a harsh croaking sound and spotted a raven perched upon the limb of a dead tree, gloating over the field of death. As Mitchell dismounted and walked up to the main gates he could hear commotion spreading inside the castle, sounds he would never have been able to hear through such thick walls before. He knocked at the gates and waited for a moment then cried out.

"Mitchell knocks! I am alive! Open the gates!"

With his heightened sense of hearing, he listened to the murmurs of fear from inside the castle.

"Open the gates!" he shouted again, impatiently, and pushed at the door with all his strength. There was a loud crack, and the great beam of wood that bolted the two doors shut snapped in half. The doors swung open.

For a moment, Mitchell looked down at his hands, eyes wide, marveling at his newfound strength. The soldiers gathered behind the gates gasped, drew their weapons, and shrank back at the sight of Mitchell's glowing, inhuman, crimson eyes. Only one stepped forward. It was his younger brother.

"Charles, it is I, your brother," said Mitchell.

Charles, still wearing his armor, was drenched from head to toe in mud from the battle. A nasty gash ran across his right cheek. He gazed at Mitchell with eyes reflecting pain, fear, and rage.

"Demon possessor!" he cried.

"What? Charles, no, I…" stammered Mitchell. "It is I, Mitchell."

"Lies! No man could have survived those wounds. We watched my brother die, and now you, demon, have possessed his body. I see the demon in your eyes. In the name of God, we cast you out!" He thrust his sword forward.

Mitchell took a step back, catching images of the confused thoughts racing around in Charles's anguished mind. What he saw there made his stomach collapse – an image of a boulder hurled by a catapult smashing through a huge section of the tower, followed by a flaming ball of pitch, his mother along with two of his sisters being burned alive.

"What… No…" he muttered, staring at his brother. "No, it can't be."

"Release my brother, demon imposter!" shouted Charles. "I will send you back to the pits of Hell where you belong!"

"I am no demon," Mitchell cried, trying desperately to disconnect with the images inside his brother's mind. "I am…" He had no idea what was happening, but he understood that there was something desperately wrong.

Afraid of being drawn into a physical confrontation with his brother and horrified by the images of his mother and sisters being burned alive, Mitchell turned and fled. Ahead of him he spotted the great black horse he had been riding. He needed to see Marigold and make sure that she was safe. He vaulted onto the horse's back and rode into the night, never looking back, even as the realization dawned on him that he might never come home again. He spurred his horse forward. As he rode, confusion filled his mind. He tried to gather his thoughts into some semblance of an understanding, but everything that had happened to him after the cold steel plunged through his chest seemed strange and blurry, like a dream that fades from memory upon waking. The dagger had pierced his heart and he had been left to bleed to death on the ground beneath the storming skies. Who could possibly survive such wounds? It was as if he were peering across a great chasm at something distant, just beyond his reach.

Had a demon really found him on the battlefield and fed him with its own blood? What did demonic possession feel like? He didn't feel as though any other entity had taken over his body. His thoughts were still his own and yet he felt something stirring deep within him, a force in his blood. Something powerful was awakening, hungering…

Perhaps I am possessed, he thought, a cold shudder shooting through him, a hunger he'd never experienced before washing over him. Maybe this was how possession began.

He spurred the horse on and soon he was approaching the palace of the Lord Protector. He slowed the beast and dismounted, jumping nimbly off its back, landing silently, weightlessly. The last of the thunder rumbled across the landscape as he tied the horse to the stump of a nearby tree and gazed up at the palace walls. All was quiet, he had arrived before the Lord Protector's scattered and wounded troops could organize themselves to return. It was time to test his new abilities. He stared up at Marigold's bedchamber window, aglow with the light of a candle. He scaled straight up the walls with little effort, like a spider. When he reached Marigold's window he peered inside. His love was lying on her bed, her face buried in the pillows, sobbing. He climbed in through the window and approached the bed.

"Marigold," he whispered. "My love, I am here for you."

Her body stiffened. She stopped crying at the sound of his voice, as though unsure of both her ears and her sanity. Slowly, her head turned, her long golden hair stuck to her tear-soaked cheeks. Her eyes were red and swollen from hours of sobbing. She blinked, trying to understand what was happening. She was wearing a white nightgown and the beautiful pearl necklace with the ruby-and-diamond pendant he had given her. Mitchell was standing in shadow, out of reach of the candlelight, and she could only make out his silhouette and a pair of glittering emerald eyes.

Emily was thunderstruck that she was now back in the scene from her recurring dream.

"I am asleep," Marigold whispered aloud to herself. "I am asleep, and this is a dream. I hope I never awaken."

"No, Marigold, you are not sleeping. I am here. Something has happened to me that I cannot explain, but I am here. It is I."

"Can it be true?" she whispered, sitting up. "Mitchell! Is it really you?"

He caught the scent of her body, the unmistakable perfume of her hair, her ivory skin, and hesitated. Desire possessed him, followed by a wrenching pang of hunger. Hunger for what, he wasn't sure. He always longed for her body, her kiss, her heart, but this was different. He realized he was aware of the sound of her heart beating in her breast and her blood pumping through her veins. The smell of her flesh grew intoxicating, and the sight of the soft, pale skin of her neck filled him with a dangerous lust, making him fall back on his haunches. His mind reeled as he fought to control himself. He would never hurt her. He took a step forward, needing to hold her.

Now Emily was living the memory through Marigold and it was identical to her recurring dream. She dreaded the encounter with the demon that she knew was to come. As in her dream lightning flashed outside and thunder cracked and rolled. The windows blew open, knocking a vase off the windowsill, shattering it. Mitchell took a step forward and his glittering green eyes changed, blazing with a deadly, inhuman, crimson glow. Mitchell reached out to caress her face.

"Marigold…"

"Your eyes!" she gasped, her face contorted into a look of horror and loathing. "Stay away from me, you are possessed! Oh God forgive me! Have mercy! I offered my soul to bring you back to me, and they brought you back from the dead… but possessed by a demon! The demons are mocking me! Oh God, if a demon has possessed your body that means your soul is in Hell!"

He reached out for her again. "Marigold…"

"No!" She stumbled from her bed and backed away from him, shaking like a cornered animal. "Get away from me, demon!"

Mitchell tried to follow her, tried to reassure her, then he caught sight of himself in a mirror. He stopped dead in his tracks. There, looking back at him was the reflection of the Mitchell he had always known, the handsome, young lord. But how it had been transformed! His bright-green eyes now blazed with an inhuman, crimson glow both mesmerizing and unsettling. A wolf-like, predatory fire burned within them. His skin was as pale as a corpse, the blue of his veins showing through it like a delicate spider's web. Most horrifying of all, he now saw what his tongue had felt on the battlefield – two deadly canine teeth. Is it true? he wondered. Am I a demon?

Mitchell approached the mirror and touched the reflection of his face. "Dear Lord, what have I become?" he whispered.

A commotion arose in the next room. Alerted by Marigold's cries, six guards burst into her bedchamber with swords drawn. "Tell my father he can burn in Hell," snarled Marigold at the stunned guards. "I won't give him the satisfaction of hanging me." She ran across the cold floor, climbed onto her windowsill and cried out, "If my love be dead and damned, then so shall I be!"

"Marigold, no!" Mitchell shouted.

She hurled herself from the window before he could reach her. Emily felt herself falling, falling, falling and saw the ground rushing toward her.

Now Emily was back in Mitchell's memories. The guards gaped, astounded, as he dove out the window after her. He saw her far below him, lying on the grass between the castle wall and the moat, her gown spread like the petals of a white rose. He landed beside her like a cat. He took her broken body in his arms. With his heightened awareness, he knew that her heart had stopped as he held her. He felt her soul leaving her body like a wisp of innocent light, floating away. She was gone.

A low howl of agony escaped his lips as he cradled her in his arms. Somewhere behind him, a wooden door opened and a cohort of guards poured out, rushing toward him with swords drawn. He gently laid Marigold upon the earth and sprang to his feet.

"Stay away from her," he snarled. "You will not touch her!"

The guards took no heed of his words and Mitchell fought with incredible ferocity, his fists crushing their jaws and breaking their ribs. When a dozen of them lay strewn about the ground or struggling in the grimy water of the moat, the rest drew back, unnerved by the devastation Mitchell had wreaked upon their fellows. Seizing this opportunity, Mitchell took Marigold into his arms and leaped up onto the back of the stallion. She belonged to him, dead or alive. The horse reared and snorted then charged like a thunderbolt into the night.

With Marigold's lifeless body draped over his horse, Mitchell rode to the hilltop above the burial ground of his ancestors, a couple of miles from his father's castle, where he and Marigold had made their blood oath. It was a peaceful place with a beautiful view across the countryside. He had gone there often as a child when he needed time alone to think. The cemetery was at the base of the hill on the western side. Mitchell lifted Marigold down and sat upon a large, flat stone where he'd often sat before. For a long time, he cradled her in his arms, tenderly kissing and caressing her face. He let out a tortured groan.

"I curse this world!" he roared at the sky. He dropped his lips close to the delicate ear of his love. "I swear to you," he whispered, his voice quivering, "I swear, I will find him." He raised his face to the cold, glittering stars above and shouted at the heavens. "Whatever foul creature did this to us, I will find him and make him suffer! I swear by all the powers that exist, I will have my revenge!"

His voice echoed throughout the cemetery. He knelt again, gently kissed Marigold's eyelids and laid her upon the ground.

He tenderly caressed her face.

"Is this dear person, this bright little world that existed within these lovely features, this dear, dear soul, in all its tenderness, laughter, life and love now snuffed out? Is the voice that could fill the world with song, now silenced? Where have you gone, my love? My bright angel? You leave behind a world now forever darkened.

"Do not fear, my love. I am coming for you, wherever your soul may be. I will wipe this foul evil off the face of the earth and then I will destroy myself and come to you. You sold your soul to bring me back, then took your own life when you thought mine had been cast into Hell so we would be together again. You embraced eternal damnation… for me. And I will do the same for you. I will never abandon you! Wherever your soul now roams in the outer darkness, or whatever pit of Hell it has been cast into, I will come to you and we will be together again forever where the lost souls of the cursed and the damned dwell. I will never abandon you, I swear it!"

Droplets of blood fell on her face. Mitchell wiped his eyes.

"What is this? I weep tears of blood? My heart flows from my eyes to be with you, my love, wherever you are."

With astonishing strength and speed, he began to dig in the dirt using his hands in the same spot they had sworn their blood oath. Before long, he had cleared out a hole big enough to serve as her grave. After one last, tender kiss, he lowered her into the earth and covered her over. "What evil was in the stars that brought this demon of destruction into our little world? What has happened to my beautiful England who has borne me upon its proud green shoulders as a kind and loving parent and now lies, dying from some disease within, its noble blood filled with poison as demons tread upon its royal, emerald earth with vile, reptile feet? What foul fiend was it that sank its sharp teeth into my throat? Marigold. One way or another, soon death will send me to thee. Until then, I drink the bitter wine of misery that makes a man so drunk on its evil vapors that the whole world takes on the malignant, oppressive atmosphere of a nightmare."

He knelt down and stared at her grave then gently patted the earth. "Sleep in peace, my love," he whispered when he had finished. "Not in a cold, lifeless tomb. The grass and violets will grow above you, and the sunlight will shine where you lie. You are my heart and my soul and my everything, in this world and in all worlds, forever… and time and death cannot touch that. I will come for you, Marigold. One way or another, I will find you again. Love gave me everything, but at such a cost. Marigold is my paradise, and my paradise lost."

Emily's memories were now Marigold's again. She found herself in the endless black void from her recurring dream, and she saw the same horrific demon approaching.

Twenty-Nine

Emily came back to the bottom of the ocean to find that Mitchell was dragging her out of the Well of Many Worlds. Once free of the mist her body solidified and returned to normal. As soon as Mitchell could see she was safe he turned to go after Baelaar, but his archenemy had disappeared into the vast, dark depths of the surrounding water.

For a moment there was silence. When Emily reached up to Mitchell her hand was shaking.

"Mitchell," she whispered. "I am…"

"Mitchell," Sylvain interrupted with a wry grin as he emerged from behind the vast shell of the dragon turtle, "you certainly have some interesting friends…"

Mitchell gazed at his long-lost friend as though he had forgotten the rest of the world even existed. "Thank you so much, Sylvain."

"It was my pleasure. I have been hoping for a chance to repay you."

"What about Tom?" Emily asked. "Where did he go?"

"Most likely Magella," said Mercurios. "He went into the Well, and that is where it leads, oh yes indeed."

"What are we going to do?" Emily asked. "We have to get him and turn him back to normal. We have to save him. Before he was possessed by that demon stone he was such a good person, you have to believe me, Tom was so kind to me, Mitchell. We have to do something to help him."

Now that it was only Mitchell, Sylvain and Emily's sphere of protection holding millions of tons of water back, the combined force field was starting to collapse. Water began spraying down on them.

"We must go," Mitchell commanded.

"Must get back to the surface or we will die!" agreed the imp.

It didn't take long to make it back to the surface of the ocean. When they reached the shore, Mitchell set down the Well and turned to face Emily. "I have to take this to a safe place where no one will find it. In the coming nights I must study it and figure out how it works."

"Mitchell, I… I have something incredibly important I need to tell you. Something I saw when I was in the Well."

"It will have to wait."

"At some point, maybe you can make some sense of whatever it is that just happened," said Sylvain. "I must admit, I haven't been this baffled since… well, since I became a vampire. However, I must depart immediately. I was at the most delightful masquerade party and actually right in the middle of some pressing business when I was… well… brought here."

Mitchell squeezed his friend's shoulder. "How can I repay you Sylvain?"

"You know there is no need." He smiled. "I hope to see you again soon. I do throw marvelous parties and you are more than welcome to bring your lovely friend." He winked at Emily and looked around. "Where exactly am I?"

"Portland, Maine," Emily told him.

"Ah… interesting. I don't suppose you can send me back to where I was?"

A look of worry crossed her face. "Oh, I didn't even think of how you would get back – I'm sorry."

"No need to apologize. I'm glad that I came."

"I can help with that," said Mitchell, pulling out his cell phone.

He called his pilot and gave instructions for him to fly Sylvain to wherever he wanted to go. A few moments later Sylvain said his goodbyes, gave them a courtly bow and disappeared into the night.

"Teleport back to your home," Mitchell said, turning to Emily.

"But Mitchell…"

"Please. Do as I say."

With that Mitchell picked up the Well and ran off down the shore, heading east.

When Emily arrived home the fire trucks were still outside and Cady Sunner was nowhere to be seen. Emily's phone buzzed. It was Detective Scannel.

"Detective Scannel, how are things?"

"We've arrested Cady Sunner."

"Really?" Emily's heart leaped with joy. She was hardly able to believe she had at last succeeded in bringing justice to her father's killer.

"We're bringing in a ballistics expert and are hoping to put him away for first-degree murder if the bullets used to kill your father match his gun."

"Amazing!"

The firemen informed Emily that it was safe to go back into the house and although the fire had completely destroyed the guest bedroom, it hadn't spread to her room except for some scorch marks around the hole in her wall. She thought about everything that had happened and worried about her mother. She had no idea what to do. There was water everywhere. She hung a rug over the hole and began cleaning up with the help of Mercurios. Hours later they were still working when she heard a gentle tapping on her window. Throwing the curtains back she opened it to allow Mitchell in.

"I've come to say goodbye." He spoke the words quietly. "I will be using the Well to search for Marigold. I am sorry, Emily."

Emily glanced at Mercurios. "Privacy please."

Mercurios exited her bedroom. Emily smiled and came close to

Mitchell, running her fingers over his chest and stomach, looking up into his eyes, enjoying the sensual feel of his powerful muscles.

"Mitchell, we swore that we would be together forever and for over four hundred years, through unthinkable suffering and hardship, you have remained true to that… true to me."

"What?"

"All my life I've felt that there was a part of me that was missing. I felt it in my bones, in the pit of my stomach, I felt it from the tips of my toes to the top of my head, I felt it in the empty aching and longing in my chest, and now I know why." Her eyes were shining, overflowing with love, desire and admiration. "Mitchell, I remember it all," she whispered. "When we were in the Well, caught between two worlds, I was dying, disintegrating, and we merged into one, it all came back to me. I remember everything of my former life… and my death." Her eyes grew distant and haunted. "After I died I was lost in that cold, terrible, lonely place! A separate dimension of… nothingness, like limbo or purgatory. It was so hard, searching, always searching, for you. I was terrified that I would exist there forever alone, never able to find you, that you were in Hell or in the Abyss, the realm of demons, and we would be separated forever, each in our lonely torment." She stared into his eyes. "But then suddenly, ahead of me, a dimension door opened and a young demon emerged from the realm of demons. The dimension door closed behind it and the demon sped off through the darkness, not noticing me. I chased after it, desperately hoping I could find a way out of that terrible place. After some time, I could see a distant point of light ahead of us. The demon was headed straight for it.

"I was able to hear the demon's thoughts. Two necromancers, a king and queen in a world called Magella, were conducting a magic ritual. They were summoning a demon into their unborn child before its own spirit could form. I realized that here was a way out of limbo or purgatory or whatever that awful place was.

"To be born into the world of the living again as an infant and live a whole new life from the beginning, possibly with no memory of anything else. The thought terrified me, but I would have done anything if there was even the remotest hope of finding you again!"

Mitchell remained silent and frowning as Emily's eyes clouded over again. "I attacked the demon, I went wild. I knew it was he or I, and that this was my only chance to escape that terrible place. You see I had started to think that it was possible your soul hadn't been cast into Hell. That perhaps you were still fighting for your soul back in the realms of the living. I had to get back. I had to come to you. I was screaming, clawing, and rending his face like an animal. He burned me and stabbed me. But I finally seized my chance. I got past him and plunged into the light before the demon could enter, and I was reborn into the realms of the living in the child that would become Emily Bliss. But, just as I feared, in being reborn as an infant child, I completely forgot my former life, my former identity.

"It wasn't the demon of Marigold that was trying to possess me." Emily stopped and stared deep into Mitchell's eyes. "Mitchell... it's me, I AM Marigold Bonneville!"

"How dare you!" he snarled, incensed, eyes blazing as he reached for the hilt of his sword. "How DARE you mock me? How DARE you speak to ME in such a way!" Mitchell thundered with savage vehemence.

Emily went pale. "Mitchell, please listen to me. How else could I know these things? The pearl-and-ruby necklace, you gave it to me for my eighteenth birthday. How else could I know that?"

"When we were in the Well, maybe we went through some kind of mind meld and you saw all my memories. Or maybe you cast a spell on me that let you read my mind."

"When vampires are cut and heal they don't scar right?"

"So?"

"But any scars you had before you were turned into a vampire, you still have them right?"

"So what?"

She looked at the palm of her right hand and then held it up to show him. "Mitchell, I've had this scar along the lifeline of my right hand for as long as I can remember. I never knew where it came from… until today. You have one just like it on your left hand. They are from the blood oath we swore on Halloween under the full moon in the year 1563. The oath we swore to bind our souls together for all eternity."

Mitchell sucked in a breath and took a step back in shock, and then slowly raised his left hand and stared at the scar that ran down his lifeline. He looked up at Emily, utterly thunderstruck.

"My god, can it be?" he whispered.

"It's just like you said to me so long ago: 'You are my heart and my soul and my everything, in this world and in all worlds, forever, and time and death cannot touch that.' Our blood oath came true, Mitchell. 'I hereby join my spirit with yours forever. In this life and in all lives to come until the end of time.' We will always find each other, Mitchell."

"Beyond all hope," he whispered, holding out his trembling hand, palm facing her. Emily could see the matching scar on the lifeline of his hand. Their palms came together and their fingers clasped just as they had all those many years ago.

"Marigold!" As though in a trance, Mitchell reached out and gently caressed her face with his free hand, then collapsed to his knees as he let out a cry of both anguish and joy and threw his arms around her waist. His shoulders heaved as he burst into an uncontrollable passion of tears. "Marigold! Oh, my Marigold!" he sobbed. "My love! My darling!"

Mitchell got to his feet, wiped the tears of blood from his eyes, took her face in his hands and showered her cheeks and lips and eyelids with kisses. After a short time he stopped and Emily opened her eyes. They stared deep into each other's souls.

"But of course," he whispered. "I felt it from the moment we met but I pushed it away because I wasn't able to even conceive of the possibility. And your eyes, they are just like hers, the windows of the soul. So many nights over the years I prayed for this moment. I had to keep fighting and searching for you, and now here you are. Can this be true?"

Mitchell kissed her passionately. Emily felt four hundred years of hope, pain, love, passion and desire pour into her. Heavenly pleasure exploded deep inside her mind and body. His tongue filled her mouth and she eagerly responded. His powerful hands moved sensuously up her back to the nape of her neck. Her whole body burned for him. Joy and life beyond all description flooded Mitchell's being, like a waterfall unleashed onto a parched desert. Through more than four centuries of suffering he had clung to the faintest hope that somehow, somewhere, he would be reunited with his love. Now that his most cherished dream had come true, he was overwhelmed.

As they kissed for what seemed like an eternity of bliss, they both knew that they would do anything to feel like this forever. They broke apart simultaneously to stare at each other, panting with hunger and love and indescribable elation, eyes wide in utter amazement that they were finally together again.

Emily's face grew serious. "You need to turn me into a vampire, Mitchell, before anything else can happen that might separate us again, especially if we are going to hunt for Baelaar and stop the enslavement of humanity, and go to Magella to rescue Tom."

"After I turn you, I insist that we marry immediately. We delayed last time and look what happened. I would suggest marrying in the chapel where I spent so many thousands of nights praying that I would find you, but since it has been somewhat destroyed by zombies we will have to find someplace nearby. I refuse to wait."

"I love it! We will be married tomorrow!" Emily unbuttoned the top of her dress, displaying soft, pale flesh of her neck. "Take what's yours, Mitchell."

He stared at her, savoring her, adoring her, his eyes transforming into two bright stars, shining with profoundest love. He took off his shirt, casting it aside and Emily's eyes hungrily drank in his perfectly chiseled body.

"Oh yes!" she murmured.

A primal lust burned in every cell of his being. For a moment Mitchell stared at the object of all of his love and desire and then in one ferocious movement he tore open her dress. Emily gasped as Mitchell licked his lips and smiled, his fangs flashing a brilliant white.

BOOK 2 of The Well of Many Worlds Series will be released Halloween 2019.

39673115R00203

Made in the USA
Middletown, DE
19 March 2019